A SPY FOR A SPY

Book 6 of the NEVER SAY SPY series

Diane Henders

A SPY FOR A SPY

ISBN 978-1-927460-06-1

Copyright © 2013 Diane Henders

PEBKAC Publishing Inc.
P.O. Box 67, Station Main
Qualicum Beach, BC   V9K 1S7
www.pebkacpublishing.com

First printed in paperback March 2013 by PEBKAC Publishing Inc.

v.9

Books in the NEVER SAY SPY series:

More books coming! For a current list, please visit
www.dianehenders.com
Or sign up for my New Book Notification list at
www.dianehenders.com/books

Humour by Diane Henders

Since You Asked...

People frequently ask if my protagonist, Aydan Kelly, is really me.

Yeah, you got me. These novels are an autobiography of my secret life as a government agent, working with highly-classified computer technology... Oh, wait, what's that? You want the *truth*? Um, you do realize fiction writers get paid to lie, don't you?

...well, shit, that's not nearly as much fun. It's also a long story.

I swore I'd never write fiction. "Too personal," I said. "People read novels and automatically assume the author is talking about him/herself."

Well, apparently I lied about the fiction-writing part. One day a story sprang into my head and wouldn't leave. The only way to get it out was to write it down. So I did.

But when I wrote that first book, I never intended to show it to anyone, so I created a character that looked like me just to thumb my nose at the stereotype. I've always had a defective sense of humour, and this time it turned around and bit me in the ass.

Because after I'd written the third novel, I realized I actually wanted other people to read my books. And when I went back to change my main character to *not* look like me, my beta readers wouldn't let me. They rose up against me and said, "No! Aydan is a tall woman with long red hair and brown eyes. End of discussion!"

Jeez, no wonder readers get the idea that authors write about themselves. So no, I'm not Aydan Kelly. I just look like her.

Oh, and the town of Silverside and all secret technologies are products of my imagination. If I'm abducted by grim-faced men wearing dark glasses, or if I die in an unexplained fiery car crash, you'll know I accidentally came a little too close to the truth.

I hope you enjoy the book!

For Phill

Thank you for being my technical advisor and the most tolerant husband ever. Much love!

To my beta readers/editors, especially Carol H., Judy B., and Phill B., with gratitude: Many thanks for all your time and effort in catching my spelling and grammar errors, telling me when I screwed up the plot or the characters' motivations, and generally keeping me honest.

To the other Phil, with appreciation: Thanks for your patience with all my dumb trucking questions. Time for some more beer-and-bullshit sessions...

To Lee A., Andrew D. and the staff at Grey Eagle Casino: Thank you for arranging for me to photograph one of your roulette wheels for the cover!

To Rick and Sandy H. at Hand Crafted Images: Your talent makes my covers extra-special, and your sense of humour makes photo sessions fun even for a camera-hater like me. Thank you!

To Steve A. and the staff at The Shooting Edge: Thank you for lending us your excellent facilities for our cover photo sessions. You guys rock!

To everyone else, respectfully:

Canadian English is an unholy hybrid of British and American English, so I apologize if spellings in this book look odd to you. But if you find typos, please send an email to errors@dianehenders.com. Mistakes drive me nuts, and I'm sorry if any slipped through. Please let me know what the error is, and on which page (or at which position in e-versions). I'll make sure it gets fixed as soon as possible.

Thanks!

CHAPTER 1

Damn, nothing rearranges your priorities like narrowly escaping a fiery explosion. Priority number one: A hot shower.

Oh God, yes.

I limped into my house and made for the bathroom with the kind of ardent longing I usually reserve for cold beer.

The pain of squirming out of my too-tight biking leathers made me catch my breath, too exhausted to even swear. Some pebbles and dirt sifted to the floor when I dropped the scuffed garments in the corner, and I leaned over to brush the last of the debris out of my hair as well. The stench of smoke clung to me like acrid cologne, overlaid by the faint antiseptic smell of a night spent in the hospital.

Straightening and twisting cautiously, I examined the dark bruises on my back and side in the mirror.

Could've been worse. At least I hadn't been blown into strawberry jam. Now if I could just make it through tomorrow unscathed...

I sighed and crept into the steamy rapture of my shower.

Some painkillers, food, and a few hours of pleasantly routine bookkeeping soothed my physical discomfort but did nothing for my apprehension. Despite my best attempts to find a positive spin, I just couldn't foresee any good outcome from my summons to tomorrow's meeting.

A Saturday meeting with the director of clandestine

operations was ominous at the best of times, and my guilty conscience magnified my worry even more. If it was something benign, Stemp would have waited until Monday...

Don't think about it. Just don't think about it.

After supper, I picked up a long-neglected book and tried to prevent my mind from skittering to nervous speculations about what the next day might hold.

Dammit, lying to Stemp had been my only option at the time, but what the hell was I going to do now? Tomorrow he'd expect me to act like the experienced secret agent I'd told him I was, not the shit-scared civilian bookkeeper I truly was.

The muffled thud of a car door slamming in my driveway made me hurry for the door, mentally cataloguing the reassuring weight of my gun in its ankle holster.

Who the hell would be driving into my yard this late in the evening?

The doorbell rang just as I reached the front door. When I peeked through the fisheye lens, a sigh of mingled relief and worry leaked out.

Two uniformed RCMP officers. An unmarked black sedan faded into the darkness in the driveway behind them, its shape suggested only by the gleam of its curves in my porch light.

I composed my expression into polite inquiry and drew a deep, careful breath before unlocking the deadbolt to swing the inside door open.

"Aydan Kelly?" The shorter, dark-haired man spoke through the screen door, his face expressionless while his hard blue eyes memorized me.

"Um..."

I tried to hide my hesitation while my tired mind riffled through the possibilities. Tell them my real name? Or use my cover identity? The police were supposed to know about my fake death, weren't they? Dammit, I should've clarified that with Stemp...

"...yes?" I ventured.

The two officers exchanged a split-second sidelong glance, their posture stiffening almost imperceptibly.

Shit!

"Um, actually, sorry, no," I babbled. "I meant, yes, this is... was Aydan Kelly's place. I'm not Aydan Kelly, I'm Arlene Widdenback. Aydan died recently and I'm just taking care of things..."

This time their shared glance included frowns. The taller officer turned a disapproving gaze back to me. "May we come in?"

"Uh..." I pushed the screen door open, forcing them to move back as I stepped out onto the porch. I pulled the interior door closed behind me and propped the screen door open with my hip. "Let's talk out here." I offered a friendly smile and a placating tone. "How can I help you?"

The taller officer eyed my bare arms, already rising into gooseflesh in the frosty late-October wind. "We should go inside. You'll be more comfortable."

"No, that's okay." I suppressed a shiver along with the urge to glance up at the surveillance camera silently recording us from its concealment in the eaves. No way I'd leave its benevolent scrutiny, not even for uniformed police officers. Especially if they decided to arrest me for something. Like lying about my identity.

As if reading my mind, the shorter officer withdrew a

photo from his inside pocket. He studied it briefly before turning it toward me. "This is a picture of Aydan Kelly. Forty-seven years old. Long red hair. Brown eyes. Five foot ten, a hundred and sixty pounds. You look just like her."

I resisted the urge to gulp as I eyed the photo and held my voice steady. "Yes, I guess we look... looked a lot alike. I've had quite a few cases of mistaken identity."

The blue eyes skewered me. "Intentionally mistaken?"

Oh. Apparently they were familiar with my sleazy cover identity. Thank God. At least now I knew how to react.

I let my shoulders slump and added a hint of whine to my voice. "No, I've turned over a new leaf. It was just the stupid reporters that got us mixed up. It wasn't my fault. I didn't do anything wrong."

I cast my eyes down and scuffed a toe at my doormat in not-too-feigned discomfort. Fear chilled my gut when my conscious mind finally registered the detail that had been nagging at me.

Brown shoes.

They both wore RCMP uniforms, but the dark-haired man was wearing brown tasselled loafers.

I jerked my gaze up in time to see them eyeing each other as if reaching a silent agreement.

"Ms. Widdenback, we have a search warrant for this house." The shorter officer flashed a closely-typed sheet of paper in my face before refolding it and returning it to his pocket. "Please step aside."

"Okay..." I backed up a pace and gauged the tensing of their shoulders when I reached for the doorknob. Why the hell hadn't I worn my waist holster tonight? They could shoot me twice over before I could grab my gun. Shit, even if the surveillance analysts had already called in an alarm, help was still at least ten minutes away.

I gulped down my pounding heart and held my voice steady. "May I have your badge numbers, please? I'd just like to call and check with your detachment."

The shorter officer scowled and took an aggressive step forward. Adrenaline searing my veins, I sprang backward into the house and slammed the door, scrabbling frantically at the lock. The deadbolt snapped into place an instant before the door shivered under a heavy thud.

Bolting for the basement, I lurched down the stairs, nearly tripping myself while I fumbled the gun out of my ankle holster.

Great, fucking great, break my neck falling down the fucking basement stairs trying to avoid being shot or kidnapped or whatever they wanted...

Find a defensible position. I dashed around the corner to flatten myself against the wall beside the stairs.

With my back pressed to the cold concrete, I trained my gun on the foot of the stairs. I'd hear them coming. I should be able to get a shot in before they spotted me.

Tension racked my shoulders while long minutes crawled by. No more sounds came from above and at last I surrendered to aching fatigue and lowered my shaking gun.

What the hell were they doing? Were they still outside? And why the hell hadn't I asked Stemp for a monitor for the surveillance cameras so I could see what was going on? Surely the Department could spare me one lousy monitor.

I strained my ears. Still nothing.

Should I just wait it out? Either John Kane or helicopters full of armed men or both would likely arrive on my doorstep in a few minutes, but it was stupid to cower in my basement if the fake officers were already gone.

I levered myself away from the wall and scuttled over to grab the phone handset. Clutching my gun, I fumbled at the phone with my other hand, trying to watch the numbers and the stairs at the same time. I had only managed the first two digits of Stemp's number when the doorbell rang again.

Jesus Christ, now what? My heart battered my sore ribs.

I jabbed the Off button with a shaking finger and crept up the stairs to jitter a safe distance away from the door, swallowing hard and weighing the possibilities. If it was the fake RCMP officers again, did they really think I'd answer the door if they rang the doorbell?

The chime sounded again, making me start violently and hiss through my teeth at the resulting pain. A knock and the sound of a too-familiar voice from outside made me bite back the obscenities that begged to be shrieked.

I stuffed my gun back into my ankle holster, yanking my pant leg over it while my lips moved in silent but earnest supplication.

God, why me? And why don't You just smite me and get it over with instead of tormenting me like this?

CHAPTER 2

The voice called again from the other side of the door. "Hello? Anybody in there?"

I blew out a short breath and unclenched my teeth and fists before opening the door, trying for a pleasant expression.

The lean, handsome Stetson-clad man staggered back a step, his face blanching.

"Aydan...?" His voice was a bare whisper.

"Tom, uh..."

What the hell was the matter with him? His frozen expression suddenly clued me in. Shit, I hadn't seen or talked to him since my supposed death last week. As the realization dawned on me, his paralysis broke.

"Aydan!" He sprang forward and swept me into his arms, crushing a yelp of pain out of me. "Aydan..." He kissed me hard before pulling away to cup my face in his callused palms, his sky-blue eyes dancing. "Aydan, thank God!"

His lips met mine again, and heat flashed through me when he pulled me against his work-hardened body. Before I could stop them, my hands slid inside the warmth of his fleece-lined denim jacket to find the lean muscle of his chest.

His kiss changed from joyous celebration to seductive invitation. To hot temptation.

Common sense kicked in a moment later and I jerked away.

Dammit, this was far too dangerous. The fake RCMP guys could return at any moment with violent intentions. I couldn't tell Tom anything about my secret life, but my secrets could harm him just the same. And Stemp's team was going to be all over the place in minutes, and how the hell would I explain that?

"Aydan, what's wrong?" Concern sharpened his voice. "You're shaking."

"Nothing, I'm fine."

Get rid of him, fast. Think, think!

"I've just had..." I fumbled for words while considering and discarding options at light-speed. "The last few days have been..."

Maybe he was safer here inside the house. At least I had a gun. If he went back outside, they could easily pick him off from the concealment of the darkness. He'd never even know what hit him.

Right. Keep him here.

"Come on in and sit down." I manufactured a smile. "Would you like something to drink? I'm just going to grab an orange juice."

I waved him in the direction of the kitchen table and headed for the fridge.

"No thanks, I'm fine." He waited until I took my seat at the table before pulling up a chair to sit beside me. "What happened?" he demanded. "Thank God you're alive! Are you all right? Are you safe?"

"Yes..." I sipped my juice, stalling. "Kind of... I, um..."

Dammit, I really didn't want to get into that.

"How did you know I was here?" I asked, postponing the inevitable.

"I didn't. I thought you were dead." He frowned. "I was coming home, and I saw lights through the trees when I turned in my lane. I thought maybe one of your friends was here packing up your things. I was going to offer to help." His hand closed around mine. "Thank God you're alive," he repeated.

"I'm really sorry you were..." I trailed off, not quite knowing how to finish that sentence. Worried? That didn't quite seem to cover it. I tried again. "I'm sorry, I should've called you. I thought everybody knew..."

"It's all right, you wouldn't have been able to get me," he interrupted gently. "I was in Arizona with my folks. We left the day after your funeral. They go down every year at the end of October, and I always go with them to get them settled for the winter."

His brow slowly furrowed and he drew back, his sky-blue gaze searching my face. "What do you mean, you're *kind of* safe? What were those police officers doing here?"

Shit, he'd seen them. And double-shit, that meant they'd seen him, too.

I eased out a breath. "Long story."

His eyes narrowed, taking in my hunched posture and cautious breathing. "You're hurt. Were they here about John Kane? Has he been harassing you again?" His grip tightened on my hand. "Aydan, did he hurt you?"

"No, no," I gabbled, hurrying to quench the anger kindling in his eyes. "No, it was nothing to do with John."

He studied my face as if searching for evidence of a lie. The tension eased from his body when he apparently found none, and he continued, frowning. "Was it about your car accident? Or the men who kidnapped your friend and tried to kill you last week? Are they still looking for you?"

"Like I said, it's a long story. Short answer: no, no, and no. The police caught those men and the car accident was just a dumb coincidence." It was sort of the truth.

"Nichele is safe." Thank God that part was true. I bit back a sigh and laid out the rest of my cover story.

"The police got Nichele back from the kidnappers and arrested them, so that took care of the guys who were trying to kill me."

Which was neither a direct outcome nor true.

I forged on. "The car accident was just some poor dumb schmuck who stole my car and crashed it. I was in Victoria at the time, so I didn't realize until I got back that everybody thought I was dead and my funeral was already over."

Not only untrue but also a cruelty to my friends for which I'd never forgive Stemp. I swallowed a burning lump of anger and kept my face under control.

Tom straightened, his brows drawing together. "How could the medical examiner make that kind of mistake? When there's a fatality accident, they don't assume the driver was the owner of the car. They verify the identity."

I shrugged. "It crashed and burned. I guess there wasn't much left."

"That doesn't make sense." He shook his head slowly. "There's usually something left. Teeth. They should have checked dental records..."

Damn, I should have known better than to try to slip this past a firefighter. I went for a diversion.

"Look, Tom..." I leaned closer, giving him the big brown eyes. "Um... this is kind of embarrassing, but... there's, um...

more to the story. I have to ask you a big favour."

His frown eased. "You know I'll do anything I can."

"Um... Other than just the local people around here... don't mention to anybody else I'm alive, okay?"

His eyes hardened into blue glaciers. "Aydan, who are you hiding from? Who's threatening you? Tell me."

I laid a hand over the fist he had clenched on the table beside me. "No, it's nothing like that. Like I said, it's... just embarrassing... um..." I couldn't quite meet his gaze. "Everybody thinks I'm a porn star. I'm hiding from the media."

"What?" The word blew out on an incredulous gust of half-laughter, half-indignation. "They think you're a *what*? Why in heaven's name...?"

Well, even if my cover story forced me to lie through my teeth, at least I could be honest about my embarrassment.

I felt heat climbing my face. "Um... Well, there's this woman, Arlene Widdenback. She's this skanky internet porn star. She's done a bunch of videos where she fu... um... with this creepy little guy no woman in her right mind would touch with rubber gloves, and she's been to jail for fraud a couple of times. She calls herself Arlene Cherry and, she, um... looks just like me. Well, mostly..."

I bit my tongue before I could mention that the only difference was the digitally enhanced volleyball-sized boobs. I chanced a glance at Tom's face and hurriedly looked down at my lap.

Damn Stemp and his goddamn porn-star cover story. I'd kill him for saddling me with this. Kill him slowly. With much screaming, the bastard.

"So anyway, when I was in Victoria, some reporter saw me and thought I was her," I added rapidly. "And now the media is all fired up about stalking her for interviews and some *moron* got the idea that somehow when I'd died in the car accident, she'd assumed my identity and I'm really her, pretending to be me to avoid publicity..."

This time I didn't look up.

"Aydan, that's..." Tom's response was cut short by the sound of the doorbell. I rose without looking at him to approach the door hesitantly, my heart pounding with renewed fear. It had to be Stemp's team by now. It couldn't be the other guys.

Could it?

Dammit, if it was the fake RCMP guys and I had to pull my gun, how the hell would I explain that to Tom?

Suddenly he was beside me, frowning. "Aydan, are you afraid to answer the door?"

"Um, no, I was just..."

Even if I could have summoned up a plausible explanation, it would have been too late.

"Stay back." He strode forward and flung open the door.

John Kane loomed outside the screen, his dark hair and clothing blending with the night. The porch light threw the scar that bisected his eyebrow into sinister relief and dramatically shadowed his strong features.

Tom was tall and hard-muscled, but Kane's six-foot-four height and mountainous shoulders dwarfed him. Braced in the doorway, Tom's lean figure in faded denim contrasted starkly against Kane's towering darkness like some medieval depiction of good versus evil.

Which was absolute bullshit since Kane was the best of the good guys and the sole reason I wasn't dead several times over. Too bad Tom didn't see it that way.

And I couldn't tell him.

"Kane," Tom said, his neutral tone not quite concealing the hard edge beneath.

Kane nodded, his face expressionless. "Rossburn." His grey gaze tracked to me, rooted to the floor while I assessed the tension between them.

Oh, God, please don't let them fight.

"Aydan," Kane said, his everybody-stay-calm cop voice matching his impassive cop face. "May I come in?"

I found my voice. "Of course. Sorry." I scurried forward to reach past Tom and open the screen door.

Kane stepped unhurriedly into the room while Tom reluctantly moved a couple of paces back. The two men eyed each other without visible hostility, but the hair on the back of my neck bristled with the electric sensation of impending combat.

"I need to speak with Aydan privately for a few minutes," Kane said mildly. "If you'll excuse us, this won't take long."

And if Tom didn't excuse us, I knew it wouldn't take long, either. In hand-to-hand combat, Kane was just as deadly as he looked. Even Tom's considerable strength and courage wouldn't have a prayer.

I didn't give him an opportunity to think it over.

"Sorry, Tom, this'll just take a minute. John and I need to go over some work stuff." I grabbed Kane's sleeve and towed him down the hall into my office without looking back.

Inside, Kane swung the door shut behind us and tilted my chin up to survey my face, his touch lingering. "Are you all right?"

"Fine." I backed away and leaned nonchalantly against my desk.

Kane's big warm hands closed around my shoulders. "Try again. Are you all right? Do you need help getting rid of Rossburn?"

I considered pulling away, but the warm strength of his grip eased my vibrating tension. I gave him a reassuring smile. "Really, I'm fine. And you don't need to worry about Tom unless there's a helicopter and armed men out there that need to be explained away."

He chuckled. "No helicopter. Just me and a few of Stemp's tactical team. We scrambled as soon as the analysts reported the uniforms on your porch. We've secured the perimeter, and the tac team is concealed in the trees down by the creek."

I blew out my relief in a sigh. "Good. So who were those guys?"

He hadn't let go of my shoulders. The heat of his hands radiated, and a whiff of gun oil and leather summoned a knee-weakening wave of memories I'd been doing my best to avoid. I made the mistake of looking up at him. His eyes darkened, focusing on my mouth.

"We're not sure yet," he said, his velvet baritone caressing my ears. "Definitely not RCMP." His gaze tracked up to hold mine. "Maybe you should come and stay in the bunker tonight just to be on the safe side." His voice deepened. "I have a T-shirt you could borrow."

I swallowed hard and tore my mind away from the invitation sizzling in his eyes. With a supreme effort, I kept my hands off his body and my eyes above his chin.

"No, I'll be fine." I pulled out of his grasp. "Let me know as soon as you find out anything. I'd better go and talk to Tom before he decides you're ravishing me in here..." My perfidious voice went husky on the 'ravishing' part.

"...and rushes in to save me," I finished hurriedly, and scuttled out the door.

When I re-entered the kitchen, Tom stopped in mid-pace. His head jerked up, his arms uncrossing as his gaze snapped to Kane striding behind me.

Kane spoke before Tom could. "Thanks for the update. Good night, Aydan." He strolled to the door and stooped to don his boots. When he straightened, he fixed Tom with a level gaze. "Rossburn." His tone was casual, but challenge lurked in its depths.

Tom's eyes narrowed, blue lasers slicing the thickening tension. "Kane."

They held each other's gaze for a long moment before the corner of Kane's mouth quirked up. He turned and strode out, the quiet click of the door puncturing the barrier of suspense that had momentarily stopped my breath.

As I eased out an unobtrusive but painful sigh, Tom turned to study me. "You're shaking again. Did he do something to upset you?"

"No, of course not. We were just talking about work." I stiffened my knees, willing my legs to stop quivering.

He frowned. "You never did tell me why the police were here."

"Um... yeah, sorry." I seized on the first excuse that came to mind. "They were just tying up the last loose ends from their investigation of that car crash. They were in some pretty hot water after getting my identity wrong."

His face softened. "You've had the week from hell. No wonder you're feeling shaky." He stepped closer to gather me into his arms. "Remember you don't have to go through these things alone. I'm here for you."

The softness in his voice and the warmth of his arms brought a flood of unexpected emotion. I pulled away, blinking rapidly at the floor. Jesus, woman, get it together.

"Thanks," I muttered. "I'm fine."

"Aydan..." Tom hesitated. "Why won't you let me help you? Is it... Are you too polite to tell me to get lost? If you don't want me around, just say so. I accused Kane of stalking you, but I just realized maybe I'm the one who's being a pest."

When I glanced up, his expression twisted my heart. "Oh, no, Tom, of course you're not!" I blurted before I thought.

I bit my tongue. Idiot. I could have ended everything cleanly right here and sent him away to live safely ever after without me.

His shoulders relaxed, the tense lines easing from his face. "What is it then?" he asked softly. "Why won't you let down your guard with me? What are you afraid of?"

"I'm not afraid..." I began, but stopped and dropped my gaze to the floor as I recognized an opportunity to steer him away. "Um..." I gave him a quick glance before eyeing the floor again. "Tom..." I hesitated, mentally trying and discarding several choices of words.

"Just say it, Aydan," he said quietly. "You don't have to sugar-coat anything for me."

His bleak expression wrung my heart. Goddammit, I was sick of hurting good people.

I took his hand and told him half the truth.

"Tom, I really like you, but I'm afraid to spend any time with you because I don't want to get involved again. Not with you, and not with anybody."

His face softened, and he stroked my hand. "Aydan, you don't have to be afraid. I'll never hurt you. Let me prove it to you."

I took a moment to relax my clenched teeth and ease out

a secret breath of frustration. "No, you don't understand. I'm not afraid you'll hurt me. I just don't have what it takes to be in a relationship again."

"I know it might feel like that right now, but it's only been a couple of years since your husband died," he said gently. "Give yourself time. Someday you'll be ready to share your life again."

I blew out a breath and pulled my hand away. "I don't want that. I just can't get involved again, and I don't want to try."

"It's okay, I understand," Tom said. He smiled down at me. "I just want you to know I'm here for you as a friend. Or anything else you want me to be." The smile lingered in his eyes. "You look exhausted. I'll leave so you can get some rest."

He moved to the door to slip on his boots and jacket before studying me intently again, one hand on the doorknob.

"Do you need a hug?" he asked softly. "From a friend?"

The sudden quaking need to curl into his arms frightened me.

I stood a little taller and held my voice very steady. "Thanks, but I'm fine."

CHAPTER 3

Trapped!

The coffin squeezed tighter, pinning my arms and legs. I thrashed uselessly, my terrified screams crushed into empty whispers by the implacable pressure of my shrinking prison...

"Aydan! Are you all right?" Kane's shout dragged me free of the nightmare.

I jerked into sitting position, the horror slithering away to coil itself back into the dark corners of my mind.

"Yeah," I croaked, my throat still raw from my screams.

Kane slipped through my bedroom door, smooth and silent as a panther. Lethal black-on-black highlights glinted off his gun as he snapped a glance around the moonlit room.

"It's okay. Just my usual shit." I groaned and slumped forward to massage my aching face, struggling to bring my breathing under control. "Sorry."

The bed dipped as Kane perched beside me. "Bad dream?" His hand stroked my hair.

I drew as deep a breath as I could comfortably manage and eased it out, willing my heart rate to slow. "Yeah." I dragged my head out of my hands to give him an apologetic grimace. "I didn't think you'd be able to hear me from outside. Sorry."

"All clear." Kane spoke into a small radio before pocketing it to draw me closer. I leaned into him, letting the cold fabric of his jacket soothe my sweaty forehead. When I pulled away, he surveyed me, his expression shadowed into obscurity against the moonlit window. "After what you've been through lately, you don't need to apologize for bad dreams. It happens to everybody."

"Yeah, but I bet you don't wake the neighbours screaming," I muttered.

He sighed. "No. I wake up punching. After my first broken knuckle, I learned to move my bed away from the wall for the first few nights after a tough mission."

"Oh." I sat up straighter, feeling slightly comforted. "Gotta hate it when you hit a stud instead of nice soft drywall."

His chuckle rumbled through the darkness. "You can say that again. Go back to sleep. I'll sit with you for a while."

Embarrassment made me squirm. "No, that's okay, I'm fine. But you and the tac team should come in the house and get warm." I shot a glance at the glowing digits of the clock radio. "God, it's after midnight. You've been out there for nearly four hours. You must be freezing."

"It's only minus five. We're dressed for it, and we keep moving."

"Well, call them on the radio and tell them to come in. I don't think those fake RCMP guys were much of a threat. If they'd been serious about it, they would've grabbed me or shot me right off the bat."

I searched his face, unable to read him in the darkness. "You can protect me just as easily and a lot more comfortably from inside the house. And anyway, you need sleep. Stemp doesn't expect you to hang around here all night, does he?"

Kane shifted on the bed. "Stemp doesn't know I'm still here. My orders were to secure the area and leave the tac team in place."

I eyed his shadowed features with exasperation. "Well, he knows now, because you just came through the camera surveillance. Go home and get some rest, for chrissake, or you won't be able to function tomorrow." My words ended in a gulp as all my worry flooded back at the thought of my upcoming meeting. I wrenched my mind back to the conversation at hand. "And next week... you're going to need every advantage you can get if you're going to be saddled with me as a partner. Or do you think Stemp will just send me out on my own...?" I swallowed papery fear.

Kane chuckled. "You've been undercover too long. You can abandon the Oscar-winning act when you're with me."

My hand clenched on the duvet hard enough to crack my knuckles. "It's not an act," I hissed. "John, you have to believe me. I was lying when I told Stemp I was an agent. I'm just a dumb civilian bookkeeper and I don't know the first thing about-"

"Shhh." His fingertips pressed gently against my lips. "It's all right. I know you can't drop your cover."

I gripped his wrist. "Listen. Please listen to me. If we go on a mission and if you don't treat me like a brainless civilian, you will die expecting me to use some fancy spy skills that I *don't have*! I can't do this!"

He went still. "You wouldn't break cover even if our lives were at stake?"

I let go of his wrist to thump my forehead with the heels of both hands. "*No!* I mean, I would if I could, but I-"

His kiss stifled my protest, but before I could react he

pulled away and stood. The moonlight silvered the curve of his smile. "Aydan, I wouldn't expect anything else. I'll willingly stake my life on a partnership with you. You're amazing." His grin flashed through the dimness. "You're also naked. I'm leaving while I still have some willpower, and before the surveillance analysts get suspicious." His wicked grin widened. "But if they didn't know I was here…"

He turned and strode out, leaving the unfinished sentence vibrating on suddenly overheated air.

I managed to get through the rest of the night without screaming, largely because I couldn't go back to sleep. Squinting in the too-bright bathroom lights the next morning, I groaned at the sight of bags under my eyes big enough to carry sandwiches.

A shower and breakfast roused me sufficiently to stumble around the house pulling together the essentials to pack into my spare waist pouch along with the replacement identification cards Stemp had issued me the previous day. At least there were some advantages to working with the Department. Instant replacement ID when yours gets blown up, for one.

I tucked my spare knives into their accustomed spot, feeling smug. Nichele had teased me for my anal-retentive tendencies when I'd bought duplicates, but I loved that lock-bladed knife, dammit. And who was laughing now?

My momentary surge of satisfaction waned fast when I stepped out into the cold morning light, and my breakfast churned in my stomach during the drive to Silverside. With nothing to distract me on the empty country highway, my mind chittered and scrabbled like a trapped rat.

How could I convince Stemp to demote me back to being an asset instead of an agent? Sure, that meant he'd kill me as soon as he found another way to decrypt files and hack computer networks, but if he sent me out on a mission, I'd probably end up dead in short order anyway. And at least as an asset, nobody else's life would depend on me.

I braked when Silverside's single traffic light turned red as usual at my approach.

I could try telling Stemp the truth, but he likely wouldn't believe it. I could see it now: 'Director, y'know before, when you thought I was telling the truth? I was lying then. But I'm telling the truth now. Really, I am.' Yeah, that would work just fine, wouldn't it?

Or maybe... What if he sent me out on a mission, and I purposely screwed it up badly enough that he'd have to demote me?

The light changed, and I groaned as I drove through the intersection. Screwing up one of Stemp's missions meant breaches of national security and innocent people dying. Not an option.

What if I just refused to go?

I parked the truck in the lot across from the Sirius Dynamics building and stared blindly through the windshield, my heart racing.

Insubordination. What would Stemp do?

My grip tightened on the steering wheel and I willed my fingers to slacken enough to ease the pain in my knuckles. I knew damn well what he'd do. My heart fluttered into my throat and lodged there, vibrating.

Jail.

Captivity.

A deluge of adrenaline turned my breathing fast and

shallow, and I fought down panic. Breathe. Just belly breathe. In. Out. Stay calm.

Okay, so insubordination wasn't an option.

A figure loomed up in the half-light outside my window and I let out a strangled yelp, jerking around in my seat. For an instant I thought I was hallucinating out of sheer anxiety, but in the next moment I registered Stemp's flesh-and-blood presence. I pried my fingers off the steering wheel and opened the door, hoping my trembling knees wouldn't drop me in the grubby snow of the parking lot.

"Kelly." Stemp surveyed me with his usual lack of expression. "Is everything all right?"

"Fine." I slammed the truck door behind me and forced my legs into what I hoped was a confident stride. Stemp matched my pace as I headed for the building, and I halted abruptly, feigning sudden realization. "Oh, I forgot my gloves in the truck."

I turned back, sending out a psychic plea for him to just keep walking. "See you later," I added, hoping he'd get the hint.

"Sooner," he corrected. "Sign in and report directly to my office in the secured area."

"Okay." The word squeezed out of my suddenly constricted throat, and I trudged back to the truck, repressing the urge to get back in, drive away, and keep on driving forever.

At the security wicket in the lobby, I dropped the pen twice before managing to scrawl a shaky version of my signature on the sign-in sheet. I held still for the retinal scan outside the heavy door to the secured area with roughly the same enthusiasm as if the small aperture contained a firing squad.

When the door released, I sucked in a deep breath before stepping into the confines of the time delay chamber. Trying to ignore the muffled thud-click of the door behind me, I took two rapid steps forward to activate the next retinal scan.

My breath hissed out between my teeth while I eyed the second hand on my old wristwatch, willing it to traverse the thirty-second arc faster. The low ceiling felt like a rock slab, poised to flatten me.

Shit, stop it! Think about open spaces.

I clamped down on the need to pant in the still air, forcing myself to take deep, slow breaths. When the click of the release sounded at last, I snatched the door open and stumbled down the cramped concrete stairwell as rapidly as I could on wobbly legs. At the bottom, I yanked the door open and lurched into the white corridor, propping myself against the wall beside the door and clamping my eyes shut.

Cool air wafted against my face, and I concentrated on slowing my pounding heart. Not trapped. I could be out of here in thirty seconds. Only thirty seconds. Lots of nice, fresh air down here. Nothing to worry about.

My adrenal glands remained unconvinced.

"Are you all right?"

Every muscle in my body convulsed and I crushed my scream into a squeak behind clenched teeth as my eyes flew open. The small man in front of me took a quick step away from my half-raised fists.

"Are you all right? Do you need help?"

His soothing tones heated my cheeks with a flush of embarrassment. It was Saturday, for chrissake. I had thought the researchers would be gone for the weekend and I'd be alone down here with my claustrophobia.

Nothing like getting caught acting like a raving loony.

I twisted my stiff lips into what I hoped resembled a smile. Judging by his uncertain expression, it might not have been as convincing as I'd hoped.

"I'm fine." I attempted a light laugh that came out sounding more like a bleat. "Sorry, you just startled me. I didn't expect anybody else to be down here. I'm just a little claustrophobic, so it usually takes me a few minutes to adjust to being down here. I was just taking a few minutes..." I bit my tongue before I could babble any more and pulled myself together. "Thanks for asking. I'm fine."

I turned and strode down the hall, hoping he couldn't see how much my legs were shaking.

Steeling myself, I tapped on the door of Stemp's office. At his 'Come', I swung the door open, and my heart sank at the sight of the stunning blonde woman seated in one of his guest chairs. Sure enough, she had her little briefcase with her.

Oh, shit.

I held my voice under tight control, but it came out shrill despite my best efforts. "Hi, Jack. What are you doing here on a Saturday?"

Her radiant smile warmed the room. "Hi, Aydan." She avoided my question with a solicitous, "How are you feeling?"

I cleared my throat and tried again for a casual tone. "Fine. Still a little sore, but okay other than the bruises."

As I shuffled closer, she rose and squeezed my hand. "I'm so glad you're all right. We came so close to losing you." A faint crease formed between her flawless brows, her big blue eyes full of concern. "You still look as though you're in pain. Are you sure you shouldn't take it easy for a few days?"

I summoned up a smile. "No, I'm fine. Thanks."

"I'm glad to hear it." Stemp spoke for the first time, his reptilian gaze dissecting me. "Dr. Travers, please hook her up to the polygraph."

I sank into the chair he indicated, controlling my breathing and keeping my posture relaxed.

Earlier, it had seemed like a good idea to convince him I'd been lying about being an agent. Now it occurred to me that he might just decide I couldn't be trusted and kill me on the spot. Especially if his questions forced me to tell him the details I'd deliberately omitted from my last report...

I resisted the urge to gulp.

Jack laid her small case on his desk and extracted the familiar band of electrodes. She shot me a brief smile as she settled it around my forehead before turning back to twiddle some knobs in the case.

"There." She stepped back, giving Stemp a nod. "You may begin, Director."

"Thank you. You're dismissed, Dr. Travers." Stemp's flat gaze flicked in her direction before returning to bore into me. "I'll call you when we're finished."

Jack stiffened. "Director... I... uh... you..." She straightened her spine, her usual crisp tone returning. "You do realize that this polygraph is experimental technology, do you not? Though all my current research indicates it's accurate, I haven't completed testing-"

"Yes, of course." Stemp waved a dismissive hand.

She stood her ground a moment longer, her blue gaze raking his impassive face. "Don't shoot her this time," she snapped before turning on her heel to march out. The door closed behind her with unnecessary firmness.

Stemp leaned back in his chair, steepling his hands and appraising me over top of them. "If you would be so kind as to place your weapon on my desk. Slowly."

I leaned painfully down to ease my gun out of my ankle holster. When I laid it on his desk, he fixed me with his snake-like eyes. "You will answer yes or no. Are you carrying any other weapons?"

I sank back into my chair. "No." Realization struck even as I spoke the word. "Uh... not really..."

A flicker of movement made me jerk my gaze up to see his gun trained steadily on my chest. "Would you care to try that answer again?"

My brain bobbed weightlessly in a sea of adrenaline while the damning red light pulsed in my peripheral vision, but apparently I had catapulted beyond fear. My voice came out sounding incongruously conversational.

"I forgot about my knives. I don't even think of them as weapons."

Stemp nodded almost imperceptibly toward his desk. "If you please. Slowly."

"Okay." I carefully unzipped the front pocket of my waist pouch and extracted my sturdy lock-bladed knife and a smaller multi-tool jackknife. I slid them onto his desk before leaning back cautiously in my chair again.

"Thank you. Are you carrying any other weapons?"

"No..." The word came out suffused with guilt while I racked my brain for anything else I'd forgotten, but apparently the polygraph was satisfied this time. Its light glowed green.

Stemp fixed me with an unblinking stare. "Do you have any other means of harming me?"

What did he think I was going to do? Break out some secret ninja skills? Use the awesome power of my mind to melt the gun in his hand? The only weapon I could possibly use against him was his big secret, and we both knew I'd never blab that.

"No."

The light shone blood-red again. My heart battered my chest while Stemp sat in silence, his gun and gaze trained on me with equal deadliness. A small, detached portion of my racing mind admired my composed tone.

"Could you rephrase the question?"

His voice was completely flat. "Why would I do that?"

I couldn't prevent myself from glancing around the room before I met his gaze and spoke softly. "Is this room secure? Could we be overheard?"

"It's secure. Stop stalling. Do you have any other means of harming me? Yes or no."

"Yes. I know about your wife and daughter in Bulgaria. That information could harm you if it reached the wrong ears."

His gaze faltered, his knuckles whitening on the gun, and for an instant I thought he'd pull the trigger. Instead, he matched my quiet tone. "True. Do you have any other means of harming me besides that?"

"No."

I eased out a breath when the light glowed green.

Stemp slowly laid his gun on his desk, his eyes never leaving me. "I can see this will be an interesting conversation."

CHAPTER 4

Stemp regarded me in silence for a long moment before speaking. "Let's begin at the beginning. Is your real name Aydan Kelly?"

"Yes."

"Have you ever used another name?"

"N..." I caught myself just in time. That would have been true a couple of weeks ago, but not anymore. "Yes." The green light flashed reassurance.

"Do you also use the names Arlene Widdenback and Arlene Cherry?"

I tried to keep my expression neutral, but I was pretty sure some venom leaked through. Someday I'd make him regret assigning me that cover...

"Yes."

"Have you ever used any other names besides those?"

"No."

I knew better than to relax into the easy questions. Sure enough, the next one was a biggie.

"Are you a secret agent?"

"N... uh... yes..." Dammit, both 'yes' and 'no' were equal parts truth and lie. I wasn't an agent, but he'd promoted me to agent status, so did that make me an agent or not?

I shot an anxious glance at the case. Green light. What would it have done if I'd said 'no'?

Stemp's next question pulled me back from my nervous speculations. "Does your direct command work within the Sirius Dynamics command structure?"

At least that was an easy one. "Yes."

"Would your direct command do anything to compromise national security or our operations?"

"I seriously doubt it." Stemp might be a dickhead, but I was pretty sure he was loyal.

He eyed me. "Yes or no, please."

"How the hell should I know? You tell me. Are you a traitor?"

He raised an eyebrow. "So we're talking about me, are we? Thank you for your vote of confidence. No, I'm not a traitor." After a short silence, he spoke again. "Let's talk about your other chain of command."

I swallowed my palpitating heart and held my voice steady. "I don't have another chain of command."

He leaned forward, resting his elbows on his desk. "That is directly contrary to what you told me four days ago."

My shrug felt more like a nervous twitch. "Yes, but then I told you afterward that I didn't have any other ops."

"Very well, Kelly. Let's find out. Do you have any other ops? Yes or no."

"No."

Stemp sat back slowly in his chair, eyeing the green light.

"Did you have another op four days ago?"

My heart pistoned against my ribs, and I couldn't prevent another involuntary swallow to moisten my dry throat. "Y-yes." My voice was just above a whisper.

Shit, shit, shit...

"You told me four days ago that if anyone else found out about your other op, the consequences to you would be..." He hesitated, apparently searching for the correct word. "...disastrous. Does that still hold true?"

"Yes," I croaked.

My mind scurried away in a desperate bid for freedom. Jack should put some more lights on that thing. A big honkin' strobe for when somebody spoke a truth of the magnitude I'd just uttered. When Stemp found out I'd been lying, 'disaster' wouldn't even begin to cover it...

His voice jerked my attention back to the situation at hand. "Would your direct command for any of your other ops do anything to compromise national security or jeopardize our clandestine operations?"

Another easy one, since I'd only had one so-called 'op' and my 'direct command' had been me, myself, and I.

"No."

Stemp glanced at the green light before scrutinizing me for approximately a lifetime. My nerves twisted into knots, anticipating the killing blow.

I managed not to betray myself with a start when he spoke again. "You seem very sure."

"Yes."

Another long pause. "You must have been working under that command for some time, then."

Yeah, for my entire life...

"Yes." I held myself under rigid control, stifling a hysterical giggle when the green light flashed again.

"Have you ever conveyed sensitive information to anyone outside your command structure?"

"No."

"Do you have reason to believe any of your other ops

would ever compromise national security or our operations?"

"No."

"Would you ever intentionally compromise national security or our operations?"

"No."

Green light all the way.

Stemp sat immobile, his monochrome colouring and expressionless eyes reminding me all over again of a rattlesnake. I held myself completely still while his gaze ripped my soul from its moorings and inspected it like a cheap T-shirt held up to the light.

"Would it be in the best interests of our clandestine operations and our national security if I chose to trust you?"

I looked him square in the eyes. "Yes."

"Would it be in my personal best interests to trust you?"

"Yes."

The green light kept shining, bright and steady.

He smiled. A real smile that erased ten years from his face and warmed his eyes to golden brown, crinkling them at the corners. "Thank you. I'm very glad to hear that."

Dumbfounded by the transformation, I closed my gaping mouth as he turned away to pick up the phone.

"Dr. Travers, we're finished with the polygraph." I could still hear the smile in his voice. "I didn't shoot her this time."

When Jack had packed her equipment and departed with a relieved smile, Stemp pushed my gun and knives toward me and sat back in his chair, his emotionless façade in place once more. As I finished stowing my gear, he spoke.

"Your next meeting will be with a psychologist. We've developed a psych profile based on your behaviour and reactions over the past eight months, but this will serve to fill in the blanks. It will also help me determine how to best use your skills."

I swallowed hard. "Uh, yeah, about that..." At his inquiring glance, I stumbled on. "Um... I... you, um, shouldn't count on me having any useful skills. Don't put me in a position where somebody else's life depends on me."

"Lives will always depend on you. They always have. You know that."

With tremendous restraint, I kept from balling my fists in my hair. "I know, but... I mean... don't expect me to know what to do." His blank expression made my fear burst out. "I'm just a bookkeeper, for shit's sake!"

"Ah." His eyes narrowed. "Yes. Your original cover. You're right, that may present some difficulties. I'll keep that in mind."

A wave of relief nearly made me melt in my chair. "Thank you."

He glanced at his watch. "The psychologist will be waiting in your office. Don't mention anything classified."

I tottered out, my mind reeling. I couldn't believe he hadn't asked the obvious questions that would have nailed me to the wall. The numb incredulity carried me up the stairs and through the time delay chamber, where I barely noticed the thirty second countdown.

As I felt my way into the ladies' room on the second floor, my brain gradually rebooted.

Stemp's paranoia had just saved my ass. So many times, I'd cursed his refusal to provide us with more details than we absolutely needed to accomplish a mission. But now, he had asked only the questions necessary to assure him of my loyalty. Only what he needed to know, no more.

All of a sudden, I didn't hate him quite so much.

When I entered my office a few minutes later, I swallowed a groan at the sight of the small balding man seated in the chair beside my sofa. Christ, wouldn't you know it? Of all the people in the whole damn building, it had to be the psychologist who'd caught me freaking out in the secured area.

He rose, extending his hand with a smile. "Agent Kelly? I'm Dr. Rawling."

"Hi." I shook his hand, looking down into his kind eyes and letting out a secret breath of relief when he didn't try to crush my hand. Too many times, I'd had to deal with short guys with compensation issues. At least Dr. Rawling didn't seem to have a problem with tall women. But surely a psychologist would deal with his own shit...

His voice interrupted my scattered thoughts. "Please have a seat, and we'll begin." He indicated the sofa, and I sat, deliberately leaning back and letting my arms rest comfortably beside me.

Relaxed, open posture. Nice and cooperative, nothing to hide. Not a raving loony.

He smiled. "May I call you Aydan?"

"Sure."

"Aydan, before we begin, is there anything you'd like to talk about? I'm not given details, of course, but I understand you've had some stressful experiences lately."

Stressful. No shit, Dr. Freud.

I cranked on a smile of my own. "No thanks, I'm fine. What do you need from me today?"

"Well, let's dive right in." He smiled again, doing his

own relaxed, open posture across from me. "Let's start with your claustrophobia."

"Okay."

He eyed me in expectant silence. I shrugged. "So I'm claustrophobic."

"How do you feel about that?"

I suppressed another groan. Be cooperative.

"It's a pain in the a... A nuisance sometimes."

"You seemed quite distressed when I saw you in the secured area."

I squirmed. "Yeah, we already established that I'm claustrophobic. It is what it is. I'll deal with it."

"Do you think it might be beneficial to learn some skills that could help you cope with it more effectively?"

"I've *got* the damn skills!"

A glance at his kind, patient, accepting expression filled me with an intense desire to launch myself off the sofa and run screaming. I clamped down on control and forced my bunched-up shoulders to relax.

"Dr. Rawling," I said in my most reasonable tones, "Thank you, but I had an excellent therapist quite a few years ago, and I do have the skills to cope with this. I've just had a tough couple of weeks, and I'm a little stressed. I'll deal with it. I just need some time."

"So you're saying that your claustrophobic reaction has been exacerbated by your recent experiences? Would you like to talk about those?"

Not fucking likely.

I squelched that response. Be cooperative, dammit.

I kept it short. "I just about got blown up a couple of days ago. And I've been tied up far too often lately."

I shut up before my voice could betray me. The hiss of

the butane torch and the smell of my own flesh burning. I had relived it again last night while I fought the implacable bonds of my dreams.

I shrugged. "I'll get over it. I just need a bit of time."

He leaned forward, radiating sympathy. "Aydan, were you harmed by the people who tied you up?"

"No. Well, nothing major," I amended, driven to honesty by those damn kind eyes. "A few bruises. One little burn. No big deal." I shrugged again before realizing I was shrugging far too often. I settled back into the sofa and rearranged my relaxed, open posture.

"Were you threatened?"

The last strained threads of my equanimity snapped. "Oh, hell no, it was all in good fun. We just had a few giggles and then they let me go. What the hell do you think?"

His calm demeanor remained unaffected. "Are you sleeping well at night?"

"Oddly enough, I tend to sleep for shit right after people try to kill me. Just oversensitive, I guess."

"Aydan," he said gently. "I feel as though you're uncomfortable talking to me. Is that true?"

I drew a calming breath and tried for a forthright tone. "Yes. I understand that you've been asked to evaluate me, but I really don't want to discuss this right now. If I think I need help, I won't hesitate to get it. I really just need a bit of time. That's all."

He fixed me with his sympathetic gaze again. "Aydan, have you heard of post-traumatic stress? It often occurs when people experience frightening events or violence, particularly if they've felt powerless during-"

"Yes." I met his eyes with a stare that probably looked more hostile than I'd intended. "Have you ever experienced post-traumatic stress?"

"I've helped quite a few people to deal with it, but no, I haven't experienced it first-hand."

"I have. Trust me, if I need help, I'll ask for it."

He smiled and rose, as composed as ever. "If you ever feel you'd like to talk things over, here's my card. Call me any time. Oh, and Director Stemp would like to see you again before you leave."

I followed him to the door and closed it behind him before lowering myself onto my sofa again, holding my tremors together with both arms wrapped around my body.

Just a little time. That's all I needed.

After a few minutes, I blew out a long breath, reaching for composure. Several deep, slow yoga breaths helped me relax my clenched muscles, and I rose and shook the tension out of my arms and shoulders before heading for the door.

I had just poured boiling water over my teabag when Stemp paused outside the lunchroom, his expression lightening at the sight of me. "Oh, good, there you are." He inclined his head in the direction he'd come. "Please come to my office for a briefing. Bring your tea if you'd like."

God, if he kept acting like a real human being, I was going to get rug burn on my jaw. I retrieved it from its dangling position and followed him down the hall.

Once we were settled in our chairs, he shot me an unreadable look across the desk. "Dr. Rawling said you had a short interview."

I nodded and busied myself sipping tea.

After a pause, he spoke again. "I said 'don't tell him anything classified', not 'don't tell him anything at all'."

I couldn't think of a useful response to that, so I sipped more tea.

The hint of humour in his voice made me look up quickly, catching the little quirk at the corner of his mouth. "I probably would have done the same in your place." The quirk disappeared as if it had never existed. "I understand you've been undercover a long time, and I know how deeply ingrained those reflexes become."

I returned my attention to my tea, guilt twisting my gut. He really did understand. According to Kane, he'd been an excellent field agent before he took over the director's position. My pretense felt like an insult to all the dedicated agents who put their lives on the line to protect idiot civilians like me.

But, shit, it was a little late to confess now, wasn't it?

Stemp's voice interrupted my uncomfortable thoughts. "Dr. Rawling is an excellent resource, and I hope you'll avail yourself of his expertise. We need you in top mental condition."

I dragged my gaze up out of my teacup to meet his eyes reluctantly. "I will if I need it. I just need a bit of time."

He nodded. "I'll accept that, for now. But if I have reason to believe you need help, I will order you to get it."

My stomach dropped. He could, too. Now that I was officially an agent, I was under his direct command. The tricky bastard had out-manoeuvred me again.

I blew out a sigh. "All right. Fine."

We eyed each other for a moment over the rim of my mug before he spoke again. "With that in mind, I have an assignment for you this weekend."

I knew he hadn't missed the convulsive tightening of my grip on the mug. Willing the blood back into my knuckles, I steadied it with my other hand, my mind stampeding into near-panic. The only day left in 'the weekend' was *tomorrow*, for chrissake.

"When I said I needed time, I was thinking of days or weeks, not hours." My voice didn't sound too bad for someone on the verge of hyperventilating.

Stemp's flat eyes appraised me. "So was I. How does a few days in Las Vegas sound?"

"Uh..."

Absolutely horrible.

My lips didn't have time to frame those words before he spoke again. "The mission itself entails virtually no risk. It's just a dead drop, and it needs to be completed before Monday at nineteen-hundred hours local time. The agent who was supposed to do it has been... unavoidably detained, so we need someone else to take over."

Dead drop? 'Dead' sounded damn risky to me. And Stemp's slight hesitation over the words 'unavoidably detained' didn't reassure me, either. Getting dead did tend to detain a person.

He was still talking. "...so you could fly down tonight and spend a few days at the Mirage, on Department expense, of course. Make the drop and come back late Tuesday." He regarded me as if expecting me to jump up and do a happy-dance.

"Uh..."

Time to come clean. I couldn't fake this, and I'd be stupid to try. If he decided to kill me for my deception, so be it, but at least my incompetence wouldn't hurt anybody else.

I gathered my courage and sucked in a deep enough breath to make my ribs protest. "I don't know what a dead drop is. I'm not undercover now and I never have been. I don't have any chain of command other than you, my so-called 'op' was just me sneaking around doing stuff on my own initiative, and I was lying to cover my ass when I told you about it."

I clutched my trembling mug tighter and met his eyes. "I'm just a dumb civilian bookkeeper. I'm sorry."

He returned my gaze with a flat stare and stony silence, and I resisted the urge to close my eyes and whimper. God, just shoot me and get it over with.

I flinched when he laughed out loud.

"Oh, well done, Kelly." He extracted a small canvas bag from his desk drawer and pushed it across the desk. "Here are your phones. Use the daily check-in protocol. I'll arrange for your security bypass at the airport, and your tickets will be ready by noon. The data stick will be delivered to your hotel room, and I'll leave the details of its drop to you. Use one of the secured phones to let me know when you've set it up."

He glanced at his wristwatch. "The analysts have flagged a few urgent files, so I've asked your team to meet you in your office. You'll have a couple of hours to decrypt the files and tie up any loose ends before you go."

"Uh... N... uh, but, wait... No." I gathered my scattered wits and tried again. "No! Listen, I'm not an agent and I don't have a clue what to do..."

I trailed off as he held up a hand. "I appreciate your dedication to your cover, but there's no need to continue the charade. I'm already convinced of your acting skill." He gave me a pleasant smile and a nod of dismissal before transferring his attention to his computer screen. "Enjoy your trip."

Stunned into passivity by the double whammy of his unprecedented smiles and the utter failure of my confession, I picked up the bag with a numb hand and stumbled out.

CHAPTER 5

Still shell-shocked, I wandered into my office and met Kane's pleasant greeting with an ineffectual twitch of my stiff lips.

The smile vanished from his face as he rose quickly from the chair. "Aydan, are you all right? You're white as a sheet."

"Fine."

His big warm hand supported my elbow, and I took a measure of comfort from his strength while I wobbled over and sank onto my sofa.

He stooped to look into my face. "You don't look fine."

It took all my willpower not to fling myself into his arms and beg him to save me. Clinging to the last vestiges of my self-respect, I clenched my hands in my lap and whispered instead.

"John, I need your help."

He shot a glance at the open door before pulling the chair closer to drop into it, leaning forward as his forehead creased into worried lines. "What's wrong?"

"What's a dead drop?"

He blinked, puzzlement replacing concern. "What...?"

"Stemp's sending me to Las Vegas this afternoon to do a

dead drop," I hissed. "I *told* him I'm just a bookkeeper and I haven't got a clue, but he didn't believe me. What's a dead drop? What am I supposed to do?"

Kane leaned back in his chair with a guffaw, the tension in his body melting away. "Nice acting job. You really had me going for a minute there." He shook his head, chuckling. "That was a good one."

Frozen in sheer dismay, I was still trying to think of a way to convince him I was serious when Spider and Jack strolled in, trailed by Kasper Doytchevsky.

Now that I knew Doytchevsky's history as a Russian spy, I just couldn't think of him as John Smith anymore. The stench of his body odour pervaded the office, and he made no more eye contact than usual.

Queasy uncertainty coiled up in the pit of my stomach. I probably should've ratted him out to Stemp yesterday. I really had nothing but his word that we were on the same side, and his socially-inept-scientist act proved how convincingly he could lie.

Must be damn nice to be a real spy with some actual spy skills.

My bitter reflections were interrupted by Spider's cheery greeting. "Hi, guys, what's the joke?"

Kane grinned. "Aydan's trying to pull her 'I'm just a bookkeeper' act."

"Give it up." Spider shot me a bright-eyed grin of his own. "Maybe if you hadn't single-handedly infiltrated an enemy base and blown it up..."

"And cracked open a massive international conspiracy..." Kane chimed in.

"...we *might* believe you," Spider continued.

"But probably not," Jack finished with one of her radiant

smiles.

"I'm really just a bookkeeper," I gritted.

Kane sobered. "You're right, of course. As far as any of us officially know, you are just a bookkeeper. Don't worry, Aydan, this ends here."

I looked around at their solemn faces and nods of agreement and felt even worse. "Thanks," I mumbled.

Spider leaned close. "But congratulations on your promotion," he whispered, and squeezed my hand. "I'm so glad you're not just an asset anymore. You can't imagine how awful it's been knowing you had a death sentence hanging over you."

The relief and happiness in his youthful face warmed my heart, and I returned his squeeze along with a feeble smile. "Thanks, Spider."

"Can we get started?" Doytchevsky's nasal voice intruded on the moment, and I turned toward him, grateful for the distraction. Deceiving Stemp was bad enough, but living a lie with people I cared about made me feel like the lowest form of pond scum.

"Yes, let's," Jack agreed. "Aydan, I'm taking over Sam's research..." Her voice wavered, and the thought of Sam's betrayal made me swallow a hard lump of anger or hurt or something. Whatever it was, it didn't sit comfortably in my stomach.

She continued hurriedly, "...so I'm going to monitor a few more of your sessions in the network."

"Okay." I probably looked as sick as she did. A glance around the room assured me I wasn't the only one. Spider's usual blithe smile had vanished, leaving his hazel eyes troubled. Kane and Doytchevsky both wore standard-issue inscrutable spy faces, but Doytchevsky's eyes glittered with rage.

When my gaze passed over him, he shuttered the expression so quickly I would have missed it if I'd looked an instant later. Jack temporarily blocked my view when she placed the band of electrodes on my forehead, and by the time she moved away Doytchevsky was absorbed at the desktop computer, back to his usual bland facade.

Spider smiled and handed me the tiny box containing the micro-miniaturized network key that turned me into the world's only human decryption machine.

I accepted it reluctantly. Hard to believe such a miniscule piece of technology had completely destroyed the safe, quiet life I'd hoped to live. Goddamn Sam.

Spider tapped a few keys on his ever-present laptop before looking up. "Ready whenever you are. What are we doing today?"

"Just a couple of quick decryptions, and then I have to get going." I suppressed a sigh. "I'm going to Vegas this afternoon."

"Oh, cool!" Spider straightened, smiling. "You deserve a nice holiday. Hey, maybe you'll see Lola there. She's at another... um... convention." A flush rose on his cheeks, and I allowed my amusement to generate a smile I hoped everyone would mistake for happy anticipation.

"Could I get you to pop into the internet for a few minutes, too?" Jack asked. "I just want to nail down a few more baseline readings."

"Sure. John, are you ready?"

He nodded, his hand going to his Sirius Dynamics security fob. I gripped my tiny key and leaned back on the sofa, projecting my mind into the blank void of the brainwave-driven virtual reality environment.

A moment later, Kane's avatar popped into existence beside mine, and we made our way down the virtual corridor to the familiar file repository.

Inside, I shuffled through the file folders, searching for the ones the analysts had flagged. Pulling my chair up to the desk, I glanced at Kane seated beside me. "Ready for another exciting day?"

He chuckled. "Boring is good. Boring means you're safe."

I could hear the smile in Spider's voice when it filtered down from above the virtual ceiling. "Please bore us as much as possible."

I laughed, too, and opened the file to begin my translation.

I read off the last line and straightened slowly, rubbing my aching neck. "That's it. Was it any good?"

"Yes." Kane had materialized a computer terminal on the desk beside me, and he looked up from it with a wolfish grin. "Oh, yes, indeed. I've been tracking this for months..." He trailed off, focusing on the screen while he typed rapidly with two fingers.

"Good," I said to his intent profile. "Jack, I'm done with the files now. Do you need me to do anything specific in the internet?"

"Just wait a minute..." Her voice sounded preoccupied, and I imagined the tiny crease between her flawless brows while she twiddled with her instruments in the real world. When she spoke again, her usual crisp diction had returned. "All right, Aydan, whenever you're ready. I don't need anything specific, so just stay in the internet for a while.

About ten minutes should do it."

"Okay." I faded into invisibility, absently wondering for the umpteenth time what vagary of the network key's design required me to be invisible while I followed the data tunnels outside Sirius's simulation network.

"Aydan!" Kane's bellow made me snap back into my visible avatar, adrenaline pounding in my veins.

"What?" I shot a wild glance around the room, but saw no cause for alarm. "What? Jesus, you scared the shit out of me."

He clasped my hand in his, frowning. "Are you crazy? Don't go into the network without an anchor."

"I'm only going outside our firewall for ten minutes, and I'm not going far. You might as well keep working."

His grip tightened, "I don't care if it's for ten seconds. You *never* go into the network without an anchor. Clear?"

"Clear." I faded into invisibility again before he could read annoyance in my expression. As I stretched my consciousness from his anchoring grasp, I wondered if I was technically still under his command now that I was an agent. Hmmm. Have to ask Stemp...

I rode the jostling stream of data packets through the firewall and floated in the shifting currents of the internet, entertaining myself by skimming through data the rest of the world naively believed was impenetrably encrypted. Lucky for them I was working for the good guys. And lucky for them I'd destroyed the only remaining network keys two nights ago, so I was now the only person left in the world who could still crack their files.

Satisfaction warmed me. Maybe I was just a dumb civilian bookkeeper, but I'd done pretty damn well...

A tsunami of data overwhelmed me, tumbling me into

chaotic limbo. Terror flooded me while I struggled to gather the scattered remnants of my consciousness.

I knew this sensation.

The fear narrowed my concentration to laser-bright strands. My virtual fishnet flared and snapped shut, capturing every vestige of the turbulent data.

You. Are. *Mine!*

I began to sift packets through the finest filters I could create.

About an eternity later, I sorted the last packet. Now for the tricky part. I had been so intent on my task I hadn't registered how exhausted I was. My net pulsed with the frenetic oscillation of the captured data, straining my concentration to its limits.

And...

Now.

I released the net. The sudden absence of data imploded my consciousness, shattering me into white-hot fragments. With the last remains of my will, I pursued the retreating packets, sniffing out their now-familiar scent/flavour until they left the data tunnel.

Gotcha.

With agonizing slowness, I began to coalesce, easing my tenuously connected bits back toward Sirius Dynamics and into Kane's waiting grasp.

I was pretty sure I'd made it. Kane's voice reassured me, but it seemed to come from random directions in a cacophony that somehow melded into comprehension. I tried to pull my consciousness into my avatar's usual form, but before I could accomplish the task, pain drilled through my eye sockets.

I jerked into a ball, welcoming the sensation with sincere gratitude. Back in my own physical body. Thank God.

"Ow, ow, *ow*, cocksucking-goatfucking-sonuva*bitch*..."

Apparently my mouth wasn't quite as thankful as my brain.

I clenched my teeth and rode out the remainder of the too-familiar pain groaning wordlessly while Kane's strong hands massaged the shards of agony out of my temples.

"Aydan, what happened?" Jack's urgent voice drove resonant spikes through my head, and I uncurled enough to flap a frantic hand in the direction of the sound.

"Sshhh," I hissed, clamping my other hand over my face to keep my eyeballs from exploding. Merciful silence enfolded me and I curled back into my protective huddle to moan quietly.

At last the pain abated to a throbbing ache and I pried an eye open. A circle of worried faces swam into focus above me.

"Aydan, are you all right? Say something." Kane's voice seemed overly loud, but I suspected he was whispering.

"I'm okay." My voice clawed its way out of my throat like a reanimated corpse from a coffin. "Just give me a minute."

I hauled myself approximately upright and propped my shaking body in the corner of the sofa. Alien memories crowded my mind, but this time I knew where they came from and which ones were truly mine.

"Aydan, what is it?" Kane stooped to peer into my face, and I realized I was grinning fiercely.

"Mine," I hissed. Laughter bubbled over into a ferocious

"Ha!" and I pumped a victorious fist. "Terry Sherman is *mine!*"

Judging by the expressions on the faces surrounding me, my non sequitur hadn't been reassuring. Spider and Jack were staring at me, pale and wide-eyed. Kane's brow was creased in concern, but Doytchevsky's eyes burned with savage joy. Everyone spoke at once.

"Terry Sherman is dead." That was Kane.

"He's alive?" Doytchevsky, his face alight with unholy elation.

"Who's Terry Sherman?" Spider, still looking frightened and confused.

I heaved myself off the sofa and staggered toward the door, my head spinning. "Spider, I dumped an IP address in the file repository. Trace it right away. Let me know as soon as you have it. I have to talk to Stemp, *now.*"

CHAPTER 6

When I tapped on Stemp's open door, he glanced up from his computer, his frown of concentration smoothing into watchful detachment.

"Yes, Kelly?" His gaze darted to Kane's bulk behind me. "Is there a problem?"

"No. Well, yes and no..."

His eyes narrowed. "Come in."

We obeyed, Kane swinging the door shut behind him.

"Terry Sherman and Tammy Mellor are still alive." The words burst out of me seconds after the click of the door latch. "They faked their death in China and they're in the States now."

Kane and Stemp exchanged a split-second glance, processing the information and all its implications.

"Where? Sit."

I sank into the nearest chair. "I don't know where exactly because Tammy doesn't know. But Spider will know in a minute or two."

"What are they doing?"

"Trying to find Sam Kraus."

"Why?"

"Tammy doesn't know."

"Does she have your memories?"

I gave him a feral grin. "No. They have jackshit. I picked her clean and gave her nothing."

Stemp sat slowly back in his chair. "A full briefing, if you please."

Excitement still electrified every cell in my body, and I drew a deep breath to calm my quivering thoughts, only wincing slightly at the pain in my ribs.

"Okay." I took another deep breath and eased it out slowly, massaging my aching temples. "I... jeez, where do I start? I just absorbed Tammy's entire lifetime of memories."

"Are you all right?" Kane leaned forward, studying my face.

"Yeah." I switched to kneading my forehead with the heel of my hand, feeling breakers of data buffeting it from inside. "I knew what was happening this time. I just... my head feels too full right now."

"Maybe you should rest for a while-"

"No." Stemp's terse command overrode Kane. "Kelly. Everything. Now."

I straightened in my chair. "Okay, first the bad news. I met Tammy head-on in the network, so that means there's still one remaining network key, and Tammy can decrypt data and sneak around invisibly in networks just like me. And everything she discovers, Terry Sherman knows. And is undoubtedly willing to sell to just about anybody for the right price."

The muscles bunched in Kane's forearm beside me as his fist closed, but Stemp spoke first.

"Are you certain you didn't exchange memories? They didn't get any classified intel?"

"Positive. I knew what was happening this time, and I

locked her mind down and filtered out absolutely everything that was mine. They'll never even know they encountered me."

Stemp nodded slowly. "Good. So they don't know we broke their operation or that we have Kraus in custody."

"No. They've been hiding and out of touch since their faked deaths, so that means Sherman thinks the rest of his good-buddy Knights of Sirius are still alive and well and selling intel to the highest bidder."

I paused, prodding my tired brain to remember the past few days' events. "Sherman would know Sam has told me all about the Knights and the way they manipulate super-users like Tammy and me to steal data with the network keys. But he won't know about the bust."

I straightened as comprehension dawned. "That'll be why Sherman sent Tammy into the network. To make contact with Sam through me. That bastard, Sam *told* him how dangerous it was for a super-user to encounter me in the network. Sherman doesn't even give a shit if Tammy ends up brain-dead..."

I cut myself off at Stemp's gesture of impatience and got back to the point. "Here's some more good-bad news." Vibrating nerves pulled me to the edge of my chair. "Sherman has invented a USB device that generates a brainwave-driven network interface. It's completely mobile. They can hack into any damn network they please, from anywhere they can get an internet connection. That's the bad news."

I gave him a smile that bared a few more teeth than usual. "The good news is I got their IP address and any minute now..."

A tap on the door interrupted me and Stemp snapped,

"Come!"

Spider's anxious face poked around the corner of the door. "I traced that IP."

"Where?"

Spider twitched under the whiplash of Stemp's demand, but spoke confidently. "A coffee shop in Boston."

"Dump the address and GPS coordinates directly to the tactical system." Stemp didn't wait for Spider's nod of comprehension before picking up the phone to begin barking orders.

Several calls later, he sat back in his chair and fixed me with his expressionless gaze. "Well done, Kelly. What else did you learn?"

"Just a whole pile of background information that probably isn't too useful. The Knights of Sirius recruited Tammy when she was eight. She was blinded in an accident when she was six and her family was poor, so when the Knights offered money and schooling, her parents jumped at the chance. Terry Sherman has been controlling her nearly all her life. All she knows is that Sherman needs her to go into the network frequently. She doesn't know she's being forced to steal intel when she's in there."

I swallowed, queasily sorting through memories that felt far too real. "She's pretty fucked up. She had no family life at all. He's... everything to her. Handler. Father. Lover..."

Revulsion twisted Stemp's face.

"No, he didn't molest her," I added quickly, mindful of his little daughter so far away. "They didn't have a sexual relationship until she was eighteen." A shudder squirmed down my backbone despite myself. "He's creepy, but he's not a pedophile."

"So that's why she doesn't know where she is," Kane

said. "She's blind."

"Yeah. Her memories are so weird. There's no visual component at all." Another shudder shook me. "They've been together for nearly forty years. She's completely dependent on him. She reads Braille at a basic level, but that's it. She'll do anything for him."

I wrapped my arms around my churning stomach. "And I mean anything. Oh God." Rising bile seared the back of my throat and I sprang up to flee for the bathroom.

I breathed slowly, open-mouthed, sweat congealing on my body.

"Aydan?" The volume of Jack's voice increased as the sound of the bathroom door heralded her rapid arrival. "Aydan, are you okay?"

"Fine," I whispered.

"What happened?"

"Just... give me a minute."

Breathe. In. Out. Nice and slow. Those memories weren't mine, and they likely weren't as traumatic for Tammy as they were for me.

Just breathe.

"Aydan, if you don't talk to me, I'll call John in here and get him to pull the door right off that cubicle. And you know he can." Jack's no-nonsense tone reminded me that she was super-mom to two high-energy preschoolers.

I managed a feeble chuckle. "It's okay, Jack. I... collided with another super-user in the network. I got a big dump of her memories. I just... I'll be okay, I just need to let them fade a bit."

"Oh, Aydan." Her voice trembled with sympathy. "I

can't imagine how bad they must be if they upset you this much. How can I help?"

God, this was embarrassing. I hauled myself to my feet and vacated the cubicle to stumble past her to the sink.

"It's okay, thanks, Jack, I'm fine. They're probably good memories for her. It was just a shock, that's all."

My voice sounded a lot more convinced than I felt, and I shot her a reassuring smile in the mirror. Except for the violent trembling of my hands, I looked almost normal. My gut clenched again and I fought down another wave of panic and nausea.

Not my memories. It didn't happen to me.

I crushed my handful of paper towels into a wad and made a drop shot in the general direction of the wastebasket, attempting nonchalance. My aim was off, and the crumpled ball teetered on the edge for a moment before toppling in.

"Two points." I stretched my mouth into a semblance of a grin and made my escape.

Or so I had hoped.

Both Kane and Stemp stood in the hallway in the relaxed posture I had come to recognize as battle-readiness. Two pairs of eyes scrutinized me as if stripping away skin and bone to peer directly into my mind. The bathroom door opened behind me, and Jack's presence boxed me in. With a supreme effort, I vanquished the frenzied urge to fight my way free and run until the memories faded.

"Sorry, my stomach was a little upset, but I'm okay now." I held my voice level and strolled toward Kane and Stemp.

Please let them get out of my way...

"Very well. Kane, Dr. Travers, please brief the rest of the team. Kelly, in my office." Stemp's face and voice were unreadable as he turned to walk down the hall ahead of me.

I pushed down my claustrophobia again. I was fine, dammit.

Settled once again in Stemp's office, I summoned up a poker face while Stemp inspected me from behind his desk. After several moments, he spoke. "You said Ms. Mellor would do anything for Sherman. What exactly did you mean by that?"

I shrugged. "Exactly what I said. He's her whole world. Except for brief messages from a biological family she hasn't seen in decades, he's her only human contact."

"And what did she do for him that you found so upsetting?"

"N... nothing you need to be concerned about."

"Kelly." His unnerving amber gaze bored into me. "I've read your mission reports. I know very little has damaged your composure in the past. If this was enough to make you vomit, then I need to be concerned. What did she do?"

"I didn't actually throw up..."

He eyed me in silence and heat rose in my cheeks, but I couldn't see any means of avoiding the question. I summoned up all my bravado and met his eyes. "You know how only the data of the memory is transferred, but the emotion is generated by the person reliving the memory, not transferred from the person who originally experienced it?"

He nodded.

I wriggled, impaled on his gaze. "Let's just say that certain activities they... enjoy... Well, probably..." I gulped and hurried on. "I mean, it was consensual, so she probably enjoyed it..."

I hesitated. Come on, let me off the hook already.

No such luck. He waited, his gaze boring into me.

I unclenched my teeth and summoned up a matter-of-fact tone. "They're into bondage and domination. Not my flavour. My emotional reaction was probably quite a bit different than hers."

Another wave of memory broke over me, making me clench my teeth and ride out the accompanying surge of panic with a long breath.

"Oh." Stemp relaxed. "Was there anything else?"

"No." I slumped in my chair, fervently wishing I could disappear into a convenient hole in the floor.

Stemp fixed me with an impassive stare. "You need help."

"I'll be all right."

"You're not all right." He leaned his elbows on the desk, his gaze trapping me in my chair. "You just had a severe physical and psychological reaction to the mere thought of being tied up and restrained. You can't perform at peak capability when you have that kind of crippling fear."

My pent-up adrenaline exploded into a wave of fury. I jerked to my feet, planting my clenched fists on his desk to keep from swinging at him.

"You don't get it, do you?" I snarled. "That wasn't the *mere thought...*" I made violent air quotes around the words. "...of being tied up and restrained. That was the fresh, true-to-life *experience* of being blind, tied up, degraded and repeatedly raped by a man who's a total stranger to me. Every detail. Every... sensation. Just a few minutes ago."

Through my rage, I registered the shock in his face. I struggled to get my voice under control but it came out in a menacing growl. "I told you, *I'll be all right.* Those memories aren't mine, so they'll fade fast. In the meantime, *cut me some fucking slack, okay?*"

We locked eyes over the desk. He dropped his gaze first.

"I didn't realize," he said. "I'm sorry."

When he met my eyes again, there was no hint of compromise in his expression. "I'll give you until you return on Tuesday. If this is still an issue next week, you *will* get help."

"Understood," I snapped, and strode out.

I managed to hold it together until I'd run the benign gauntlet of the unseen tac team down by the creek and the surveillance cameras on my front porch. Alone at last, I swung the door of my walk-in closet shut behind me and curled into a ball in the darkness, pulling my fleecy robe over my head to shut out the world.

Don't think. Just breathe.

When my pulse rate returned to almost-normal and my tremors diminished at last, I hauled myself upright and flipped on the light. Squinting at my watch, I groaned at the sight of the time. A two-hour drive down to Calgary, check in at the airport two hours before my international flight... that left me exactly half an hour to pack and get my ass out the door.

First things first. I hurried to my computer. When I found the description of a dead drop online, I breathed a sigh of relief.

I could do this.

I flung some clothes into my suitcase and hit the road.

CHAPTER 7

Hoping Stemp's 'security bypass' meant what I thought it meant, I trailed into the Calgary International Airport half an hour late with the guilty weight of my Glock dragging at my ankle, my fake passport burning my pocket.

I chose to be reassured when a security guard began to tail me as soon as I entered the airport. That's what they'd done last time.

Or maybe I was about to be arrested and charged with terrorism...

But no. Customs passed me through without any alarms, and a guard singled me out of the lineup at security and ushered me aside for my 'private search'. Easing out a sigh of relief when they turned me loose, I began to relax while I strolled down the concourse to the boarding area. Tammy's memories were already receding into tolerable distance. Maybe Stemp was right. Maybe a vacation in Vegas was exactly what I needed.

A snack appeased both my growling stomach and my residual nerves, and I felt almost optimistic when I boarded the plane.

My improved mood faded rapidly when I entered the bustle of the Vegas arrivals lounge. Jostling along with the crowd toward the baggage carousels, I tried to close my ears to the electronic cacophony of the slot machines, but it nibbled at my nerves like a persistent rodent.

I survived a kamikaze cab ride to the hotel, and by the time I staggered into the hotel lobby and took my place in the queue, I was beginning to feel a reluctant kinship with the wackos who pull guns and empty them indiscriminately in public places.

Shit, this was the United States. If I pulled my gun I'd probably be riddled with six different calibres of bullet holes in seconds, just from the little old ladies at the slot machines.

I shook my head to dislodge the thought and trudged up to the desk to claim my cardkey.

My room door closed behind me at last, and I was just drawing a breath of relief in the silence when my cell phone vibrated. I yanked it out of my waist pouch, eyeing the display with trepidation.

My breath blew out in a whoosh. Thank God. A bit of upbeat conversation was exactly what I needed.

I punched the Talk button, grinning. "Nichele! How are you?"

"Hi, Aydan."

Uh-oh. That subdued greeting didn't sound like my flamboyant friend. Fear clutched my heart.

"Nichele, what's wrong?"

"Nothing."

"Bullshit."

"No, really. Nothing." She sighed. "Well, kind of something, I guess. Dave just broke up with me."

"What?" I flopped down on the bed, dumbfounded. "Um, Nichele..."

"I know, it's stupid. We were only together for a couple

of weeks. But he said I'm too good for him because I'm a rich stockbroker and he's just a fat, broke trucker. He said a beautiful woman like me should be with some handsome young guy like Dante."

"Um... you told him about Dante?"

"We ran into him at my club and I introduced them."

Poor Dave. I dragged my attention back to Nichele's story.

"...anyway, I told Dave I don't care about any of that stuff, but he said it wasn't fair to expect me to be alone all the time while he was on the road. I told him it was okay, we could be friends with benefits, but he said it wasn't respectful to use a woman like that and he'd never do that to me..." She paused to draw a breath.

"Yeah, that sounds like Dave."

"...and then he kissed me like he loved me. And he left."

"He probably does love you, Nichele. I told you not to break his heart."

"I *didn't!* I told you, I've changed."

I massaged my aching forehead. "I've lost count of all the guys you've fallen in 'love' with and then dumped two weeks later. And that's not counting all your hookups and booty calls. How many guys do you have on the booty call speed dial these days, anyway?"

"Just Dante."

"Nichele, the only reason you're upset over Dave is because he dumped you before you could get tired of him and dump him first. He's right, there's no way in hell it can work between you, and it'll be kinder if you just let him go now. Call Dante. Take the Italian stallion for a nice long ride tonight, and you'll be all better in the morning."

"I don't want Dante. I want Dave."

I thumped my head against the pillows a couple of times. "Just sleep on it, Nichele, okay? You know he's not your type and you know if he stayed you'd just get tired of him and dump him. He's such a sweet guy, don't hurt him-"

"He is sweet, isn't he? I can't believe his first wife divorced him." Nichele sighed. "But he said he didn't blame her. He's always playing those country songs about lonely truckers and what a hard life it is for their wives."

"Jesus, Nichele, I know how much you hate country music. I'm surprised you're not out at the club trying to drive it all out of your brain."

She chuckled, but it didn't sound very humorous. Then she sighed again.

Shit. Nichele never sighed. Well, unless she saw a hot guy in an expensive suit. But that was just the hiss of escaping lust. Not like this sigh.

"I kind of miss it," she said in a small voice. "Dave always sang along with the mushy ones."

I passed a hand over my face, caught between amusement and a sense of impending doom. "Dave sings?"

"Actually, he's a really bad singer." Her giggle ended in a gulp. "He was so sweet, though, because he was singing them for me."

Shit. Doom. Definitely doom.

"Jesus, Nichele."

"I know. What am I going to do?"

"Just sleep on it, okay?"

"That sucks. Come on, Aydan, you've got to help me get him back."

"No."

The silence on the other end of the line made slow dread creep into the pit of my stomach. Silence only meant one thing. She was summoning up some devastating personal leverage to bend me to her will, just like she'd been doing since we were five years old.

"Okay," she said.

Her innocent tone sent a cold chill down my spine. When she spoke again in her usual bright and bouncy tone, I knew I was screwed.

"So what are you up to, girl? Did you get some panty-puddling makeup sex with Hot John?"

Panty-melting was closer to the truth, but I really didn't want to discuss it.

"John is permanently off my to-do list." Go for a diversion. "Actually, I'm in Vegas," I added.

"*What?*" Her squeal made me yank the phone away from my ear. "Aydan, why didn't you say so? Girl, that's perfect, I'll hop the first flight down and we can cruise the strip for man-candy!"

"I thought you wanted Dave."

"I'm taking your advice, girl. Vegas is just what I need! Where are you staying? Do you have an extra bed in your room? This is going to be soooo much fun! I'm packing now!" Muffled thumps on the other end of the line indicated she was telling the truth.

I suppressed a groan. "Nichele, no. You can't. I'm here on business and I won't have any time-"

"It's Vegas, girl, there's always time to play in Vegas! I love Vegas!"

"I hate Vegas. I hate cities, I hate crowds, I hate noise, and I'm too cheap to gamble. And I have to work. Just-"

Her theatrical sigh came through loud and clear. "You need to get laid again, don't you? Why don't you booty-call your ugly Hellhound guy, what's his real name? ...Oh, yeah,

Arnie. You're never this cranky when you're getting some."

I balled my free hand in my hair and yanked. Hard. "Not that it's any of your business, but he ended it. We're just friends now."

"You got dumped, too? Well, don't worry, girl, I'm coming down there to find us some serious action."

"No!"

Her blithe chatter didn't falter. "Oooh, I can hardly wait! Where did you say you were staying?"

"I didn't."

"Aydan, come on, girl, give! Where? Hurry up, I need to make reservations."

"Nichele, no."

"Where! Or I'll post those pictures of you from college..."

"Fine, go ahead. The whole world thinks I'm a porn star anyway, so a few drunken college photos won't matter."

"Aw, come on, Aydan." A bit of hurt crept into her voice. "Don't you want to see me?"

My heart smote me. "Of course I do, it's just that I'm really busy and I want to be able to spend time with you..."

"You'll make time. You're 'way too serious, you need me to lighten you up a bit. Admit it, girl, you always have more fun when I'm around."

I couldn't help smiling. "Yeah, I do, but-"

"I promise I'll let you get your work done before I force you to have fun against your will. So where are you staying?"

"Mirage, but Nichele..."

I should have known she wouldn't take no for an answer. By the time I disconnected, she had booked her flight online, packed, and extracted a promise from me to meet her in the hotel lobby the next morning at eleven-thirty.

For a few moments, I lay recovering from Hurricane

Nichele until anxiety prodded me upright again. Pacing from door to window and back again, I forced my over-stressed brain into planning mode.

Okay, I had to find somewhere to hide a USB stick. A place that was quick and easy to access, but not easily discovered by anyone except the person who would retrieve it. A place that could be easily described to Stemp. A place I could get to without arousing suspicion, because, dammit, now Nichele would be shadowing me. And when the hell was the damn USB stick going to be delivered?

I gave the bed a couple of indecisive kicks. At least this shouldn't be actively dangerous, but it was going to be damn tricky. If that stick fell into the wrong hands...

My mind skittered away from that possibility. Stemp hadn't mentioned what the stick contained, but I was pretty sure it wasn't cupcake recipes.

I jittered back and forth a few more times before blowing out a breath. Might as well go for a walk and start scoping out potential hiding places.

Back in the casino area, I leaned next to the elevators, getting my bearings. The nonstop hum of voices and chiming of slot machines wove into an irritating fabric that abraded my already-frayed nerves. A constant stream of people wandered by, eyes glazed with alcohol and greed. I shuddered and turned my attention to the casino layout.

No hope of hiding anything here with surveillance cameras blanketing the whole area. I pushed off from the wall and joined the flow of the crowd, longing for wide-open country.

The urge to run quivered in my belly, and I split off from the casino to make for the exit. Outside, the backlit waterfall glowed red while I wove through the crowd of spectators, barely noticing the light show in my search for likely-looking places to leave a USB stick.

I blew out a pent-up breath and rubbed at the frown lines on my forehead. Too many people. And there were probably surveillance cameras outside, too.

Letting the movement of pedestrians carry me down the sidewalk, I peered around with increasing desperation. So many damn people! Where could I hide a USB stick without being noticed? Stick it in a friggin' palm tree?

Yeah, that'd be unobtrusive, wouldn't it? 'Don't mind me, I'm just inspecting this palm tree for...' what, fungus or something?

I shook my head and kept walking. Maybe I should get off the strip and find someplace quieter. But then I'd be even more obvious without the cover of the crowd...

Overwhelmed by the unrelenting lights and noise and motion, I felt the Vegas stare settling onto my face. I was about to abandon the effort when my blank gaze slid across some newspaper vending machines on the opposite side of the street.

Inspiration flashed like an Elvis impersonator's rhinestones, and I cut through the crowd to the nearest crosswalk.

Ambling up to the painted boxes, I was reaching for my change purse when I remembered I had only Canadian cash. I retraced my steps to one of the many ATM machines I'd spotted and subtracted some money from my bank account, making a mental note to ask Stemp about expenses when I got back.

God, talk about a babe in the woods. If I didn't drop dead of sheer incompetence, it'd be a miracle.

A whiff of barbecued meat made my stomach roar its

displeasure at the long interval since my snack in the Calgary airport, and I rejoined the moving throng on the sidewalk to follow my nose. Unwilling to take the time for a full meal, I settled for a quick slice of pizza instead and pocketed the change, feeling smug.

Back at the vending machine, I plugged in the coins and opened the door to extract my newspaper, casually running my hand along the upper inside edge of the box.

Perfect. There was a small lip above the opening.

I let the door close and tucked my paper under my arm to stroll down the street again. A bit of double-sided tape and I'd be all set.

The tape proved more difficult to obtain than I'd anticipated. Averting my eyes from the sidewalk carpeted with business cards featuring mostly naked women, I wasted nearly an hour searching through shops that contained a bizarre amalgam of tacky souvenirs and insanely expensive clothing and jewellery.

When I caught myself fantasizing about charging through the mob of pedestrians like a bull escaping the pack at Pamplona, I knew it was time to quit.

Calm. Just stay calm.

Clinging to the last vestiges of my patience, I made my way back to the Mirage and gratefully shut myself into the silence of my room.

The ring of the phone jerked me out of a violent nightmare. Heart rattling my rib cage, I floundered across the bed to fumble at the receiver with a shaking hand. A wide-awake voice answered my slurred 'hello'.

"Ma'am, we've had complaints about noise from your

room. The callers said it sounded like screaming. Are you all right?"

"Shit."

"Pardon me?"

I thumped my forehead with my free hand. "Sorry. I... uh... I turned the TV on, and somebody had left the volume turned up to max. Please tell everybody I'm sorry."

"That's quite all right, ma'am, as long as you're okay."

"I'm fine. Thanks. Sorry."

I hung up the phone and collapsed face-first onto the mattress, groaning into the unsympathetic bedding. For shit's sake, did I really have to embarrass myself this frequently? A glance at the glow of the clock-radio turned my groan into a whine. Only two A.M.

I rolled over and straightened the churned-up covers into a semblance of order before settling on my back, belly-breathing in an attempt to regain some composure. A wistful memory of Hellhound's muscular bulk made self-pity well up.

If we were still friends with benefits, I could invite him down here and he'd put a smile on my face that would last for days. And he'd soothe my nightmares with strong arms and whiskery kisses. And he'd watch my back while I hid the USB stick, his keen vigilance hidden behind his devilish grin and dirty jokes.

Or if Kane was here...

I hissed out a breath between my teeth and flipped over, giving the pillow a couple of vicious punches.

Dammit.

CHAPTER 8

After dozing fitfully for the rest of the night, I hauled myself out of bed much later than usual and staggered into the shower. Letting the hot spray drum against my closed eyelids, I dragged my sleepy brain into action.

If Nichele was arriving at eleven-thirty, I only had a couple of hours to procure some double-sided tape. And where the hell was the USB stick? And how the hell was Stemp planning to deliver it to me...

A knock made me jerk my head out from under the shower to listen. When it came again, louder this time, I swore and snatched up a towel to hurry dripping to the door. Peering through the fisheye lens, I saw nothing but flowers.

I opened the door a crack, leaving the security bar in place.

"Ms. Widdenback?"

My nod was slightly belated while my exhausted brain processed my cover identity and reminded me to react.

"Flowers for you."

Suspicion flared. "Who are they from?"

The uniformed delivery boy consulted the card. "It says, 'Dearest Arlene, Good luck and best wishes, Charles'."

"Oh." Realizing he was waiting for some useful response

from me, I added, "Just put them on the floor outside the door."

"But…"

I gave him a don't-mess-with-me look. "I'll bring them in when I get dressed."

"Okay…"

I closed the door on his uncertain face and peered through the fisheye lens. After hesitating for a few moments, he placed the vase on the floor as instructed and walked away. A few moments later, the ding of the elevator indicated he'd gone.

Paranoia kept me glued to the peep-hole for another couple of minutes, but there was no movement in the corridor. When I was sure nobody was out there, I unlocked the door and whisked the flowers into the room, locking the deadbolt and security bar behind me again.

A rapid examination of the vase and flowers revealed nothing. Dammit, there was no way Stemp would send me flowers out of the goodness of his heart. 'Dearest Arlene', my ass. The USB stick had to be in here somewhere.

I started again, systematically inspecting every inch of the vase and pressing every lump and bump.

I was shivering by the time I discovered the tiny plastic-wrapped wafer attached to the stem of one of the roses, well below the water line. I had been expecting a drive about the size of my thumb, but this was closer to fingernail size. I debated for a moment before turning away, carrying it with me.

Halfway back to the bathroom, I turned to scrutinize the flowers one more time. They were beautiful. And I didn't trust Stemp any farther than I could throw him.

Bye-bye, Charles.

I returned the flowers to the corridor and locked the door behind them before diving back into the welcome steam of my interrupted shower.

I was combing out my wet hair when the next knock came. Swearing, I grabbed another towel and headed for the door.

Bright orange tiger lilies obscured my view through the fisheye lens.

What the hell?

I retreated momentarily to grab my gun and held it concealed behind me while I cracked the door open again.

"More flowers, Ms. Widdenback," the delivery boy said cheerfully.

"Is there a card?"

"It's in an envelope."

"Pass it to me and leave the flowers in the hall."

This time he didn't question me. I took the envelope, relocked the door, and listened for the elevator before opening the card.

'10:15 front entrance'.

I turned the card over, but there was no signature. Shivering again under the cold wet strands on my shoulders, I carried the card and my gun back into the bathroom and laid them on the vanity, puzzling over the message while I plied the hair dryer.

Who the hell would expect me to meet without identifying themselves? How stupid did they think I was?

And anyway, screw them. It was already ten o'clock, I wasn't dressed, and I was starving. Whoever they were, they could just wait.

Who knew I was here, anyway? The flowers had been addressed to Arlene Widdenback, so it was someone who knew me by my cover identity.

A blip of hope made my pulse quicken. Maybe it was Kane. Maybe he'd realized I wasn't joking and I really needed his help. Kane was an excellent agent. He wouldn't risk identifying himself on the card.

I studied it again. The writing was unfamiliar, but that didn't mean much. It could have been written by a flower shop employee.

I threw on some clothes and hurried for the lobby.

Loitering just outside the front entrance, I fiddled with my phone as if texting. Kane should be easy to spot, head and shoulders above the bustle of people, but my surreptitious surveillance wasn't rewarded by six and a half feet of male hotness.

I toggled back to my date/time display. Ten-fifteen on the dot. Where the hell was he?

"Excuse me, could I bother you to take my photo by the fountain?"

I managed to conceal my guilty start and turned to face the source of the familiar nasal voice.

Shit. I should have known by the tiger lilies.

"Sure, no problem." I summoned up what I hoped was a polite but distant smile and turned to take Doytchevsky's proffered camera.

His food-stained clothes and body odour had been replaced by a tidy beige button-down shirt, neatly-pressed khaki pants, and a hint of innocuous aftershave. Without his repulsive trappings, he was a pleasant-looking and eminently forgettable middle-aged man.

The perfect spy.

I followed him across the pavement and applied myself to the camera while he posed with bland expression.

"I'm sorry to trouble you, but would you mind taking another from around the side where the light is better?"

"No trouble," I agreed, falling into step beside him.

"What the hell are you doing here?" I hissed through my smile.

He gestured casually at the waterfall, smiling in return. "Where's Terry Sherman?"

"I don't know."

"You're lying."

We dodged a particularly large group of tourists and their clicking cameras. As soon as we were clear, I replied, still hanging onto my I-don't-know-you-but-I'm-being-polite smile.

"It's the truth. Spider tracked the IP to a coffee shop in Boston. He dumped the location to the tactical system. That's all I know."

"Fine." He reached for his camera.

"Not so fast." I held onto the camera and waved a hand toward the railing and the waterfall. "You're getting your picture taken."

I leaned closer, pointing to the back of the camera as if asking how it worked. "Leave Sherman alone," I muttered. "Let Stemp take him down. If you go charging in and fuck it up, I'll tell Stemp how you knew all along about the Knights and their treason. You'll rot in jail for the rest of your life."

His hand locked around my wrist, and I had to prevent myself from recoiling from the suppressed violence in his eyes. His voice was a poisonous hiss. "He's *mine*! My last chance for revenge on the Knights. If you kill him or let him escape, you will *pay*."

"I don't have anything to do with this. I'm sure as hell not going to kill him, and Stemp's not going to let him escape."

"You blew the others to bits."

"That was an accident."

"Don't have any more *accidents*." He stepped away to pose against the rail, smiling for the camera.

I clicked the button before handing it back to him, wondering if the photo would capture the burning hatred banked behind his insipid facade.

Shaken, I wandered through the pedestrians in the direction of the entrance. What would he do now? A backward glance showed him moving away, but a moment later he turned, leaning against the low railing to snap another picture. Watching me. I'd have to be extra careful dropping the USB stick. Christ, nothing like making my life even more complicated.

Speaking of...

I tried to dodge behind a cluster of tourists, but it was too late.

"Aydan!" Nichele bounced up and down beside the hotel entrance, waving. Heads turned to survey the short, curvy brunette in her elegant clothes and stiletto heels.

Goddammit, what was she doing here so early? I barrelled through the crowd toward her before she could blow my cover any worse, my mind ricocheting through a list of increasingly unlikely excuses to prevent her from using my real name.

Thank God, she shut up as soon as she realized I'd seen her. I used the intervening seconds to seize on the most plausible story I could manufacture.

"Hey, Nichele, this is great! What are you doing here so early?" I feigned happiness while she gave me her usual bearhug.

"My plane was early, and I had a limo pick me up." She handed the driver what looked like a hundred-dollar bill. Judging by his reaction, it probably was. "No, that's okay, I only have the two. We can manage," she demurred when he reached for her bags.

I hefted one of them. "Speak for yourself. What have you got, rocks in here?"

"It's got wheels, silly," she chided, giving me her sparkling grin. "Don't wimp out on me. I'm nearly a foot shorter than you, I'm wearing heels, and I can handle them just fine."

"Yeah, yeah," I grumbled, following her into the hotel. "Hey, listen, Nichele..." I bent down to her level. "Don't call me Aydan, okay? There was this creepy guy coming onto me last night and I told him my name was Arlene so he wouldn't be able to find my room."

She laughed. "Don't you know anything? The hotel wouldn't give out your name or your room number."

I did my best rueful grin. "Yeah, I know, but..."

"And why did you use *Arlene*? Wasn't that the name of that porn star everybody thought was you?"

"I know, I know, it was just the first thing that popped into my head. Please, Nichele?"

She laughed again and patted my arm. "Well, duh, of course I'll cover for you. You're such a goofball, girl." She caught the eye of a uniformed hotel employee. "Be right back."

In moments, she was back, brandishing a cardkey and a triumphant grin. "Come on, Ay... Arlene, let's go!"

As she turned to tow her bag across the polished tile, I snagged her arm. "The elevators are this way."

"Not the ones we're going to." She shot me a

mischievous look. "Come on."

"Seriously, Nichele? The penthouse?" I stared around at the lavish furnishings.

"Sure, why not? It's Vegas. Sometimes you have to live a little." She abandoned her suitcase in the foyer and stalked through the living area, her stiletto heels leaving deep dents in the thick carpet. "Hmmm, which bedroom do I like better?"

I came around the corner in time to catch her bouncing experimentally on the bed in the room to the left.

"God, Nichele, this ensuite bathroom is bigger than my friggin' living room! You need a GPS just to find the shower."

"Maybe I like the other one better." She zipped out the door and across to the other end of the suite, and I followed the sound of her voice. "This one's nicer. I get a better view of the Paris from here."

I sank into one of the deep upholstered chairs and propped my aching head in my hands. "This chair is more comfortable than my bed. If I wasn't so damn hungry I'd go to sleep right here."

"Aydan, are you okay?" When I looked up, Nichele was frowning concern at me. "You look wiped. When did you eat last?"

My stomach responded with a ravenous growl. "Last night. I didn't have time for breakfast this morning."

"*You* didn't have time for *breakfast*? Girl, that's like the Pope not having time to pray! Here..." She scurried across the room, returning in seconds with a room service menu. "Pick something, and I'll tell them to rush it."

"It's okay, let's just go down and get something from one of the restaurants..."

I was too late. She was already on the phone. "...two orders of Eggs Benedict and a Belgian waffle with strawberries and whipped cream and couple of mimosas..."

I waved a hand. "I don't like mimosas."

Nichele shot me a quelling look. "They're for me. You're getting..." She turned back to the phone. "...Milk. And green tea. And a fruit platter. I've got a hundred bucks for whoever brings it up here in less than fifteen minutes." She clicked the phone off and laid it back in its cradle with a decisive nod.

"There." She flapped her hands at me as if shooing chickens. "Go and lie down. You can have one of your famous ten-minute naps."

"Nichele..."

"Go! Hurry up, girl."

I went.

Later, I sprawled in the comfort of the upholstered chair, cradling my belly with the hand that wasn't holding my mug of tea. "Urgh. I think I hurt myself."

Nichele looked up from the remains of the Belgian waffle. "Good. You needed it. You look 'way better. Drink your tea and then go off to work. You've got four hours before our Stripper 101 pole-dancing class, and then there's just enough time for supper before we go to see the Chippendales. And we're going to go party with the Chippendales boys afterward, so make sure you wear something sexy."

I stared at her mischievous grin, all-too-familiar

horrified amusement dragging my jaw toward the floor. "Nichele, no! I don't have time! Can you seriously see me pole-dancing? And I only have jeans and workout shorts with me, so forget the sexy party clothes. Just go by yourself. You'll have more fun without me."

"No. You need some fun in your life. Besides, how much work can you really do? This is *Vegas*!" She eyed me, frowning. "What kind of work *are* you doing here, anyway? I thought all your bookkeeping clients were in Silverside."

"Uh..."

Shit! Another damn hole in my cover story. What the hell would a small-town bookkeeper do in Las Vegas?

"Um..." Inspiration bloomed in my brain. "One of my clients owns a sex shop, and she's down here at a trade show. She's hopeless with numbers so she offered to buy my plane ticket if I'd keep track of her sales while she was here."

"Aydan, *really*?" Nichele's squeal of delight made me wince with the certain knowledge of imminent catastrophe. "A sex shop? In a tiny town like Silverside? Ooooh, I *totally* have to meet this woman! I'll come with you!"

"No..." My protest died on my lips at the sight of her enthusiasm. What the hell. She'd love Lola, and Lola would get a kick out of her.

And maybe, just maybe, it would distract Nichele long enough for me to plant the tiny USB stick that was burning a hole in my change purse.

CHAPTER 9

I was just opening my mouth to speak again when my cell phone vibrated. I slipped it out and grimaced at the two-word text message: 'Call home'.

Stemp's signal.

"Nichele, I have to run downstairs and grab some stuff before we go. Let's meet down in the lobby in a few minutes."

She sprang up from her chair. "I'll just come down to your room with you."

"Uh..." My mouth forged ahead before my brain could catch up. "I need to take a dump. You won't want to stick around and smell that."

Nichele clapped her hands over her ears. "Eeeuw, girl! That was waaay too much information!"

I shrugged. "You picked me out of thousands."

"Lord knows why." She grinned. "Okay, meet you downstairs."

Back outside the exalted realm of the penthouse, I hurried to my room, guiltily eyeing the flowers still on the floor outside my door. They really were beautiful. But they could be bugged, and not with the kind of insects that roamed a garden. I should've brought my bug detector.

Dammit. What kind of agent forgets to bring critical equipment on a mission?

A moron civilian, that's what kind.

I left the flowers where they were and locked myself into my room before extracting one of Stemp's secure disposable phones from my bag.

The phone rang once before he answered. "Yes."

I spoke into his waiting silence. "It's Arlene."

"The two men who were impersonating RCMP officers broke into your house last night," he said. "We've just finished questioning them. They were sent by Fuzzy Bunny."

Cold fear stopped my breath, but when I managed to speak a few moments later, my voice sounded much calmer than I felt. "Don't they think I'm dead?"

"Yes. They believe Aydan Kelly is dead and that you are Arlene Widdenback the fraud artist and internet porn star. They were searching for a re-engineered fob that allows untraceable access to a brainwave-driven network. They believe the late Ms. Kelly stole it from their agent, so they were searching your house for it."

I spared a moment for a breath of relief, immediately followed by worry about the state of my house. I wrenched my mind back to the conversation at hand when I realized Stemp was still talking.

"...so it appears your cover is intact. We'll send uniformed officers to your neighbours, ostensibly to ask if they saw anything, but actually to disseminate the information that two men were arrested for breaking and entering at your farm. That news should find its way quickly to Fuzzy Bunny. We expect they will arrange a fatal incident at the Remand Centre to dispose of their compromised agents, but not before they learn that the fob was not in your possession. Your farm should be left in peace now, so I've recalled the tac team, though your surveillance cameras are still active as always."

"That's... good... I guess. Um... did they take anything else?"

I held my breath. Shit, I *really* should've brought that bug detector with me. Stemp didn't know I'd 'acquired' it. It was going to be damn hard to explain illicit Sirius Dynamics technology in my house...

"No. We intentionally waited to capture them until after they had finished and left your house. They were empty-handed."

I sagged with relief, thankful he couldn't see me, and changed the subject. "I got the flowers."

"Do you have a drop location?"

"Yes, but I might have a complication."

"What?" he snapped.

"Somebody might be following me."

"Abort. I'll arrange an extraction and send Kane to rendezvous with you. Are you in immediate danger?"

"No, and I'm not sure I'm being followed anyway. Even if I am, I know who it is. There's no danger to me." I tamped down my desire for rescue along with a much hotter and considerably less wholesome desire. "There's no need to send Kane."

A longish pause crackled on the line. "You're sure you're in no danger. No possibility of capture."

"Positive."

"Kelly, you know very well that in our line of work there is no such thing as 'positive'."

I blew out a sigh. "Yeah, I know, but I'm pretty sure."

"Check in again as soon as you know more."

"Okay."

I hung up and dropped the phone into my pocket for later disposal before extracting my own phone to dial Lola's cell.

"Hi, Aydan!" Her throaty purr made me smile.

"Hi, Lola. How's the trade show?"

"Great! But how did you know I'm here? Were you talking to Linda?"

"No, Spider said you were at a 'conference' in Vegas. And he blushed."

Her bigger-than-life laugh warmed me. "That kid is just as cute as a button. He can't get used to the idea that his girlfriend's grandmother spends her days dabbling in sex toys."

I grinned. "I notice he never discusses Linda's share in the business."

"No, I suspect he doesn't object to product-testing with his girlfriend. But their sex life is none of my business," she added virtuously.

"Since when?" I demanded. "You don't hesitate to pry into my sex life."

"Which reminds me, I've still got that chocolate-scented leather thong. I bet Big John would love to wear it for you-"

"Well, so what's new at the trade show?" I interrupted, perhaps a shade too heartily.

"That's a surprise. Wait'll you see what I'm bringing back this time!"

"How about if I come over and see it first-hand? I'm in Vegas right now."

"Really? That's great! Come on over, then. We're at the Sands. I've got some free passes, so I'll leave one at the ticket counter for you."

"Thanks, Lola. Um... can I ask you a favour?"

"Sure, honey."

"I... uh... I kind of fibbed to one of my friends. I wanted a relaxing weekend by myself, so when she said she was coming to join me, I told her I was working. But she came anyway, and now she thinks you bought my ticket down here so I could keep track of your sales from the trade show."

She chuckled. "Honey, I hope your life never depends on your ability to lie. I'm not selling anything. I'm on a buying trip. But don't worry, I'll cover for you. I'm glad you're finally taking a holiday. You've been working too hard lately."

I breathed a sigh of relief. "Thanks, Lola, you're the best."

Down in the lobby, I surveyed the crowd without spotting Nichele. Backing away from the busy central area, I propped myself against a wall, smiling with the exasperated fondness that usually accompanied my interactions with her. She'd be here. Probably with some new way to make me laugh while simultaneously wanting to throttle her.

A few moments later, her chirpy voice emanated from the centre of a large group of dark-suited Asian men. "There she is!"

Faces turned my way and the suits parted to reveal Nichele's curvy figure stunningly arrayed in a wisp of a dress and platform stilettos that added six inches to her diminutive stature. Her glossy dark hair was piled atop her head in an elegant updo, her nails and makeup impeccable as always. I couldn't decide whether she looked like a movie star or an astronomically-priced hooker.

Or hell, maybe just a regular office worker. Fashion isn't exactly my forte.

"Arlene!" Nichele gave me a fingertip wave. "Come and meet Aki and Hiro and Takao and Kin and all their friends." She beamed at the man nearest her. "Arlene is a movie star, too!"

Oh, God.

I plodded over, feeling like an ox in my hiking boots, faded jeans, and T-shirt, my waist pouch slung on my hips. The group offered me a courteous half-bow like some land-locked synchronized swim team.

I managed a jerky nod in return, hoping I wasn't doing anything overtly offensive. If I was, they were too polite to react. Their eyes widened as I loomed up beside them, tall enough to look down into their dandruff if they'd had any.

"Nice to meet you," I mumbled. "Come on, Nichele, let's go."

"May we take photographs?" one of the men asked with a barely-noticeable accent.

"Of course," Nichele said graciously at the same time I said 'no'.

"I'll be happy to take pictures of you with Nichele," I added hurriedly.

The subsequent deluge of cameras kept me occupied for some time while Nichele posed smiling with each man, all of them beaming as though they'd just landed a prize tuna. Fortunately, none seemed inclined to insist on a photo with a red-haired amazon, and at last I got close enough to Nichele to seize her arm and drag her away from her new-found admirers. The receding click of cameras followed our retreat.

"Jesus, Nichele-"

"Oooh, Aydan, did you see their suits? They were *fabulous*! All Armani and Gucci and Hugo Boss! And they were all so charming and polite!" She turned to smile and flutter coquettish fingertips at them.

I kept a tight grip on her wrist, but I had to laugh in spite of myself. "You're such a suit slut. What is it with you and guys in suits?"

"Oooh, I just looove men in suits. Yummy!" She shot an unrepentant grin up at me. "And I just looove getting men out of their suits... wait, where are we going?"

"The Sands convention centre. It's just a few blocks away."

"Aydan," Nichele said with the patience reserved for small children and idiots. "I'm not going to walk on the *sidewalk*, girl. I have nine-hundred-dollar Louboutins."

"Can you take penicillin to cure that?"

"Very funny. I'm talking about my *shoes*." She waved a cab to halt. "Come on, get in."

We arrived at the Sands about thirty seconds later, and I smothered amusement while Nichele gaily tipped the driver approximately ten times the price of the actual fare.

Tickets in hand, I smiled down at Nichele while she prowled beside me toward the exhibition hall, as comfortable in her sky-high heels as I was in my hiking boots.

"What's with the movie-star duds?" I kidded.

"It's a sex-trade show. You have to dress up."

I snickered. "It's a sex-shop trade show, not a sex-trade show. It's like any other trade show, just a bunch of booths with stuff for sale..." We handed our tickets to the doorman, and my jaw dropped as we stepped inside.

"...okay, I was wrong."

CHAPTER 10

"Oooh, booth babes," Nichele squealed, dragging me toward the three buff men in bow ties and gold lamé thongs posing just across the walkway. Their animated expressions brightened further at the sight of Nichele, and blindingly-white teeth flashed in seductive smiles.

"Hi, what are you selling?" Nichele purred at the nearest one.

I missed his answer when his compatriot turned to get something from the table behind him, revealing naked buttocks apparently sculpted out of highly polished black granite. I managed to jerk my gaze back up to his face just before he turned.

Nichele didn't even try. Her openly appreciative gaze lingered low before traversing unhurriedly upward. She gave him a slow grin, head cocked at a saucy angle. "Sorry, I didn't hear what you said."

He returned her grin and her up-and-down scrutiny, holding out an unidentifiable object. "It's a prostate massager. A little treat for the man in your life."

Nichele's smile slipped a little. "I don't have one at the moment."

He leaned closer. "Do you want one?" He shot a wicked

glance at his companions. "Or three?"

Nichele laughed, her sparkle returning in an instant. "I'll think about it. I still have a lot of shopping to do."

"You know where we are."

She giggled and towed me away.

I leaned down to hiss in her ear. "Nichele, you're not seriously considering-"

"No, of course not, silly. He didn't mean it anyway. He was just flirting." She stole a glance over her shoulder. "But he was really hot."

I straightened, marginally relieved, and tried to find an inoffensive place to look. The ceiling was the only area not bulging with acres of semi-naked flesh, so I settled for letting my vision blur slightly and not looking too long in one place.

Beside me, Nichele's head swivelled avidly, taking it all in. "Wowza, girl, I should hang with you more often. You have more fun than I thought."

"More than I can stand," I muttered.

"Aydan!" Lola's throaty voice came from behind me, and Nichele and I both swung around.

Nichele recovered first. "Shhh, you have to call her Arlene. She's hiding from some creepy guy who was coming onto her."

I regained my composure. "Hi Lola, this is my friend Nichele. Nichele, Lola."

I eyed Lola's tiny figure, her slightly-wrinkled cleavage bulging out of a skin-tight black leather jacket loaded with fringe and chrome studs. The ensemble was completed by a black leather micro-mini, fishnet stockings, and lace-up black stiletto boots crisscrossed with ferocious straps and buckles. A black leather cap slouched on her startlingly purple spiked hair.

A woman her age should have looked ridiculous in the outfit, but stereotypes simply didn't apply to Lola. I shook my head, grinning. "You look dangerous. Where's your Harley?"

An impish leer creased her wrinkled face and she waved at a stout elderly man dressed in biking leathers. "Right over there. And I plan to take him for a nice long ride when this show's over."

Nichele let out a whoop of delight. "Oooh, I like you already! Is his name really Harley?"

"Yep. I met him a few years ago, and we usually hook up at shows. The biker getup is our private joke." She eyed me critically. "You're calling yourself Arlene? Honey, I thought you were trying to distance yourself from that whole thing."

"I know, it was stupid, it was just the first name that popped into my head when this guy started bugging me."

Lola smirked and planted an unsympathetic elbow in my ribs. "Go on, you secretly like being a porn star. Admit it."

"Who's a porn star?" a gruff voice inquired from behind me, and I turned to face Harley. His expression went comically blank for a moment before splitting into a huge grin.

"Arlene Cherry!" His bellow made every head in the vicinity turn.

"No, no!" I hissed frantically.

"I'll be double-dog-damned, Miss Cherry, it's an honour to make your acquaintance!" He seized my hand and planted a kiss on my knuckles. "I didn't hardly recognize you in that getup. Lola, honey, why didn't you tell me you knew a star?"

Lola's evil smile told me I couldn't expect any rescue from that quarter. Nichele's grin was equally unhelpful.

"I, uh, I'm travelling incognito," I muttered, and fled.

A couple of camera flashes convinced me not to dawdle. Hoping for a convenient taxi, I flung a glance around the front of the convention centre as I shot out the doors. I didn't see a taxi, but I did catch a glimpse of Doytchevsky disappearing behind a column.

Bastard. He *was* following me.

I hoofed it for the Mirage.

When I arrived sweating profusely and muttering vile imprecations under my breath, Nichele met me at the doorway, every hair in place, as cool and elegant as ever.

"Why didn't you take a cab?" she asked. "There was one right there."

"Yeah, whatever," I snarled. "Listen, did you see a middle-aged guy in a beige shirt outside the convention centre when you left?"

"No."

Of course she hadn't seen him. He was a fucking spy. I bit down my irritation.

"Nichele, can you do me a favour? Watch for a middle-aged guy in a beige shirt and khakis..."

"You mean like that guy?"

I followed her gaze to see Doytchevsky leaning into a taxi on the street, almost completely concealed by the trees and shrubs lining the driveway.

I whirled back to face Nichele so he wouldn't see me looking. "Yes! That's him! That's the creepy guy who's following me. Can you stall him so I can get away?"

Nichele's devilish grin reminded me of why she was my best friend. "Oooh, yeah, I can stall him. This is going to be *fun*."

I was turning away when I heard her summoning her army. "Oh, Hiro, Aki..."

Just in case Doytchevsky had some way to track my cell phone, I hurried to the elevators and stopped in my room long enough to jettison it.

Down the stairs and out the back door.

Showtime.

Despite my confidence in Nichele's stalling tactics, my heart pounded while I hurried away from the Mirage, heading for the shopping centre I'd spotted in my earlier wanderings. There had to be a roll of double-sided tape in there somewhere.

At the mall, I acquired the tape and ditched Stemp's phone. In the ladies' washroom, I peeled off a tiny piece of tape and tested its stickiness on my finger.

Good. It would still be strong enough to hold the USB stick even after I'd handled it.

I stuck the precious wafer to my change purse and left.

Strolling down the sidewalk, I tried to look nonchalant while sweat beaded on my backbone. Shit, was everybody looking at me? Everywhere I turned, it seemed as though people were just glancing away as I met their eyes.

God, what if word got around about Arlene Cherry, and some crazy fan was following me? Or what if the media showed up with TV cameras?

I gave myself a mental slap to the head. Nobody cared about some sleazy middle-aged internet porn star. Arlene Cherry had a tiny cult following, nothing more. The media couldn't care less unless there were explosions, and the chances of encountering a fan were slim to none.

I gulped. Except for Harley. Shit. I glanced around again, still doing my nonchalant stride.

Nobody's looking. And so what if they are? So Arlene Cherry buys a newspaper, so what? It wasn't like some fan was going to go around fondling everything I touched.

A shudder shook me. Eeuw. I really shouldn't have thought about that.

The newspaper machines came into view long before I was ready. I forced my feet toward them, keeping my shoulders loose, concentrating on an easy gait.

Shit, I couldn't be stiffer if I had a pole shoved up my ass. Relax, dammit!

I shot one more glance around me and eased out a breath when no eyes flicked away. Hoping I wasn't overdoing my act, I scrounged in my waist pouch. Thank God, the taped USB stick caught my forefinger on the first try, and I held it against my change purse, hoping its tiny black-on-black shape was invisible to passersby.

The clink of change in the slot sounded like crashing cymbals, and I forced myself not to peer fearfully around me. Just a harmless pedestrian getting a harmless newspaper. No need to look around.

Newspaper in hand. A quick flick against the inner lip of the opening, and the USB stick was secure. The door clanged shut, and I tucked the newspaper under my arm to stroll away, heart thundering.

Nobody batted an eye.

It couldn't be that easy.

I quivered into the nearest restaurant and chose a table with a view of the vending machines, unable to believe nobody had followed me. Sneaking frequent peeks over my unfurled newspaper, I watched the machines for nearly an hour while I dawdled over the worst hamburger I'd eaten in a long time.

Must be too late in the day for newspapers. Nobody gave the machines a second glance.

At last I paid my bill, dropped my newspaper in the trash, and trailed back to the hotel, still shaking.

Nichele pounced on me the instant I walked through the front door. "Where have you been? I've been calling and calling your cell!"

"Sorry, Nichele, I slipped out to grab some food and I got delayed." I assuaged my guilt with the thought that it was true, though not exactly the truth.

"Well, hurry up and get your shorts. We're due at our pole-dancing class in half an hour!"

I groaned. "I'm bagged. Why don't you just go without me?"

"If you get some exercise, you'll feel better." She gave me an imploring wide-eyed look. "We never get a chance to just go out and have fun anymore. I felt terrible when I thought you'd died and I hadn't spent any time with you for months. Come on, Aydan. It'll be fun. Please?"

I could never resist those puppy-dog eyes. I suppressed another groan. "Okay. I'll go get my shorts. Be right back."

When I stepped off the elevator on my floor, I froze at the sight of the corridor outside my room. There were more flowers. And an anxious-looking middle-aged man whose face lit up at the sight of me.

The elevator doors closed before I could jump back inside, and I made my way warily down the hall.

"Miss Cherry?" The man greeted me, ducking his head as if afraid I'd yell. "May I have your autograph? P-please?" He thrust a paper and pen at me, his hands shaking. "I'm a big fan. I can't believe I'm really meeting you."

I momentarily considered having a movie-star tantrum to get rid of him, but he looked so cowed I couldn't bring myself to do it. I accepted the paper and pen with resignation. "What's your name?"

"P-Paul..."

I smoothed the paper against the wall and scrawled, 'For Paul, love and best wishes' and signed it with a big loopy 'Arlene Cherry' and a heart. Just to be on the safe side I added a couple of Xs and Os at the bottom and handed it back.

"Oh, thank you, Miss Cherry!" He looked as though he was going to faint or pee his pants or something.

"You're welcome," I said, and dove into my room before he could do either.

Safely behind my locked door, I watched through the fisheye lens until he trailed away down the hall, holding the paper in front of him as if somebody had just handed him the Holy Grail.

As soon as he vanished into the elevator, I snatched up another of Stemp's phones.

He answered immediately. "Yes."

I matched his curt tone. "The drop is done."

"Already? Where?"

I described the location, and I could hear keys clicking in the background while he apparently communicated with the person who'd do the pickup.

When he came back on the line, his tone held a hint of criticism. "That was very short notice."

"Sorry. It turned out I was being followed. I had an opportunity, so I took it."

"And your tail?"

"I got rid of him."

After a short pause, Stemp spoke again. "Do you need a clean-up crew?"

My stomach lurched when I realized what he was asking.

"No."

"Very well. Let me know if anything else develops."

I clicked off the phone and started packing.

CHAPTER 11

Doytchevsky materialized out of the crowd as I towed my suitcase across the lobby. "That was very cute with the Jap pack earlier," he growled sotto voce. "Where's Sherman?"

"I told you, he's at the other end of the country as far as I know." I kept walking.

"Where are you going?"

"Checking out." I stepped up to the desk to complete the paperwork.

When I stepped away, he closed in again. "You're meeting him, aren't you? Where is he? Tell me!"

"No! I don't fucking know where he is! Get lost, or I'll call Security and have you thrown out."

He gave me a single venomous glare before melting into the crowd to disappear out the door. I gave a whole-body shudder and pulled out my cell phone.

"Arlene! ...*Arlene!*"

The second time Nichele called across the lobby, I registered the need to respond. Jeez, a real spy would spot my so-called cover in an instant. I needed to get better at that.

I dragged my suitcase over. "Hey, Nichele, I was just going to call you."

She eyed the suitcase, her expression crumpling into disappointment. "You're leaving?"

"No, I'm just leaving my room. There were a bunch of flowers and an Arlene Cherry fan outside my door. Can I come and play in the penthouse for a while?"

Her face lit up. "Girl, I thought you'd never ask!" She leaned closer, grinning. "Was he cute?"

"No."

She tossed her head. "Well, screw him, then."

"Don't even joke about that."

Her peal of laughter made me smile in spite of myself. She seized my hand, still giggling. "Come on, I'll get you a cardkey."

We were just turning away from the registration desk when Lola appeared, dwarfed by a bulging shopping bag. The biker gear had been replaced by a sleek and sexy hot pink wraparound dress, strappy hot pink sandals, and artful makeup that accented her sparkling eyes and vivid hair.

"Over here!" Nichele beckoned, and Lola wove expertly through the crowd in her high heels.

"All set," she panted, hefting the bag into Nichele's waiting grasp. "See you later. This is going to be fun!" She and Nichele exchanged a grin that chilled my blood before Lola turned and left with an airy wave, still smirking.

"Why do I have a bad feeling about this?" I demanded.

"Because you're a paranoid freak, that's why." Nichele headed for the penthouse elevator. "Hurry up," she tossed over her shoulder. "We'll drop your suitcase and you can grab your shorts. We have to get to our class."

Inside the luxurious suite, I retreated into the bedroom for a few moments of frantic thought. I usually wore a baggy T-shirt over my workout shorts to conceal my waist holster, but I had only the vaguest idea of what a pole dancing class might entail. And 'Stripper 101' didn't sound good.

What if I had to put on a costume or something? Or worse, take something off? Or what if somebody grabbed me around the waist and felt my gun through my T-shirt?

"Aydan, hurry up! We're going to be late!"

Dammit. I consulted my wild-eyed reflection in the gigantic mirror. Maybe I should just feign a sudden attack of sickness. The way my gut was churning, it might not require much acting.

Nichele's sad-puppy expression rose from my memory, and guilt suffused me. She'd flown all the way down here just to spend time with me, and I'd done nothing but whine and bitch. And after coming so close to losing her a couple of weeks ago...

"You are a fucking idiot," I growled at the mirror before shoving my gun and holster into the depths of my suitcase.

When I emerged, shorts in hand, Nichele eyed me critically. "You aren't going to wear that baggy old T-shirt are you?"

I sighed. "It's all I've got."

"I should have known. Here, take this tank top."

I eyed the scrap of fabric with alarm. "I can't wear this. You're half my size."

"It *stretches*, girl!" She hoisted her hands under her boobs, giving them a cheerful bounce. "And anyway, my girls are bigger than yours, so it should fit just fine."

"I'm not going without a bra."

"I didn't say you should." Nichele shot me a grin. "In fact, if gravity hit you as hard as it hit me, you definitely shouldn't."

"But this has spaghetti straps..."

"Jeez, girl, if I hadn't known you all my life, I'd think you grew up Amish or something! Everybody wears a bra under spaghetti straps now." She reached up to snag the neck of my T-shirt, stretching it out to peek at my bra strap. "Your leopard-print will look great with that black tank. Come on, let's go."

"But..."

She propelled me out the door, and I resigned myself to my fate.

In the change room, I surreptitiously surveyed our giggling, chattering classmates while I put on my gym shorts. Blowing out a sigh, I pulled my T-shirt over my head and reached for the tank top.

"Ohmigod, Aydan, what *happened*?"

I turned to face Nichele as her horrified gaze slid over my black-and-blue torso. Shit, I'd grown so accustomed to the dull throbbing of my ribs, I'd forgotten I'd have to explain the bruises.

"Nothing. I just slipped and fell."

"God, girl, you look like a poster child for abusive relationships."

"Yeah, well, if you figure out a way for me to press charges against my front steps, let me know."

"Are you sure you're okay? Did you get x-rayed?"

"Yeah, I'm fine. Just sore."

"No kidding. Ouch." Nichele grimaced and turned to reach for her own shorts.

I wriggled into the skimpy tank top and tugged its deep scoop neck up as high as possible, but apparently I had no reason to feel self-conscious. A couple of girls drifted out into the classroom wearing barely-there bras and g-strings that made my thong look like granny panties. Wearing my shorts and tank top, I was definitely overdressed.

I blew out a breath between my teeth. My sense of nakedness had nothing to do with clothing or lack thereof. Without my gun, I felt horribly exposed.

"Come on, Aydan, hurry up!" Nichele beckoned from the doorway.

Dammit, I couldn't even enjoy a simple outing with my best friend without suffering separation anxiety over a firearm. What a fucked-up life.

I cranked back wooden lips in what I hoped was a convincing smile. "I'll be right there. Just gotta pee."

I grabbed my waist pouch and hurried into a bathroom stall. Clutching my folding knife in a sweaty fist, I rapidly inventoried my clingy garments. It wasn't a huge knife, but it would be far too obvious if I carried it in the back pocket of my shorts. No room in my shoe. Only one place left.

I swore silently and wedged it into the bottom of my right bra cup. Its cold hardness hurt, but at least the push-up padding concealed its outline. Please, God, let it stay put.

A rush of glorious relief flooded me when I remembered the small roll of double-sided tape still in my waist pouch. I briefly considered taping the knife between my underwear and the crotch of my shorts, but rethought the idea with a sudden mental image of doing some stripper-type move with my legs spread.

A snicker burst out before I could smother it. It'd be really tough to explain a large elongated bulge in that area...

A couple of pieces of tape later, the knife was secured in its uncomfortable berth and I readjusted my boob one more time, grimacing, before heading for the door.

The class was actually a lot more fun than I'd expected. Despite the persistent discomfort of the knife in my bra and the protests of my still-aching ribs, the time flew by with laughter and music and a tension-relieving workout.

Back in the changing room, Nichele shot me a mischievous glance. "You had fun, didn't you?"

I laughed. "I had fun. You were right."

"I'm gonna write that on the calendar! 'Today Aydan admitted I was right...'"

"Yeah, yeah."

Back in the penthouse, I was just sinking into one of the soft chairs with a sigh of relief when Nichele poked her head out of the bedroom. "If you want a shower before we go for dinner, hurry up. Our limo will be here at five-thirty and our reservation is for six."

Yawning, I slouched down in the chair and stretched my legs out. "I'm just going to have a PPA shower. I've got lots of time."

"A what?"

"PPA. Pussy, pits, and ass. Five minutes, tops." I yawned again, sinking deeper into the plush upholstery and leaning my head back.

When a small but insistent foot nudged mine a couple of times, I opened my eyes with a groan to see Nichele standing in front of me.

"Go have your shower now. Then if you still have time, you can have a nap before we leave."

If I hadn't been so tired, I would have recognized the

implied threat. Instead, I hauled myself out of the chair and trailed obediently into the bathroom, oblivious to the suffering about to befall me.

CHAPTER 12

"Jesus *Christ!*" I clutched my hammering heart through my towel and slumped against the bathroom doorframe. "Jesus, you guys, *don't ever do that!*"

"Do what?" Nichele inquired, exchanging an innocent glance with Lola, perched beside her on my bed.

"Don't sneak into my room like that, for fucksakes! What if I'd freaked out and shot you or something?"

Nichele laughed. "With what? Your mammary cannons?" She jumped to her feet, throwing back her shoulders and jutting her chest in my direction. "Stick 'em up! These babies are loaded and I'm not afraid to use them!"

Beside her, Lola collapsed backward on the bed, howling with laughter.

"Shut up, you pair of deranged midgets," I growled, starting to smile despite my still-thudding pulse. "And get out so I can get dressed."

"Why do you think we're here?" Nichele reached over to haul Lola upright. "Lola, deploy the bag!"

"Right!" Lola sprang off the bed with entirely too much energy for a woman her age and delved into the distended bag at the foot of the bed. "Try this one."

A scrap of glittery fabric landed on the bed beside

Nichele. She pounced on it and held it up, smoothing it into what appeared to be a very inadequate T-shirt.

"Oooh, I like this one." She shot me an authoritative glance. "Put on some underwear, and then try this on."

I sidled over to my suitcase, eyeing the garment with trepidation. "I don't think it's my size."

"You won't need your jeans."

I paused with my underwear and jeans dangling from my hand. "Trust me, I'm pretty sure you don't want to see my bare ass hanging out of this thong. I'll put on my jeans and then try on your little T-shirt thing."

Lola and Nichele laughed simultaneously, Lola's throaty chuckle harmonizing with Nichele's lilting grace notes.

"It's a *dress*." Nichele giggled. "Here, put it on."

I backed away, feeling behind me for the safety of the bathroom door. "Oh, no. No, no, no. No fucking way." I clutched my jeans in a death grip. "You are not going to stuff me into that thing and parade me around like some..."

I trailed off, eyeing their outfits and for once in my life, stopping myself before I said something tactless.

Nichele's lush curves were barely contained by a brilliant red sequined dress approximately the length of a tube top I'd once owned in junior high. Elegant and obviously expensive jewellery glittered at her throat, wrists and earlobes. The effect was stunning with her satin skin and ebony hair, but unless she'd used some double-sided tape of her own, Vegas would get some cheaper thrills than usual if she made a sudden move.

Lola had changed into a brief purple number that matched her hair. The thigh-high slit in the skirt flattered her still-shapely legs, while the wrapped top emphasized more cleavage than I could summon up with any of Victoria's

Secrets, wrinkles notwithstanding.

"No," I said as firmly as possible. "Just no."

Nichele sighed and exchanged a glance with Lola. "Okay. Next."

"This one'll knock your socks off," Lola enthused, holding up another vestige of fabric. "Don't you think, Nichele? Won't she look great in this with her long legs?"

"Ooooh, yes!" Nichele turned an eager face toward me.

"No."

"How about this one?"

"No!"

"Aw, come on, Aydan," Nichele cajoled. "Just try something on. How about this one?"

"No, Nichele! It wouldn't even cover my ass!"

Lola chimed in, holding up another handkerchief-sized garment. "How about-"

"No! You know I hate dresses. You know I really hate short dresses. You know I really, really hate short dresses with-"

"Okay." Lola sounded deflated. "We get the picture. Fine. I did bring one other one, but it's plain and dumpy." She extracted a handful of slithery teal-blue fabric and held it up with a grimace as it unfurled into an actual dress.

"That's perfect. I love it." I snatched it out of her hand and retreated to the bathroom.

The dress fit, if I had actually wanted a teal-blue second skin. But at least the skirt came half-way down my thighs, and the plunging neckline didn't plunge past my bra. If I sucked in my gut and stuck out my chest and held my breath, it wasn't too bad.

And I couldn't disappoint Nichele and Lola after they'd tried so hard.

When I emerged cautiously, they both let out whoops of delight. "I knew it! It's perfect," Lola chortled. "Here, honey. Here's some pantyhose and shoes. I know you can walk in stilettos, but I'll have mercy on you."

She handed me a pair of teal-blue shoes with moderate heels and ankle straps, and I heaved a sigh of relief while I hiked on the hose and buckled up the shoes. "Thank God. I was afraid you were going to hand me those thigh-high-"

I broke off as I glanced up in time to catch the conspiratorial look Nichele and Lola exchanged.

"Wait a minute..." I scowled and advanced threateningly on Lola and the shopping bag. "Let me see that."

I grabbed the bag and upended it. Nothing but more micro-dresses and a light wrap suspiciously colour-coordinated with my dress. A handbag that matched my shoes. No other shoes or accessories at all.

I'd been had.

"You pair of little *rats*! You tricked me!"

They both burst out laughing. "And it worked, honey," Lola wheezed, wiping her eyes. "That's the one we wanted you to wear in the first place, but we knew you'd never go for it otherwise. This way you were *grateful* for that dress. And it looks smashing on you."

"I'll give you smashing, you little runt..." I couldn't hold onto my grumpiness in the face of their laughter. A chuckle crept out despite my best efforts. "You two are deadly. I should never have introduced you. Where the hell did you get all that stuff? I hope you didn't buy it."

"No, I borrowed it from some of the vendors I know from the trade show," Lola said.

"You're evil. Both of you. And you're buying me drinks tonight to make up for this."

"Done! Come on." Nichele began to drag me toward the door.

"Wait a sec." I hung back, my mind kicking into overdrive. "At least let me put some things in the purse you guys so *thoughtfully* provided." I gave them a sarcastic bow. "And you scared me so badly with those teeny little dresses, I need to pee again." I planted a hand on each of their shoulders and steered them toward the bedroom door. "Out. Give me a few moments alone with my humiliation."

I closed the door on their laughter, and, as an afterthought, quietly engaged the lock before turning to study the tiny handbag. I'd learned my lesson. I wasn't going anywhere without my gun. But even if I could cram it into that little purse, there wouldn't be room for anything else.

Shit.

With my short, tight dress, both the waist and ankle holsters were out of the question. I hunched beside my suitcase, fingering my gun and pondering. Maybe...

After a few minutes' experimentation with the elastic chest strap from my workout heart rate monitor, I devised a passably secure harness to hold the gun against the inside of my thigh. Tugging the dress down, I surveyed the result in the mirror, hopes rising. Neither harness nor gun was visible when I was standing. Watching myself in the mirror, I sat carefully on the bed, the gun butt nudging my crotch. Not comfortable, but as long as I kept my legs glued together, nobody would ever know.

I stood and did a trial run of drawing the gun. Awkward, but doable. And better than going without.

I strapped it back into place, transferred my phone and wallet into the miniscule handbag, and straightened my spine.

Quality time with my best friend. It was worth it. And at least I'd discovered a foolproof way to remember to keep my knees together.

Nichele and Lola exchanged off-colour badinage in the elevator while I smiled and nodded, hoping they'd accept any preoccupation on my part as a natural consequence of being forced to wear a dress.

When the doors opened into the lobby, a transformed Harley swept us a courtly bow, resplendent in a black tux. He offered his arm to Lola, and Nichele and I followed them across the lobby, exchanging a smile while the stout man and his purple pixie cuddled close together, utterly absorbed in each other.

"Hi, Aki! Hi, guys!" Nichele did her little finger-wave, and I clutched her wrist at the sight of her Asian entourage smiling and bowing from across the lobby. "Don't worry," she whispered. "I'm not going anywhere. I don't want to be late for our dinner reservation."

"Good, 'cause I'm starving." I released her and offered Aki and the boys a nod. A movement in my peripheral vision made me jerk my head around in time to see Doytchevsky slip into the lobby from the casino area. His gaze travelled up my legs and lingered at chest-level before meeting my eyes. He gave me a brief, contemptuous smile before fading back into the casino once more.

I squelched the shiver that snaked down my back and turned back to Nichele's bright chatter. Trying to ignore the blaze of cameras, I managed to follow the others into the limo without flashing either my gun or my assets, and drew a breath of relief when we pulled away.

By the time the Chippendales show was half over, my stomach ached from sucking in my gut around the lavish meal Nichele had insisted on buying earlier, and my head pounded in time to the heavy beat of the music.

Nichele pushed another beer in my direction. "Isn't this great?" she shouted. "Hey, Lola, get a load of that one!"

Lola let fly with a wolf whistle that threatened to cleave my brain in two, and I sucked down a long swallow of beer, hoping to apply some anaesthesia.

Approximately an eternity or possibly an hour later, the show came to a thunderous close and I blew out a sigh of relief. I appreciate eye-candy as much as the next woman, but my enjoyment of the scenery had been seriously limited by the gun rammed into my crotch. I stood, trying not to wince when circulation began to return to some extremely sensitive places.

"Back in a few minutes." I nodded toward the ladies' room for Lola and Nichele's benefit and hobbled in that direction, cursing quietly but sincerely.

When I returned, somewhat more comfortable, Nichele was vibrating beside the table. "Come on, Aydan, hurry up! We don't want to miss the party with the Chippendales boys."

Oh yes, we do. We really, really do want to miss that.

I summoned up a smile instead of uttering my killjoy thoughts and turned to Lola. "Are you coming, too?"

"Nope." She grinned up at me. "Harley's been getting all fired up watching the girls while we watched the boys. Now you kids run off to your party. Harley and I have plans for a little party of our own." She let one eyelid droop in a lascivious wink. "See you. Don't do anything I wouldn't do."

We watched her tiny figure weave through the crowd to the exit, and Nichele giggled. "I just *love* her. I'm so glad you introduced us. Come on, let's go."

I spared a brief but fervent wish for my bed, and followed.

Christ, maybe I was having an epileptic seizure. But I was marginally reassured by the coldness of the glass in my hand. Probably not seizing if I could still hold onto my beer and perch on this damn uncomfortable stool. Strobe lights pummelled my eyes while the music battered my brain as if some evil poltergeist was using my skull for a kettledrum.

I cranked my aching head slowly around, but I didn't see any ghosts, evil or otherwise. On the opposite side of the bar, Nichele's red sequins flashed and glittered through the dimness while she laughed and danced and flirted. I groaned and gulped some more beer.

"Hey, beautiful."

A chiselled chest gleamed inches away from my eyes. I dragged my gaze up to his face. Long blond hair, bright blue eyes, and a seductive smile. Gorgeous. Half-naked. And I was pretty sure that wasn't a gun strapped to his thigh under those tight pants.

And he was young enough to be my son, if I'd ever had children.

I suppressed another groan. "Hi." I manoeuvred my beer past his pecs to take another drink.

"Are you having fun?"

"Oh, sure."

More beer.

"You don't look like you're having fun. Maybe I can help." He moved a little closer, hips circling suggestively. "Do you like my nipple ring?"

I focused slowly on the nipple in question. With an effort, I contained my urge to wince and cross my arms over my chest. "Ouch."

"You can touch it if you like."

"No thanks."

"Go ahead." He straddled my knees, which were pressed uncomfortably together thanks to my gun. His thighs slid against my legs with slow, rhythmic strokes. The nipple ring came closer. "Go ahead. It feels reeeally good if you take it in your teeth and tug a bit..."

A sudden memory of bright metal tearing through flesh made me recoil with a cry, slopping beer over his bulging crotch. I slid awkwardly off the stool, clenching my legs on my gun.

"Sorry." I backed away, fighting to control my shallow breathing.

"It's okay. You can help me dry it off." He gave me a provocative grin.

"No thanks, I have a headache." For the first time in my life, I abandoned an unfinished beer. I threw a wave in Nichele's direction and got the hell out of there.

Outside the door of the lounge, I sagged against the wall to avoid a cluster of noisy drunks and switched to belly breathing. After a couple of breaths, I drew myself up and shook off the residual horror of the flashback.

Nipple rings just grossed me out, that's all. Totally

unrelated to that memory.

I deliberately guided my mind back to the sight of the gleaming ring, breathing through another surge of adrenaline while I worked to lessen my reaction. Just a run-of-the-mill piercing. Repulsive, but innocuous.

There was no reason to think it would ever be viciously torn from his body while he screamed and struggled and bled...

Fine. I was fine, dammit.

Just a piercing. He liked it. It wasn't hurting him.

Just breathe.

I tottered down the walkway toward the small food fair. Over-tired, that's all. A snack would help.

I was hovering between the kiosks trying to decide between two unappealing varieties of greasy food when a hard object jammed painfully into my bruised back and a voice spoke in my ear.

"Let's go. Nice and slow."

CHAPTER 13

Another deluge of adrenaline completely breached the weakened dam of my self-control. I let out a yell and whirled, my arms windmilling in mindless attack.

Doytchevsky jumped back, narrowly avoiding a backhand to the face, and glared at me. "What is your problem?" he demanded loudly enough to carry to the staring vendors and patrons nearby. "It's just me."

I staggered toward the nearest chair and he moved solicitously to my side, reaching as if to support me.

"Back off, dickhead," I barked, and dropped into the chair, panting and shaking.

"I'm sorry, honey, I really didn't mean to scare you." Doytchevsky was still maintaining his 'misunderstood husband' act. "It was just a joke. It was a pop can." He held up the offending object.

I grabbed his shirtfront and yanked his face down to my level. "If you ever, *ever*, try anything like that again, I will tear... you... *apart*!" I jerked the shirt for emphasis with each word. "Got it?"

"Don't make a scene," he whispered. "Let me go." He pried my fingers loose and slid into the chair opposite me.

I jerked forward to glare into his eyes. "Why the fuck

shouldn't I make a scene?" I hissed. "And what the hell did you think you were doing? You're lucky I didn't fucking shoot you, you moron."

"You're lucky I didn't shoot *you*. That wasn't a pop can."

"Asshole!"

"I'm sorry," he repeated loudly before dropping his voice to a whisper. "Look, I'm going to keep following you until you tell me where Sherman is. So we might as well work together. We both want the same thing anyway. Give."

"Or what?" I snarled. "You'll threaten me again? We both know damn well you won't shoot me. You need me. And we both know damn well you can't do anything to me or Stemp will nail your ass to the wall. Now I'm going to tell you this one more time in small words so you can understand, and I want you to listen very, very carefully. I don't know where Sherman is, but I'm pretty damn sure he isn't in Vegas. I'm not meeting him. I'm not hunting him. And if I see your rat-face again, *anywhere*, I'm going to call Stemp and tell him everything, including how you've been stalking and threatening me. Got it?"

He stood, his glare so malevolent that I had to prevent myself from recoiling. An instant later, his expression smoothed into its usual blandness.

"We'll talk later when you're not so upset," he said, and walked away.

I sat breathing carefully. Beer and exhaustion and stale adrenaline provided toxic fuel for my splitting headache. I dry-swallowed a couple of painkillers and vibrated quietly in the chair until I thought my legs might hold me again.

At last, I staggered to the nearest kiosk and bought an order of french fries, forcing them down without tasting them. The pounding in my temples eased, and I finally summoned up enough energy to head for the escalator. Descending into the insistent noise and movement of the casino, I clenched my teeth, massaging my forehead.

God, this place was like my own private version of hell. I tried not to limp while I navigated through the crowded casino, cursing the blister on my heel and the fiery friction of the gun against my inner thigh.

Outside, the thought of closing myself into a cab was more than I could bear. I turned away from the crowd milling at the entrance and retreated down the sidewalk to an oasis of relative peace and quiet.

Letting out a long breath, I stepped off the concrete and pressed my back against the coolness of a sheltering pillar. Above me, the gigantic illuminated sign flashed out its welcome.

Huh. More like a warning. 'Caution: Migraine Zone'. I sighed again and savored the relative softness of grass under my aching feet, letting the tension ease from my shoulders.

The sound of footsteps and an advancing shadow made me shrink back a little farther from the sidewalk. Just let me have a few moments of peace and solitude, for God's sake.

The footsteps slowed. Good. Maybe they were going back.

The motionless shadow loomed across the sidewalk in silence.

Watching. Or listening. A sudden chill made me ease my hand down toward my gun.

The shadow moved suddenly, but before I could decide whether to draw my gun, my stalker stepped around the corner of the pillar.

My jaw dropped.

"Hi," Kane said.

"Uh... hi."

God help me, he was breathtaking in that dark suit. It must have cost a fortune to tailor the jacket to fit his powerful arms and shoulders while emphasizing that taut midsection. Nichele would faint.

Hell, I was damn close to fainting. Or something.

Kane grinned and leaned a shoulder against the pillar beside me. "You're stunning in that dress." His gaze trailed heat from my throat to my knees. "I hope you're as dangerous as you look. Where's your gun?"

I tamped down the urge to say 'search me' and shot him a grin instead. "You don't want to know."

He leaned closer, his eyes darkening. "Oh, I think I do."

I straightened, holding onto control with all my might. "What are you doing here? I told Stemp I didn't need you." I glanced up at his nonplussed expression. "Sorry, I didn't mean it like that," I added.

His smile came back. "It's all right. Stemp didn't like the idea that you were being followed, so he sent me. I was already in transit by the time you called the second time and told him you'd eliminated your tail and made the drop."

He sobered. "I don't blame you for being irritated. I'd be mad as hell if Stemp second-guessed one of my missions like that, but you're quite a bit more valuable than I am. He can't afford to take chances with your safety."

"Mm." I twitched a shoulder and changed the subject. "I presume you found me by tracking my cell phone?"

"Yes. When I got here and discovered you'd checked out of the Mirage, I got Stemp to coordinate with the local law enforcement to run back the security camera footage. I saw you meeting Nichele and Lola, so I wasn't surprised you were out on the town." He leaned closer, frowning. "And I saw

Doytchevsky accost you in the lobby. That didn't look like a friendly exchange. What's he doing here?"

Shit! I stared up at Kane for a moment, my mind racing. If I told him about Doytchevsky's private obsession with finding Sherman and the rest of the Knights, it would raise all kinds of awkward questions. Little things like 'why didn't you put this in your report'. I made a split-second decision just as he spoke again.

"Aydan, you can tell me."

I shrugged. "There's nothing to tell. You remember how he asked me out to lunch a while ago? Well, it seems he got the wrong idea and followed me down here thinking we might have a little vacation together. I set him straight, and he wasn't very happy about it."

Kane's frown deepened. "Don't you think it seems obsessive to follow you to Vegas on the strength of one short meal where you ate a couple of bites and then threw up in the bathroom until he left? Is there something you aren't telling me?"

It took all my self-control to meet his eyes. "He's just a creep, that's all." At least it was true, though it didn't exactly answer his question.

Change the subject.

"So what are you doing here in your James Bond outfit?" I teased. "I hope you're playing high-stakes roulette and drinking martinis, shaken not stirred."

His smile made the irresistible laugh lines crinkle around his eyes. "That would be clichéd. I'm playing high-stakes poker and drinking single-malt scotch."

A vivid memory of the taste of scotch lingering on his lips made me swallow, the tip of my tongue skimming my own lips before I could prevent it.

His gaze fixed on my mouth, his eyes dilating. Even several inches away, I could feel his body heat radiating against the exposed skin of my cleavage.

His voice dropped to a panty-vibrating rumble. "What are you doing here in your Bond Girl outfit? I hope you're drinking champagne and planning to seduce a secret agent."

My insides melted into a puddle of lust.

Shit, this was exactly what had gotten me in trouble the last time...

He leaned closer and my breath caught when blazing hunger consumed me.

Too much beer, too many hot memories. Goddammit, if he kissed me, I'd rip his clothes off right here and now and bang him up against this sign...

"John, stop!" I blurted desperately.

The naughty twinkle vanished from his eyes and he stepped away so quickly the abrupt withdrawal of his body heat nearly made me reach for him to regain it.

"Do you mean that?" His suddenly serious gaze searched my face. "Aydan, if I'm stepping over the line and making you uncomfortable, say so and this stops right now."

I swallowed the dryness in my throat, my lecherous memory roaming wantonly over that glorious chest, those delicious biceps, that perfectly-sculpted ass, that rock-hard...

I shook myself and dragged in an unsteady breath. "Yeah, you're sure as hell making me uncomfortable," I muttered.

He stiffened. "I'm sorry. I won't-"

"But I don't think the discomfort of unsatisfied lust is going to land you in a sexual harassment tribunal," I interrupted. I gave him a smile as the tension eased from his posture. "John, you know damn well it's all I can do to keep my hands off you..."

His lips curved into that teasing smile again as he stepped closer. "So don't."

"...but you know I have to," I finished, determinedly not looking at the tempting laugh lines around his eyes.

"Of course you have to when somebody might see us," he said in reasonable and far-too-convincing tones. He advanced another step, only inches of superheated air separating our bodies.

"But we're alone. Here in Vegas with no mission. Nobody watching. If you want me..." His voice dropped to that deep rumble that threatened to dislodge the underpinnings of my self-control. "...you can have me." He held me motionless with his gaze, my willpower evaporating into wisps of vapour under its heat. "Remember that time in the woods? Up against the tree?" His fingertips traced lightly over my collarbone before drifting higher to tilt my chin up. "Tell me you remember." His eyes were a rim of grey around bottomless black. "I know I do."

His husky baritone sent electricity sizzling from my eardrums directly to all points south. God, yes, I remembered. With every cell in my body.

"I... That's not what I meant." I fought the waves of desire generated by the proximity of those lickable lips. And all the rest of that lickable real estate.

Shit, stop thinking about it.

I stepped back far enough to suck in some air that didn't contain the brain-scrambling scent of gun oil and leather. "What I meant was, I don't want to get involved with you, and having sex with you again would really, really not help that."

"So don't get involved."

I jerked away from him, frustration putting more of an edge into my voice than I'd intended. "For fucksakes, John, I'm not worried about *me* getting involved with *you*. I won't. That's what I'm worried about. I don't want you to get hurt."

"You won't hurt me."

"Goddammit, yes I *will*!" I balled my fists in my hair and tugged savagely. "Why can't you just-"

"Aydan." The tease was gone. Nothing left but deadly-hot testosterone-drenched male. "I live a dangerous life." The deepening growl of his voice made my argument shrivel in my suddenly-dry throat.

He closed the distance between us, his mountainous shoulders looming over me. "I know what I want. I'm willing to take risks to get it." His intense gaze made my knees begin to tremble despite my best efforts. His hand slid behind my head, powerful fingers closing in the hair at my nape to pull me closer. "Those risks are mine to take if I choose."

I gulped, groping for a reply in the boiling vat of lust that had apparently replaced my brain. I managed a shallow gasp before he spoke again, a fraction of an inch away from my lips.

"I choose."

His kiss made breathing irrelevant. Made everything irrelevant except the mind-melting need to feel his hard contours against my body and-

He broke the kiss and pulled away, a wicked grin tilting his lips at my involuntary moan of protest. He eyed my panting and trembling with undisguised satisfaction. "Sooner or later, you'll see the wisdom of my choice."

I swallowed hard and scraped together a semblance of intellect. "I thought you said it was up to me whether anything happened between us or not."

His grin widened. "It is. But I never said I wouldn't try to influence your decision." He pulled me into another incendiary kiss before releasing me. "Think about it," he whispered before striding away, tossing a devilish grin over his shoulder.

Jesus, like I was going to be able to think about anything else.

I was dragging myself across the polished tiles of the Mirage's lobby when Doytchevsky appeared beside me, smirking. I glared at him from behind the headache that had returned full force during my cab ride. If I kept walking, I'd have exactly enough energy to make it to the elevator.

"Fuck off," I growled, and kept moving.

His smile widened. "No, I don't think so." He brandished his camera. "You're going to want to see this."

I stopped. Summoned up every fibre of forbearance I still owned.

"Doytchevsky." My tone made his eyes widen. "In three seconds, I'm going to pull out my gun and shoot you. Three. Two..."

He thrust the LCD display of the camera in front of my face.

"...W... What the *fuck*?"

CHAPTER 14

Doytchevsky's smile widened as I stared at the photo. His hand closed around my arm, jarring my mind back into motion. His voice held sheer triumph. "Let's go up to your room and talk about this. If you tell me where Sherman is, I'll make these pictures go away."

I straightened and clamped my hand around his wrist, letting him have the full force of my grip despite the jab of pain from my arthritic thumb. A tiny spurt of satisfaction warmed me at his start of surprise.

Yeah, I'm stronger than I look, buddy.

I pushed at his wrist, and when he let go I released him as if I'd been clutching a sewer rat. Which, come to think of it, I had.

I leaned close, glaring at him from the lofty advantage of my heels. "We're not going anywhere. And we've got nothing to talk about."

He gave me an irritatingly superior smile. "So you won't mind if I send Stemp a nice photo of you and your boyfriend getting all hot and heavy on company time."

I shot the photo a contemptuous glance. Kane's massive shoulders blocked most of the details. Only the back of his head and a sliver of my hair were visible.

I went for a sneer. "You're not much of a photographer. So you snapped a couple of random people that look a bit like Kane and me. You think I give a shit?"

"I think you will. That was just the last one." He toggled the camera's display.

Shit, shit, shit!

The bastard had caught the whole exchange. My mind raced while he flipped through the photos in a stop-action montage showing Kane closing in, stepping away, moving closer and kissing me.

If Stemp saw this, Kane was in deep shit. I had no rank or privileges to be revoked and I was the only person in the world...

I stopped myself. The only person in the world except Tammy Mellor, anyway... who could decrypt and hack networks. Stemp needed me.

But all Kane's long career in military and law enforcement, all his medals and commendations and exemplary service wouldn't save him from disciplinary action for inappropriate behaviour on the job.

Goddammit, I *told* him he was going to get hurt...

Doytchevsky toggled to the last photo and shot me a victorious grin. "Are you feeling a little more cooperative now?"

My old defensive reflexes snapped into place with an almost-audible click. Pretend you don't care and they can't hurt you.

I felt the familiar mask of indifference slip onto my face. "Why should I? I've got nothing to lose."

He frowned. "Maybe not. But your boyfriend does."

"That asshole's not my boyfriend." I shrugged. "I'm going to bed."

I was turning away when he grabbed my arm again. "You're bluffing. I'm going to send these straight to Stemp tonight, and by tomorrow morning Kane's disciplinary hearing will already be scheduled."

"Tell it to somebody who cares. And I'd like to hear you explain to Stemp why you followed me down here in the first place. Good luck with that."

He eyed me with contempt. "I'm not that stupid. I'm here for a technology expo, which I've duly registered for and attended, according to their records. If I just happened to be doing a little sight-seeing one evening, well..."

I hid my icy trickle of fear. So much for that line of defense. Before I could respond, he spoke again.

"We both know you're bluffing, so give it up. You wouldn't be kissing him if you didn't care about him, and you know how much he has to lose if this goes to Stemp."

Holding onto my façade with all my might, I gave him a blank stare. "Go take your camera to bed and flip through those pictures again while you whack off, you pathetic little louse. After you wipe your jizz off the display, you'll notice I wasn't kissing him. He was kissing me. I don't give a shit about him. You've got nothing."

I turned and walked away.

Safely up in the penthouse, I stripped off the shoes and dress and pantyhose, wincing at the bright red abrasion on my inner thigh. In the privacy of my ensuite bathroom, I glared at my reflection and mouthed obscenities I didn't dare scream out loud for fear of triggering another call from the front desk.

It didn't help.

Rage and fear overwhelmed me, and I flung the dress onto the floor, kicking it violently around and around the bathroom. At last, I leaned my sweating hands on the vanity, my breath coming in hiccups that wanted to turn into sobs.

Goddamn Doytchevsky, goddamn Vegas, goddamn that goddamn stupid dress, and god*damn* Kane for putting himself in that kind of danger!

I couldn't even call him. Doytchevsky could easily get my cell phone records, and a call to Kane immediately after the confrontation with Doytchevsky would be even more incriminating than the pictures. I stared at my hollow-eyed, dishevelled self in the mirror, emitted a small whimper, and trudged out of the bathroom to creep into bed.

"Aydan. Hey, Aydan, wake up!"

I groaned and pried my face away from the pillow to see Nichele's red dress backlit in the open door of my bedroom. Shit, I should've locked that.

"If you're not waking me up because you're dying, I'm going to kill you." My voice emerged in a raw croak. "What time is it?"

"It's six A.M. Come on, Aydan, you're always up by now. Hurry up, we have to go."

"Go? What? Where?" I jacked my head a little higher and groaned again when I eased my aching fingers out of their death grip on my gun. I must have fallen asleep clutching it. Christ, had I even moved since I fell into bed less than four hours ago?

I pushed the gun a little farther under the pillow and rolled over to squint at Nichele's figure vibrating in the doorway. "Nichele, what the hell?"

"Dave's not answering his cell phone. I just know something bad has happened to him! We have to go and find him."

I fell back on the pillow. "It's six in the morning. The poor bastard's probably in the shower or something. Or still sleeping. Go away and let me sleep, too."

The mattress bounced under the weight of one small but determined woman. My eyes popped open when she seized my wrist and pulled.

"Come *on*, Aydan, I'm not kidding. I'm really worried. I've been trying to call him since yesterday morning. He's a *trucker*. You know he never goes anywhere without his cell phone."

"Nichele..." I marshalled my sleepy brain into a semblance of tact and gently disengaged her fingers. "I'm not trying to be mean or anything, but do you think maybe he's ignoring your calls? Maybe he just wants a clean break."

She gave a little flounce of frustration. "No! Aydan, he'd never do that! This is *Dave* we're talking about. And I left him a voice mail and told him it was an emergency. I *know* he'd call me back. You know it, too."

I sat up, my heart beginning to thump a little harder. She was right. When I'd been in trouble, Dave wouldn't leave me no matter how hard I tried to drive him away. And we hadn't been in a relationship.

"Okay, Nichele, calm down. Let's think about this. Did you try his home phone?"

"He doesn't *have* a home phone." Her voice was beginning to tremble. "He doesn't even have a *home*. He just lives in that big stupid truck he's so proud of."

"Oh." I flashed back to Dave's tiny but impeccably clean custom-built sleeper. The miniscule sink and toilet, the narrow bed, the small built-in cabinets containing his few neatly folded clothes.

My heart swelled. When he'd rescued me literally off the street a few weeks ago, I hadn't realized he was inviting me into the only home he had. And he'd left it behind for me without a single complaint. Never even mentioned how important it was to him.

I owed him my life, and then some.

Stay calm.

I took a deep breath. "Maybe his cell phone died and he had to get a new one."

"I *thought* of that! But it's his business phone, too. His *everything* phone. He'd forward the number to his new phone. Aydan, something's wrong, I know it, I *know* it!"

"Nichele, just calm down for a second-"

"Aydan, oh my God, what if James found him?" Her dark eyes went liquid with terror. "What if-"

I seized her shoulders and gave her a little shake. "Nichele, stop! Now you're just scaring yourself. James is in jail and he's going to stay there for a very long time. You're safe. Dave's safe. It'll be okay."

"But what if he got out?" Her usually confident voice was a teary whisper. "You know how smart he is. And how mean he is..." Her voice wavered into silence.

I pulled her into a hug, tightening my arms around the delicate shoulders that had so recently been black with the bruises of James Helmand's fists.

"Nichele, it's okay, I promise. They won't let him out."

I was sure of it. The regular justice system might be rife with loopholes, but when people got arrested by Stemp and his team, they usually stayed arrested.

"And anyway," I added, "He never met Dave, and the two

of you weren't together at the time. There's no way James would even know to look for him."

Nichele pulled away, straightening her spine and dabbing her eyes. "You're right, I know you're right. But... Aydan..."

I switched to another tack. "Did you call the police? Can you file a missing-persons report?"

"I don't think they'll listen. It's not even twenty-four hours." She gulped. "He's a healthy guy and he doesn't need any medications or anything. A trucker with no fixed address. When they find out he dumped me, too, they'll just blow me off."

I squeezed her hand. "If you file a report, I'm sure they'll look. Call them. They wouldn't blow it off."

"Okay, I will. But we're wasting time." She sprang off the bed. "Come on, get packed. We have to start looking for him."

"Nichele, let the police deal with it, okay?"

"I'm not just going to sit here and wait! Come on!"

"Slow down. How could we look for him? He could be anywhere in North America by now. Do you even have any idea where he was going? Did he have a load this week?"

"He was going to Vancouver again. I think he pulled out right after he left... me..." Her voice quavered on the last words.

I blew out a long breath. "Okay, I'll see if I can get my flight changed."

"Forget that, Aydan, I'll buy us tickets on the first plane out of here. I don't care what it costs."

Shit, there was no way I could get through the airport carrying my gun without Stemp's intervention.

"Just go pack." I hauled myself out of bed to take her by

the shoulders and point her in the direction of the door. "Let me see what I can do."

The bedroom door safely locked behind me, I snatched one of Stemp's secure phones out of the bag and pressed the speed dial.

Only one ring sounded before Stemp's brusque voice spoke. "What took you?"

"What...?"

Never mind. I shook myself back to the present. "I need to get back to Calgary on the first flight out of here."

"Already done. Report to my office as soon as you can get back to Silverside." He followed up with a spate of flight numbers and disconnected.

Shit, that couldn't be good.

I stood staring at the phone in my hand for a few seconds, my heart slowly sinking. Doytchevsky wouldn't have. He *wouldn't* have, that rat-bastard. Would he?

Oh, shit.

CHAPTER 15

Beside the baggage carousel in the Calgary airport, Nichele turned to look up at me, her unprecedented lack of makeup leaving her sallow and haggard. The deep shadows under her eyes emphasized her lost-puppy expression.

"Aydan, please, just come with me so we can leave right away. Your client can't be more important than Dave. If you have to drive all the way up to Silverside, it'll be evening before you get back. We don't have time."

I squeezed her trembling hand. "Look, Nichele, it's better this way. In the first place, it gives the police a little longer to look for him. In the second place, you haven't slept, and you can't help anybody if you're so exhausted you can't function."

When she started to shake her head, I gave her hand a little squeeze and locked eyes with her. "Nichele. Here's what I need you to do. Go home..."

"But, Aydan-"

"No, listen. Go home and get on the internet and start making a list of all the gas stations and truck stops and everything along the TransCanada Highway between here and Vancouver. Then call, um..." I racked my brain for the names of the places Dave had stopped on our last trip and came up empty. "Call the gas stations and restaurants on the north side of the highway in Revelstoke and Hope. That's where he stopped when he drove me last time. Get packed…"

I played the wardrobe card, hoping she wasn't too far gone to perk up at the thought of clothes. "You'll need totally different clothes for a road trip than you did for Vegas."

She pulled herself up out of her dejected slouch with a little nod. "Okay."

"And if I'm still not back by then, you need to sleep. Or at least lie down and rest. But I'll probably be back," I lied. "Okay?"

"Okay. See you later." She trailed away towing her two big bags, her tiny form looking even smaller than usual.

I blew out a breath between my teeth and headed for the exit.

I signed in at the Sirius Dynamics security desk, my mind still buzzing with all the scenarios I'd considered during my two-hour drive. If Doytchevsky had delivered the incriminating photos to Stemp, my best solution would be to tell Stemp I was on another obscure "mission", and that I'd asked Kane to stage the kiss as part of my cover.

But if he hooked me up to the damn lie detector, it was all over. And if I tried to avoid the lie detector, he'd be even more suspicious. Goddammit.

I flashed my security prox card at the doors to the office area and trudged through.

But I didn't really have any other option. I couldn't think of any other plausible reason why Kane would kiss me except for the truth. And the truth could kill his career.

Dragging my feet up the stairs, I spared a brief thought

to the possibility that it might be something else entirely. I racked my brain for any other transgressions I might have committed, but nothing came to mind.

Shit.

I drew a deep breath and tapped on Stemp's door.

He looked up, frowning. "Come in. Close the door behind you."

When I complied, he waved me into the chair in front of his desk. "Please sit."

I almost handed over my gun out of sheer reflex, but he didn't ask for it. Instead, he eyed me briefly, still frowning, before he spoke.

"Agent Kelly, I owe you an apology. I wasn't aware of this situation, and I'm sorry it came to the point where you felt impelled to file a formal complaint. I'm also sorry you felt so intimidated that you couldn't come to me directly."

"Uh...?"

What the hell was he talking about? I searched his concerned expression for a clue.

"Rest assured that we will treat this very seriously indeed. Kane has been suspended without pay pending his hearing, and he is under direct orders not to contact you in any way during the intervening time. A breach of those orders will result in a court-martial, and almost certainly dishonourable discharge and imprisonment. Please notify me immediately if he attempts to contact you or harass you in any way."

I didn't have to fake my confusion. "Wait, what? What are you talking about?"

Stemp's frown deepened. "This, of course." He gestured to a sheaf of papers on the desk in front of him. "Your sexual harassment complaint."

"My *what*?" My voice rose to a squeak. "I didn't file any complaints. Harassment or otherwise."

That scum-sucking *bastard!* Doytchevsky hadn't just damaged Kane's career, he had annihilated it.

Just to hurt me.

Icy rage froze my reaction into needle-sharp focus. "Let me see that." My voice was completely calm and level.

Stemp pushed the papers across his desk.

I skimmed the typed sheet, fury pulsing behind my eyes. A glance at the photos on the other sheets proved Doytchevsky had chosen with deadly intent. In the first of the sequence, I stared wide-eyed up at Kane looming around the corner of the pillar. In the second, my face was frozen in an expression that could have been fear while Kane leaned closer, grinning.

A small voice commented from the corner of my brain. Shit, now I knew how I looked when I was fighting lust. Not pretty.

The third was even more damning. Kane towered over me while I backed away with both hands pressed against the pillar behind me as if seeking protection. This time there was no mistaking the fear in my face, but I *had* been afraid, dammit. Afraid I was going to jump him right there on the sidewalk.

Another shot showed my face twisted with anger. The next was a closeup of Kane's hand clamped on my neck, my eyes enormous while he stared down from inches away. And then the kiss, with my hands braced against his chest as if fighting him.

Shit, shit, shit!

"These are fake." My voice was dead level. "And you don't seriously believe I wrote this letter." I slapped the sheet with the back of my hand. "This is bullshit! *'I can't take it anymore. I don't know what to do. He keeps forcing me...'* What a load of shit!"

I glared at Stemp. "Do you honestly believe I'd write a pathetic, limp-wristed, cowardly load of piss-poor *whining* like this? If I had a problem, I'd bring it up with him, and if that didn't solve it, I'd get mediation. And if I was going to actually file a complaint, I'd have a complete list of dates, times, and documentation! This is *bullshit!*"

Stemp's poker face was impenetrable. "I understand how intimidating it must be to face up to a man of Kane's size and martial arts skill. I understand that you may be having second thoughts out of fear, and I assure you, we'll protect you-"

"No!" I rocketed to my feet. "Get the damn lie-detector. Hook me up right fucking now and ask me if Kane has ever, *ever*, acted inappropriately. Do it! Now!"

Stemp rocked back in his chair, a faint twitch of humour flickering for only an instant at the corner of his mouth. "You forget who gives the orders here."

I froze, my anger draining away into cold, lethal purpose. Very slowly, I unlocked my joints enough to plant my fists on his desk. My voice was low and deadly.

"You. Will. Not. Screw. Him. Over."

Stemp's expressionless façade never wavered. "No, I will not screw him over. Given my knowledge of your psych profile and your reactions in the past, not to mention your..." His lips twisted. "...*insistence* on the lie detector, I'm inclined to believe your story. But if you didn't file this complaint, who did? Your signature is on it. And how do you explain this?" He gestured toward the photo of Kane's and my entwined bodies.

I collapsed back into my chair, trembling with unspent adrenaline. "I staged this with Kane for my other op. I knew I was being followed, but it never occurred to me this could happen. Fucking moron. I should have known. I should have been more careful."

Apparently Stemp was sufficiently convinced by the profound sincerity of the latter sentences to accept the lie contained in the first. He raised an eyebrow.

"You have another mission now?"

"Oh, hell yeah," I snarled.

Hunting Doytchevsky to the ends of the earth and crushing him into a disgusting little grease spot.

"Can you give me details?"

"No. Just get rid of that stupid fake complaint and I'll deal with this."

Stemp eyed me levelly. "There's a problem."

My stress level ratcheted up another notch. "What problem?"

"I can't."

"Can't what?" My nerves stretched to breaking.

"I can't suppress the complaint."

CHAPTER 16

I stared at Stemp, my blood draining into my socks. "What do you mean, you can't suppress the complaint?" My voice was a bare whisper.

He returned my gaze, looking almost as sick as I felt. "I can't. It's already been escalated up the chain of command. There's a strict protocol in place for handling complaints like this. It's too late."

"But it's bullshit! I'll write another letter denying it. I'll write as many letters as it takes..."

"It wouldn't help," Stemp said. "Once the process is in motion, it can't be stopped even if the initial complaint is retracted. The hearing still has to be held." He gestured toward the damning photos. "And what are you going to say about these if you can't disclose your other chain of command? That it was consensual? That would damage both of you."

"It's still better to say it was consensual. At least the sexual harassment thing won't go on his record..."

I trailed off at the sight of his face. "God, no. It all goes on his record?" My stomach twisted itself into a hard knot. "So you're saying he has to go through this... this... travesty? And even if the claim is proven false, it isn't expunged?

That's... that's..."

"Bullshit, I know," Stemp finished quietly. "Whoever is doing this has an excellent knowledge of how to cause the most damage with the least effort. And I intend to find out who it is. This came in by fax from the business centre at the Mirage late last night. I'll get the surveillance camera footage and-"

"Don't," I interrupted. "I'll deal with it."

The quirk of Stemp's mouth didn't look quite as humorous as before. "I gather you're accustomed to holding rank in your other chain of command. However, you do *not* outrank me."

"Sorry," I said quickly. "I didn't mean it that way. But really, just let it go, please..."

Stemp's gaze pinned me to the chair. "I have allowed you a great deal of latitude and placed a great deal of trust in you, but in this case my top priority is damage control for all of us. I will not stand by while a good agent gets railroaded by the system."

He drummed his fingers on the desk, visibly switching to tactical mode. "Some collateral damage is inevitable, but maybe the charges could be downgraded to a minor sexual misconduct. Kane might be allowed to keep his pension, though probably not his rank. Best-case, if you deny sexual assault, we might convince the tribunal that it's simply an adverse personal relationship and he could avoid charges. He will be removed from your project and reassigned no matter what we do, of course."

He shot me a wry look. "I presume you'll handle any potential consequences to yourself through your other chain of command. But to protect both you and myself, I have to investigate the complaint as fully as possible. If I do not, the only alternative would be to disclose my unauthorized knowledge of your other activities."

He grimaced. "I doubt either of us would be pleased with the consequences of that."

Sudden realization smothered the cutting comment I'd been ready to make about covering his own ass. In his world, unauthorized knowledge frequently turned out to be fatal. He didn't know I was lying through my teeth.

His trust made my gut clench with shame.

Stemp struck while I was vulnerable. "You know who sent the photos and the trumped-up complaint."

It wasn't a question. Completely blindsided, my mind refused to summon up a convincing lie.

Just say no, dammit. Meet his eyes and say no.

The guilt swamped me. I couldn't do it. And I was already too late. My silence had spoken louder than words.

Trapped! Panic trickled into my veins.

"Can you tell me?"

Oh thank God, a loophole. I could just say it was part of my other op and he'd drop it.

The words wouldn't come.

I dragged myself upright and met his gaze. "It's John Smith. Well, Kasper Doytchevsky. That's his real name."

CHAPTER 17

Stemp's eyes narrowed. "Why would Doytchevsky want to make it look as though you'd filed a sexual harassment charge against Kane?"

I slumped in the chair, unable to even sit upright. Resignation made my voice flat.

"Long story. I left some details out of my last report."

Stemp's face froze over. "What details? And why?"

I blew out an exhausted breath. "Doytchevsky was a Russian secret agent during the Cold War. He was working as a handler for their network super-user Irina..." My mind went blank. "Um, Irina Somebody-or-other. She's dead anyway..."

"Popov. Or perhaps you were thinking of Doytchevsky?" Stemp supplied drily.

"Uh, right, they were married. You already knew that?"

"Yes."

"Oh."

Shit, I'd been killing myself to keep Doytchevsky's secret and Stemp already *knew*? Son of a bitch...

"Anyway," I stumbled on. "Irina started feeling irresistible compulsions and hearing voices in her head. She thought she was going crazy. She was eventually diagnosed with schizophrenia."

Stemp's eyes sharpened at this revelation. Maybe he didn't know as much as I thought he did.

"It wasn't schizophrenia," I went on. "It was her Knight, Rex Rimmel, controlling her inside the network, but nobody knew that except Rimmel and of course he wasn't about to blab."

I sighed. "She committed suicide eventually, but not before Doytchevsky started to piece together her ramblings. He became obsessed with finding out what had happened. Eventually he captured Rimmel and tortured him until he spilled all the Knights' secrets. Then Doytchevsky killed Rimmel and made it his life's mission to destroy the rest of the Knights."

"You were aware Doytchevsky had prior knowledge of the Knights of Sirius and you omitted it from your report?" Stemp's expression didn't change, but his tone chilled my heart as though an icicle had slipped between my ribs.

"You had already granted him a top-level security clearance, and he'd held it for years. I made a full report about the Knights' activities as soon as I could. His knowledge didn't pose any additional risk."

"That was not your decision to make."

I eyed his impassive face. "I'm sorry, I know it doesn't look good, but I was forced into a decision." I took a chance. "You know how things don't always go quite the way you planned in the field."

His lips thinned. "True. Go on."

"I needed information from Doytchevsky for one of my other missions. As leverage, I threatened to report his prior knowledge of Knights' treason and told him he'd go to jail as an accessory, but I promised to keep it a secret if he gave me the information."

"But you antagonized him somewhere along the line."

"Um, yeah. He wasn't happy when I wiped out the Knights and took away his chance for revenge."

There was also the small matter of how I'd abducted him, chilled him to hypothermia, and threatened to torture him. That might have made him a little cranky, too...

I banished that thought and continued. "So the omission from my report didn't jeopardize our security, it just protected him from potential charges. And it should have ended there."

"But it didn't."

"No. When I discovered Terry Sherman was still alive, Doytchevsky saw his last chance for revenge on the Knights. He's been following me around because he believes I'm hunting Sherman, and he wants to get there first."

I sighed and slouched down in my chair. "He's convinced I'm in contact with Sherman. That's why he's been trying to threaten and coerce me to give up Sherman's location. He showed me those pictures last night trying to blackmail me into cooperating with him. I didn't think he'd take a chance on having his secret revealed, so I bluffed and told him I didn't care if he sent you the pictures. Obviously I underestimated his obsession." I rolled my aching shoulders. "And Kane is paying for my mistake."

Stemp leaned back in his chair, his expressionless gaze focused in middle distance while his fingers drummed a slow rhythm on the desk. At last, he spoke slowly.

"You're right, this changes nothing in terms of the current state of our national security, so I'll let your omission slide." He shot me a flat stare. "This time." His gaze slid into the distance again. "Maybe we can use Doytchevsky's obsession to our advantage and test his loyalty at the same time. Since we're perennially under-staffed in the first place, and now that Kane is suspended into the bargain..."

Guilt churned in my stomach. If only I'd done something differently. But what, for chrissake? I'd been telling Doytchevsky the truth all along.

"...we'll see whether Doytchevsky's skills are still sharp. You and he will work together to capture Sherman."

My attention snapped back with a jolt. "What?"

"Yes." Stemp gave a single brisk nod, obviously satisfied with his solution. "You can feed him information and let him do the legwork while you relay progress reports to us. That will free up resources for our other operations and also ensure, shall we say, *enthusiastic* progress in the search for Sherman. When you've narrowed down a location, notify me and we'll move in to capture Sherman. If Doytchevsky proves himself to be acting in the best interests of our country in the process, he'll never need to know we had this conversation. If he proves less than loyal..." He trailed off and lifted one shoulder a fraction of an inch in what served as an eloquent shrug for him.

"But, um..."

Please no. I raised the first objection that came to mind. Well, the first valid objection. 'He's a sleazeball and I want to throttle him' probably didn't count.

"He doesn't trust me as far as he can throw me. And when he realizes I've dropped the harassment charge, he'll know I was lying-"

"Which is why you won't drop it," Stemp said smoothly.

"I sure as hell *will* drop it!" Outrage made me louder than I'd intended.

Stemp subdued me with his snake-eyed stare. "Whether

or not the accusation is dropped at this point will make no difference to either the scheduling or the outcome of the hearing. You'll be able to explain yourself then. In the meantime, letting it stand gives us a tactical advantage."

"But Kane deserves to know..."

"If Kane has been falsely accused, he already knows. If, however, there is something else I should know about your interactions with him, now would be a very good time to tell me, Kelly."

I bit my tongue. Hard. "I didn't mean that, I just meant..." I eyed his stiff face and took another tack. "We're not really going to 'narrow down' a location. If I can track Sherman through the internet, we'll have an IP address that will tell us exactly where he is."

"Yes, but we can't move fast enough to capture him using that method. I did send personnel to the address you gave us earlier, but they didn't arrive for several hours, and of course there was no sign of Sherman by then."

"But I need to be here in order to get into the network to get the IPs."

"And you'll feed that information to Doytchevsky in the field. Pretend to be cooperating with him. You'll place a tracking device on Doytchevsky so we can keep tabs on him, and I'll monitor the operation from here."

Place a tracking device on him. Yeah, right. Like I'd intentionally touch that slimebucket, except maybe to punch his lights out...

Oblivious to my internal kvetching, Stemp continued. "At a guess, I assume Sherman is making his way back here to rendezvous with Kraus, but we won't know for sure until we get several different contact points so we can plot his progress. If I'm right, then the longer we wait, the easier it will be to capture him."

He reached for the telephone. "I'll get Webb to come over right now so you can try to make contact again."

"Um, actually, I have to go."

His reptilian gaze pinned me in place. "Go? Where?"

"You said I had time off until Tuesday night. I'm taking it. I've already spent..." I glanced at my watch. "...three hours that I didn't have, and I'll lose another two getting back to Calgary."

"What's in Calgary?"

None of your damn business.

"Personal," I said instead, and returned his stare as emotionlessly as I could manage.

We eyed each other in silence for a few moments. "Very well," he said at last. "Since time is actually on our side for this operation, I'll agree to that. It will also allow you time to plant the tracking device. Stop at Stores on your way out. I'll requisition more disposable phones and the tracking device. Check in minimum daily. If you don't..."

I shrugged and completed the sentence. "...you'll come and find me. And I won't be glad to see you."

"Something like that."

After a short wait at Stores, I collected my gear and hurried out into the lengthening shadows toward my truck, shivering in the cutting breeze. Dammit, five o'clock already.

I hopped into the truck and fired it up, letting the engine idle while I punched Nichele's number on my cell phone.

She answered on the first ring. "Aydan, where are you? What's taking so long?"

"Sorry, I had this big emergency, and I just got done-"

"You're still in Silverside? Aydan, we have to get started!"

"I know, I'm sorry, I'm on my way. Did you-"

"I made all the calls and I have a list of all the numbers. I'm packed and ready to go. The police haven't got anything yet," she reeled off in her 'business' voice.

If I hadn't been so worried, I'd have taken a moment to enjoy my usual amusement at the hyper-efficient dynamo concealed by her fluffy off-duty persona. But under the circumstances, I didn't feel much like laughing.

"Good, Nichele, then get some rest. I'm leaving now, and I'll be there as soon as I can."

"Wait, one more thing." She hesitated. "I called Hellhound. Arnie, I mean. I thought since he's a private investigator, he might be able to help. He said he would, but... Aydan, I'm sorry, I thought you guys were still friends. I didn't know..."

"We are still friends. What are you talking about?"

"Um, don't be too sure about that. He said he'd work with me, but he doesn't want to have anything to do with you."

My heart plummeted to my toes before a wave of rage washed over me. God *damn* Doytchevsky. He had hurt me in ways he couldn't have even imagined.

Nichele's plaintive voice brought me back to reality. "Aydan, I don't know what to do."

Somehow I held my voice steady. "Don't worry, Nichele, it's just a misunderstanding. I'll call him and figure it out. Just get some rest. I'll see you soon."

I hung up before she could question me and stared at the flashing message indicator on my phone. I hadn't taken time to check my messages before, but now I had a pretty good idea what they contained.

Hands shaking, I punched the button to view my single text message.

It was from Stemp. 'Call home', sent at three A.M. the previous night. He must have texted me right after the fax came in. God, did the man ever sleep?

Never mind, it was irrelevant now. And anyway, I was only stalling, avoiding the three voicemail messages from Arnie's number.

I took a deep breath, closed my eyes, and pressed the button.

His first early-morning message sounded puzzled and hurt. "Aydan, I just talked to John. What the fuck? Call me."

Next message, a few hours later. "Aydan, what the fuckin' hell? Call me!"

The last one was from a couple of hours ago. This time his voice ground through the speaker like icy gravel. "I been tryin' to cut ya some slack for stabbin' my best friend in the back an' flushin' his whole goddam career down the fuckin' shitter. But if ya don't even have the guts to call me, then fuck ya." It sounded as though he'd hung up with a sledgehammer.

I stared through the windshield, trembling. Tears rose in my eyes while the soulless voicemail prompt yammered in my ear. 'To erase this message, press seven. To save it, press nine...'

I gulped and punched seven before flinging the phone onto the seat beside me. Resisting the urge to curl into a ball and cry my heart out, I smeared a hand across my eyes and let anger straighten my spine.

You won't destroy me that easily, Doytchevsky. You

vicious little shit.

I seized my phone again and punched Arnie's number.

No answer.

Dammit, it was his cell phone. He always carried it. I hit redial.

Again.

After the third try, I realized he wouldn't pick up. A razor-sharp wire of pain tightened around my heart.

It couldn't be too late. I couldn't lose him like this.

I pressed the button one last time and waited for his usual gruff voice prompt. "Helmand. Leave a message."

That impersonal tone gut-punched me. What if his laughter and teasing and friendship were gone from my life forever?

Please don't let it be too late...

"Arnie..." My voice broke and I had to stop and try again. "Arnie, I..." Unwelcome logic reminded me that cell phone calls weren't secure. "I can't talk about it on the phone. I'll be there in a couple of hours. If... if you're going to be home. If..." I swallowed the stupid tears again. "If you're still willing to listen..."

Oh, shut the fuck up and stop being so damn pathetic. I punched disconnect, scrubbed my hands over my face, and slammed the truck into gear.

I'd make him listen. Once I explained everything, it would be all right.

He had to listen.

He just had to.

CHAPTER 18

Standing in the lobby of Arnie's condo building, I pressed the call button for his unit with a shaking finger.

His familiar rasp rattled the tinny speaker. "What."

"It's..." My voice was a dry whisper. I swallowed. "It's Aydan."

My only response was the click when he hung up.

The pain was so intense I stood frozen, my arms wrapped around my body. As if hugging myself could make it better.

Stupid.

I should have known. I shouldn't have let myself count on him.

They always hurt you.

Always.

I managed to move at last. Just as I was turning away, the door lock buzzed its release tone. I reflexively snatched the door open and slipped inside to stand trembling in the main lobby.

Had he changed his mind? Or had another resident released the latch? If I knocked on his door, would he slam it in my face?

I shook myself. Nothing to lose. If he threw me out, so

be it. If he was mad enough to hit me...

But he wouldn't. Arnie would never do that, no matter how angry he was. I gulped at the memory of his scarred knuckles and prize-fighter's face. If he did lose his temper...

He wouldn't. I knew he wouldn't. And anyway, it didn't matter.

I turned my feet toward the stairs. Even if he beat me to a bloody pulp, it wouldn't hurt as much as losing him because I was too cowardly to try.

Outside his door, my hand didn't seem to want to knock. I focused my will on it, but it hovered stubbornly a few inches from the panelling.

Just knock on the damn door, for shit's sake.

My eyes welled up again. I was swiping at them in an attempt to preserve what little dignity I had left when the door flew open.

I let out an involuntary squeak and threw up my arms to protect my face as Hellhound charged. The impact slammed a cry of pain out of me, his powerful arms grinding my bruised ribs while we staggered off-balance.

In an instant, the pressure released and he steadied me. "Jesus Christ, Aydan, what the fuck? Are ya okay?"

I opened my eyes to see his concerned face peering down at me. "I thought ya left. I was runnin' to catch ya. Are ya okay?" he repeated.

His gentle hands on my shoulders nearly undid me completely.

"I..." The word choked out on a half-sob.

Get it together.

I pulled away, swallowing hard. A couple of slow deep breaths, grappling for control.

"Aydan?" His fingertips touched my cheek as tenderly as

his soft rasp caressed my ears. "Aw, darlin', what happened?"

I resisted the urge to throw myself into his arms and never let go. I wiped my eyes, holding my voice as steady as I could. "Can we talk?"

"Yeah." His voice rose to a shout. "Ya goddam dumbass furball!"

I took no offense. Hiding my emotion behind a grin, I helped him corral the large, battle-scarred cat that had escaped his apartment to make a determined foray toward the stairs.

"Hey, Hooker," I murmured, cuddling my armload of long, tickly fur. "Who's my big guy?" I scratched behind his torn and tufted ears, and his booming purr filled the hallway.

I relinquished him to Hellhound, who roughly massaged the big cat's scruff and muttered 'dumb-ass furball' with unmistakable fondness. The furball in question slitted his eyes in bliss and pushed his scarred nose into Hellhound's beard, his purr rumbling while we stepped into the apartment.

As soon as the door closed behind us, Hellhound lowered the cat to the floor. When he straightened, I met his eyes. "Arnie, I didn't do it. I didn't file that complaint."

"What?" He scowled. "Kane saw it. He said it was your signature. Photos an' everythin'."

"It wasn't me. I'd never do that to him." I clutched his sleeve. "Arnie, please tell me you didn't really believe I'd do that!"

His arms folded me in. "I didn't wanna believe it, darlin', but it sure as hell looked bad."

"Thanks for giving me the benefit of the doubt even when there wasn't any doubt." I gave him a squeeze and pulled away before I could get too comfortable in his arms. "Can you call John and tell him? If he even talks to me he'll get court-martialled. And if Stemp finds out I've told anybody it's fake, it'll make things even worse."

Hellhound frowned and headed for his dilapidated chair, waving me in the direction of the sagging but still comfortable couch. "But he's gonna wanna know what the hell's goin' on. Who filed the complaint if it wasn't you? How'd they just happen to get pictures the one an' only time he ever made a move on ya in public?"

He reached down beside his chair, fingering the strings of the guitar propped beside it as if taking comfort from his beloved instrument.

"An' all this right after he asked ya if he should back off an' ya said it was okay. An' ya promised he wasn't gonna end up on sexual harassment charges. An' why the hell didn't ya just tell Stemp it was bullshit and drop the whole thing?"

He straightened, his brows drawing together. "Hell, never mind Kane, *I* fuckin' wanna know. Christ, Aydan, this's rippin' my fuckin' guts out."

"I'm sorry, Arnie! Stemp already knows it's bullshit, he just won't let me tell anybody. I told him Kane and I staged the kiss, and I think he believed me. The guy that faked the complaint was trying to blackmail me by saying he'd get John in trouble for making a move on me on the job, but..." My stomach wrung itself in a corrosive mixture of rage and remorse. "I guess he decided to go for the gold with a sexual harassment complaint instead. Prove he was serious."

Hellhound jerked forward. "Aydan, who's blackmailin' ya? An' why?"

I sighed. "It's complicated. I, um... had a kind of a... promotion at Sirius Dynamics and I was in Vegas on... um...

business."

He settled slowly back in his chair, his shrewd gaze searching my face. "Stemp finally brained up. Ya ain't an asset anymore, you're an agent. Ya had a mission, an' it went bad," he translated.

I shot him a half-serious glare. "Stop doing that. Go be a dumb biker."

He grinned. "Sure, darlin'." His smile drained away. "So what kinda shit are ya in? How deep?"

"Not as deep as it could be." I sighed. "My business in Vegas actually went okay. It was done by the time John got there. I knew I'd picked up a tail earlier, but I thought..."

I pounded my forehead with the heel of my hand. "No, I didn't fucking think *at all*, goddammit. Moron! It never even occurred to me the bastard would still be following me, and I should have known better. I tried to tell John to cool it, but he wouldn't listen..."

"So what's this asshole got on ya?" Hellhound eyed me levelly. "Ya got your hand in a cookie jar somewhere?"

"No! He's got nothing on me. He just wants information and he was trying to use those photos as leverage to make me tell him."

He relaxed. "An' ya didn't play ball."

"No. I tried to bluff, and I lost." I gulped. "John lost. There aren't any consequences for me." I buried my face in my hands. "I really fucking hate this stupid life."

The couch dipped and Hellhound's arm tightened around my shoulders. "It's okay, darlin', it ain't your fault."

I collapsed against him. "It *is* my fault. I should have thought. I should have warned John about the tail and I didn't, and now he's going to lose everything over one lousy kiss..."

"Well, shit, if he's that bad a kisser, maybe I should talk to him. Give him some pointers."

I straightened out of my slump to see his grin. I wedged an elbow into his ribs. "You know what I meant. And anyway, keep your secrets to yourself. If all the men in the world could kiss like you, women would be doomed."

"Aw, thanks, darlin'."

Our eyes met, and the memory of his kisses sent a wave of primal need coursing through me. God, how I missed his easy presence in my bed. His teasing mouth, his adept hands, his musician's unerring feel for rhythm and tempo. That slow smile with his eyes half-closed, just before his skillful touch toppled me into glorious free-fall. The wonderful safety of knowing he wanted nothing more from me than a few hours of mutual pleasure...

I realized I was tilting toward him, lips parting.

I jerked upright. "Sorry."

"It's okay." He rose, not meeting my eyes. "I'm gonna call Kane."

"Wait!"

"What?"

"I have to go. I can't be here when you call."

Hellhound shrugged, his gesture encompassing the small apartment. "Who's gonna know?"

"Anybody who's tracking my cell phone."

He stiffened, his gaze darting to the beaten-up behemoth of a coffee table. "Do I need my gun?"

"No, it's okay." At his dubious expression, I clarified. "I just meant it would be bad if anybody could prove I was here while you were talking to John. I'm going to leave. Give me twenty minutes before you call him. I have to call Nichele anyway, so I'll do that from somewhere far away from here, at the same time you're talking to John. Just in case."

"Okay..." He moved closer to take my hand. "Aydan, we promised each other no lies. Are ya really tellin' me the truth?"

I clasped my other hand over his. "No lies. I promise. Everything I told you is the truth."

"An' what didn't ya tell me?"

I squeezed his hand, willing him to understand. "I told you as much as I can without putting you in danger."

"An' how much danger are ya in yourself?"

"None that I know of."

He disengaged my grip to slide his hands up my arms. "Then why're ya shakin'?"

"I..." I gulped down rising tears along with the urge to blurt out an admission of the nightmares and flashbacks. To beg him to sleep with me just so I could take comfort from his closeness.

I held my voice level. "I'm just bagged and I need to eat."

"Shit, Aydan, it's damn near eight o'clock an' ya didn't eat yet?" He eyed me with concern. "I got some leftover Chinese food in the fridge..."

"No, it's okay. I really need to go so you can call John."

"Come right back. I'll call ya as soon as I'm done."

I considered, my thoughts stumbling over each other in calorie-deprived exhaustion. "Okay. That'll work. My last cell phone call was to you, so it'll look like you're returning my call. See you later. Remember, wait twenty minutes before you call him."

I turned to go.

"Hey."

When I turned, he folded me into a gentle hug, his muscular bulk making me feel small and protected. "Drive safe, darlin'. Make sure ya get somethin' to eat." His lips brushed my forehead.

"Thanks," I choked, and stumbled out before I could cling to him.

When I emerged from the building, snow was beginning to sift down and the breeze had turned into a biting north wind. I bolted for the truck and hunched shivering in the driver's seat, cursing until the first puffs of welcome heat wafted into the cab.

East of downtown, I pulled into the first fast-food restaurant I found and wolfed down a burger and fries whose flavour was virtually indistinguishable from the packaging. Spitting out a fragment of paper, I reminded myself to slow down and pay attention to what I was eating, and then promptly ignored my own advice while my mind shuttled from one problem to the next.

What if Stemp found out I'd told Hellhound the sexual harassment charge was fake?

Worse, what if Doytchevsky found out? What if he was following me even now?

I stopped my feeding frenzy long enough to shoot a worried glance out the window. I had taken a seat with my back to the wall, near an exit as usual, but I was far too visible in the brightly-lit restaurant.

I shrugged and let it go. Whatever. So he follows me and sees me visiting Hellhound. I was pretty sure everybody thought we were sleeping together anyway, so no problem.

But Kane. My stomach clenched around the greasy food. What a horrible betrayal. How could he forgive me for the damage to his career, his life?

He couldn't. I wouldn't expect him to. It was more than anyone could expect.

But there had to be a way to fix it. Somehow, I had to find a way.

And what about Dave? God, please let him be all right.

The snow was beginning to accumulate, brightening the slick, dark pavement. What if he had driven off a mountain road, was even now lying injured and alone in the icy wreckage?

Dammit, no, that wouldn't happen. He drove an eighteen-wheeler, for chrissake. It wasn't like people would fail to notice a wrecked semi. And the police would have known about something like that right away. He was probably fine...

I gulped the last of my drink and pulled out my phone. Nichele would be frantic.

When she answered, her voice sounded strained and exhausted. "Hi, Aydan."

"Hi, Nichele, I'm back in Calgary and I'm just on my way over to Arnie's place. Did you get some rest?"

"I couldn't. But don't worry, Aydan, I don't expect you to go out when the weather's like this. Go over and see if you can patch things up with Arnie, and we'll talk in the morning."

I held the phone away from my ear to frown at it. That was a hell of an about-face.

"Are you sure, Nichele? Are you okay?"

"Yeah... But it's dark and the roads are really bad..." Her voice wavered as if on the verge of tears. "...and I don't want you to take a chance driving tonight. I'll call you in the morning. Maybe by then I'll have good news."

"Okay, if you're sure..." Relief battled guilt. "I'll come

over to your place as soon as I'm done talking to Arnie."

"Oh…" When she spoke again a few moments later, it was in her usual bantering tone. "Girl, if you show up on my doorstep tonight, I won't even let you in. You get your ass over to Hellhound's and into his bed, or else!"

I laughed. "Thanks for the pep talk. Try to get some sleep, okay?"

"Try to get some hot sex, okay? Bye-bye!"

I hit disconnect and stared at the phone. What the hell was she up to?

The phone's vibration made me start, and I hurriedly punched the answer button.

Hellhound's welcome rasp soothed my ear. "Hey, darlin', come on over."

I bit my tongue to keep from asking about Kane. Damn cell phones. "I'll be there in about fifteen minutes," I said instead.

"Hang on, did ya get somethin' to eat?"

"Yes." I eyed the grease-smeared paper wrappings with distaste. "'Something' is about the only way to describe it. I'm on my way."

CHAPTER 19

By the time I parked in the visitor's slot at Hellhound's condo, I was thankful all over again for Nichele's unusual attack of good sense. The roads weren't exactly bad, but they were definitely getting slippery. Even with the two hundred pounds of sandbags I always left in the truck box for winter traction, the rear end was developing an uncomfortable tendency to slide when I braked.

Shivering inside the front doors, I pressed Hellhound's call button with a gush of relief. Thank God he had believed me. Thank God I didn't have to dread his reply this time.

When the lock released, I hurried up the stairs. By the time I gained the third floor, he was waiting in his doorway with Hooker tucked under one arm. The big cat squirmed and fixed me with an expectant yellow gaze, apparently hoping I'd provide sufficient distraction for another escape attempt.

"Nice try, buddy," I said, and gave him a chin-scratch as Hellhound stepped aside to let me in.

"Where's mine?" Hellhound asked plaintively, raising his chin.

"Right, I can't neglect the big pussycat." I slid my fingers into his beard and rubbed his chin while he rumbled raspy satisfaction. "You're two of a kind."

"Yeah, we both look like we been chasin' parked cars," he quipped as he locked the door behind me. He released Hooker and made for the kitchen. "Ya want a beer?"

"Oh, hell yeah." I slid off my boots and dropped my coat on top of the half-wall that served as his impromptu coat closet. Padding over to his couch, I sank into my favourite corner and pulled one of his hand-crocheted afghans around me.

"Ya want a coffee or somethin' instead?" Hellhound appeared around the corner and gestured with the frosty bottles. "This ain't exactly gonna warm ya up."

"I don't care." I reached for a bottle. "You have no idea how much I need this right now... shit."

"What?"

"I better not. The roads are getting bad, and-"

Hellhound grabbed my hand and wrapped it around the bottle. "An' ya ain't goin' anywhere tonight. If ya really gotta go somewhere, I'll drive ya, or ya can get a taxi. Drink up."

"Thank you." I poured a long swallow down my throat. "Oh, thank you, God."

"You're welcome."

"Wise guy."

He flopped into his broken-down chair, stretching his legs out and taking a long swallow of his own beer. "Jesus, darlin', this day's finally gettin' better." He grimaced. "'Course most of it sucked shit, so it wasn't like it was gonna get much worse."

"Be careful saying things like that."

He grunted agreement and swigged from his bottle again.

"What did John say?" I clenched my icy bottle, bracing

myself.

"He said don't worry, it wasn't your fault. Ya warned him an' he shoulda known better."

"What else did he say?" I cuddled deeper into the blanket and savoured another crisp, cold mouthful, secure in the knowledge that Hellhound's photographic memory would disgorge a complete and accurate account of the conversation.

"He wanted to know if ya were okay, an' if ya were in any danger. He wants to know who's framin' him, an' why this person would think harmin' him would be leverage against ya. 'Cause nobody should think he's anythin' to ya but a co-worker." He shot me a piercing look.

"He's right, nobody else would think that." I considered for a moment and decided it was probably best not to mention it was Doytchevsky. If Kane went after Doytchevsky while under suspension, he could end up in even more trouble than he was already.

I sighed. "I can't tell him who it is, but the guy who took the pictures thought since we were kissing, I must care about John." I pressed the cold bottle against my forehead. "Oh, shit. The sexual harassment thing *is* my fault. I must have given him the idea."

"What? How?"

I clutched a handful of hair and tugged. "I was trying to convince him I didn't care, and I said something stupid like 'I don't care if that asshole gets in trouble, he was kissing me, I wasn't kissing him'. Something like that. I can't remember exactly, but I'm sure it put the idea in his head."

"Hm." Hellhound's fingers found the guitar strings again, brushing them lightly. "Don't see how ya coulda done anythin' different, though, darlin'." He tipped another measure of beer down his throat. "Anyway, no point in rippin' yourself up over it. It's done. But here's somethin' that's worryin' me." He frowned. "If the photos were his leverage, he just gave 'em up. Why would he do that?"

"I don't know. Just to prove he was serious, I guess."

"But that doesn't make sense, darlin'. If he's already hurt ya, what's he got left? If ya didn't give him what he wanted when he was holdin' a threat, why the hell would ya give him anythin' now?" His fingers closed on the neck of the guitar. "Unless he's got somethin' else in his back pocket that's gonna hurt ya even worse. An' he wants ya to know he ain't afraid to use it."

I shivered with a chill that had nothing to do with cold beer. "He's got nothing on me. He doesn't even know me..." My throat squeezed shut on the words.

He had been friends with my husband for years. He knew more about me than anyone except maybe Nichele.

He was a spy with decades of experience. He was probably as dangerous as Kane. Hell, more dangerous. He was a nutcase into the bargain. And I'd been lulled into believing his geeky, harmless façade.

"Oh, fuck, I'm too dumb to live!" I beat my forehead against my draw-up knees. "I'm such a fucking moron! Goddammit!"

"Jesus, darlin', what?" Arnie eyed me worriedly. "What's wrong?"

"I have to go. Right now." I sprang up and pushed my unfinished beer into his hand.

"Whoa, hold on!"

By the time he put down the beer bottles, I already had one arm in my coat and one foot jammed half-way into one of my boots. Hopping and flapping, I caromed off the half-wall by the door. "OW! Fuck-goddamn-sonuvabitch-motherf-"

"Stop! Aydan, stop." Arnie's powerful arms closed around me and I tried to pull free, one arm still trapped by the coat. His grip tightened painfully on my bruises.

"Ow!"

His arms flew open, his eyes widening. Completely off balance, I staggered and tripped over my own half-shod foot.

In the slow instant of clarity that precedes impact, my brain offered up the helpful observation that this was really going to hurt.

Fuck, did it hurt.

Sprawled on Hellhound's door mat, I tried to swear, but my breath caught inside a cage of pain. I managed a faint mewling sound, which was neither comfortable nor satisfying.

"Aydan, Jesus, darlin'..." Arnie dove to his knees beside me. "Don't try to move. Just lie still. Did ya hit your head?"

"No." This time I managed a whisper. "I'm fine."

"Can ya move your legs?"

I demonstrated my competence by rolling over with a groan to toss aside the boot that had been crushed into my aching side. "Ow. Fuck. I'm fine. And I'm still an idiot." Wincing, I hauled myself upright despite his protests. "And I still have to go."

"Ya ain't goin' anywhere."

He had gotten between me and the door.

Shit.

Muscular legs planted like tree trunks, bulging tattooed arms crossed over his bulky chest, he stared down at me with all the sweet compliance of a bull facing a matador. "Now you're gonna tell me what the fuck's wrong, an' then *if* I agree that ya gotta go, we'll figure somethin' out."

"Arnie, please, just let me go. I don't have time for this."

"Well, shit, darlin', that's too bad. 'Cause I got all night." He glowered at me. "So ya better start talkin'."

I didn't dare take time to argue. "He's probably following me. He's probably listening in on my cell phone calls. That means either you or Nichele will be his next leverage. If I leave right now, there's still a chance that you might stay safe."

I yanked on my coat, wincing and swearing at the fresh pain, and stuffed my feet into my boots. "Arnie, please, I have to go."

"Who beat ya up?"

"Nobody. I fell."

"Bullshit."

"It's the truth!"

I eyed him desperately. I'd never be able to get past him. And at the moment I really didn't feel athletic enough to escape from a third-floor balcony.

"Please, Arnie! I really did fall."

"Ya promised not to lie to me."

"I swear I'm not lying."

He sighed. "Okay, Aydan, here's the thing. Ya gotta know I ain't gonna let ya run outta here just 'cause you're tryin' to protect me. I been workin' with Stemp's covert ops guys for longer than ya even know. Twenty-one years in the army. Combat." He waved a hand in the direction of his damaged face. "Ya know the rest a' my shit. I ain't some delicate little flower."

"I know, Arnie, but this guy's nuts. He's obsessed. I think he'll do anything it takes, hurt anybody it takes, to get what he wants. I don't want him anywhere near anybody I care about and... you aren't listening, are you?"

"Nope. All I heard was 'Okay, Arnie, you're right. I'm gonna take off my coat an' drink my beer an' stop doin' fuckin' stupid shit like runnin' off to fight some fuckin' nut job all by myself'. I'm pretty sure that's what ya said, wasn't it?"

The last of my energy deserted me and I sank to the floor to bury my face in my hands. "I can't do this. I just can't do this anymore."

He knelt beside me, smoothing my hair. "Then maybe it's time ya stopped tryin'. Come on, darlin'. Take off your coat an' drink your beer."

A few beers later, I squinted at Hellhound and giggled. "Shit, I guess I'm tore... more... tired... than I thought. I'm fuggen wasted."

He chuckled. "Good. That's what I wanna hear. Come on, darlin', let's get ya to bed."

"'S'okay, I'm fine here." I snuggled a little lower on the couch.

"Nah, I still gotta get some work done tonight." He jerked his chin toward the tiny bedroom that held his computer. "The light'll be right in your face. An' if you're hurtin' from that fall, ya shouldn't be crunched up on the couch. Come on. Up ya get." I accepted his outstretched hand and let him pull me to my feet.

"I'm okay," I protested. "I can walk just fine. I'm just at that silly-drunk stage... oops..."

He steered me around the coffee table, which had inexplicably planted itself in my path.

"...and anyway, I need to pee," I finished.

"Here ya go." The bathroom appeared in front of me. "Don't lock the door."

I peered at the mirror and recoiled from the slack-jawed, droopy-eyed apparition that confronted me. "Right."

I successfully navigated the bathroom and managed a more-or-less straight line in the direction of the bedroom, stripping off my T-shirt as I went. Arnie turned from closing the blinds as I slumped against the door to fumble at my jeans.

"Jesus fuckin' Christ, Aydan!"

Suddenly he was beside me, and I squinted up at his shocked expression. "Wha...?"

"What the hell did ya fall off of, a fuckin' skyscraper?"

"Oh." I peered down at my blackened torso and giggled. "No. A pallet of C4. I mean, before I blew it up. Well, I blew up two of them, but I only fell off one of them."

With an effort, I focused on his face. He was frowning.

"I fell off my dirt bike, too," I added helpfully. "Twice. Well, the first time the esk... 'skplosion blew me off it. But at least I didn't fall out the window. The guard fell out... well, I kind of pushed him out..." I giggled at the memory. "He bent over and I put my foot on his ass and..." I mimed a shove with my foot.

Arnie seized my shoulders and righted me when the room slid sideways. I giggled again. "...but *I* didn't fall out. I climbed out. And he didn't get hurt. I saved him." My throat constricted suddenly at the memory. "But I couldn't save the dog."

Tears prickled behind my eyes. "Oh, Arnie, I blew up a *dog*. It was such a nice dog, too. Hardly bit me... at all..."

I fought a ragged breath that wanted to turn into a sob. "...and I... can't sleep... and... I... keep seeing..." To my horror, a couple of tears spilled over, trickling down my cheeks. "Shit... sorry..." I scrubbed at my face, grappling for control.

"Aw, darlin'..."

His arms closed around me, warm and strong and safe, and I jerked away to flee for the bathroom before I lost it completely.

Cranking on the cold tap full blast, I hunched over the sink, cupping my palms to splash icy water on my face over and over, diluting the hot tears. At last I got myself together and stuck my mouth under the tap for a few swallows. Turning the water off, I appropriated Arnie's towel before slithering down the wall to sit on the floor, still clutching the towel.

God, what a pathetic loser. Get shit-faced and drip tears all over the guy who'd probably end up paying for my incompetence with his life. If I thought Hellhound actually owned a razor, I'd go looking for it to slit my wrists.

A tap on the door made me groan.

"Aydan?"

"Yeah."

"I'm gonna come in now, okay?"

I buried my face in the towel. Why the hell not? It wasn't like I had any dignity left anyway.

"Okay."

The door bumped my foot, and I shuffled over to allow enough room for Arnie to slip inside. He manoeuvred his bulk nimbly into the small space and sat on the floor beside me, and I let my head fall against his shoulder. We sat in silence.

"Aydan?" he said at last.

I roused myself from my stupor. "Yeah."

"My ass's killin' me on this damn hard floor, an' I gotta take a leak. Can ya get outta the bathroom now?"

Somehow it was the perfect thing to say.

I laughed and threw my arms around him. "I love you!" The words slipped out unguarded and I froze.

Great, just great. Top off the night by saying the only words guaranteed to make him run screaming.

He grinned. "Well, hell, darlin', what's not to love?"

I let out my breath in a whoosh. "Thanks for not taking that wrong."

He shrugged. "I trust ya."

Warmth bloomed in my chest, stealing my breath at the magnitude of the compliment. "Thanks," I mumbled.

We levered ourselves up from the floor accompanied by a duet of groans and obscenities. Hellhound straightened slowly. "Fuck, darlin', I'm too old for this shit."

I rubbed my aching ass. "Tell me about it."

I closed the door behind me and limped for the bedroom.

CHAPTER 20

I swam gradually to wakefulness, so comfortable and relaxed I thought I might ooze through the mattress. Soft snoring from behind me identified the warm weight draped over my hip as Hellhound's arm, and I squeezed my eyes shut again and snuggled a little closer.

The snoring stopped.

I held still, keeping my breathing slow and deep. Maybe he'd go back to sleep and I could lie here forever...

His hand eased off as if trying not to wake me. Damn.

A moment later, my breath caught when he caressed my hair aside, his lips pressing smooth heat and whiskery roughness against my nape. The tingling kisses trailed slowly down my spine as if counting the vertebrae, and I moaned and shivered, my body opening into the slow ache of need.

Forget faking sleep. I rolled over and pulled him to me.

He took my mouth in one of his mind-melting kisses, his tongue promising all the many ways he could make me very, very happy. Starving for his touch, I pulled his hand to my breast, arching against him.

He drew back, his hand still hovering hot over my breast, his palm barely brushing it in an exquisite feather of sensation.

"Oh, God, Arnie, please don't stop!" I tried to pull him into another kiss, but he propped himself on his elbow to look down at me.

"Darlin', what kind of a friend would I be if I got ya drunk..."

His palm moved in a small circle, making me gasp.

"...an' took advantage of ya the very next mornin'..." He eased lower in the bed. I watched, transfixed, while his mouth moved closer to my breast.

"...while you're still feelin' weak..."

Closer.

Please.

Oh, please.

"...when I know ya been tryin' to stay outta my bed..."

His breath was hot on me, his lips a mere fraction away. Another tiny movement of his palm made me whimper as every nerve fibre strained toward his touch.

"God, Arnie, you know I never wanted to stay out of your bed." My voice came out jerky and breathless.

Touch me, please, please...

"Sure seemed like it to me." His moustache grazed my nipple when he spoke, an electric jolt of sensation.

"*Ahh!* I thought..." Another gasp disrupted my words when he exhaled slowly, the warm current curling around sensitive tissue. "Oh *God*... You dumped me... I was trying to do what you wanted..."

"I busted my ass to get ya together with Kane." He gave me that sleepy-eyed grin I knew so well. "Ya told me it wouldn't work. He told me it wouldn't work. Well, hell. I ain't a fuckin' saint."

His lips closed on my breast, the hot suction exploding

through my nerve endings. My body bucked under his mouth, a cry bursting out of me.

"Hmmm." He pulled away just far enough to apply another moment of magnificent whisker torture when he spoke. "Guess ya missed me."

I clutched at him, panting. "You have no... *idea*..." The last word turned into a moan when his lips and tongue went into action again, his dexterous fingers playing my other breast at the same time.

The delicious shocks of pleasure reflected each other, amplifying into a pulsing current. My hips jerked to the rhythm, begging for his hand as it drifted off my breast to search lower.

Teasing fingertips circled close, then closer still, light touches that made my body strain toward him in desperate anticipation while his mouth drove me wild.

When his hand slid between my legs, I couldn't prevent my cry, my hips driving up to meet him.

He raised his head from my breast to smile, watching me while his unerring fingers found the perfect position and rhythm. "Missed hearin' ya moanin' like that," he rasped. He dropped his mouth back to my breast, stroking heat into me all the while.

The sweet pressure built, my body moving to his delicious rhythm while his tongue and fingers coaxed me to the edge.

My breath stopped, the first tremors of orgasm holding me suspended for an exquisite instant before the flood of sensation swept me up and tumbled me into the glorious chaos of ecstasy.

Gasping, I rode the waves until they began to diminish at last. I dragged my eyes open to see Hellhound's smile, his hand still moving lazily, rocking me on the last ripples of pleasure.

"Oh... God... Arnie..." I reached for him. "I need you..."

"Darlin', you're too beat up. I don't wanna hurt ya." He stretched out beside me, trailing kisses across my shoulder. "I can wait."

"I can't." I lurched to my trembling knees to reach for the bedside table. He rolled onto his back, his smile widening while I fumbled with the slippery condom wrapper, swearing with desperate lust.

"Here, darlin', let me."

I feverishly blessed his adept hands while he quickly dealt with the wrapper and its contents. Before he could change position, I swung astride.

"Ah, *darlin'!*" His rasp mingled with my groan of satisfaction as I slid onto him.

"Slow... Give it to me slow, darlin'... wanna take my time..."

His hands cupped my ass and I moved mindlessly under his guidance while the hot tension coiled up inside me. Through half-closed eyes, I saw him watching me with his heavy-eyed smile. I bore down and rocked back, catching my breath at the feel of him deep inside me.

His hands slid up to gently roll my nipples between his fingertips. Still tingling from his mouth, the intensity of the sensation made me cry out, clenching around him.

He gasped, his hips driving up.

"Oh *God* Arnie..."

The hunger seized me and I rode him hard, his hands clutching my breasts, the friction of his palms driving me higher. My orgasm struck like a hurricane, arching me backward in gusts of pleasure that redoubled when he gripped my hips and thrust up into me again and again until a groan wrenched out of him, his body spasming under me.

I collapsed forward to sprawl atop him, savouring the luscious aftershocks while our panting gradually slowed.

"Ah, darlin', I missed havin' ya in my bed," he growled at last, his hands stroking lightly down my back. "If I ever try that noble-sacrifice bullshit again, tell me what a dumbfuck I am."

I propped myself above him on my elbows, my hair falling around us like a private tent. "You aren't dumb." I brushed a kiss across his lips. "It was a sweet gesture, and you were trying to be a good friend to both Kane and me, and if you ever try it again I'll beat you severely."

He chuckled. "Mmmm. Kinky."

I toppled off to stretch out beside him and he cuddled me close, caressing my hair away from my face and planting a gentle whiskery kiss on my forehead.

"Now, darlin', tell me about these bad dreams."

I wrapped an arm around him and snuggled against his chest. "I didn't have any. Thanks to you."

"Yeah, ya did." He stroked a hand over my hair. "About every half hour for the first little while, an' then they started to taper off. I just kept wakin' ya up as soon as ya started to cry an' struggle."

"Oh." I concentrated on tracing the lines of his tattoos with my fingertip. "Thanks. I don't even remember. I must not have woken up all the way. I'm sorry I kept you awake."

"It's okay, darlin'." I could hear the grin in his voice. "Ya paid your debts this mornin'."

I laid a trail of kisses down his solid belly. "You're too easy to please. You should hold out for better payment."

"Hmmm." His voice dropped to a rumble. "Didn't say I

wouldn't take payment in advance. But seriously, darlin'..."
His hand found my chin and tilted it up so he could study my
face. "It ain't like ya to have a meltdown like last night. If
you're havin' problems, ya need to get some help."

I sighed and burrowed closer, avoiding his gaze. "I
know. I think it was just because I had too much shit
happening in the last few days and I hadn't had enough
sleep. I always have to go through some bad dreams, it's just
part of the process. You said yourself they were starting to
taper off by morning."

"Yeah..." He didn't sound convinced, but he let it drop.
"So your two pallets a' C4 wouldn'ta had anythin' to do with
that massive barn explosion east a' Silverside a few days ago,
would they? Gas leak, my ass."

I giggled. "Your ass couldn't manage a gas leak that big."

"Ya ain't been around when I been drinkin' beer an'
eatin' bean burritos."

"That wasn't intended as a challenge!"

We both snickered for a few moments before he sobered.
"Three dead, three injured, they said on the news. Ya said ya
blew up a dog. Ya didn't say anythin' about people."

My heart twisted again at the thought of the dog. "Yeah.
The people were trying to blow up Sirius Dynamics and my
farm and Kane and Spider and half of Silverside. They
deserved it. The poor damn dog didn't."

Arnie's hand drifted lightly down my side, barely
touching the blackened skin. "An' ya were so close ya got
blown off your bike? That's too damn close, Aydan."

"I don't know if it actually blew me off the bike. I might
have just hit a big lump of dirt at the same time it went off. I
was going pretty fast, and it was dark." I traced a few more
tattoos.

He sighed. "I'd give ya shit, but I know it wouldn't help. Think we should phone Nichele? It's nearly nine. I figured she'd be callin' by now."

"No, let's wait. Maybe she finally fell asleep, and if she did, I don't want to wake her. If I don't hear from her by ten, I'll call."

"Mmm." He shifted onto his side. "A whole hour to kill." His lips drifted down my neck in tiny whisker-kisses that made me shiver. "Wonder what we should do."

"Mmmm. I don't know..." I drifted a hand down his chest. "Any ideas?" I slid my hand a little lower.

"Oh, yeah. I always got ideas when you're around." He rumbled a raspy purr, moving to the rhythm of my stroking. "Gonna be a minute for that, though, darlin'. Seems to me ya only had two crummy little orgasms so far..."

"Two amazing, gigantic, mind-bending orgasms," I corrected, letting him ease me onto my back.

"Yeah, so you're still down about five."

I surrendered to the slow delight of his kiss. Long moments later, he pulled away a fraction. "...An' then there's all the orgasms I missed givin' ya the last coupla weeks," he mumbled against my chin, kissing his way down my throat to find the sensitive hollow of my collarbone.

A flick of his tongue made me gasp and clutch at him, and he chuckled, tracing kisses across my breasts before sliding lower in the bed. "Ya like my tongue this mornin', do ya?"

More kisses, sprinkled lower.

My breath caught. "I love your tongue. I would *marry* your tongue."

He chuckled. "Well, I ain't quite done with it yet."

He moved down again and the kisses marched lower,

blazing a line of heat directly to...

His lips diverted to my hip, making me whimper protest.

"What's the matter, darlin'?" He lifted my leg over his shoulder, running a strong hand down the outside of my thigh and trailing a line of slow whiskery nibbles and kisses up the inside.

My eyes drifted closed, my breath coming faster while the scorching kisses crept higher.

Higher...

A small moan escaped me, my body begging for the first touch of his tongue. His hot breath laved me from close range, torturing me with glorious anticipation...

My phone vibrated.

My eyes popped open. "Seriously, Nichele? *Now?*"

Hellhound chuckled. "Let it go. She'll understand."

"I shouldn't... *oh!*" My body spasmed with bliss when his fabulous tongue went into action. "No, wait, Arnie, I... *ahhh*... I should... *ahhh!*"

I abandoned Nichele to her fate.

CHAPTER 21

I dragged my eyes open, my body still thrumming with satisfaction. "I'd better call Nichele. She's going to kill me."

Hellhound chuckled and pulled me closer. "Nah, but she'd prob'ly have killed ya if ya picked up the phone instead a' comin' your brains out. Smart woman."

"Who, her or me?

"Both a' ya. I like 'em smart." He nibbled my neck. "An' sexy."

"Don't start again. You know I can't resist you."

I squirmed reluctantly out of his arms and stumbled over to snatch up my phone before diving back into bed. "Jeez, why do you keep it so cold in here?" I punched the voicemail button.

"'Cause it makes the chicks cuddle up closer," Hellhound teased as I burrowed back into the warm blankets.

The voice message made my jaw drop. "Shit, it's Dave!" I punched the speaker button so we could both listen.

"...so call me as soon as you get this, 'kay?"

Hellhound shot me a puzzled frown, but I was already dialling Dave's number.

His voice crackled out of my speaker on the first ring. "Is Nichele with you?"

Arnie and I exchanged a worried glance. "No, haven't you talked to her? Thank God you're all right! Where are you? What happened?"

"Inbound west of Golden now. Nothing happened. Had lunch in Revelstoke a couple of days ago and put my phone down when I paid the bill. Didn't miss it 'til Kamloops. I had a short turnaround planned in Vancouver, so I figured I'd just pick it up on my way back through. Didn't know the cops were looking for me 'til I heard some guys talking about it on the CB last night. Aydan, where is she?"

"I don't know." Cold fear sank into the pit of my stomach. "She was supposed to call me this morning so we could start looking for you. I haven't talked to her since last night about eight-thirty."

Oh, God. Leverage. What if Doytchevsky had her...

"She was on the road by then."

"What? Shit! Goddammit, that's how she knew the roads were bad..." I cut myself off. "Tell me everything you know."

"Don't know much. Called the cops soon as I heard they were looking for me, must've been around nine-thirty last night. They said they'd let her know I was okay. The Coquihalla was a bitch... sorry, was bad last night, but I pulled off as soon as I could and called Nichele. Didn't get an answer, so I left her a message, said I was fine but I didn't have my phone yet and I'd call her in the morning. Just picked up my phone about an hour ago and I've been trying ever since."

I sprang up to pace. "Did she leave you any messages?"

"Yeah, a bunch. Her first couple of messages just said 'call me', and then her next one said it was an emergency. What was the emergency?"

"Nothing, she was just worried about you and wanted to make sure you'd call as soon as you could."

"Shi... Crap! So then there were some more messages, and the last one was last night around nine. She said she'd made it to Lake Louise and to hang on, she was gonna find me. And now she's not answering her cell."

"Dammit, she always answers her cell!" I hugged myself, shivering, and Arnie got out of bed to press against my back, wrapping a blanket around both of us. "We'll start looking from this end," I began, but Dave interrupted.

"No. Don't need any more amateur drivers on the road. It ain't the worst I've ever driven, but it ain't good. Got a heavy load on so I can get through just about anything. I'll watch for that piece of sh... little Miata. I kept telling her to get a real car..." His voice choked off.

He cleared his throat. "Just call the cops, 'kay?" he said gruffly. "Cell phone's patchy out here. Better if you talk to them. Call me as soon as you hear anything."

"Okay, Dave. Drive carefully. Stay safe."

"'Kay."

I hung up and backed closer to Hellhound's warm bulk, shivering more from nerves than cold while I poised my finger over the keys. "What's the police non-emergency number?"

His arms tightened around me. "Hang on, darlin', why don't ya at least get dressed? You're shakin' like a leaf again."

"I need to get my suitcase from the truck."

"Gimme your keys an' I'll go get it for ya." He stepped away, draping the blanket over my shoulders and reaching for his jeans. He straightened, frowning, and despite my worry I took a moment to appreciate his muscular nakedness.

"Hang on," he said. "Why're ya drivin' that piece a' shit truck when ya got a brand new all-wheel-drive car?"

"It's not a piece of shit. And the car blew up," I said absently, heading for the living room to search out his phone book.

"*What?*" Still clutching his pants in one hand, he strode around to confront me, obviously unconcerned by the wide-open blinds in the living room. "What the fuck, Aydan, ya said ya were ridin' your dirt bike."

"I was. The car blew up earlier. Somebody rigged a bomb to my ignition so it exploded as soon as the car started." I peered around the living room. "Where the hell is your phone book?"

Hellhound gripped my arms, frowning down into my face. "Aydan, for fucksakes..." He took a deep breath. "Okay, an' ya didn't go up with the car because...?"

"I got lucky. It was cold that day, so I used the remote starter."

"Jesus." He folded me into his arms and held me close for a moment. "Remind me next time, if I don't really wanna know, don't ask. Phone book's under the couch. Back in a few minutes." He pulled on his jeans. "Don't blow anythin' up."

By the time he returned, I was nervously pacing the living room while Hooker uttered hoarse meows of complaint from beside his empty food dish.

"Did ya talk to the cops?" Hellhound asked.

"Yes. The police said Nichele's car was in a non-injury accident west of Lake Louise last night around ten. As far as they know, she was fine and the car got towed, probably to Lake Louise. So where the hell is she, Arnie? Why isn't she answering her cell?"

"I dunno," he began, but I interrupted.

"What if D... the guy I was talking about last night was following her?" I yanked my fingers through the tangles in my hair. "What if he ran her off the road and then kidnapped her?"

"That doesn't make sense, darlin', the police woulda told ya if she wasn't there. If they said it was a non-injury accident, they musta talked to her."

"But..."

My phone vibrated, and I jerked it up to squint at the display.

"Oh, for *shit's* sake!" I stomped over to my suitcase.

"What now, darlin'?"

"I have to call Stemp." I rummaged in the suitcase, shivering while I pawed through its icy contents. I extracted one of Stemp's secured phones and hesitated.

"I'll wait outside," Hellhound said, and stepped into the hallway, closing the door behind him.

I sent brief but profound thanks for him winging skyward, and punched the Talk button.

"It's Arlene," I replied to Stemp's usual brisk 'yes'.

"We need you back at Sirius Dynamics."

The phone creaked under the clenching of my hand. Christ, could *anything* go right this morning?

"I can't."

A brief pause hummed on the line before he spoke again. "Unacceptable."

"Tough," I snapped. My phone vibrated again, and I squinted at the display. Chateau Lake Louise. "I have to go," I said, and hung up on Stemp.

Heart pounding, I pressed the Talk button on my phone.

"He's safe!" Nichele's jubilant voice made my knees give way.

I collapsed onto the sofa. "Nichele, where the hell are you? You scared the shit out of me!"

"I'm at the Chateau Lake Louise! It's soooo beautiful here..."

"What the hell, Nichele! Why didn't you answer your cell?"

"It broke when I hit the ditch. I had it on the seat beside me and it smashed into the dashboard. But he's safe, Aydan! Dave's safe!"

I slumped on the couch, trying to decide whether to yell at her or dance a jig. "Don't ever do that again, Nichele! Don't ever run off without telling me what you're doing. What happened? What the hell were you thinking?"

"I'm sorry, Aydan, I just couldn't wait for you to get back from Silverside. I just kept thinking what if Dave was hurt somewhere, trapped in his truck, and I just started driving. It was really icy and I went off the road, but a nice man stopped and called the police and tow truck for me. By the time I got back here it was after midnight and I thought you'd be with Hellhound, so I just went to bed. I was so wiped, I just woke up a few minutes ago."

I shuddered at the thought of who the 'nice man' could have been. "Listen, Nichele, I'm really glad you're all right, but I need you to just stay there, okay? Just wait until I call you. Promise?"

"I promise. I'm really sorry you were worried."

"It's okay. Bye."

I went over to stick my head out into the hallway. Hellhound levered himself away from the wall, eyeing me questioningly.

"Nichele's fine," I told him, stepping back to let him in the apartment.

He frowned. "An' ya know that from callin' Stemp?"

"No. Just hang on a second, I have to call Dave." I dialled again.

When he answered, I said, "Nichele's fine. She's at the Chateau Lake Louise."

I could hear the smile in his voice. "Yeah, I know. She called me a few minutes ago. Tried to call you, but it went to voicemail and I didn't want to leave a message."

"Okay." I drew a deep breath. "Dave, can I ask you something personal?"

"'Kay..." he said cautiously.

"Sorry, this isn't really my business, but it's important. Do you... um... *like* Nichele?"

He laughed. "Yeah. We back in third grade now?"

"Do you like her well enough to put up with her for a few days?"

When he spoke again, the laughter was gone from his voice. "I'd put up with her for the rest of my life if she'd have me."

My heart squeezed. "Oh, Dave. I'm sorry. I mean... Not that I'm sorry you like her, just..."

"What's this about, Aydan?"

"Could you please do me a big favour? Could you stop on your way through Lake Louise and pick Nichele up..."

"Well, sure," he interrupted.

"No, it's more than that. Keep her with you. Don't let her go home. Don't let her go to work. Don't let her drive her car, if it's still driveable. Don't let her use her credit cards anywhere. Just keep her with you, go on your regular runs, and don't let her out of your sight."

"Shi... crap, what's wrong?"

"Nothing. Just... she'll be safe if she's on the road with you. Can you do that?"

"Sure thing, Aydan. Are you on a mission?" His voice tightened. "You need help? I'll be in Calgary in about three and a half hours..."

"No, I'm fine. Thanks, Dave, but what I really need is for you to protect Nichele."

"I will," he said firmly. "What should I tell her?"

"Tell her... um... tell her James Helmand escaped from prison."

Tension knifed into his voice. "Shi... crap, did he?"

"No. It's just a cover story."

I heard the whoosh of released breath. "Good. I'll do it. Be careful, 'kay?"

"I will. Thanks, Dave. You, too."

Seconds after I hung up, I realized I'd let him use the word 'mission' without denying I was a secret agent.

Shit.

I knew he'd been harbouring a fantasy about me as Jane Bond, secret agent, but I had been sure Stemp's debriefing after our last adventure had convinced him I was nothing more than a protected witness. Obviously I'd been wrong.

Well, too late now. And I could trust him. Dave would keep his mouth shut.

I called Nichele back and told her to expect Dave, and then hung up again, sinking back onto the couch with a sigh.

"Everythin' okay now, darlin'?" Hellhound sat down beside me and laid an arm across my shoulders.

I stared at the latest text message blinking on my phone. 'Call home'.

The white text didn't look any different from any of my

other messages, but the two words practically vibrated with fury.

"No, not quite everything." I rubbed my aching forehead and hauled myself up to get another phone out of my suitcase. "Sorry."

I shot Hellhound an apologetic glance, and he shrugged. "No problem, darlin'."

He stepped out into the hallway again, and I sank back onto the couch and tucked my cold feet up under me before poising my finger over the phone.

I squeezed my eyes shut and pressed the button.

"Ms. Widdenback." Stemp sounded pissed.

"Um, hi. Sorry about before." I shook myself and summoned up what I hoped was a crisp, professional tone. "I had a situation. It's fixed now. What do you need?"

"I need you back at Sirius Dynamics as soon as possible."

I sighed. "Okay. I don't know how long I'll be. The roads are bad and my truck isn't great on ice."

"Call when you're about half an hour out."

"Okay."

I hung up and collapsed slowly forward to bury my face in the sofa cushions. The warm lassitude of Hellhound's bed was already a distant memory. Why couldn't I just have one day? One lousy day...

I huffed a sigh, spat out the cat hairs that found their way into my mouth as a result, and dragged myself off the couch to let Hellhound back into his own apartment. Again.

"I'm comin' with ya."

I reached up to kiss Hellhound. "Thanks, but I'll be fine. We've had enough drama with people out on the highway today."

"Yeah. That's why I'm comin' with ya." He dropped his duffel bag by the door and tenderly tucked his guitar into its case. "I know ya take good care a' your vehicles, darlin', but that truck's almost as old as you. An' it's rear-wheel-drive, an' light in the back. It'll suck on ice. I'll follow ya in my Forester, just in case. 'Least I got four wheel drive."

"But it's a two-hour drive even if the roads are good. It'll be a lot longer today." I stuffed my feet into my boots. "Just stay here where it's warm and safe..."

He silenced me with a kiss. "Shut up, darlin'. It ain't always about you. I gotta go see Kane. He's chewin' horseshoes an' spittin' nails, an' ya gotta have some way to talk to him so he doesn't get court-martialled." He shrugged into his parka and dropped another kiss on my lips. "Come on, let's go."

I grabbed my suitcase and followed him out, secretly relieved.

By the time we got close to Silverside, my shoulders were aching with tension. I slowed, braking cautiously and steering into the skid as the truck slithered to a skittish halt beside the road.

Prying my stiffened hands loose from the wheel, I delved into my pocket for the last of Stemp's phones.

A tap on my window made me jump, nearly dropping the phone. I hurriedly rolled down the window when I saw Hellhound outside, snowflakes already beginning to collect on his beard.

"Everythin' okay?" he asked.

"Fine. I just have to check in with Stemp. I figure we're

about half an hour out now. I have to go straight to Sirius Dynamics when we get there."

"Okay, darlin', when we get to town I'll just head over to John's. Call me when you're done at Sirius."

"Thanks." I leaned out the window to plant a kiss on his already-cold lips. "Get back in your SUV where it's warm."

He grinned and strode away, and I thankfully closed the window on the bitter wind.

I didn't spare any pleasantries when Stemp answered my call.

"I'm about half an hour out."

"Good. Use the back entrance."

He disconnected, and I glared at the phone before rolling down the window to fling it out into the ditch. Not exactly an environmentally responsible method of disposal, but I had to get rid of it anyway. And it eased my irritation to pretend it was Stemp freezing his ass off in a snowbank. Jerk.

In Silverside at last, I slid to a stop at the traffic light, red as usual. Hellhound's Forester pulled up beside me, and he waved before turning down the side street that led to Kane's house.

The truck's tires spun, the rear end fishtailing slightly as I feathered the gas to get moving again. A few minutes later, I pulled thankfully into the parking lot behind the dilapidated bowling alley.

Easing my hands off the steering wheel, I turned the truck off and sagged for a few moments in the seat, taking slow breaths and letting the tension unwind from my shoulders. Only one more short drive, and then I'd be home again. All my friends safe. Thank God.

Shooting a cautious glance around the deserted parking lot, I slid out of the truck and hurried over to let myself in the back door of the bowling alley. Inside, the din of machinery and clatter of pins made me stuff my fingers in my ears while I traversed the walkway behind the lanes.

I was reaching for the door to the electrical room when a flicker of movement in my peripheral vision made me whip around to face the masked, black-clad figure.

I almost got to my gun in time.

CHAPTER 22

I woke in blackness so profound that I blinked wide-eyed in momentary terror that I'd gone blind. I gasped a couple of shallow fearful breaths before logic reasserted itself. Blindness wasn't black. Tammy's memories were good for something, at least.

My relief was short-lived. When I tried to move, I realized I lay on my side, my wrists bound behind me and my ankles tied together. Icy terror drenched me when I tried to move and my knees and hands bumped against constricting walls. Rearing my upper body, my shoulder struck a hard surface only inches above me.

Coffin! I was in a coffin!

Panic seized me, my heart drumming so hard its rhythm burned behind my straining eyes. My breath whistled shallowly in my throat.

Exerting every ounce of my self-control, I prevented myself from thrashing and screaming mindlessly.

Don't panic. Just breathe.

This was real life, not a dream. The coffin wouldn't shrink. There was air. I hadn't suffocated while I was unconscious, so I wouldn't suffocate now.

Stay calm. Breathe. Think.

I fought the surging adrenaline. Think. What happened?

My captor had used a trank gun. But what had he done with me once I was unconscious? He must have dragged me back out of the bowling alley and into a vehicle. The only other ways out of the service corridor led through the public area of the bowling alley or into the secured area below Sirius Dynamics.

And how long had I been unconscious? Hours? Days?

Terror threatened to overtake me again, and I beat it back. No time for that, dammit.

Don't panic. Evaluate.

I squirmed, stretching to full length. My feet touched bottom, and my hair brushed against a surface above me.

Coffin*coffinCOFFIN*...

Breathe.

I concentrated on yoga belly breathing, fighting to control the jerky spasms that seized my lungs. Nice and slow. In. Out. Think about ocean waves rolling in.

A few moments later, I succumbed to the urgency again.

Out! I had to get out...

Another exploratory squirm, and a surge of fierce elation parted the waves of fear. They'd taken my gun, but they'd left my waist pouch on.

Stupid assholes. They'd regret that when I got out. And I *would* get out. I clung to the thought.

I squirmed again, rotating my hips in the confined space. I bared my teeth in a grimace of triumph when I managed to wedge the pouch against the wall of my prison. Slowly, so slowly, I wriggled and twisted until the pouch rode up over my hip.

Careful now. If the buckle let go, all would be lost.

A whimper of fear escaped my lips and I clamped down hard on it. I could do this.

I contorted my arms, straining against the ties on my wrists to grasp the belt of the waist pouch and pull it around to my back.

Almost there...

Almost...

I gasped relief when I felt the zipper on the front pocket. Groping at the zipper tab, I managed to ease it open. My keys fell out, jangling to the bottom of my prison. I clamped frantic fingers over the pocket.

Oh God, please, God, don't let my knife fall out.

I gulped, fighting to steady my trembling hands before twisting my fingers around to delve into the pocket.

Careful.

Slow and careful...

My shaking fingertips found the knurled grip and teased it closer.

Easy now...

Seconds later, I clutched the glorious hardness of my folding knife.

Sweat prickled my body while I struggled with terrible slowness to open it without dropping it. At last, I managed to manoeuvre the blade against the binding on my wrists. A few moments of sawing, and I blessed my obsession with sharp knives when my arms sprang free.

Clutching the wonderful knife, I heaved my hands in front of me and reached into the pouch again for my tiny LED flashlight. Its beam made me clamp my eyes shut, clenching my teeth on the screams that tried to rip from my throat.

My shrill keening might have been suppressed screaming

or the whistling of my breath in my too-tight throat. After a few moments I wrestled myself into silence again.

Darkness was better. In the darkness I couldn't see the walls of the crate inches from my face...

I clamped down on my panicked panting again.

I was fine. The walls weren't caving in. There was air. I had a knife. I could get free. Just as long as I stayed calm.

Just stay calm.

Okay. I'd take another look. I needed to know how long I'd been imprisoned.

I braced myself. I'd just look at my watch. I wouldn't look at anything else...

I flashed the light on and squinted awkwardly past my chest, twisting my wrist to see my watch. Before I had a chance to panic again, I flicked the light off.

Quarter after three. But was it three in the afternoon, or three in the morning? Was it still Tuesday?

If it was still Tuesday afternoon, I'd been unconscious for only about an hour. Somehow that felt right. If I'd been lying on my side for over twelve hours, I'd be in a lot more pain than I was. And I'd probably have peed my pants.

I squirmed, wishing I hadn't thought about that.

Unless I'd been out for who-knows-how-long, and they'd put me into the box right before I woke up.

Do. Not. Panic.

I shook my head, trying to awaken some useful plan. First things first. I strained to reach my feet, knees jammed against the wall of the box, shoulders grinding into the other side. At the extreme tip of my knife, I felt something that might have been the tie on my ankles.

Sweating and shaking, I picked at the tie one tiny nick at a time. My body screamed disapproval of the contortions, but I kept at it, focusing all my will on the task.

No time to panic. Pain doesn't matter. Just keep working on that tie...

At last, I strained my legs and the binding gave with an audible snap. I collapsed, panting, my beloved knife clenched in my hand.

Forcing myself to concentrate, I lay in the blackness, pretending with all my might that I wasn't in a box.

Think.

Who had captured me? And why?

The black-clad figure had been taller and bulkier than Doytchevsky. Could it have been one of Fuzzy Bunny's men?

I fought down panic again.

Stemp would know by now that something had gone wrong. He'd have found my truck in the parking lot, maybe discovered some drag marks in the snow. If there was any evidence to be found, he'd find it.

My fingers toyed with the empty space that should have held my cell phone. Why would they take my cell phone out of my waist pouch, but not take my knife? And why hadn't they just taken the whole pouch? That was stupid.

A faint sound made me freeze. Had it come from outside? I strained my ears.

Another faint sound, then a scraping noise so close to my head I jerked away instinctively. Another scraping noise from the foot of the box. Was that the sound of...

...latches?

When the first sliver of light appeared above me, I was already in motion, lunging up to slam the lid open.

Light half-blinded me, but not enough to obscure the blurry dark shape stumbling back from the box. A scything sweep of my knife hand ended in meaty impact and a heavy dragging sensation before my blade flew free.

A scream tore the air and I blinked tears away from my burning eyes to see a black-clad man tumble to the floor. He screamed again, writhing and clutching his leg. A bright jet of blood fountained from his upper thigh.

I pounced on him, clamping my hand over his mouth, jamming my blade against his throat. "Shut up."

He froze, quivering violently, and the smell of shit filled the air. My stomach lurched.

Screams and blood and shit. I fought the flashback with all I had.

"Put pressure on it." My voice was an unrecognizable rasp. "Get your hand on it, asshole. Put pressure on it!" His shaking hand moved to obey. "More. More, goddammit!"

The crimson stream slackened, and I eased my grip off his mouth. "Where am I? Who are you working for? Now, or I'll slit your throat!"

He vanished.

A wave of vertigo seized me as the white walls of Sirius's secured area bloomed around me.

"Well done, Agent Kelly." Stemp nodded approval from across the room. "Very well done indeed."

I lurched out of the chair, clawing at the back of my neck for the generic network access fob I was sure I'd find. Dr. Rawling flinched away, his face blanching as I pulled the small device free and flung it at Stemp with all my might.

"You fucking *asshole!*" My hand slammed down on my empty holster.

"You weren't planning to shoot anyone, were you?" Stemp inquired, inclining his head toward the desk where my gun and waist pouch sat.

"Aydan, I know you're upset right now..." Dr. Rawling

quavered.

"Upset?" My voice cracked. "*Upset?* Fuck no, I'm not upset. I'm fucking *livid!*" I jerked back to face Stemp. "I'm going to rip your fucking head off and shit down the hole, you fucking sack of shit!"

Stemp's gun flicked up to point steadily at my chest. "Is that a fact?"

"Aaaargh!" I whirled and seized the chair, flinging it against the wall with all my strength. Instead of shattering satisfyingly, it rebounded and crashed into my shin.

"*Aaaargh!* Fucking goddamn sonuva*bitch!*"

I hopped impotently, clutching my shin and swearing at the top of my lungs. After a few moments, the superhuman strength of adrenaline ebbed, and I trailed off to face Dr. Rawling's white face and wide eyes. Beside him, Stemp returned my gaze impassively. I turned away to retrieve the chair and set it upright again. Trembling violently, I collapsed into it.

"Here." Stemp laid aside his gun and rose to offer me an insulated paper cup. The aroma of hot chocolate wafted from the small hole in its lid.

I glared, and he sighed. "Take it. You need it."

"Fuck off." I braced my feet wider against my tremors, struggling to hold myself steady in the chair.

"Drink it. That's an order."

Slow breaths. I clutched the chair like a lifeline and fought the sobs that tried to climb my throat.

He was right, goddamn him to hell. I did need it.

I held out a shaking hand, and he pressed the warm cup into it. By clenching it in both hands, I managed to hold it to my lips, thankful for the spill-proof lid when the hot liquid sloshed inside.

Stemp returned to his seat and shot a wry glance at Dr. Rawling. "Now you understand why I insisted on a virtual reality simulation instead of a real-life scenario. If that man hadn't been a construct..."

The doctor turned a still-pale face in my direction. "What if he had been there to rescue you?"

That possibility was part of what was fuelling my tremors. I gulped another mouthful of chocolate, clutching the hot cup in icy hands. "I'd have patched him up and gotten him out. Somehow."

"And if he didn't tell you what you wanted to know?"

I avoided considering the answer by glaring at Stemp. "So what the fuck was that all about? Slow day at the office? You thought maybe I'd entertain you by crushing myself to death inside a sim?"

"You couldn't have crushed yourself. I programmed the sim externally so the parameters of the box were unalterable." His level gaze measured me. "And this was necessary. Unlike Dr. Rawling, I don't have the luxury of hours or days of psychological assessment to determine your fitness for duty. I needed to know if you were mission-ready today. Now I know you are."

"I told you that! If I say I'm fine, I'm fucking *fine*," I snarled.

He nodded, obviously unperturbed. "So you say." He flicked a glance at Dr. Rawling. "Thank you for attending. You're dismissed."

The doctor nodded wordlessly and rose, supporting himself on the back of his chair with hands that shook almost as much as mine. I indulged in a moment of vicious satisfaction. Talk to me about post-traumatic stress now, asshole.

As he tottered out, whitefaced, my satisfaction faded into shame. The poor man hadn't done anything to me. Stemp was the asshole.

I transferred my scowl to its deserving recipient. "That was a shitty thing to do to him."

Stemp shrugged. "I didn't expect a bloodbath. I thought you'd break. Rawling was only here to pick up the pieces afterward."

"You fucking dickhead." My words came out exhausted and flat, and I took another shaky sip of hot chocolate, hoping to revive some righteous anger.

He eyed me expressionlessly. "My job isn't to be popular. My job is to make sure all my staff can perform at peak efficiency. Otherwise, good people die."

He was right, and it only made me hate him more.

"Well, good job, then," I spat.

"Thank you. When do you plan to put the tracer on Doytchevsky?"

Shit, I'd forgotten about that.

"When I'm damn well good and ready."

He rose, apparently unperturbed. "You need to attempt another contact with Sherman. The team is assembled in your office. I'll stand in for Kane. Let's go."

I stood, refusing to clutch at the chair for support. "I have to go to the bathroom. I'll meet you up there." I drained the cup and crushed it in my fist, wishing it was his skull.

He turned and left without another word, and I collected my gun, jacket, and waist pouch before wobbling down the corridor to the ladies' room.

The trip through the time-delay chamber was a small slice of hell. I braced my forehead against the door, eyes closed, focusing every ounce of my being on taking slow, steady breaths. When the door finally released, I held myself under rigid control and strode over to the security wicket.

"Just going outside for a second. Be right back." I dropped my security fob in the tray and made a beeline for the exit.

Outside, I trembled on the sidewalk, clamping down on the frantic urge to run. The swirling snow stung my face while the bitter wind whipped my hair around my head in wild gusts. I closed my eyes and sucked in huge lungfuls of freedom.

After a few minutes I retreated to the warmth of the lobby, wiping moisture off my cheeks that might have been tears or snow.

"Rotten day," the security guard commented as I collected my badge again.

"No kidding," I agreed with profound sincerity. I didn't bother to point out that I wasn't referring to the weather.

CHAPTER 23

Standing in the doorway to my office, I took stock of its occupants and concealed my feelings with a non-committal, "Hi everybody."

Spider's face lit up. "Hi, Aydan, how was your holiday? Lola said you guys had a blast."

"Yeah." I accompanied the word with what I hoped was a cheerful expression. That was a little tricky when I was wishing slow, painful death on two of the four people in the room.

Stemp and Doytchevsky were apparently trying to outdo each other for the Most Deadpan award, but Jack rose with her usual warm smile. "Welcome back. I thought you were away until Wednesday."

"So did I," I muttered. "Change in plans," I added, trying to look as though that was a good thing. Sinking onto the sofa, I eyed Stemp. "What do you want me to do?"

"The same as last time. I'll come into the network with you and act as your anchor."

I hid my disgust the best I could.

"When do you expect John back?" Jack inquired, fixing Stemp with a concerned gaze. "I hope his personal leave is nothing serious. Was there an illness in his family?"

Doytchevsky's eyes glittered with triumph while Stemp replied, "I'm not at liberty to discuss the circumstances, but Kane has considerable leave time accumulated. If he chooses to use it, he could be away for several months."

"Oh." Jack's radiance dimmed.

"I'll stand in this week, but if it looks as though it will turn into a long-term absence, I'll assign another agent." Stemp turned a bland face toward me. "Shall we begin?"

I drew a deep breath and let it out slowly, stepping mentally into the white void and concentrating hard on concealing my animosity.

I wasn't quite as successful as I'd hoped. I banished the spiky armour that encased me and waved the snarling, fire-breathing dragon into oblivion. Damn virtual reality anyway.

"What was that?" Spider's voice filtered through the interface in a mixture of delight and astonishment.

"Sorry. Guess I'm tired. I was watching a medieval thing the other night," I lied, avoiding the appraising gaze of Stemp's avatar.

"That dragon was so cool!" Spider enthused. "Do you mind if I save that into a separate sim file?"

"It's all yours." I plodded resolutely toward the virtual file repository.

Inside, I materialized a couple of chairs and sank into one of them. Get this over with. I grasped Stemp's outstretched hand and whisked into data stream before I could recoil at his touch.

Just outside the firewalls of Sirius Dynamics, I floated aimlessly in the busy currents of the internet. This was stupid. What was I supposed to do, just hang around in the hope that Terry Sherman happened to be riding Tammy's mind around the internet at this exact moment looking for me?

But I didn't have a clue where they might be, and stretching off into nothingness was even more of a waste of time than hanging around close to home. He knew where to find me. If he wanted to...

Even though I'd been half-expecting it, the deluge of data drove a shock of fear through me. Clinging grimly to Stemp's distant grip, I captured Tammy's turbulent presence and began to sort through it again.

It took forever. My exhausted consciousness strained to hold her, sifting memories only to lose them and start over.

Read. Sort. File.

Over and over.

When I finally packed the last bit of data away and opened my net, the implosion shattered me. I tried to gather myself into a data stream to pursue the retreating packets, but my weakened consciousness bobbed uselessly, millions of barely-connected shards too scattered to coalesce.

With the last of my will, I seeped back toward Stemp's distant grip.

"Kelly!" Stemp's voice echoed as if from the end of a long tunnel. "Agent Kelly! Aydan!"

I could feel the pull now, as if he was drawing me back bit by bit.

Let him pull.

I floated, barely conscious of his distant shouts.

"Aydan!" The calls were closer now, Stemp's and Spider's voices mingling.

I concentrated with all my might, and Stemp swam into focus. "Just hold on. I'm going to get you out now," he said.

I couldn't perceive my avatar's appearance, but it

couldn't have been good. Stemp's hands trembled finely when he lifted me, belying his calm voice. "Stay with me. We're going through the portal now."

Moments later, pain crashed through me and I jerked into a ball, hugging my head and sobbing curses. When gentle hands began to massage my temples, I pressed my face into the sofa cushions to hide my tears.

"Aydan?" Spider's tremulous voice penetrated my misery.

I groaned and dragged myself more-or-less upright, swiping my sleeve across my face. "Yeah."

"Did you get the IP?" Doytchevsky's nasal voice drilled through my aching brain.

"No." I opened my eyes and singled Stemp's expressionless features out of the ring of faces. "I couldn't trace it back. It was all I could do to sort through all our memories and hold mine back."

He frowned. "Are you certain you didn't give anything away?"

"Positive."

"Good enough." He gave me a look that might have been compassion. "We'll try again tomorrow. Go home and get some rest."

I sighed. "There's a problem."

"What?"

"We missed them." I slouched forward and closed my eyes, rubbing at the persistent pain in my temples. "I thought... *Tammy* thought they were going to travel by ground to stay hidden. But instead Sherman booked a flight under fake names. They flew in on Sunday, drove up here to Silverside yesterday, discovered that their headquarters was flattened, and ran."

A pregnant silence ensued, and I didn't open my eyes.

When Stemp spoke again, his even voice betrayed no emotion. "Do you have any idea where they were going?"

"No. And I don't even know what their car looks like..."

"Because Tammy is blind," Stemp finished.

"Yeah. I know they were travelling as George and Janet White, but that's all. And they probably won't use those names again anyway."

"Do you know what car rental agency they used?"

I pried my eyes open at last to face Stemp's question. "No."

"We'll start there nevertheless." Stemp turned to Spider. "Webb, hack into the rental car agencies at the Calgary airport. Look for a rental for George or Janet White. If they rented a car with an onboard GPS, we might be able to locate them with that. If you can't find either name..."

"I'll check all the arrival times from Boston on Sunday and cross-check with the names of people who rented cars at those times," Spider finished. "Aydan, do you know what time they arrived in Calgary?"

I squeezed my eyes shut and clutched my throbbing head while I laboured through twice as many memories as any brain should hold.

"Aydan!" Jack's sudden voice made my eyes pop open. "Your nose is bleeding. Are you all right?"

I swiped at the tickle under my nose and stared stupidly at the red smear on my hand for a moment before accepting the tissue from her outstretched hand.

"Yeah..." I struggled to marshal my thoughts back into some semblance of concentration, but it was no use. "Sorry, Spider, either Tammy didn't know or I can't dig out the memory. My brain is too full." I dabbed at my nose. "They know the other three Knights were killed, though. They searched out the news items on the barn explosion. But they don't know Sam's in custody, and Sherman still wants to contact him."

"Good," Stemp said. "That's enough for today. You need to go to the hospital now."

"No, I'm f-"

"That wasn't a suggestion," he interrupted. "Dr. Travers, please hook Kelly up to your diagnostic equipment and compare her current brainwave pattern to your baseline data. I'll call the hospital and they will be expecting you as soon as you finish here." He rose. "Will it be necessary for me to escort you?"

I slumped back on the sofa. "No. I'll go."

A couple of hours later, I escaped when the doctors admitted they couldn't find anything wrong with me other than slightly elevated blood pressure and high levels of stress hormones.

I muttered 'No shit, really?' under my breath and trudged through the gathering dusk to my truck. The snow had stopped, but the bitter wind sliced through every tiny aperture in my clothing.

Shivering, I fumbled my key out of my waist pouch and unlocked the door by feel in the half-light. Focused on getting out of the miserable wind as quickly as possible, I realized my mistake a fraction of a second after the door closed behind me.

"Both hands on the wheel." Doytchevsky unfolded himself from the foot well of the passenger side and the muzzle of his gun stared me down.

After a split-second of adrenaline-drenched indecision, I obeyed. I was pretty sure he wouldn't shoot me with an actual bullet, but the trank gun in his hand meant business. One wrong move, and I'd wake up a lot unhappier than I was at this moment. Which was extremely unhappy indeed.

He nodded approval. "Smart."

"What the hell do you want?"

He shivered. "I hate this damn truck. I've spent far too much time freezing in it."

"Well, nobody's stopping you from leaving," I snapped. "Don't let the door hit you in the ass on your way out."

He gave me a smile that chilled me in ways the cold vinyl upholstery couldn't match. "Oh, I'm not staying. I just want to have a little chat. Did you and Stemp enjoy my photography?"

I hid my fear and anger in a shrug. "I told you I don't give a shit. That's Kane's problem."

He shot me a look of pure satisfaction. "Yes, it is, isn't it? Thank you for giving me the idea. I've been searching for a creative way to make him suffer."

Wait a minute. Make *him* suffer?

Shit, maybe Arnie was right. It wasn't all about me.

I went fishing. "What's your problem with him? I'm the one he's harassing."

I held my breath, hoping he'd bite.

He did. His face twisted with hatred. "You mean besides the fact that he murdered Robert? My best friend?"

Oh. Right.

Maybe it was time to build a little rapport.

"*Your* best friend. *My* husband," I said flatly.

"Yes." He had the grace to look slightly abashed. "I suppose it was naive of me to think I could use Kane as leverage against you. Nevertheless." He straightened, the trank gun unwavering in his grip. "I'm finished playing games. Where's Sherman?"

I hissed out a short breath between my teeth. "I told you, I don't fucking know."

"That's too bad. Tell me, are you fond of your little purple-haired sex granny?"

My heart clenched into a fist-sized stone.

Oh, God. I'd been so busy worrying about Nichele, I'd forgotten Doytchevsky had seen Lola with me in Vegas. And she was a highly-visible target in this tiny fishbowl of a town.

"Yes." My voice came out high and tight.

"So you wouldn't want anything bad to happen to her."

"No." I tried to draw a long, slow breath, but my lungs felt as though they had been encased in steel. "Kasper, I swear I will do anything you want. I'll tell you as soon as I get even a hint of where Sherman is. But I honestly... don't... *know*." I met his eyes, willing him to believe me. "I'm sorry. Please believe me. If I knew, I'd tell you. Please don't hurt Lola." I didn't have to exaggerate the quiver in my voice.

He eyed me for a few moments. "Nice acting. Too bad I know you're lying."

"I'm not!" In the dim light, my knuckles glowed white on the steering wheel. "Kasper, *please!* Think about it. Why would I lie to you? I hate the Knights as much as you do. More. Look what they've done to my life. Why the hell would I protect Sherman?"

"So you can kill him yourself."

"*Kasper!*" I thumped my forehead against the steering wheel, holding back tears of frantic frustration. "I blew up three of them. That's all I need. You can have Sherman. I'll tell you where he is as soon as I know, I swear it!"

On second thought, now was not the time for bravado. I let the tears leak out. "Kasper, please." My voice was a hoarse whisper.

"Aw. Real tears. I'm touched." He gave me a sardonic smile. "All right. See that you keep your end of the bargain. Or I'll pay a visit to your little granny. Maybe I'll try out some of her merchandise on her. I'll be sure to take lots of pictures so you can share the experience."

My stomach clenched, sending a wave of sickness up to half-strangle my voice. "I swear I'll tell you as soon as I know."

"You do that." He unlatched the door and backed out, still holding me at gunpoint. "Oh, and if you mention this conversation to anyone, your little granny will pay in ways you won't even want to imagine. Have a pleasant evening."

For several minutes after he faded into the darkness, I sat with my hands glued to the steering wheel, swallowing quaking nausea. At last, I pried a shaking hand loose to turn the key, taking scant comfort when the engine roared to life.

Hunched trembling in the driver's seat, I took long, slow breaths. When I could fake calm, I made a quick call to Hellhound to let him know I was on my way home, then sat staring at the frost on the windshield.

Just breathe.

At last I put the truck in gear, peering through the small but widening clear spot in the glass.

The drive on the dark, icy highway was made bearable by the knowledge that in only a few miles I'd be home. When my garage door rolled down behind me, I slumped forward to rest my aching forehead on the steering wheel, slowly peeling my grip off the steering wheel finger by finger.

The urge to curl up in the warm stillness was almost

overwhelming, but after a few minutes I pulled myself upright and crept out of the truck.

Home at last. Thank God.

I plodded out of the garage and clung to the handrail while my shaking legs hoisted me up my snow-covered steps. Long moments later, my cold, clumsy fingers finally managed to guide my key into the lock.

When I stepped through the front door, a horrible stench froze me to the floor.

Oh, no.

Please.

No.

As if of its own volition, my hand found the light switch.

My knees gave way and I thudded to the floor.

CHAPTER 24

The sound of my doorbell slowly penetrated my consciousness. It rang a couple of times, followed by a knock, and Tom's voice called from outside.

"Aydan? Hello! Anybody home?"

It took a couple of tries to get my voice working. "Come in."

The door swung open and Tom spared a fast glance around the kitchen before dropping to his knees beside me. "Aydan, are you hurt? What happened?"

"I'm not hurt." My voice reverberated in the empty hole where my heart had been. "I just... I can't..." It took all my strength to raise a hand and gesture at the devastation of my home. "I forgot about the break-in."

His face hardened as he took in the gutted cabinets, the smashed dishes and putrefied food scattered across the floor. The open chest freezer filled the air with its strained humming, but the fridge had given up, its doors gaping sadly around a dark and lifeless interior.

Long tremors shook me and I looked away, my battered mind seeking solace in the summer-blue of Tom's eyes.

He pulled me against his chest, blocking my view of the room. "It's going to be okay, Aydan. Don't worry, we'll fix it." He held me for a moment before drawing away to study my face. "Come on, let's get you out of here. Can you stand?"

Too overwhelmed to even react to his sympathy, I groped for a simulation of composure. "I'm okay. I just... it was just the shock..."

"Let's go." He wrapped a gentle arm around me and helped me rise.

"No, it's okay, I should get started on this mess."

"No, you shouldn't." He steered me firmly toward the door. "You're coming home with me."

"The freezer..."

He strode across to close its lid, his boots crunching over shards of glass. "There. The rest will keep."

Despite my ineffectual protests, he guided me out the door, gently pried the keys out of my still-clenched hand, and locked up. The last of my will deserted me, and I let him walk me to his truck and help me into the seat in silence.

At the end of my lane, he got out to close the gate behind us. When his door admitted a blast of cold air, my brain ground into a forward gear again.

"I can't leave," I said as he got back behind the wheel. "Arnie's on his way."

Tom reached across to extract my phone from the pocket of my waist pouch and press it into my shaking hand. "Call him and tell him to come to my place instead."

"No, I..."

"Yes. Do it." His voice was kind but firm, and I surrendered and dialled, too spent to argue.

Numbness descended while I huddled in the seat,

watching the beautiful, deadly ground-drift sculpting the snow into pointed fingers across the road. Tom's heavy dual-wheeled truck forged through the drifts, their delicate appearance belied by the solid bump when we struck them.

"Sorry?" I roused myself when I realized Tom had asked me a question.

He turned down his lane, wallowing through the snow at the corner. "I said, I saw your truck go by earlier, so I knew you were home. I tried to call you but it just rang and rang."

"Yeah..." The lights of his farmhouse looked warm and safe when we pulled up in front. "I guess they must have broken the phone. I didn't hear anything." A shudder shook me.

He nodded and shut off the ignition, sliding out to stride around to the passenger side and open the door for me.

When he unlocked his front door and ushered me in, the tidy hominess struck at my heart like a physical blow. I stumbled, and in an instant his hand was strong under my elbow.

"Sit down for a minute." He swivelled me onto a wooden bench beside the door and I sat, breathing slowly to hold my emotions in check. When he knelt in front of me to unlace my boots, embarrassment restored some of my energy.

For chrissake, suck it up. Surely I didn't need to be rescued and comforted like a child just because my house was a mess.

"Thanks, Tom, I can manage." I bent to undo the other one, but my shaking fingers tangled the laces.

His warm hands nudged my cold ones out of the way. "I'll get these. Take off your coat."

I slid reluctantly out of my jacket, trying to hold my shivering in check.

He rose. "Come and sit by the fireplace."

Mustering all my energy, I managed to pry myself off the bench. I sank gratefully onto the sofa, and he shook out a fleece blanket that had been folded across the opposite chair and settled it over me. Reaching for the stack of split logs beside the fireplace, he laid a couple more on the fire before turning to smile down at me.

"I'll get you some tea. You like herbal in the evening, don't you?"

"No, it's okay, don't bother. I'll be warm in a minute."

"It's no bother. And you need it." He strode away, and in a few moments I heard running water and clinking crockery from the direction of the kitchen.

Wrapping my arms around myself, I huddled under the blanket and diverted my mind by taking stock of Tom's living room.

It suited him.

The floors were dark-stained planks, the walls panelled in a lighter shade of wood that made the room feel cozy and rustic with the rough stone of the fireplace. A bright Navajo-patterned rug warmed the floor between the sofa and two deep chairs upholstered in what looked like dark brown denim. Stacks of books occupied the table in the corner, a mix of hardcovers, paperbacks, and what looked like textbooks.

The pleasant tang of woodsmoke scented the air, and I drew a deep breath, easing tension from my shoulders.

Tom arrived with a steaming mug a few minutes later, and I extricated both hands from the blanket to accept it, hoping my tremors wouldn't spill it.

He tucked the blanket back over my shoulders. "I hope you like chamomile."

"Thanks, I love it." I inhaled the steam and forced a smile. "This smells so good."

He returned my smile. "My mom grows it, so this is the summer's crop."

"Oh, I didn't know you could grow it here. I'll have to try it..." I broke off at the sound of a muffled thump from outside. "That's probably Arnie."

Tom headed for the door and I took a nervous sip of the tea, hoping there wouldn't be fireworks. Tom hadn't gotten a good impression of Hellhound in his badass biker's leathers when they'd first met in the summer, and I was pretty sure Hellhound hadn't appreciated being held at the business end of Tom's shotgun a few weeks ago.

Only a few weeks ago. It felt like a lifetime.

I tensed at the sound of the door opening.

"Come on in." Tom's tone was cordial, and I turned to crane my neck over the back of the sofa as Hellhound stepped inside, looking wary.

His face brightened when he spotted me. "Hey, darlin'." He shed his boots and parka and turned to Tom. "Thanks for not meetin' me with the shotgun this time."

Tom laughed. "Thanks for not giving me a reason to. Go on in. Do you want coffee?"

"Yeah, thanks." Hellhound hesitated. "Don't get me wrong, I appreciate the invite, but what's the occasion?"

Tom stopped halfway to the kitchen, frowning. "You don't know?"

Hellhound matched his frown. "Know what?" He shot me a look. "What'm I s'posed to know?"

"Sorry, Arnie." I gave him an apologetic grimace. "My house got broken into over the weekend. I had forgotten about it until I walked in."

"Ya *forgot?* Jesus, Aydan..."

"It's a disaster zone..." My voice broke at the memory, and I turned away, swallowing hard and pretending to sip my tea.

"Aw, darlin'." A moment later, he sank onto the sofa beside me, and I put my mug aside to burrow into his arms.

Okay, so maybe I needed a little comforting after all.

He held me close, stroking my hair. "How bad? Did ya see it?" he asked, raising his voice in the direction of the kitchen. Hiding my face in his chest, I huddled closer, letting Tom answer.

"Bad. Looks like they dumped everything out of the kitchen cupboards and the fridge and freezer."

At the sound of Tom's approaching voice, I pulled away and sat up, reaching for my mug.

"Black okay?" Tom asked, handing Arnie a mug. At Arnie's nod, Tom settled into the chair opposite us cradling his own mug, and I inhaled the pleasant coffee scent while they sipped.

"Broken glass and rotten food everywhere," Tom added. "The fridge is probably done for." He turned to me. "Did you look through the rest of the house?"

"No. I just walked in the front door..." I shut up and hid my face in my mug.

Arnie's arm tightened around my shoulders. "Don't worry, darlin', I'll finish my coffee an' then head over an' start straightenin' up."

"Have you eaten? You're welcome to stay for supper," Tom offered. He smiled at me. "That's why I was calling you in the first place. I made a big pot of chili and I was looking for help to eat it." He turned to Arnie. "There's lots."

A grin spread across Arnie's face. "Well, hell, I never

turn down chili. Thanks."

We made stilted small talk while we gobbled Tom's excellent chili, Hellhound feigning interest in Tom's horses while Tom feigned interest in Hellhound's Harley. When those topics were exhausted, Hellhound turned to me.

"So when did they break in?" His eyes added the unspoken question, 'And what about the surveillance cameras', but I stuck to the stated topic. Tom didn't know about the cameras.

"Saturday night or Sunday morning. The police called me in Vegas to tell me."

Tom smiled. "It must have been a good trip to make you forget about bad news like that."

"Not really. I just had worse things to worry about."

Concern wrinkled his forehead. "That doesn't sound good. What happened?"

"Do you remember Dave Shore? The guy who was with us when you, um..." I bit off the words 'held us up with your shotgun' and substituted, "...met us down by the creek a few weeks ago." After all, Tom had only been trying to protect me.

Remembrance lightened his frown. "Yes. How is he? Did he get that chest pain checked out?"

"Yes, it was just a muscle spasm, thank God. Anyway, my friend Nichele..."

"The one who was kidnapped," Tom put in, nodding.

"Yes. She was in Vegas with me. She's dating Dave now. He has his own trucking business, and she was afraid something had happened to him because she knew he was on the road but he wasn't answering his phone. There was a big kafuffle and a lot of drama over nothing and in the end everybody was fine, but I completely forgot about my house."

Tom reached over to squeeze my hand. "You just can't win for losing, can you?"

"Not lately. But at least everybody was okay."

Arnie scraped the last of the chili out of his bowl and rose. "Thanks, that was great, but I wanna get started on Aydan's place. Hope ya don't mind if I eat an' run."

Tom stood, too. "No, of course not."

"Hang on, I'll get my coat," I said, trailing Arnie toward the door.

He shot a glance at Tom before returning his attention to me. "Nah, stay here, darlin'. If it's as bad as ya say, lemme do the rough stuff first."

"No, it's no big deal. I'll come."

He dropped a kiss on my forehead. "You're still shakin'. Ya better stay here an' take it easy for a bit."

"He's right," Tom said from behind me. "Just stay here and rest. You can both stay the night here, and tomorrow we can all work on it."

"Good, thanks," Arnie agreed, slinging on his parka. "Gimme your key, darlin'."

"It's on the bench over there." Tom spoke over my protest. Arnie collected the key and slipped out, leaving me alone with Tom's smile.

"You've been overruled." His eyes crinkled into weathered laugh lines. "Go sit by the fire and I'll bring you a beer."

I surrendered gracefully. "You just said the magic words."

A couple of beers and some easy conversation later, my eyelids drooped as if my eyelashes had been dipped in concrete. I smothered the latest of many yawns. "I'd better call Arnie and see how it's going."

"Hold on, I'll get you the phone." Tom forestalled my half-hearted attempt to rise by springing up, and I subsided on the couch, feeling faintly guilty. But not guilty enough to get up.

Another cavernous yawn seized me as he returned, holding out the handset.

Arnie assured me that the cleanup was going well, but when I asked how much longer he'd be, his voice took on a cautious note.

"Think I'll stay here tonight."

I sat up, anxiety nibbling at me. "Why, what's wrong?"

"Nothin'." He hesitated. "It's a guy thing."

"What the hell is that supposed to mean?"

"Territory, darlin'. Tell Tom I said thanks but no thanks. Bet ya ten bucks he looks happy."

I laughed. "You're kidding, right?"

"Nah. See ya in the mornin'. G'night."

"Um... good night..." I hung up, not sure whether to frown or smile.

"Is everything okay?" Tom leaned forward, searching my face.

"Everything's fine. He just said he was going to have a late night, so he'll stay there. He said to tell you thanks anyway."

Tom settled back in his chair. "There was no need for him to do that. He could have stayed here."

But I was going to have to shell out ten bucks. He did look happy.

I set aside my empty beer bottle regretfully. "I'd better go, too. My suitcase is still sitting in my kitchen and all my things are at... home..." The last word ended on a bit of a gulp as I considered what condition the rest of my things might be in.

Tom leaned forward to take my hand. "You don't need to face that tonight. Who knows if you even have a bed to sleep in. I'll run over and get your suitcase, but you should stay here tonight."

"No, Tom, that's too much trouble..."

He gave me his attractive crooked smile. "It's only a mile. And it's no more trouble for me to go over and pick up your suitcase than it would be for me to drive you over there if you were going home."

"Oh. Uh..." I groped through a haze of beer and fatigue with the feeling I was missing some key point in the argument, but I failed to discover any useful rebuttal.

I abandoned the effort. "Thanks. Don't bother about the suitcase, then. I don't need it if you've got a spare toothbrush."

"No problem." He rose. "Can I get you another beer?"

Another yawn caught me unaware. By the time I'd finished exposing my tonsils, I knew I was done. "No, thanks. If it's okay with you, I think I'd rather call it a night."

After a short flurry of towel and washcloth and toothbrush and extra blankets, I found myself installed in a tidy guest bedroom, holding a pajama top Tom had earnestly assured me he'd never worn.

As if I'd care. I was so exhausted, he could have handed me a potato sack and I wouldn't have known the difference.

When I slipped it on, a whiff of his clean-cotton outdoorsy scent made me reconsider. Okay, so I did know the difference.

I curled between the cold sheets, shivering, and pulled the pajama top closer to my nose.

I couldn't sleep.

Of course.

Vibrating with bone-weary tension, I lay listening to the night noises. The front door opened and closed quietly as Tom headed out to do his evening chores. Some time later, I heard the door again when he returned. Then soft movements from the main part of the house, followed by running water from the bathroom and the closing of his bedroom door.

Then silence broken only by the soft grumble of the furnace and the creaks of a sleeping house.

Dammit, I should have gotten him to take me home. Even if we'd had to sleep on the floor, a night that started with Hellhound always ended with total relaxation and a good sleep.

Trying to calm myself, I imagined the feel of Arnie's warm bulk beside me, the comforting weight of his arm around me.

Just relax.

Go to sleep, for chrissake.

I knew it was a nightmare even while I fought the tightening walls of my prison. Helpless to prevent the screams that ripped my throat, I battered my body against the shrinking space. The profound blackness flowed into my mouth, choking me...

"Aydan! *Aydan! What's wrong?*"

I jerked up in bed, flinging my arms out to fend off the blinding light. As reality dissolved the dream, I realized I was still keening brokenly, and I smothered the sound when Tom spoke again.

"It was just a dream, Aydan. You're safe. Just a dream." His voice was softer now, and he beamed the flashlight at the floor as he came around to the side of the bed. "I'm Tom Rossburn. You're at my house. You're safe." He stooped to look into my face. "You were having a nightmare. Do you know where you are now?"

"Shit." I pawed my tangled hair away from my face, resisting the urge to hide under the pillow from sheer humiliation. "Tom, I'm so sorry. I'm fine. Go back to bed. I promise I won't do that again."

Because I'd damn well stay up for the rest of the night. Poor guy, I should have warned him... No, dammit, I should have insisted on going home. Idiot.

I peered up at him in the reflected glow of the flashlight. "I'm really sorry."

"It's okay." He smoothed my hair. "I'm not surprised you're having nightmares after what you've been through. Go back to sleep. I'll sit with you."

"No, I'm fine, really."

Now I knew the reason for the superfluous pajama top. He wore only the bottoms, and I couldn't help admiring his chest and shoulders, the sinewy muscles defined even in the dim light.

Before my gaze could linger embarrassingly, he clicked off the flashlight. "Lie down." His gentle hand pressed me back on the pillow. "Just relax." He tucked the blankets around my shoulders. "You're safe. I'm here, and I'll watch over you. Go to sleep."

"I can't sleep while somebody's watching me. Thanks anyway."

He hesitated for a moment as if trying to decide whether to insist. "Okay. Good night."

"Good night. Sorry."

"It's okay." He moved away into the darkness and I rolled over, willing myself to stay awake.

I woke without opening my eyes, my cheek pressed against the warmth of Hellhound's chest, the safety of his arm encircling me. I sighed contentment and slid my hand over his hard muscles, sleepily tracing a line of kisses over his chest and up his neck to...

...morning stubble?

My eyes flew open and I peered through the semi-darkness at Tom.

CHAPTER 25

"*Shit!*" I bounded out of bed and spun to face Tom's expression of consternation. "Shit, Tom, I-"

"I'm sorry Aydan, it's not what it looks like..." He scrambled off the bed.

On top of the covers. Still wearing his pajama bottoms. Thank God.

"No, shit, I'm sorry, I didn't mean-" I gabbled, tugging at the hem of the pajama top to make sure it was where it belonged.

My babble was overridden by Tom's anxious voice. "I'm sorry, Aydan, you kept having nightmares and I was sitting with you a while, I must have fallen asleep..."

I raised my hands, palms out. "Hold on. Let's take a breath."

He fell silent, watching me worriedly.

I followed my own advice, sucking in a long breath and letting it out slowly. "Okay. Sorry, I didn't mean to freak out-"

"You don't have any reason to apologize, I shouldn't have-"

"No, it's fine." I raised my voice a little to make sure he was listening. "It's okay. I'm not upset, I know you weren't trying to put the moves on me, I just... I wasn't awake yet and I thought you were Arnie."

I dragged my courage up from where it was attempting to ooze out the soles of my feet and met his eyes despite the burning in my cheeks. "I didn't... um... grope you or anything last night, did I?"

He laughed, his shoulders relaxing. "Not that I noticed."

Relief made me close my eyes momentarily. "Thank God." When I opened them again, I caught his disconcerted expression. "It's not that I'd mind groping you... I mean..."

Now my face was really on fire. "Not that I... I just meant if I was going to grope you, I'd want to know it was *you*. And I'd want to be awake when I did it."

He chuckled. "I'd rather be awake when you did it, too." He extended his hand, still smiling. "No harm done?"

"No harm done." I took his hand and squeezed it. "Thanks for babysitting me. I had a good sleep."

"Good." He glanced at the bedside clock. "Well, I'd usually get up in twenty minutes anyway. I'll get dressed and start breakfast." He padded out, closing the door behind him, and I collapsed onto the bed to beat my head against the pillow.

We got through breakfast without too much awkwardness, and by the time we loaded the dishes into the dishwasher, we were back to our usual easy camaraderie.

Tom stretched and moved toward the door. "I have to do some chores, and then we can go over to your place and get started. Why don't you go back to bed for a while? I'll be about an hour, and you can probably use the extra rest."

"Thanks, Tom, but..." I eyed my watch. "I'm sorry,

would you have time to drop me off before you start your chores? I have to go to work this morning and I need a shower and change of clothes. The cleanup can wait 'til tonight."

"If that's what you want." He frowned. "Are you sure you should be going to work today? Can't you take the day off?"

I sank onto the bench with a sigh and reached for my boots. "No. I've got a really important project... with a deadline," I added, hoping I sounded convincing. "I have to go in today."

"Okay."

When we pulled up in front of my house a few minutes later, I reached for Tom's hand. "Thank you. I really appreciate you going to all this trouble for me."

His callused hand tightened on mine. "It's no trouble at all. All I did was give you some food and a bed for the night."

"It was a lot more than that. Thanks." I squeezed his hand and slipped out of the truck before I could do something truly stupid like kissing him.

I turned to plod through the snow toward the garage, and the truck's passenger window hummed down. "Is everything okay?"

"Fine. I'm just going to get my spare key from the garage. Arnie isn't much of a morning person. If he worked late last night, he's probably still sleeping."

"Okay. See you later. Have a good day."

"You, too."

Yeah, right. As his truck churned away through the snow, I pulled my jacket tighter around me and hunched my shoulders against the icy wind. My chances of having a good day were approximately on par with a snowball's chance in...

"What the *hell?*"

I stood in the doorway of my garage, my mouth gaping. A moment later, reality sank in and I closed the door behind me, a grin stretching my face.

"Yes!" I did a fist-pump and happy-danced across the garage to the shiny blue Subaru Legacy parked in the far bay.

Okay, so it wasn't red like the one that had blown up, but the blue was very pretty indeed. I glided a palm over its sleek fender and tried the driver's door. Letting out a hum of satisfaction when it opened, I slid into the driver's seat, delighting in the new-car smell and the well-bred subdued thump of the closing door.

"Mine, mine, mine," I sang, caressing the steering wheel. I blew myself a kiss in the rearview mirror and let out a giggle before reluctantly getting out again.

Just in case my truck's feelings were hurt, I offered it a pat on the fender as I went past. "You're still my favourite truck," I assured it, and went to unearth my hidden key.

All was silent when I let myself into the house. My mop and bucket leaned in the corner, silent guardians of the clean kitchen floor. The remaining undamaged contents of my kitchen were laid out neatly on the table and counters, and a quick inventory made me breathe a sigh of relief. A few plates and mugs had survived, and none of the appliances or cookware seemed to have been damaged.

The living room looked exactly as it had before the break-in, and for a moment I thought it had been spared. But a closer inspection revealed that although everything was in its place, my dead husband's photo had a gash across it and the glass was missing. Other items showed damage, too, and I realized Arnie must have consulted his phenomenal memory to replace everything exactly as it had been the last time he'd visited.

My heart swelled with gratitude and I smiled as I tiptoed down the hall, following the sound of quiet snoring. Peeking into the bedroom, I discovered that his herculean effort hadn't extended that far.

The bed floated like an island amid mounds of my tangled clothes. Hellhound sprawled on his back in the middle of the bed, one muscular tattooed arm flung out across the white sheets like a splash of paint on a clean canvas.

As if some sixth sense had alerted him to my silent presence, he let out an aborted snore and his eyes snapped open.

"Hey, darlin'," he mumbled, his eyelids drooping again as he relaxed. "Mornin' already?"

"Afraid so," I agreed, and picked my way through the chaos to slide into bed beside him.

"Mmm." He wrapped his arms around me and treated me to a kiss that left me breathless. "Missed ya last night."

"I missed you, too. Thanks for all your work. It looks so much better."

"No problem." He grimaced. "Still a helluva lot to go. No wonder ya were upset after walkin' in on this shit."

"Yeah... it wasn't really that, though." I cuddled closer and tucked my head under his chin so he couldn't see my face. "I had... a really bad day yesterday..." My voice trembled into silence, and I took a slow, deep breath to dispel the memory.

His gentle fingertips smoothed my hair away from my cheek. "What happened, darlin'?"

I drew another deep breath and let it out slowly. "I... can't tell you. But it was pretty much my worst nightmare..."

Renewed anger at Stemp displaced my residual fear and stiffened my spine. I leaned up on my elbow to drop a kiss on Arnie's lips. "Anyway, I'm okay now. The bastard probably did me a favour. Now I know I can handle it."

A memory of Doytchevsky's vicious smile made me shudder.

Dammit, I could handle him, too. As long as I kept my promise, Lola would be fine. And Stemp had ordered me to cooperate with Doytchevsky anyway.

Arnie eyed me with concern. "Don't like the sound a' that, Aydan. Are ya really okay? Or are ya just hidin' it like ya always do?"

"I'm okay."

Maybe if I said it firmly enough, I could start believing it, too.

He frowned at me for a moment before speaking again. "What the hell really happened here? What the fuck were the surveillance analysts doin', sittin' around with their thumbs up their asses while these assholes trashed your place?"

I sighed and flopped down beside him again. "The analysts knew I wasn't home, so they didn't scramble right away. When they found out the intruders were from Fuzzy Bunny, Stemp decided to let them finish their search to convince them I didn't have what they were looking for. He thinks they'll leave me alone now."

Hellhound sat up abruptly. "What the fuck, Aydan? They know where ya live, they're breakin' into your place, an' Stemp's doin' fuck-all? He's got his head up his fuckin' ass!"

"No, probably not." I tugged gently on his arm to get

him to lie down again. "He knew they wouldn't find what they were looking for, and it'll make them believe my cover story. It actually makes me safer."

"Bullshit." He scowled down at me for a few moments before succumbing to my pull. He slid an arm around me and cuddled me close. "Ya shouldn't hafta do this shit."

"I don't want to, but I have to."

His arms tightened around me. "Let somebody else do it. Stemp's got lots of other-"

"I'm the only one that can do it."

"Bullshit."

I blew out a long breath. "Unfortunately, it's not. I'm literally the only person in the world who can do it."

Hellhound drew back, studying my face for a long moment. At last, he spoke. "Well, shit."

I made a face. "You can say that again."

He dropped back onto the pillow beside me and we lay in silence for a while before he turned to face me. "How can I help?"

I kissed him. "You've already helped."

"Ya know that ain't what I mean."

"I know. But there really is nothing else you can do besides what you're doing." I kissed him again, longer and slower, before drawing away to smile at him. "And you're very good at what you do."

He grinned and pulled me against him.

"Ya got too many clothes on, darlin'," he mumbled against my lips a few minutes later.

"Very true." I kissed him and made as if to get out of bed. "But I have to go to work. I only came home to shower and change."

His hand wandered up under my top. "Guess that means

ya gotta take your clothes off, then."

"I guess it does."

Somewhat later, I flopped onto my back and stretched luxuriously, still warm and tingling. "This day just keeps getting better. First I find a new car in my garage and then I find you in my bed."

Hellhound leaned up on his elbow to run a hand over my stomach. "I figured you'd be all tuckered out from ridin' a cowboy last night." He followed his hand's path with whisker-kisses that made me twitch and giggle. "What's the matter, couldn't he get his little dogey rounded up?" he rumbled against my belly button.

I reached over and smacked his ass. "Be nice. I didn't give him a chance to try. That cowboy's happy trails are off limits for me."

Hellhound grinned. "Hey, if it gets ya naked with me, it's all good. An' if ya spank me, hell, that's just bonus."

"Pervert." I bounced my eyebrows at him. "If you're a very, very good boy, maybe I'll spank you again."

"Hmm." His growl vibrated my belly as his mouth moved lower. "How good do I hafta be?"

I squirmed regretfully out from under him. "You're already so good I'm going to be late if I don't get out of here in the next twenty minutes." I perched on the edge of the bed, smiling at his smug expression. "What are you going to do today?"

He yawned and stretched, letting me enjoy the flex of his bulky muscles. "Gonna head over an' sit on Kane so he doesn't do anythin' stupid. He's goin' nuts. Gonna need a new punchin' bag by the time this's over. I barely managed to talk him outta followin' ya yesterday."

A chill slithered down my spine. "Thank God you did. Don't let him follow me. No matter what."

Hellhound sat up, his gaze sharpening. "Why not?"

I bit back my urge to pour out the story of Doytchevsky's threats. Kane could help me, but dishonourable discharge and prison was too high a price if he got caught.

"He just needs to stay far away from me. And... just... tell him to watch out. There's somebody out there who wants to harm him. I don't know how far he'll go."

"Tell me who it is."

I sighed. "I can't. Just... if Kane starts interfering, innocent people are going to get hurt. Tell him I said so."

Hellhound swung his legs over the edge of the bed to sit beside me, his arm settling around my shoulders. "What about you?"

"I'm fine."

He turned my chin to face him. "Look me in the eye an' tell me ya ain't in any danger."

"I'm not in any danger that I know of. Tell Kane that, too. Tell him I'm fine, and as long as he doesn't interfere everything will be okay."

Arnie searched my face in silence for a moment before letting out a long breath. "I sure hope ya ain't lyin' to me."

I met his eyes. "I've never lied to you. And I never will."

His smile made his ugly face almost handsome. "Thanks, darlin'."

Another lingering kiss later, I rose reluctantly. "I've got to go. At least it'll be an easy drive this morning in my nice new car. When did it get here?"

"I called Stemp before I came in the house last night. Didn't wanna show up on his cameras without warnin'.

When he found out I was gonna be here, he said he'd send it out. Guess it'd been ready for days but ya ain't been here."

"Thank you so much. For everything." I gave him another quick kiss and pulled away before he could tempt me any further.

CHAPTER 26

My new car's all-wheel drive handled the snowy road with assurance, leaving me time for intense thought. I wanted nothing more than to tell Stemp everything, but Doytchevsky's malevolent smile hovered in my mind's eye.

He had to be bluffing. He wouldn't risk attacking a little old lady. That would attract too much attention, especially in a small town. And holding a captive would make it impossible for him to hunt Sherman.

I swallowed sudden nausea. Which meant he wouldn't leave Lola alive if he did carry out his threat. She would just disappear, never to be seen again...

But surely it was only a threat. He couldn't be so crazy that he'd torture and murder an innocent woman just to get what he wanted...

I unclenched one hand from the steering wheel to turn up the heat against my sudden chill. He had been nurturing his obsession for years. I shuddered, remembering the glitter in his eyes. That was the look of a man who was past the point of reason.

But Stemp was known for instant action. If I told him, he'd take Doytchevsky down before he could ever get to Lola.

My breakfast squirmed uneasily in my stomach. Stemp

was a ruthless bastard. He might risk Lola if he thought it would give him a strategic advantage. What if he decided not to act? And what if Doytchevsky found out I'd reported him?

My mind cowered away from the thought of Lola's impish smile and too-big laugh lost to screams and pleas for mercy.

That wouldn't happen, goddammit. I wouldn't let it happen.

A sudden blinding thought made the breath catch in my throat.

What if I killed Doytchevsky?

Tremors spread up my arms until I was shaking so violently I pulled the car over onto the shoulder and stopped. Staring through the windshield, my mind ricocheted around the possibilities as if trying to escape the inevitable conclusion.

I had a gun.

I could tell Stemp that Doytchevsky had attacked me and I'd killed him in self-defence. Stemp would believe me. No trial. No consequences. Everybody I cared about safe.

The hardness of my gun pressed against my waist like some alien creature intent on invading my body.

Simply kill a man in cold blood, and this could all be over.

Decree a death sentence just like Stemp. Plan and carry out a murder just like Kane.

For the safety of others.

I gulped down rising bile, clinging to the stability of the steering wheel. Could I do it? Walk up to him and just... pull the trigger?

My churning gut answered the question. Not in cold blood. I would shoot without hesitation if he attacked me or if he was harming another person, but I wasn't a murderer.

Not yet.

I leaned my forehead against the steering wheel. What made that tiny switch click inside a person's brain? When had Kane become capable of killing a man like my husband without confronting him, without any direct personal threat? What made him able to dispassionately execute someone for the sake of the 'greater good', whatever that meant?

Was that stone-cold killer lurking inside me, too?

Unwilling to even think about the answer, I jammed the car into gear again.

I was being silly. If anybody could keep a secret, it was Stemp. Doytchevsky would never know I'd ratted on him. Everything would be fine. I'd tell Stemp, he'd arrest Doytchevsky, and Lola would be safe.

And even if Stemp didn't act, pinpointing Sherman's location was the next-best option. Play along and give Doytchevsky what he wanted. I could do that. No bloodshed required.

I spent the rest of the short drive planning my strategy and trying to ignore the insistent pressure of my waist holster.

Stemp laced his fingers together, leaning back in his chair. "No. I'm sorry."

I held my temper in check with all my might and tried again. "But he threatened her. That's illegal."

"I thought I had made my position clear." Stemp's flat tone sounded Lola's doom. "National security is and has to remain my top priority. While I sympathize with your concern for your friend, arresting Doytchevsky on such a minor charge would be a waste of our setup. We'll go forward with our original plan. Your friend will be safe because you'll be ostensibly cooperating with Doytchevsky." He rose. "You have your orders. The rest of the team is waiting."

Clamping down on the need to yell and pound my fist on his desk, I rose, too, blocking his way. "If anything happens to Lola..."

"I see no reason why anything should as long as you carry out your mission." He stepped around me without a change of expression. "Let's go."

I strode toward my office, ignoring Stemp beside me and trying to arrange my face into something approaching normalcy.

I might as well have saved myself the effort. When I turned the corner into my office, the sight of Doytchevsky made my lips draw back in an instinctive snarl. I groaned and dropped my head to massage my temples, hoping nobody had noticed.

"Do you have a headache?" Jack inquired. "Would you like some ibuprofen? I have some in my purse."

"Thanks, Jack, I've got some of my own." I managed a smile as I sank onto my small sofa. "And I hope it won't be a long session today anyway. I have an idea."

"Good, because I couldn't match up any car rental records," Spider said. The despondent note in his usually chipper voice made me give him another look.

"Are you okay, Spider?" I studied him with concern.

"Yeah." He didn't meet my eyes. "I'm just tired because I'm moving back into my house. It's a lot of work."

"Your house is finally ready! It must be great to get back into it after all this time."

Jack looked confused, and I elaborated. "Spider's house burned down this past summer." I didn't add that we'd both almost burned with it.

"Yeah, the house is great," Spider mumbled. "What's your idea?"

I hesitated, worry nagging at me. Something was very wrong in Spider's world. But now wasn't the time or place to find out what it was. I blew out a breath.

"Stalking Sherman in the network is risky. Every time we connect, there's a chance I won't be able to hide my presence. And even if I can get an IP address, it doesn't help us if they're on the other side of the country."

"I presume you have a solution besides aimless whining," Doytchevsky interrupted.

Asshole.

"Yes." I smothered my irritation and carried on. "Sherman faked his death because he was afraid the other Knights would retaliate after he warned Sam about their betrayal. So he's been lying low and avoiding the Knights' internal communication system. But now he knows all the other Knights are dead. Maybe he'll feel safe enough to try to contact Sam through their old system."

I focused my eyes midway between Stemp and Doytchevsky, hoping my animosity wasn't too visible. "I think it's time for Sam to leave a message."

Stemp nodded slowly. "That could work. Can you fake the message?"

"I think so. But that would mean we'd have to admit... well, 'Sam' would have to admit that he knew Sherman had faked his death."

"And Kraus would only have that knowledge if he'd encountered them in the network." Stemp completed my thought. "But you said you had hidden all trace of your contact."

"Yeah." I slouched against the cushions. "So I guess I could say... well, 'Sam' could say he'd found a way to shield my mind."

"That could work," Doytchevsky said. "Sherman will want to know how Kraus did it. We can reel him in by offering to exchange technology. Trade their wireless network generator for Kraus's shielding technique."

Stemp nodded. "Very well. Kelly, whenever you're ready."

This time I managed to project myself into virtual reality without swords or dragons. When Stemp's avatar appeared beside me, I turned and strode down the virtual hallway to my familiar file repository. Inside, I sat and took his hand, vanishing into the internet before I could let my revulsion show.

It took me a while to find the Knights' secret communication system, hidden within its shell-game of shifting IP addresses. Floating outside their firewall at last, I summoned my courage, wishing my current form was capable of taking a few deep calming breaths.

Gathering myself, I dove for the firewall.

And missed.

The maelstrom ripped me into millions of data bits tumbling helplessly in the vicious undertow. Flinging panicky tendrils of myself in all directions, I managed to gain enough of a grip to pull myself free.

Bit by bit, I extricated and reassembled myself, trying to ignore the terrified pounding of a heart I didn't even possess. Huddling into my consciousness, I hovered in the data flow outside the firewall.

The anchor of Stemp's presence was long gone, and I bit down on panic. Spider and Jack would know what was happening. They would remember from last time. Spider would find a way to call me home. I wasn't lost.

I'd be fine.

Calming the frantic oscillation of my data bits, I regrouped. I had done this before. I could do it again. Nothing bad would happen.

Just keep believing that.

I turned to face the firewall again, its deceptively benign presence mocking me.

Body-surfing. Think about body-surfing.

Before I could chicken out, I flung myself forward again.

The serenity of the data flow inside their firewall was so blessedly welcome I would have emitted a sob of relief if I'd had a voice. Drawing my consciousness together, I floated for several moments in the placid currents, recovering.

When I had regained a semblance of calm, I turned my invisible presence toward their messaging system. Preoccupied with composing my lure, I jerked to a halt when I realized it already held a message.

From Sherman. For Sam.

If I had been capable of grinning, I would have. I left a short reply and turned for home.

I surged through their firewall and floated uncertainly at the edge of the internet's vastness, feeling very small. Afraid to venture too far without an anchor, I hitched my consciousness to the firewall's IP and stretched outward. Sniffing down tunnels in search of a familiar trail, I cursed the constantly-shifting connections and withdrew to the comparative safety of the firewall.

Its IP address changed beneath me. Goddammit, now I

had to figure out where I was again. And even if I knew where I was, I didn't know if I could find the Sirius servers, concealed even more effectively than the Knights' system.

After several more fruitless forays into the maze of connections, the fear that had been nibbling the edges of my consciousness developed larger, sharper teeth. I pulled my consciousness closer, fending off panic.

Surely Spider would be searching for me by now. But what would he be searching for?

Stretching into the public tunnels again, I sniffed for 'Aydan Kelly', but found no welcome stream of searches. Besides, Spider wouldn't use my real name.

Why the hell hadn't I remembered this would happen? I should have arranged everything with Spider in advance. Dammit, I should have known better.

I diverted my mind from useless recriminations. Just focus. The last time we'd tried this, we had agreed on camels as a search term.

Come on, Spider, talk to me.

Far too damn many people searched for camels on the internet. Clinging to calm, I began the painstaking task of following up each data request.

At last, almost at the limit of my perception, a stream of data packets whizzed by. Camels.

Then another. Camels.

Relief swelling in my heart, I relinquished my hold on the Knights' server and dove into the data flow, following the camel trail home.

When I materialized in the virtual file repository inside Sirius's network, Stemp greeted me expressionlessly. "Welcome back, Kelly."

I tried to hold onto my hatred for him, but my smile of

relief and triumph broke through despite me. "Thanks." I turned and hurried for the portal.

Back in the reality of my office, I ground out some perfunctory profanity until the pain receded from my head. As soon as I could focus my eyes again, I straightened, unable to suppress my grin.

"Thanks for the camels, Spider."

"No problem."

Slightly dampened by his monotone response, I turned to Stemp. "Sherman beat us to it. He's already trying to contact Sam."

"What did he say?"

"He just said 'Are you safe? Can we meet?' So I told him I'm fine and asked him when and where."

"Idiot!" Doytchevsky exploded. Everyone stared at him, and he quickly converted his enraged expression to haughty disdain. "Everybody knows you don't let him choose the location. You want to maintain control of the situation on your own turf."

Heat climbed my cheeks and I bit down a rude retort. He was a jerk, but he was also right, goddammit.

"Well, it's a start." I rose, holding my temper firmly in check. "I'm going to grab a snack, and then I'll go back and check for an answer in a little while. Maybe I can suggest a location then."

The others stood, too, and began to move toward the door.

Stemp's voice stopped me. "Kelly, we need to discuss your travel expenses."

I turned to face his impassive façade with distaste. "It's hardly worth it, is it?"

"I beg to differ. While I appreciate your dedication to

your cover..." I could have sworn I detected a sour tilt to his mouth, but he kept talking and I couldn't be sure. "...this department does not have an unlimited budget. In the future, clear your expenses with me before proceeding."

All my hostility came rushing back. My lingering humiliation and pounding headache did nothing to mitigate it.

"Fuck, you've got to be kidding me! I buy one lousy hamburger, and I do mean *lousy*, a piece of pizza, a roll of tape and a newspaper, and you're climbing up my ass for expenses?"

Oops.

Probably shouldn't have blurted that out in front of an audience. Spider and Jack and Doytchevsky stood bunched near the doorway, watching avidly.

Stemp stiffened. "And new clothing and shoes and fine dining and a penthouse suite and sex shows and VIP tickets to male strippers and your latest *videos*..." He infused the word with biting contempt.

I stood gaping at him. "What... the... What the hell are you talking about?"

His eyes narrowed. "Don't insult my intelligence. It's all over the internet."

My knees decided to take a vacation and I dropped onto the sofa. "Oh, God. Please don't tell me..."

I trailed off at the flash of fierce exultation in Doytchevsky's face. An instant later it vanished behind his usual bland expression, but I realized the horrible truth.

I dragged my gaze up to Stemp's implacable face. "Show me."

CHAPTER 27

Too soon, I realized the full extent of my own stupidity. Nothing like setting myself up to watch porn with my boss and co-workers. Particularly when the porn starred me.

It started innocuously enough, with some news blurbs about Arlene Cherry in Las Vegas. There were a few photos of Lola, Nichele, and me coming out of the penthouse elevators in our dresses and high heels, including an unfortunate picture of my ass as I scrambled into the limo. Luckily the blue dress covered the subject. But just.

Another shot showed me fleeing the trade show, the mostly-naked men posing and smiling in the background.

Then the video footage started. My mouth dropped open.

A few minutes later, my face was hot enough to singe my eyebrows. Spider stared at the ceiling, blushing so furiously his face was almost purple. Jack turned away to fiddle in her purse, Doytchevsky grinned, and Stemp remained utterly deadpan.

"Turn it off!" I recoiled from the screen of Spider's laptop. "That's fucking disgusting."

"Well, it's definitely fu-" Doytchevsky cut off his snide comment as I whirled, my fist clenching on the need to punch that smile off his face and right down his throat.

I controlled myself with an effort and turned to Stemp, willing the hot blood away from my cheeks. "I didn't do any of that! I did do a pole-dancing class..."

For which I intended to smack either Nichele or myself; maybe both...

"...But I had all my clothes on. The dress and shoes were borrowed, my friend paid for the meals and the penthouse and the Chippendales, I had a free ticket to the trade show, and I absolutely did not do anything even *remotely* like that with that Chippendales guy!"

I faced Stemp with all the poise I could muster. "You don't seriously think I could do that in a public place without getting arrested, do you?"

"What happens in Vegas stays in Vegas," Doytchevsky murmured.

"Shut *up*, you prick! You-"

Stemp interrupted before I could really get going. "How do you explain it, then?"

I shot Doytchevsky a venomous look. "Obviously somebody was following me around with a camera and they altered the video afterward. God knows there's enough Arlene Cherry crap already out there, they could have faked this easily enough." A thought struck me. "And a couple of the women in that class hardly had any clothes on to start with. All they'd have to do was transplant my face onto one of them and edit out their underwear..."

I stood and wrapped the remaining shreds of my dignity around me. "Anyway, it doesn't matter. I didn't do any of that shit, and my total expenses come to about twenty bucks. So bite me."

I strode for the door, keeping my back straight, chin

high.

Stemp spoiled my not-so-grand exit. "In my office, Kelly."

I blew out a sigh and trudged down the hallway.

With his door closed safely behind us, Stemp and I faced each other in silence. I tensed when his hand dipped into his desk drawer, but he was only extracting one of Sirius's portable bug detectors. He systematically scanned his entire office before speaking.

"Doytchevsky?"

I grimaced. "Probably. He was following me around with his camera, and he has the computer skills to fake the video. And I don't know who else would do that."

"Why would he?"

"I haven't a clue. It's a hell of a lot of effort if all he wanted to do was piss me off. And he didn't try to manipulate me with it. I didn't even know he'd done it until you told me." I tried not to look too accusing. "How did you find it?"

He eyed me as if debating whether to take offense at my implication that he spent his days surfing the net for porn. When he spoke, his voice was as emotionless as ever.

"Webb's facial recognition algorithm flagged it."

I winced. "Poor Spider."

A hint of humour tugged briefly at the corner of Stemp's mouth. "Perhaps I should assign one of the other analysts to that duty."

"No thanks. I don't want anybody else looking at that shit. At least I know Spider isn't getting off on it."

One of these days I'd kill Stemp for this porn-star cover. Put a richly-deserved bullet right between his eyes...

Or not. I quickly modified the thought. After my

revelation in the car, the idea of shooting someone in cold blood made my skin crawl. Okay, fine, I wouldn't really kill him, but I'd make him suffer...

"...what?" I refocused when I realized he'd spoken.

"I said this works well. Free reinforcement for your cover identity."

I scowled. "Excuse me if I don't do a dance of joy."

"You're excused. And by the way, thank you for keeping your expenses down." Stemp surveyed me across the desk. "You do realize we expect an agent to expense three reasonably-priced meals per day. It's not necessary to starve yourself."

Christ, I couldn't get used to him flip-flopping between a human being and a total asshole.

"Fine, then I'll bill you for the french fries, too," I retorted.

He actually laughed.

A moment later, his impersonal mask descended again. "Why didn't you specify a location to Sherman?"

"I didn't think of it." I dropped my gaze to study the telephone squatting in solitary splendour on his barren desk. When he made no comment, irritation prickled my already-smarting ego. "I'm just a bookkeeper, for shit's sake. I didn't know any better."

"Ah. Yes."

His dry tone jerked my gaze up to search his face for derision, but his expression was as impenetrable as always. He changed the subject.

"Doytchevsky's foray into X-rated video concerns me. If he has an agent's background, he could be a considerable threat as a sexual predator. Has he said or done anything to make you think you might be a target?"

"No." I grimaced. "I'm pretty sure he hates my guts. I seriously doubt he's forming any unhealthy attachments."

Stemp eyed me in silence for a moment. "I wasn't talking about attraction. If he hates you enough to act on it, sexual violence is an easy way to make you suffer."

I swallowed my instinctive surge of fear. "Thanks for reminding me."

When I emerged into the hall, Spider detached himself from the doorway of the lunchroom as if he'd been waiting for me.

"Hey, Aydan, I'm going over to the Melted Spoon. Do you want to walk with me?" His voice still held a minor key, and I hurried to accept the invitation, renewed worry tightening my throat.

A few minutes later we were picking our way along the icy sidewalk. I spared a glance away from my footing to peer up at his lanky six-foot-two.

"Spider, what's wrong?"

"I, um... I heard some stuff..." He hesitated, and my heart sank.

"What kind of stuff?"

"About... um, about Kane. And you."

"What did you hear?"

He stopped and turned to face me, his hazel eyes dark with unhappiness. "I heard he, um..." He blushed. "...Sexually assaulted you and now he's being court-martialled and he'll go to jail." His words tumbled out. "Aydan, is it true? All the rumours say that's what it is."

"Spider..."

I hesitated, wondering how much to tell him, and his lips

quivered. My heart twisting, I stared up at his miserable countenance. He practically worshipped Kane. Hell, just about everybody did. And Kane was worthy of their respect and admiration, dammit.

"But... I thought he... I thought you liked each other..." Spider sounded like a lost child.

Sympathy overwhelmed my good sense. "It's not true, Spider. Kane and I are on a mission and we have to pretend that's what's happening, but it's not true. Kane would never do that."

He flung his bony arms around me. "Oh thank God, Aydan! I couldn't believe it, but..."

I patted his back. "I'm glad you didn't believe it. But don't tell anybody, okay? I mean nobody."

He drew away, blinking. "But it would be okay if I told Linda, right? I already talked to her about it..."

"No, Spider!" I clutched his arm, already regretting my indiscretion. "Nobody."

God, I sucked at this spy stuff. A real spy would have kept her mouth shut and watched his heart break with the belief that his hero was a coward and a criminal.

No, dammit, I couldn't do that. And anyway, it was too late.

"Promise me, Spider!" I shook his arm. "Don't tell anybody!"

He stared down at me, wide-eyed. "Okay... But, Aydan..."

"No buts. If anybody asks, tell them you asked me and I said I couldn't talk about it, but you thought I acted as if the rumour was true. If anybody else finds out, innocent people will die. Promise me!"

He straightened, squaring his skinny shoulders. "I

promise."

Spider and I were the last ones to trail back into my office. Stemp and Doytchevsky were already seated to the left and right of the sofa like a pair of particularly unprepossessing bookends, and I took my place in the middle.

Jack looked up from her small case and gestured with its headband of trailing wires. "I want to monitor your brainwaves when you go in this time."

"Okay…" I raised a questioning eyebrow in her direction. "But you know I'll probably flatline when I get into the Knight's system, right? Don't freak out this time."

A flush stained her cheeks. "I won't. It was… just such a shock the first time you did it. I've been studying the records from your earlier sessions, and I've tweaked my instrumentation. I want to see if I can detect some brain activity even after you've… left. It will give us a better idea of whether you're actually in trouble or just experiencing a normal… well, normal for you… disconnect."

I laughed. "I'm glad you don't actually expect me to be normal. There's not much hope of that."

She chuckled, too, as she placed the wires on my head. "There's no such thing as 'normal', really. We're all just points along a continuum."

"And some of us are farther out than others," Spider teased.

I stuck out my tongue at him, and the return of his usual mischievous grin warmed my heart.

Inside the virtual file repository, I materialized a couple of chairs and sank into one of them, reaching for Stemp's hand with resignation.

"An anchor doesn't really work for this, does it?" he asked.

"Not really. When I get jumbled in the Knights' firewall, I can't hold on anyway."

"Can I come in and anchor you there?"

"I doubt if it's even possible." I raised my voice, even though I knew the rest of the team could hear us just fine through the interface. "Kasper, is it possible?"

"How would I know?" His nasal voice set my teeth on edge.

"You're supposed to be the damn expert here..."

Stemp's grip tightened on my hand, and I clenched my teeth to prevent myself from saying something I might regret. I turned to face Stemp. "Even if you could follow me into the internet, you wouldn't be invisible."

"True, but would it matter as long as we were outside the Knights' firewall?"

"No... probably not... Spider?" I appealed to the virtual ceiling.

"Even if it's actually possible, it would be a really bad idea," he said promptly. "In the first place, it leaves both of you without an anchor here. In the second place, Aydan doesn't always know what connections she's passing through. You could get stopped or separated by firewalls or intrusion detection software. There's no telling how that could harm anybody other than Aydan. Don't even try it."

I blew out a breath. "Okay, then. I'll be looking for camels on my way back."

I faded into invisibility and dove into the data stream.

CHAPTER 28

This time, the Knights' server was even harder to find. I cast about through endless data tunnels, frustration building. Occasionally I caught a whiff of something that might have been it, only to lose the scent when the IP addresses shifted again.

At long last, I ferreted it out. Floating outside their firewall, I felt Stemp's distant anchor only as a tenuous shred of connection. God, how far away was I? What if I couldn't detect Spider's homing beacon when I came out?

Fear closed in, disrupting the ordered data of my consciousness. Clinging to my courage, I faced the firewall. I had to do this. Somehow, I'd get home.

I made it through on my first try, surging invisibly into their network. Sherman had left a reply, but I didn't like the look of the message. Concentrating fiercely, I memorized its cryptic contents.

Please let me retain it. I floated, repeating it to myself again. Damn, it must be nice to be Hellhound, with his effortlessly accurate memory.

I steeled myself and slipped back through their firewall into the internet, refusing to panic at the trackless complexity. Just stay calm and look for camels.

When a string of camel searches erupted practically in my face, I jerked back. No way that could be Spider. Probably some little kid doing a school report or something.

But the search terms were so repetitive. Could it be...?

No way. It couldn't be that easy.

It was. Seconds later, I materialized in Sirius's file repository.

Stemp rose, looking surprised. "That was quick."

"Yeah." I couldn't hold back a grin. "When I went in, the IP felt like it was on the other side of the world, but it must have shifted while I was inside their network. It dumped me out practically next door." I turned for the exit portal. "Let's get out of here."

The instant I straightened in the reality of my office clutching my thundering skull, Doytchevsky's voice bored into my brain. "Did you get it?"

"Yes." The word ground out between my gritted teeth, and I massaged my temples, desperately missing Kane's strong hands.

"Well, what is it?"

"Just shut *up* for a minute, would you?" I hissed. "Goddammit..." I thumped my head against the back of the sofa, trying to release the knotted muscles at the base of my skull.

"Don't! Aydan, please don't!" Spider's pleading voice was accompanied by the clasp of his hands around my head, his skinny fingers more tentative than Kane's firm touch, but welcome nonetheless.

I groaned and dropped my head forward, stretching my neck. "Thanks, Spider."

I sat up at last, rubbing my forehead. "Sherman replied, but he's using some kind of code. His message was..." I hesitated, making sure I had it right. "...Office, 2455874.187500, RXM, 634257."

"That's useless! Why didn't you decrypt it?" Doytchevsky demanded.

I held back the urge to snarl. "That *is* the decrypted version."

"Well, it's no damn good. You should have-"

Stemp raised a silencing hand. He shot a glance at Spider, whose fingers were flying over his keyboard. "Webb?"

"Let me make sure I got it right." Spider read back the numbers and letters.

"That's it." I rolled my shoulders, cracking my neck. "For all the good it does."

"It might be better than you think." He studied his screen with the bright-eyed enthusiasm he always exhibited when confronted by a technological puzzle. "Hang on."

After a few moments of rapid typing, he surfaced again with a smile. "Well, 'office' is easy enough. It probably means exactly what it says. And I think the first number is just a Julian date."

"A what?"

"It's an alternate calendar system to the Gregorian calendar we use today. Lots of programmers use it. It's just a continuous count of days and fractions since noon Universal Time on January 1, 4713 BCE-"

"Never mind that," Stemp interrupted. "Can you convert the date?"

Spider looked slightly crestfallen. "I already did. It's tomorrow at four-thirty in the afternoon."

"Good. What about the rest?"

Spider hunched his shoulders, frowning at his screen.

"That might be a problem. If Aydan couldn't decrypt it, it's probably a cipher with a cryptovariable that we don't have. They're likely using a codebook of words or phrases that correspond to letters or numbers. We could start crunching it through our system, but it would take forever."

"We don't have forever. We need it before tomorrow." Doytchevsky glowered at me. "Idiot. If you had just told him a time and place, we'd be fine. Now we can't do anything without giving ourselves away because Kraus would know the code."

"And if I'd specified a meeting without using their code, Sherman would've known right away I wasn't Sam and vanished forever," I snapped.

I turned to Stemp. "Let me talk to Sam. He never did actually commit treason, and I think he regrets the way things turned out. I bet he'll help us."

Stemp fixed me with his reptilian gaze. "He undoubtedly regrets the way things turned out. Being incarcerated tends to have that effect. And the only reason he didn't commit treason was because he lacked the opportunity."

I shrugged, still wanting to believe in Sam despite the small cynical voice in my head that agreed with Stemp. "Regardless of his motivation, he'll likely cooperate if he thinks it'll help him."

"True." Stemp considered in silence for a moment. "I'll talk to him. If he gives me the right answers, we'll be able to put a team in place and take Sherman without any difficulty. Well done, Kelly."

He rose, glancing at his watch. "You'll be visiting your bookkeeping clients today, won't you?" At my nod, he addressed all of us. "Briefing at fifteen-thirty when Kelly returns."

Stemp strode out and I heaved myself to my feet, avoiding Doytchevsky's scowl. He didn't accost me, though, and I hurried out of the building, not sure whether to feel relieved or worried.

I keyed open the back door of Blue Eddy's Saloon and slipped inside. A voluptuous cascade of piano music curled around me and I released a breath that felt like I'd been holding it for days.

Dawdling toward the source of the sound, I let the music soak into my skin, washing away the ugliness and fear of the past week. By the time I poked my head into the bar, I was actually capable of giving Eddy a real, honest-to-goodness smile.

"Hi, Aydan!" His grin lit up the empty room while his clever fingers poured out music as if they required no input from his brain at all.

"Hi, Eddy." I strolled over to perch in my favourite spot on the corner of the stage, leaning against the wall. "If I sit here for the next ten years or so, will you just keep playing?"

He laughed. "Sure, no problem. As long as I get a beer break every now and then." The music continued, never a false note. He gave me one of his semi-serious looks, eyes twinkling. "I missed you last week."

"Thanks. I missed you, too."

He shot me a grin. "You only missed my piano-playing."

I feigned indignation. "That's not true. I missed your burgers, too. And your beer."

He chuckled.

I rose and added, "You know you're the bright spot of my week. But I guess I'd better stop goofing off and make up for lost time."

He sobered, the music trailing off. "Hey, Aydan, I wasn't complaining. I know how busy you are, and I'm happy with any time you can give me. You're doing a great job with my books."

I resisted the urge to hug him. "Thanks, Eddy. I really needed to hear that today." I planted my hands on my hips and gave him a mock glare. "Now get those hands back on that piano and get to work. You've only got half an hour before the bar opens."

He grinned. "Yes, ma'am." The rollicking notes burst free again, and I let them dance me into his cramped office.

An hour and a half later I emerged, my good humour restored by excellent blues music and the safe, predictable world of bookkeeping. My spirits rose even further when Eddy waved from behind the bar and pointed to my usual table in the corner. A platter reposed in the centre, wisps of steam still rising from the hand-cut fries and enormous burger.

I wandered over and sank into the chair, smiling. Eddy would probably refuse payment, concocting his usual story about food ordered by a customer who later changed his mind. His friendship and generosity were doubly sweet after my miserable morning.

I slouched happily in the chair and applied myself to the delicious food, letting the blues lull me into pure contentment. Eddy raised a beer bottle and an interrogative eyebrow in my direction but I shook my head regretfully, miming hands on a steering wheel. He grimaced understanding and turned to serve another customer.

I was just returning my attention to my plate when a middle-aged man in a suit and tie caught my attention, moving purposefully toward me. Something about him looked vaguely familiar, but a rapid perusal of my mental files came up empty.

He smiled and raised a hand in greeting as he approached, and I gave him a tentative smile in return, wishing once again that I had Hellhound's photographic memory.

Shit, how did I know this guy?

He slid into the chair opposite me and offered his hand. "Hello, Ms. Widdenback."

"Uh... hi." I shook his hand, hiding my alarm in a smile.

Everybody in Silverside knew me as Aydan Kelly. My so-called fans called me Arlene Cherry. Who the hell was he?

"I'm sorry, but I don't remember your name," I prompted.

"You can call me Paul."

Paul. Why did that ring a bell? But not a very loud one, dammit. Who the hell...

He smiled. "I'm not surprised you don't remember me. I'm sure you must have spoken to hundreds of fans in Vegas."

"Oh!" I tried to cover my dismay with an expression of enlightened recognition. "You were the man in the hall outside my room. How did you find me?" I tried to make it sound like an expression of casual interest, but I was pretty sure my chagrin leaked through.

Shit. Like it wasn't bad enough to have to deal with horny fans; now I had a creepy stalker into the bargain. His cowed expression in Vegas had obviously been an act. Now he radiated assurance.

Marvelous. Just what I needed. A *confident* creepy stalker.

He smiled as if reading my mind. "Don't worry, I'm not stalking you."

Before I could respond to that conversational gambit, he spoke again. "I completely understand your desire to maintain a low profile, and you've certainly been successful. Everyone in this town seems to know you as Aydan Kelly."

Shit!

I rose. "Paul, I'm afraid I'll have to cut this short. I have a meeting."

"Hear me out, please."

Had he intentionally twitched aside his suit coat to reveal that shoulder holster concealed beneath? I shot a glance around the bar, adrenaline surging.

Not packed, but the usual lunch patrons were scattered here and there. Eddy was in the most danger, closest to my table with his back turned while he joked with a couple of the regulars.

I had to get the hell out. If it turned into a shooting match, there would be fewer innocent targets outside in the snow and cold.

"Let's talk outside." I turned and walked away, the hairs on the back of my neck bristling with the expectation of an attack.

CHAPTER 29

The attack didn't come. I slipped out the back door unscathed, letting out a breath at the sight of the few cars in the deserted parking lot. No passersby at all, thank goodness.

I leaned one shoulder against the building, my hand resting casually on my hip as close as possible to my holster, my fingers buried in my sweatshirt to hide their trembling. 'Paul' leaned against the building as well, facing me with his arms crossed over his chest. That placed his hand close to his holster, too.

But he probably didn't know about my gun, tucked away under my baggy sweatshirt. Maybe he'd be lulled into carelessness...

"What did you want to talk about?" I held my voice level, my tone polite.

"I'd like to talk to you about Aydan Kelly."

I put on an expression of regret. "That was a terrible accident. So sad."

"Yes." His lips twisted into an ugly little smile. "How did you arrange it?"

I didn't have to fake my astonishment. "What? I didn't arrange it. It was an accident."

"And her home and assets were coincidentally transferred into your name. And you coincidentally took her name and her clients."

"Um... No, it wasn't like that at all..." Another burst of adrenaline threatened to redline my heart rate. I flung out the first idea that came to mind.

"Aydan and I were business partners. Um... friends. Almost like sisters. We even looked alike. We used to play tricks on people all the time when we were younger..."

My mouth ran on while my brain churned furiously through wild and ridiculous excuses. "She transferred everything over to me because... um..."

I seized with relief on a cover story I'd used before Arlene Cherry. "...because her crazy ex-husband was stalking her. We put everything in my name so he couldn't find her, but then she died..."

I trailed off at the sight of his cynical smile.

"I bet he killed her!" I exclaimed, frantically grasping for something, anything plausible.

How convincing did I have to be? Who the hell was this guy, anyway?

"Are you a cop?" I blurted.

"No."

Damn. Police would have been embarrassing but easily handled by a short conversation with Stemp.

Not-police meant I was in deep shit.

"But you wouldn't have any reason to worry about talking to a cop, would you?" he asked silkily. "Because you haven't done anything wrong, have you?"

I tossed my head, hoping I looked like a defiant-but-guilty petty fraud artist. "Of course I haven't. I'm just taking care of Aydan's affairs. It's the least I can do in her memory."

Paul laughed. "How touching. How did you manage to dodge the investigation? Surely the police asked some embarrassing questions when they discovered such a..." he coughed politely. "...*timely* transfer of assets."

I let my gaze drift down to my toes. "They couldn't pin anything on me," I muttered. "Her car didn't show any signs of tampering. And there's no law against putting all your money in a friend's name. And it's not my fault all these hicks keep calling me Aydan."

"But you wouldn't want anyone to tell them otherwise, would you?"

I glared at him. "I don't give a shit. Everybody around here has heard the story about how some sleazy reporter mistook Aydan Kelly for Arlene Cherry. Everybody in this stupid little backwater town will swear I'm Aydan." I tossed my head again. "They love me. They'll never believe I'm Arlene Cherry."

"Except for the fact that they all went to Aydan Kelly's funeral. Because she was really dead. Killed in a car crash."

My mouth went dry. "Um... well, funny you should mention that... um... it was kind of funny the way it happened..."

His hard little smile was back. "Is that so? I enjoy funny stories. Do tell."

God, I couldn't remember which side of my cover I was on. Aydan Kelly pretending to be Arlene Widdenback pretending to be Aydan Kelly, but actually trying to convince him I was Arlene Widdenback the fraud artist...

I lobbed a silent prayer skyward and started babbling.

"Well, they kind of might've gotten the idea that Aydan didn't really die in the car crash. That somebody stole her car and crashed it and by the time they realized it wasn't really her who had died, her funeral was already over. So everybody was really happy to have me back. Um, I mean..."

Shit, did I just tell him the truth? Idiot, *idiot!*

"I mean, um, I didn't have the heart to tell them I wasn't Aydan because they were so upset when she died. So when people started recognizing me, I just let them... You know, because I love these people and I'd never want to hurt them..."

"Despite the fact that they're all hicks in this stupid little backwater town." His eyes glinted amusement.

"No, no, of course I didn't mean that, I was just joking, I love everybody here..." I mumbled, hoping I looked like a woman backpedalling frantically to save her own ass.

Hell, I *was* a woman backpedalling frantically to save her own ass.

This time Paul's smile looked genuine. And interested. "You've set up a very cozy little game here. I'm impressed. My organization may have some... opportunities for a woman of your talent."

"I'm not looking for any opportunities at the moment. I'm very busy. Thanks anyway." I straightened, easing my weight off the foot that was slowly falling asleep under my apparently casual posture. "Well, it's been nice talking to you, Paul. I hope you have a nice trip back to wherever you came from."

"Oh, I'm not going just yet." That nasty little smile was back. "I notice you spend quite a bit of time at Sirius Dynamics."

A hard, cold lump formed in my belly and I stared at him, shivering in the icy breeze. Christ, he'd been following me for who-knows-how-long. At least since Vegas. He probably knew where I lived, too.

And he had made the connection between Arlene Widdenback and Aydan Kelly. Just like the two fake cops from Fuzzy Bunny.

Electric fear jolted through my body.

Oh, God. They'd found me.

The horrible death I'd imagined for Lola would be mine instead. Only much slower and much more painful. And the torture wouldn't end until I told them everything they wanted...

"Do you suppose Sirius Dynamics would be interested to discover you're not really Aydan Kelly?"

His question nearly made my shaking legs collapse with relief. He believed my cover story. He thought he was threatening a small-time con artist.

Drawing a modicum of strength from the knowledge, I threw myself into my part with a sullen glare, my mind winding up to maximum RPM.

I had to keep him thinking I was Arlene Widdenback. But he'd never believe I could fool Sirius's security.

I said the only plausible thing. "They already know, so stick it."

He laughed. "You don't seriously expect me to believe they know you committed fraud and they let you keep working there in Ms. Kelly's place."

I shrugged. "They're weird. I went in to... um... help with Aydan's work load... after, um..."

"After you assumed her identity and were welcomed with open arms by the rest of the town," he prompted helpfully.

I shot him another surly look. "Whatever. Anyway, they have some kind of fancy security system, so they nailed me right away. They yelled a bit, but then they shut up and asked if I wanted to work for them."

I pasted on a sneer. "Stupid hicks in a stupid little town. You should see what they're paying me. And for doing nothing. I sit around surfing the net all day and they throw money at me."

Which was actually kind of true when I thought about it...

"Why?"

I snorted. "Who gives a shit? They're paying me for nothing. Duh."

His brow creased into a calculating frown. "Oh, I'm sure they're not paying you for nothing. Did they tell you not to use Aydan Kelly's name?"

A tendril of triumph warmed my blood. He was buying it. Just go easy now. Give him a reason to believe...

"No, I can do whatever I want. They're keeping their mouths shut." I let my mouth twist into a sardonic smile. "One of the higher-ups *likes* me. I keep him happy, and he looks out for me."

"Is that so?" The hint of contempt in his tone told me I had him. His next words confirmed it. "You do realize they're paying you to impersonate Aydan Kelly. Setting you up as a target. If nobody else kills you in the interim, you'll probably have an unfortunate accident as soon as they're done using you."

I tossed my hair back. "How stupid do you think I am? Of course I have an insurance policy."

He leaned closer. "And what might that be?"

"That would be none of your business. Goodbye." I pushed past him toward the door.

"How does ten thousand dollars sound?"

I turned slowly to face him. He studied me with the eyes

of a man accustomed to purchasing souls, balancing avarice against cash on the scales of damnation.

I didn't know a thing about the going rate for criminal activities, but I was pretty sure he wouldn't lay out his top offer first.

I barked a short laugh. "Get real. Ten grand isn't even enough to buy you my used toilet paper. Throw me a hundred and I *might* bother to ask what you want."

He smiled, obviously unsurprised. "I see you're a woman of principle. Fifty is the most my organization is willing to pay."

Yikes. Whatever it was they wanted, they wanted it badly. And if his 'organization' was Fuzzy Bunny, I really needed to know what they were after.

I tried to look like a cheap, greedy crook who was trying not to look cheap and greedy. "Pay for what, exactly?"

"A certain item we believe Aydan Kelly had in her possession before she died."

"What item?"

"Do we have a deal?"

I gave him a pitying smile. "Hardly. You tell me what it is, and then I'll decide whether it's worth my time to look for it or not."

He returned my smile with one that might have looked pleasant if not for the hardness in his eyes. "You decide if you'd like fifty thousand dollars. If so, we'll talk." He extracted a gold case from his pocket and handed me a business card. "Don't wait too long."

He turned and strode away.

I slumped against the building for a few moments before tottering back inside to run my hands under the hot tap in the women's washroom until I stopped trembling.

By the time I returned to my table, the fries had congealed into cold grease and even the remaining half of the burger had lost its appeal. I stuffed it down anyway before engaging in my usual friendly wrangle with Eddy, who steadfastly refused to let me pay for it.

Smiling again, I headed for Lola's store.

Outside the small strip mall that housed Up & Coming, I angled into a parking stall and debated for a few moments. I should report to Stemp immediately, but I couldn't talk on an unsecured cell phone. Should I drive back to Sirius?

But then I'd have to manufacture an excuse for my late arrival at Lola's.

I hissed annoyance. Note to self: Get more of Stemp's secured phones and carry one at all times.

Christ, what other dumb mistakes was I making? I had always admired Kane's abilities as a secret agent, but now I had a more realistic idea of exactly how good he was. Make one little misstep; overlook one little detail, and you're dead.

I groaned and dragged myself out of the car, belatedly realizing that a real agent would have carefully surveyed her surroundings before popping up like a brainless gopher.

Casting a jittery glance around me, I scurried for the shelter of the building.

Inside the store, there wasn't a penis in sight.

That couldn't be good.

Worry seized me as I surveyed the shelves, taking in the tasteful and innocuous displays of lingerie and candles and CDs. Movement caught my eye, and I hurried over to the cash desk as Linda straightened behind it.

"Hi, Aydan!" She dusted off her hands on the seat of her

gaily-patterned nurse's scrubs and tucked a couple of wayward wisps of hair back into her shiny brunette ponytail. "What do you think? I just got it all rearranged."

I studied her perky features for any sign of distress and saw none. "Hi, Linda. It looks great. Um, where's Lola?"

Linda laughed, looking like a mischievous twelve-year-old despite her twenty-some years. "Why, do you think she'll disapprove?"

I forced a chuckle. "Probably. Where did you hide Big John the Wonder Horse? She'll miss him."

"Oh, he's still here." She shot me an impish grin that was an exact replica of her grandmother's. "I wouldn't deprive Granny of his company." She waved a hand in the direction of the shelves behind me. "I put him and his buddies on the back side of the display units so they aren't the first thing you see when you walk in. I know Granny loves the shock value of a giant silicone penis, but she promised we could try things my way for a while."

I grinned down at her wholesome, makeup-free complexion. "If you two didn't look so much alike, I'd never believe you were related."

"All short people look alike to you," she teased. "All you can see is the tops of our heads."

"True, but I'm pretty sure I'd recognize Lola's purple hair." I hesitated. "So, um, is she around?"

"She should be in any minute. I'm picking up some extra hours at the hospital this week, so I'll be heading over there soon." Her blue eyes sparkled. "I'm saving up so Spider and I can buy ourselves something special together when we move into his new house."

I briefly considered asking what she was saving for, but decided I might not want to know, given the nature of her business. I gave her a smile instead. "That's great! Congratulations."

She gave a happy little bounce, her ponytail bobbing. "Thanks!"

I only had to fake absorption in the books for about ten minutes before Lola arrived. She was rather conservatively attired in a snug pink leather pantsuit, and she rubbed both hands briskly over her butt as she hustled through the door.

"Holy cats," she growled in her throaty voice. "I just about froze my tutu off out there. Hi, Aydan!"

My relief burst out in a grin, the tension releasing from my body. "Hi, Lola. Nice leather."

"Thanks." She shot me a wicked grin. "It's not quite as nice as the chocolate-scented stuff..."

I clapped my hands over my ears. "La, la, la, la... I can't hear you. La, la, la..."

After a few more minutes of indelicate and thoroughly enjoyable banter, I turned my attention back to the books, finally able to concentrate now that I knew she was safe.

I had been working steadily for nearly an hour when the door chime sounded. Hunched over the desk engrossed in a bank reconciliation, I paid little attention as Lola moved out of my sight line to greet the customer. A moment later I snapped upright, fear flash-freezing my blood.

I'd know that nasal voice anywhere.

Lunging to my feet, I peeked out into the shop just in time to see Doytchevsky direct a spine-chilling smile down at Lola.

"I'm looking for personal recommendations," he said. "Why don't you show me some things you like?"

CHAPTER 30

My hand closed convulsively over my holster, and Doytchevsky's gaze jerked up from Lola's face to meet my eyes.

He smiled.

A slow, deliberate, poisonous smile. Then he turned back to Lola, nodding encouragement while she engaged him in her usual flirtatious sales pitch.

The pop of my knuckle and a jab of pain from my arthritic thumb prompted me to ease my grip on my gun. Frozen in the doorway, I watched with sickness coiling up in my stomach while Lola extolled the virtues of her products.

Doytchevsky shot me another malevolent glance. "What about restraints?" he inquired in a voice clearly intended to carry to my ears. "Do you have any handcuffs? And I'll need spreader bars, too."

Lola twinkled up at him. "Oh, aren't you the naughty one? This way..."

Nausea wrenched my guts into knots, and I clung to the door frame. He wouldn't... couldn't... try anything here in plain sight. Would he?

I couldn't take the chance. Swallowing hard, I watched his every move with my hand hovering near my holster.

Even though I knew he was deliberately tormenting me, I didn't dare leave him alone with Lola.

His performance went on and on, discussing the details and uses of each item with Lola at length, punctuated by pointed glances at me. At last he finished paying for his purchases, and an oily smile spread over his face as he stepped away from the desk. He hefted the bag and met my eyes.

"See you back at the office," he said, and strolled out.

I gulped down burning bile. Gulped again.

Dashed for the bathroom, my guts wrenching.

Sweating and shaking, I leaned my elbows on the toilet seat and breathed carefully.

Do not throw up.

Just breathe.

Do *not* throw up.

"Aydan! Honey, are you okay?" Lola's anxious voice called from the other side of the door.

"Yeah. Just an upset stomach." My voice was a feeble croak.

Breathe.

"Should I call Linda?"

"No, I'm fine."

I would kill him. I knew that now.

My guts twisted again and I dry-heaved.

"Aydan, open the door." Lola tapped gently. "Come on, honey, open up."

Breathe.

"Just a sec." I hauled myself to my feet and wobbled to the sink to stick my mouth under the tap for a sip of water.

Sip.

Breathe.

I sipped one more time before opening the door.

"Come and sit down." Lola wrapped an arm around my waist and guided me to the desk chair before perching on the desk to study me.

"Thanks, Lola, I'm all right now. I guess I must have eaten something that disagreed with me."

She stroked my hair back from my damp forehead, her sweet wrinkled face set in lines of concern. "Aydan, honey. Tell the police."

"Uh... what?" I eyed her in confusion.

She slid off the desk to put her arms around me. "I know it's scary, honey, but you have to tell them. Don't let him hurt you anymore."

"Um, I don't know what you're talking about."

She placed firm hands on my cheeks and looked into my face. "I saw what he was doing to you. How he raped you with every word. Aydan, it isn't anything to be ashamed of. You haven't done anything wrong. You can make him stop. Just tell the police."

I pulled away. "No, Lola, you've got it wrong. I wasn't... he didn't..."

Her wise gaze held me. "Aydan, I've seen that look on a woman's face before. When he picked up those handcuffs and looked at you, you went as white as paper."

Tammy's memories. I closed my eyes and drew a long, slow breath. Then another.

Lola's arms closed around me, rocking while she murmured a half-lullaby that brought back a heart-piercing memory of my mother, dead for over thirty years.

I determinedly rerouted my mind. Now I understood why Doytchevsky's threats had upset me so much. The impact of Tammy's memories had diminished considerably since I'd first acquired them, but I still knew first-hand what Lola would suffer if Doytchevsky took her. That, and much worse.

Drawing on long-ago counselling sessions, I put my feelings into perspective. I knew how to deal with this. It was just a matter of identifying and reframing that emotional reaction.

I drew a deep breath. Now that I understood, I'd be fine. And Lola would be fine. I would protect her. No matter what.

Another deep breath.

All better now.

But I kept my eyes closed, treasuring Lola's comforting embrace just a few short minutes.

At last I sat up, promised Lola I'd deal with the situation, and tottered outside to collapse into my car. I sat trembling while I contemplated the double meaning of that promise.

I'd deal with him, all right. It was just a matter of when and how.

And the sooner, the better.

Parked in the lot at Sirius Dynamics, I slumped in the driver's seat, preparing myself.

I wouldn't let Doytchevsky hurt Lola.

I would do what had to be done.

I took a deep breath and retreated to the dead place inside my heart, still bastioned by the old cold scars of my first husband's abuse. That place would serve me now.

I would feel nothing.

Walking toward the building, I wasn't surprised when Doytchevsky stepped out from between two cars to confront me. Nor was I angry. Nor afraid.

Nothing.

I eyed him, calculating. Too many witnesses. Better leave it until later, when my story of self-defence wouldn't be contradicted.

"What do you want?" My voice was completely emotionless.

The icy observer in the back of my mind noted the flicker of uncertainty in his face.

Yeah, something's changed, buddy. But you won't have to worry about it for long.

"You're going to feed Sherman an alternate location without telling Stemp. Same day, an hour earlier, different place." He spoke with his usual supercilious sneer, but he was off balance. I could smell it. The scent of my prey.

"Where."

He spouted an address and I recited it back to him, letting my gaze bore through him like the bullets I would soon fire.

When he nodded confirmation, I turned away.

"Remember the stakes." He spoke from behind me. "You'll do exactly as I say and tell nobody."

"I remember."

Seated in my office, I watched Doytchevsky out of the corner of my eye.

Soon.

Stemp strode in and began the briefing with his usual briskness. "Kraus cooperated. I filed a copy of their codebook in the repository in case we need it in the future, but Webb has already decoded Sherman's message. 'Office' refers to a vacant commercial office space they hold in Calgary; Webb was correct about the date; and the remaining letters in the message are security codes required for access." He paused. "And also an encoded instruction to bring you to the meeting. I don't know why he wants you, but it helps us. With you there, I won't have to place another agent on the inside. When he sees you, he'll think all is going according to plan and we should be able to take him completely by surprise. We just need you to reply to Sherman's message accepting the meeting."

"Okay." I closed my eyes and summoned up the virtual corridors of the network. Seated in the file repository, I took Stemp's outstretched hand, feeling none of my earlier animosity.

Numbness was better. Easier.

The turbulent journey into the Knights' server shook me, but the fear was distant. I stood apart from myself, recognizing the shivery adrenaline burn without judging it. Allowing myself a virtual shrug, I assembled Doytchevsky's altered information into a message and floated it into the data stream as carelessly as a child's paper boat.

It didn't matter. In just a few hours, Doytchevsky would be dead and everyone would be safe. Lots of time to tell Stemp afterward.

I navigated the convoluted route back to Sirius's network safely encased in my cool protective shell. When Stemp rose, his eyes asking a question, I said simply, "It's done".

Some routine decryptions let me relax into the mindless work of transcription for the rest of the afternoon. Pain skewered my brain when I stepped through the portal at last, and my mouth framed the usual profane complaints while my mind ticked over its checklist.

I'd grab a bite to eat first. Low blood sugar made my hands shake, and I'd rather keep this tidy. Besides, I wanted to give Doytchevsky time to get home for the evening. No need to chase him when I knew where he lived.

Should I shoot him in the apartment or drive him out into the country first? My black humour seized on the joke. Shoot him in the *apartment*. Ha. I'd shoot him in the heart. And the head. Double-tap.

"Aydan?"

"...huh?"

I jerked my attention back to my office where Spider hovered in front me, looking apologetic.

"Sorry, you looked like you were really deep in thought and I hate to disturb you," he said. "But can you give me the network key so I can take it down to the secured area? I want to get going." He blushed. "Linda and I have plans tonight. We're celebrating moving into my house."

"Oh!" I blinked, realizing everyone else had left while I wallowed in my unholy reverie. "Sorry." I unclenched my fist from around the tiny network key and handed it to him, absently returning his cheerful wave as he left.

Linda and Spider... why did that remind me of something? And what was it...? I backtracked through my afternoon and the memory returned with a jolt.

Christ, how could I have forgotten my exchange with 'Paul'? I sprang up from the sofa to hurry for Stemp's office.

When I tapped at his door, he beckoned me in and I swung the door shut behind me. Without waiting for an invitation, I took a seat and dipped into my waist pouch for Paul's card.

When I passed it across the desk to Stemp, he studied it for a moment before raising an eyebrow in my direction.

"Should I know who Paul Hibbert is?"

"I'm pretty sure he's working with Fuzzy Bunny."

Stemp's eyes sharpened. "Details."

I laid out the encounter from beginning to end, reciting the events as if by rote while the killer in my brain sat back, biding her time. "I guess the good news is that my cover is secure," I added. "I'm pretty sure he bought the whole thing. What do you want me to do?"

Stemp smiled. "Well done, Kelly. At this time, I think it's best to leave things exactly as they are. Get in touch with Mr. Hibbert and reiterate that you're not interested in working with them and that you don't have any items of value. If he is from Fuzzy Bunny, he should believe you since their search of your house came up empty. Offering to work with them would prolong contact and increase the risk of breaching your cover. It will be better if they simply lose interest in Arlene Widdenback."

"Okay. I'll call him tonight." I retrieved the card and left, my mind already returning to the details of planning a murder.

My legs carried me through the lobby and my mouth exchanged pleasantries with the security guard while I signed out. My hands were steady when I paid for a greasy burger at the takeout place. The good food at Eddy's would be an unnecessary distraction.

I ate without tasting. Maybe I'd better force him into my car and drive him out into the country. If a stray bullet went through the wall, one of the other residents might get hurt. That would be bad.

The burger sat like a stone in my stomach when I rose, but no queasiness rocked it. My hands and feet felt light and tingly and my mind floated somewhere above and to the left of my skull, guiding my movements by remote control.

Then I was climbing the stairs to Doytchevsky's apartment, my hand resting cold and inert on my gun, dead flesh animated by a frozen heart.

Outside his door, my fist rose to knock without hesitation. A buzzing like angry bees echoed in my skull.

Abrupt awareness of every sensation in my body. The pressure of my feet on the floor, cloth whispering against my skin, blood surging through arteries and veins.

The door opened and I knew no more.

CHAPTER 31

Something bad had happened.

I knew it with every fibre of my being before my brain could even formulate the thought. Somebody groaned.

Close.

Too close.

Another groan. I belatedly connected the sound with the sensation in my throat.

When I dragged my eyes open, nothing made sense. My cheek pressed against something rough. Two large, blurry objects stood planted inches from my nose and I blinked, trying to bring them into focus.

Slowly remembering that everything was blurry at that range without my reading glasses, I turned my attention to more distant objects. A strange sensation nagged at the edges of my mind.

A moment later, the nagging resolved itself into two distinct and unpleasant realities.

Hands bound.

Pain.

I gasped, jerking my face off the carpet to stare up past the two blurry objects that were Doytchevsky's feet and legs, up into his smiling face.

"Good, you're awake. Stupid woman. Did you seriously think I'd open the door unarmed? Stand up."

Fueled by a surge of adrenaline, I snapped a gaze around the room in a single lightning assessment.

Hands pinned tightly behind my back. Probably a nylon tie by the way it was cutting into my wrists. Lying on the floor of Doytchevsky's bedroom. Fully clothed, thank God.

"Stand up."

A jerk on my wrists yanked my hands painfully up behind me and I heaved onto my knees, then rocked precariously onto my feet, clenching my teeth on another groan.

"Step back." Another yank, and I staggered backward, unsuccessfully trying to ease the burning pull in my shoulders.

"Good. Now we're going to talk." Doytchevsky gave me one of his vicious smiles. "Look around you."

I looked, my heart lurching into my throat to drum a choking rhythm.

All the wares he had purchased at Lola's shop lay displayed on his bed.

I reached for the safety of numbness and met his eyes. "So what?"

As if I hadn't spoken, he smiled again and gestured with the cord in his hand. "This is one of my favourite restraints. It's so simple and yet so effective. The rope goes up over the closet rod to pull your hands up behind you. If I pull hard enough, it will tear all the muscles in your upper arms and dislocate both your shoulders." He shrugged. "Mind you, the closet rod isn't high enough to do that unless you fall, but I can certainly cause you a great deal of pain by raising your hands only a few inches."

As if to illustrate, he pulled harder. A grunt leaked out from between my teeth and I rose to my tiptoes, trying to ease the pressure on my shoulders. I twisted my hands in the bindings, ignoring the slicing pain of the ties on my wrists. My fingers groped for a knot on the taut rope.

His lips twisted into a sneer. "Don't bother. It's tied at the top. I'm not an amateur. Unlike you."

"What do you want?" I ground out. "I did what you asked."

"And then you tried to shoot me."

My joints screamed agony when the tension on my arms increased again, leaving me panting shallowly and straining on the tips of my toes while he tied off the rope to the leg of his bed. Cold sweat prickled my body, my pulse thudding behind my eyes.

He straightened, smiling. "There. That's better. Now I have both hands free." He picked up a dark hood from the bed, pulling it over his head to obscure his face. His eyes glittered through the slits. "You see, trying to shoot me was very naughty, and now you have to be punished."

"I wasn't trying to shoot you," I lied desperately, averting my eyes from the short whip he picked up from the bed. "I was coming to give you a report."

He laughed. "Oh, good one. A report. As in a gunshot. Aren't you clever."

"I wasn't trying to be- *agh!*" The whip cut across my thigh, making me cry out at the shock of pain.

"You'd better think twice before you do anything to me." My voice came out dead level, the terrified screaming of my other self muffled by the silence of my protective shell. "I'm not going to shut up about this, so you'll have to kill me. And Stemp's going to notice if I suddenly go missing."

"You think you're untouchable?" The whip hissed through the air, slashing a red-hot line higher on my leg. I yelped and jerked involuntarily, my shoulders cramping in agony.

He pushed his head close to mine. "You're not. I will punish you. And you will beg for more. Thanks to the current popularity of bondage sex, everyone will believe Arlene Cherry has released a new video." He jerked his head in the direction of a camera and tripod in the corner, its recording light glowing like a satanic eye in the half-light. "I can edit the video so this looks consensual. So it looks like you asked for it. Begged for it. Every mark on your body will be accounted for."

The whip whistled and struck high on my thigh with a crack, electric pain flaring from crotch to knee. Despite my effort to stay silent, a cry wrenched out between my teeth.

He chuckled. "It's surprising how sounds of pain sound so similar to those of pleasure." He stepped away to adjust the camera. "First I'll strip you naked. Cut your clothes off piece by piece. Then I'll whip you. Thoroughly. I think you'll be shocked at how much pain I can inflict." He shrugged. "Then perhaps I'll get creative."

I steadfastly refused to look at the contents of the bed, pushing the terror down deeper and locking it away.

Feel nothing.

He could hurt my body, but he couldn't break me. There was nothing inside me that hadn't been broken a long, long time ago.

The hooded figure stepped toward me, knife in hand.

"You're afraid, aren't you?" he said softly. "Tell me you're afraid."

"So are you." The words came out of my mouth before I

even realized I was thinking them. "You want revenge for your wife and your best friend, but you know neither of them would want you to do this. You know they'd both be sickened by it. Sickened by you."

"Shut up!"

My deadened voice continued as if announcing a particularly uninteresting weather report, my mouth speaking the words even while my mind cowered in helpless terror. "You're a ruthless bastard and a killer, but you don't really want to do this. You've made your point. I know you're serious, and I'll cooperate. Now you need to let me go so you can get to the man you really want to hurt."

His hand shot out to clench my throat. "As you once said to me, I'll do whatever I have to do." Blood pounded in my ears, blackness hazing the edges of my vision. His voice receded, each word dropping softly into my darkening pool of consciousness. "Never believe otherwise."

I jerked back, his fingers gouging hot channels across my neck, pain searing my shoulders.

He grabbed a fistful of my hair, yanking my face close to his. "If you say one word, if I even think you might be *considering* telling anyone, I'll put your little granny right where you are now. And I will do whatever is necessary."

Almost too fast for my eye to follow, he stepped away, the knife flashing toward the rope as he drew his trank gun again.

Cold.

I was cold.

Long spasms of shivering amplified the burning ache in my shoulders. My thigh throbbed with slow, hot pulses of pain.

I dragged my eyes open, muzzily taking stock of my dark surroundings. After a moment of slow incomprehension, I realized I was staring at the roof liner of my car with my seat reclined. A feeble effort to turn my head allowed me to identify the dark alley where I'd parked behind Doytchevsky's apartment.

Another effort to drag my head around. Keys in the ignition. Pouch secured around my waist. Gun in my holster.

Reaching for the keys was an exercise in torment, the strained muscles of my shoulders screaming protest. When the engine caught, I let my arm drop and my eyelids fall shut.

When I opened my eyes again, the car was still running, the heater blasting, but my shivering hadn't abated. Groaning, I forced myself to brave the pain and pulled my seat upright again.

I drew in a slow, quaking breath, fighting the tremors. Not daring to examine my emotions, I shoved them back into their prison and barred their door.

My cynical inner commentator snickered.

Oh, goody. I'd learned another valuable spy-skill. If you're planning to shoot a spy, don't knock on his front door. Duh.

Swearing and whimpering, I dragged my aching arms back into action and put the car in gear.

My swearing ratcheted up a notch when I turned in the lane at my farm. Tom's big half-ton and Hellhound's SUV were both parked in front of my house.

Shit, shit, shit.

I pulled into the garage and let the door roll down behind me, pushing my mind into planning mode.

I was pretty sure Tom wouldn't start a fight with Hellhound unless he thought Hellhound was actively threatening me. And Hellhound would definitely finish a fight, but he wouldn't start one.

That meant they were probably working together, cleaning and tidying. My mind cringed away from the thought of them wading through the detritus of my life. It was my stuff, dammit. It was private.

I shook off my unreasonable feelings.

They were trying to help. It wasn't an invasion. Just deal with it.

My best strategy would be to plead exhaustion. Tom would leave without protest, and Hellhound... I considered for a moment. He'd leave if I asked him to. He usually stayed at the Silverside Hotel when he was in town anyway. He'd understand if I said I needed space.

I unzipped my waist pouch to stow my keys and groaned. One more thing I'd forgotten. Paul's card.

Fine. Deal with it right now.

I extracted my phone and dialled. After a couple of rings, a male voice spoke on the other end of the line. "Ms. Widdenback. Good to hear from you."

"Yeah. Look, I just wanted to tell you thanks but no thanks. I've been through all Aydan's stuff and there's nothing here worth the kind of money you're offering."

A pause.

"You're a tough negotiator, Ms. Widdenback. All right. Seventy-five thousand dollars."

I bolstered my sagging jaw with my free hand. Shit. Now I understood why people sold secrets despite the risk.

"No, you don't get it. I don't have anything."

Another pause.

"It would be a small electronic device."

Sheer perversity made me goad him. Well, that and an increasing desire to confirm that they wanted what I thought they wanted.

"Aydan had a CD player. You mean like that?"

"No. A small chip. Like the little memory cards for digital cameras."

Weariness overcame me. Fine, they were after the fob. Old news. Time to end this.

"Aydan didn't have anything like that."

"Fine. One hundred thousand, and that's our final offer."

I sighed and let my head drop forward to rest on the steering wheel. "I'd love to oblige, but I really don't have what you want."

Another long pause.

"Call me if you change your mind." He hung up, and I wearily tucked my phone back into my waist pouch, hoping that was my last interaction with Fuzzy Bunny.

Next problem. Deal with the men in my house. I willed my aching arm up to the door handle and froze.

Goddammit!

My sleeve had ridden up as I reached, and the light of the garage revealed shallow cuts and smears of blood on my wrist. I pushed back my other sleeve. Double damn. More cuts.

I spat on a tissue and dabbed away the dried blood, careful not to reopen the cuts. My wrists looked better when I was done, but the red lines practically glowed on my white skin.

I thumped my forehead against the steering wheel. Now what? It'd be damn hard to come up with a plausible explanation for ligature marks on my wrists. If I was only trying to fool Tom, I'd brazen it out with the implication I'd been having kinky sex. He'd be too embarrassed to pursue the conversation.

But Hellhound knew me too well.

I sighed and crept stiffly out of the car. I'd make sure the sleeves stayed down. Hellhound wouldn't question me. He knew I'd keep my sweatshirt on if I had my waist holster concealed under it.

I only had to act as if nothing was wrong.

Easy.

I had years of practice.

When I stepped in my front door, the kitchen was deserted but the sound of the radio floated up from the basement. I drew a deep breath. Relax the diaphragm so the voice sounds natural.

Calling out a cheery hello, I started down.

Hellhound appeared at the foot of the stairs a moment later, a smile lightening his face. "Hey, darlin'. Where the hell were ya? I left ya a message to call me."

Paste on a smile. Be sure to crinkle the eyes so it looks like a real one. My old habits rushed back easily.

"Sorry, I got hung up at work and didn't get a chance to check my phone."

Shit, did I really say 'hung up'?

I banished the thought and descended the rest of the way to give him a quick hug, forcing my arms up and tucking my head under his chin to hide my grimace of pain.

I pulled away. "Hi, Tom! Wow, you guys have worked wonders down here!"

Oops, a little too chirpy. Tone it down a bit.

"You must be sick of this by now. It must be after eight."
I started to glance at my watch before aborting the
movement. Dammit, don't expose the wrists. I converted
the motion to a vague wave of my hand. "Why don't you call
it a night?"

I carefully avoided meeting Hellhound's quizzical gaze
and smiled at Tom. "I hope you aren't neglecting your
horses for this."

He smiled back, the weathered laugh lines framing his
eyes. "No, I usually do my chores a little later."

Shit. How could I manoeuvre him out tactfully?

"Why don't you come upstairs for a beer before you go?"
I offered, hoping I wasn't emphasizing the word 'go' too
much. "I see you guys brought my beer fridge in from the
garage. Thanks."

"You're welcome. At least you'll have something until
you can replace your kitchen fridge."

"Yeah, an' it got the beer handy," Hellhound added,
grinning. But his gaze lingered on me a little too long.

Shit.

"Come on, let's go up and have a beer." I turned and
hurried up the stairs.

Reassured by the sound of their feet on the steps behind
me, I made a beeline for the fridge, hoping they hadn't done
any male bonding that would encourage them to sit around
and drink beer together all evening.

Apparently not.

When I turned, holding out the bottles, Tom shot an
awkward glance at Hellhound. "Thanks, Aydan, but I'd
better be going. You must be tired after such a long day at
work, and I've got a few things I need to do at home. I'll call

you tomorrow."

He pulled on his boots and reached for his jacket.

"Oh, I didn't mean to chase you away," I lied as graciously as I could. "Are you sure you won't..."

"No, thanks. Good night." He gave me a smile before settling his Stetson on his head and striding out into the night.

Hellhound and I stood in silence until the sound of the truck's engine faded.

Then Arnie turned to face me, his keen eyes seeing too much as usual. "Okay, what really happened?"

CHAPTER 32

My heart sank as I stared back at Hellhound. "Um, nothing. Like I said, I got hung up..."

"Bullshit. What's wrong? Ya look kinda..." He frowned down at me. "...spacey. An' you're sweatin' an' shiverin' at the same time."

"Oh." Habit pulled a laugh out of me, my best fake smile crinkling my eyes. "Yeah, I'm out of it. It was a hell of a long day and I feel like shit. Maybe I'm coming down with something. I think I'll just go to bed."

Come on, take the hint.

He studied me for a long moment. "Okay. I'm gonna have a beer. Hand me one a' those, would ya?"

"Sure, take two. Good night." I thrust the bottles in his direction and was already turning away when his hands closed over mine, trapping the bottles between us.

"Aydan."

Something in his voice froze me to the floor. I turned slowly to see the incriminating injuries exposed on my extended arm.

His voice was very quiet as he took the bottles and returned them to the fridge. "Ya wanna try tellin' me the truth now?"

My fake self performed like a trouper. "Oh, that's no big deal." My voice came out light and easy. "I just..."

"...got hung up," he finished grimly. He captured my other hand, gently pulling back the cuff of my sweatshirt. "Hung up by your wrists, looks like. That why ya can't lift your arms?"

"No, I can. See, I'm fine." I attempted a casual wave of my arm and almost succeeded without wincing.

His face hardened. "Where else are ya hurt? How come you're limpin'?"

"Oh, that's nothing, I..."

"Do I hafta strip ya naked to find out?"

The echo of 'strip you naked' lashed me like Doytchevsky's whip, all the suppressed terror bursting through my defences. An instant later I dammed the breach and shoved it all safely away again, but I was too late.

Arnie's eyes widened and he rocked back. His hand tightened convulsively on mine. His voice emerged in a hoarse whisper. "Aw, shit, Aydan."

I hastened to reassure him. "No, don't worry, it's not what you think. I'm fine, it was no big deal. Just a guy who wanted to make sure I didn't shoot him while he made his point. He just made a few threats and then let me go."

"What guy?" His hand tensed, his shoulders bulging with knotted muscle.

"Arnie, let it go, okay? I'm not in any danger. He still needs me, he just wanted to make sure I'd cooperate."

A buzzing sound made me relax. Saved by the vibration.

Arnie shot me a look and extracted his cell phone from his pocket. He glanced at the display before punching the talk button. "Yeah."

He listened for a moment. "Yeah, she's here." Another

pause. "I dunno. Somebody hung her up by her wrists for starters." He reached to brush my hair back, examining my neck. His face darkened. "An' choked her, by the look of it. I'm tryin' to get the whole story outta her now."

My fingers flew to the burning skin on my neck. Damn, I'd forgotten there would be marks there.

The phone emitted an extended crackle of indistinct words. Hellhound stood rigid, his gaze boring into me while he listened. The plastic let out a small creak under his whitening knuckles.

His brows snapped together, his shoulders bunching and swelling. A moment later, his sudden shout made me flinch.

"*Fuck!* Motherfuckin' son of a whore's-" He cut himself off, and when he spoke again his voice rasped hard as iron. "No! Stay there. Stay there or I'll kick your fuckin' ass!"

Another tirade crackled from the other end, and Hellhound interrupted. "I got this. No, I *got* it. Lemme deal with it here... No! Promise me you'll stay there at least 'til I call ya back. Yeah, soon's I can. Gimme your word you'll stay there 'til then... Gimme your fuckin' *word*, for fucksakes!"

Another pause, and he drew a deep breath. "Okay. Soon's I know. Yeah. *Yeah!* I give ya my word."

He slowly returned his phone to his pocket, his movements stiff with anger. His scowl was so black that I had to swallow the dryness in my throat before I could speak.

"Um... is everything... um, are you okay?"

He drew a deep breath, visibly calming himself. When he spoke again, his voice was as gentle as the hand he closed around mine. "Come on, darlin'. Let's go sit down for a few minutes."

His quietness struck fear through me.

It was something bad. Something really, really bad. I couldn't deal with any other bad things. Not now.

I fled to the safety of numbness and the dead voice spoke from my lips. "Okay."

I let him tow me into the living room and lower me to the sofa without speaking. My body sat stiffly on the cushions while my battered soul curled into a tight ball behind the wall of my heart.

Nothing left to break. No need to feel.

Arnie sat beside me, still holding my hand. "That was Kane." He sounded as though he was chewing gravel.

"I figured." The dead voice spoke again. "Just tell me."

"Aydan..." He half-reached as if to stroke my hair, but his hand stopped in mid-air and drifted uncertainly down again. "Somebody hacked Kane's computer. Every time he turned it on today, he got massive dumps of porn. Not just any porn, though. It's all you. Arlene Cherry." He eyed me unhappily. "It's pretty damn realistic shit. If I hadn't slept with ya myself, I'd think it was the real thing."

"Yeah, I know."

My flat tone seemed to bother him even more. He shifted on the couch, his face creasing into worried lines. I spoke before he could.

"Somebody's trying to frame John for the sexual harassment tribunal. Make it look like he's obsessed with me. I told Spider that John and I were on a mission, so just call Spider. If anybody can clean it up, he can. He'll keep his mouth shut."

That didn't seem to help as much as I thought it should have. Arnie nodded absently.

"Okay. But, Aydan..." He faced me, squaring his shoulders. "Another one just showed up on his computer a few minutes ago. Wasn't the usual Arlene Cherry stuff." He held me with his level gaze, lines of strain etched around his eyes. "Ya wanna tell me why you're scared to get naked with me tonight?"

"Uh, I'm not, I... um..." I scrambled for an explanation, my brain refusing to cooperate. "I was just..."

Screw it. I went with the truth. "He hit me a few times... um... with a whip. I didn't want to have to explain the marks."

His shoulders slumped and he bowed his head, his voice rasping bleak defeat. "Christ. Fuckin' sick bastard. Tell me who it is. I'll hunt the fucker down an' kill him with my fuckin' bare hands."

I had expected him to be upset, but not as devastated as this. Slow comprehension oozed into my brain. "Wait. The video that came to John tonight. Was it... was I naked? Tied up and whipped and... um, other stuff?"

"Yeah." His hand trembled on mine. "Come on, darlin', let's get ya to the hospital. It's gonna be okay."

"No, wait. That wasn't real. It didn't happen."

His head rose, hope dawning in a face that had aged years in the past few moments. "What d'ya mean?"

"I mean the video was fake. I wasn't naked. He didn't rape me or anything. He just tied me up and threatened me. Whipped my leg a couple of times to make his point. That's it. No big deal. He probably did a close-up at the beginning to make it look like it was all me, and then spliced in some other footage."

His grip on my hand tightened almost to pain. "Aydan." He searched my face with desperate eyes. "Ya ain't lyin' to me, are ya? 'Cause what Kane saw... he said it was... really fuckin' sick."

I leaned forward to kiss him, gently extricating my hand from his grasp to cup his face between my palms. I looked deeply into his anguished eyes. "I promised I'd never lie to you. I'll take my clothes off right now if you want, so you can see for yourself."

He dropped his gaze, his hands clenching in his lap. "Aydan... darlin', ya know I trust ya, but... if ya can..." He faced me again, his expression raw and pleading. "I gotta see for myself. I gotta *know*."

I reached for the hem of my sweatshirt and winced at the pain in my shoulders. "Help me with my shirt."

A few moments later I stood naked in front of him, and the tension melted from his body.

"Aw, darlin', thank God," he said hoarsely. He pulled me into a hug, his face buried in my hair, his hands stroking my skin over and over. After a long moment he pulled away, turning to reach for the throw blanket I kept on the back of my couch. He draped it around my shoulders and kissed me gently. "I gotta call Kane. Hope he believes me. I dunno if *I'd* believe me, if I was in his place."

I wrapped the blanket around me and sank onto the couch. "I don't see why he wouldn't. Just tell him you saw me completely naked and there wasn't a mark on me. Well, except for the bruises from the explosion. The only new stuff is those welts on my leg."

"Uh. Yeah..." He lowered himself to the sofa beside me and scrubbed his knuckles in his beard, staring at the floor. "Look, he flat-out told me not to hold back from bein' with ya if that's what I wanted. An' a little competition ain't bad, we been one-uppin' each other since we were kids. But this... now's prob'ly not a good time to mention me gettin' ya naked, ya know?"

"Um. I see your point. But, Arnie..." I wrapped the blanket tighter around myself, still shivering. "We have to convince him not to come over here."

Sudden realization struck me dumb for a moment.

Arnie tensed. "What, Aydan? What's wrong?"

"Shit! I played right into his hands. Set John up. Oh, shit, Arnie..." I buried my head in my hands. "He's been ahead of me right from the start, and he just... I just..."

His hands closed on my shoulders. "What? What's happenin'?"

I straightened, fear for Kane snapping my mind into focus. "You were right, it's not about me. Remember how I said I thought somebody was trying to hurt John? The sexual harassment charge was just a start, but he wants to destroy John. Not kill him. Make him suffer for the rest of his life. And I just gave him the means to do it."

I silently blessed Arnie's brilliant mind as his eyes sharpened with comprehension. "Shit. This fucker's smart. He keeps ya in line with the threats, but then he makes up this fuckin' sick shit an' sends it to Kane, knowin' it'll make him come runnin' straight to ya. I bet he's just waitin' to follow Kane with his fuckin' camera. Documented evidence of disobeyin' a direct order, an' Kane gets court-martialled an' loses everythin'. Dishonourable discharge, jail time, no pension, no benefits..."

"Everything he's ever worked for destroyed," I finished. "Arnie, we've got to convince him it was fake. Just tell him you saw me naked and be done with it. So he gets upset, so what? It's better than the alternative."

"Hang on, darlin'." His eyes narrowed and he let go of me to stare into space, burnishing his knuckles against his beard again. After a moment, he snapped his gaze back to me. "Did this guy ever see ya naked?"

"No." I shuddered. "Thank God."

"So he wouldn't know about the bruises."

Hope made me sit up straighter. "No. I bet that video shows nice pink skin."

Hellhound squeezed my hand. "Let's hope so, darlin'." He reached for his phone.

Moments after he dialled, he interrupted the crackle on the other end. "It's okay, it was faked."

He listened and shot me a brief smile. "Nah, she wouldn't lie to me... Yeah, he hung her up, hit her a coupla times, an' just for that the fucker deserves to die, but the rest was faked."

Another crackle.

"Yeah, I'm sure. *Positive*... Listen... No, *listen*. Did she have any bruises on her-"

A furious eruption at the other end of the line made his fist clench. "No, I ain't a fuckin' sicko, I'm askin' 'cause I'm gonna prove to ya it was fake! Nah, right at the start, before he was hittin' her!"

He listened for a moment, his shoulders relaxing, and then he spoke quietly. "Then ya know it was faked, 'cause ya gotta know she was beat to ratshit in that barn blast. Ya woulda seen it in the video if it was really her."

Silence, followed by a subdued crackle.

"Nah, it's okay. We figure he's just tryin' to push ya into breakin' orders so he can watch ya get nailed in a court-martial. So stay put. I'll keep ya posted. Yeah. Later."

Hellhound pressed the disconnect button and collapsed back onto the cushions. "He bought it."

"Good." I clutched the inadequate blanket closer.

"Darlin', you're still shiverin'. I'll get ya a cuppa tea-"

"No, it's okay. I think I'll have a hot bath instead." I started to rise.

"Not so fast." He pulled me close and I gratefully huddled into his body heat. He wrapped warm arms around me and planted a gentle kiss on my forehead. "We gotta do somethin' about this asshole. Any guy that'd hit a woman is a fuckin' sick piece a' shit. Do we call the cops or Stemp?"

I sighed. "Neither. He probably figured he owed me. I... We had a little run-in earlier and he came out second-best. And anyway, I'm under orders to cooperate with him."

"*What?*" Tension strung his muscles tight. "You're just s'posed to let him... Aydan, that's fuckin' sick!"

I pulled away to face his scowl. "It's complicated and I can't tell you any of it, but..." I ransacked my tired brain and failed to find any explanation that wouldn't divulge classified information or put Lola in danger. "I just have to," I finished ineffectually.

"That's bullshit!"

"Arnie..." I searched his face, trying to find words to make it better.

God, I couldn't deal with his fears tonight. My own were more than enough for me to handle.

I retreated behind my shield. "I honestly believe he won't harm me, and my orders are to go through with this. That's just the way it is."

He stiffened, his scowl darkening. My old instincts leaped to barricade my emotional defences, hiding from the storm that was sure to come. I felt my face smooth into its indifferent mask.

His black look melted instantly. "Aw, darlin', don't..." His fingertips floated across my cheek. "I ain't mad at ya, I'm mad at this whole fuckin' bullshit situation."

"It's okay." The worry on his face tugged at my heart despite my effort to stay detached. I sighed and pressed close to hug him. "Really, it's okay. I'm sorry, I just..."

"Ya got no reason to be sorry, darlin'. It ain't your fault."

"Thanks." I sat up to give him a kiss. "I'm still freezing. I'm going to head for the tub."

He surveyed my face. "D'ya want me to stay?"

"Um, I... uh..."

"It's okay, Aydan, ya ain't gonna hurt my feelin's. If ya want some space, just say so."

"I... want you here, but I want space..." I wrapped my arms around myself. "To tell the truth, I'm a little weirded out by coming home to you. I mean, I want you here, I'm glad to see you, but... it's just that it's kind of too... couple-ish, you know? Like we're married or something."

He laughed. "Jesus, darlin', bite your tongue!" I forced a chuckle, too, and he sobered and added, "I'll go to the hotel tonight if you're sure you're okay."

I blocked out the thought of the black nightmares swirling around my cold, empty bed. They were only dreams. They couldn't hurt me.

I swallowed. "I'll be okay."

"Darlin'..." He studied my face. "Ya prob'ly ain't gonna sleep for shit if you're alone tonight. If ya want me, I'm here."

His sweet, ugly face made tears prickle the back of my eyes. He looked so big and warm and safe on my couch. I only had to nod. He'd bring in his guitar and soothe me with his music. Comfort my aching body and hold the bad dreams at bay all night long.

And then what?

Ask him to stay the next night, and the next?

No. Never again. Dependence only sets you up for pain.

I stood, blinking back the burning behind my eyes. "Thanks, but I'm okay."

He rose, too, and followed me into the kitchen where I stood with my arms wrapped around myself so I wouldn't cling to him while he put on his boots and jacket. He pulled me to him and kissed me gently. "G'night, darlin'. Call me if ya want me to come back, even if it's the middle a' the night."

I gulped, tears rising like floodwaters.

His face softened. "Aw, darlin'..."

I pushed him away and slammed the gates on my emotions, summoning up my easy smile and bantering voice. "You'd better get going. I'm freezing my butt off and there's a hot bathtub calling my name."

He hesitated. "Okay. G'night."

When the door closed behind him, I switched off the lights and crept to the window. Shivering in the shadows, I watched until his SUV disappeared into the darkness.

The night went as I'd expected. Despite my warm bath and some relaxing pre-bedtime music, the nightmares swooped down on me in waves and I woke screaming again and again.

By morning, it was a relief to leave my churned-up bed. I stood for a long time letting the hot spray of the shower sluice over me, but twisting my stiffened arms behind me to fasten my bra was a torturous profanity-filled ordeal nonetheless. By the time I slumped into my chair at the breakfast table, I was mired in self-pity.

Listlessly swirling my spoon in my cereal dish, I contemplated the upcoming day. What the hell was I supposed to do now? Doytchevsky was still alive and well, a fact that filled me with both relief and despair.

If he had opened the door without a trank gun in his hand, could I have pulled the trigger in cold blood? And if I had, could I have lived with myself afterward?

I blew out a sigh, knuckling my aching eyes. Irrelevant. My priority now was to tell Stemp about the location change. I groaned and thumped my forehead with the heel of my hand. In the previous day's trauma, I'd completely forgotten to get more secured phones.

Fine. Just fucking fine. I'd go straight to Stemp's office this morning to give him my report, and I'd ask him for phones at the same time. And report Doytchevsky's latest threats, for all the good it might do.

I poured the soggy cereal down the garbage disposal and headed for the door.

Trudging through the snow with my eyes downcast, I almost missed it. My peripheral vision barely caught the flutter from the front of the garage as I approached the side door.

What the hell?

I detoured to the main door where a sheet of paper was taped, its corners lifting in the breeze. The first glance froze me in mindless denial.

This couldn't be happening.

In the next instant, my brain rebooted and I spun, clawing at my jacket for the gun I'd *stupidly* tucked inside it, under my goddamn sweatshirt.

Gun in hand, my frightened panting emitted bursts of steam in the frosty air while I scanned my yard, eyes and ears straining.

Nothing but the usual silence of my remote country

home.

A line of footprints in the snow led from my gate to the garage door and back again. He must have left his car outside the gate and sneaked in here sometime in the night.

"You filthy fuckwad sonuvabitch ..."

My mouth continued to spew the foulest insults I could muster while I yanked the paper off the door, my heart stuttering against my ribs in sick dread.

I ran a shaking fingertip over the tuft of purple hair taped beside the photo of Lola bound and blindfolded in a chair, her face contorted with fury or terror. The plain laser-printed font somehow made the four words even more horrible: 'You talk, she pays.'

CHAPTER 33

I crushed the paper into a ball and hurled it at the ground with all my strength before dashing for the car. Tearing a fingernail on the door handle, I flung myself inside, pitching my gun onto the passenger seat beside me. In moments, I was barreling down the snowy road, the steering wheel jerking in my hands as the tires hit the drifts.

I'd kill him. I'd fucking kill him.

I couldn't kill him. He had Lola.

Where?

I jammed on the brakes at the highway, cursing and hammering my fist on the steering wheel. Why the hell hadn't I brought the photo? I should have looked more closely at the background. Was that Doytchevsky's apartment, or somewhere else?

Idiot, idiot, goddammit...

Too late for that.

I stomped on the gas pedal and yanked the car around the corner, tires spinning and whining on the still-slippery pavement.

Somehow the all-wheel drive kept the rubber on the road all the way to Silverside. I shot a fast glance at the main intersection as I raced toward it. No cars at all.

Fuck the red light.

Moments later, I slid to a halt in Doytchevsky's alley. I had snatched my gun up off the seat before the first shred of logic wafted into my brain. I froze with my hand clenched on the door handle.

Slow down. Don't be stupid about this.

Find him. Kill him. Find him. Kill him. My pounding pulse drummed the words in my brain.

I forced myself to take a slow, deep breath.

Kill the fucking bastard!

Shut up.

Another calming breath.

The other residents of the apartment might be up and heading for work by this time in the morning. Now would be a bad time to get caught waving a gun.

And anyway, that method hadn't exactly gone well for me last night.

I had to talk to him. But I didn't dare phone him. Damn unsecured phone lines. I had to go up there.

Okay. Just stay calm. Stay smart.

I stuffed my gun into my holster and pulled my sweatshirt down over it before getting out of the car and forcing my quivering legs to stroll into the building. Climbing the stairs, I twisted my stiff lips into a smile to return the cheerful 'good morning' from a woman shepherding two small children. Thank God I hadn't come charging in here like Rambo on uppers.

I tapped on Doytchevsky's door before standing back, both empty hands held at shoulder height where he could see them easily through the fisheye lens.

My heart thundered as though I'd run all the way from the farm.

"What do you want?" Doytchevsky's voice was muffled by the closed door.

"I just want to talk." I hoisted my trembling hands a little higher.

The door swung open on an empty room.

Shit, he must be standing behind the door. I walked in slowly. No sudden moves. Stay calm and Lola would be fine.

The door clicked closed as I began to turn.

A small, flat report.

The floor rushed up to meet me.

I woke lying on Doytchevsky's bed, my throbbing arms pinned behind my back again. All the terror of the previous night rushed back and I twisted frantically against the knife-like pain of another nylon tie around my wrists. He had tied my ankles together, too. I jerked and thrashed, the bed thumping against the wall.

"Lie still!"

An open-handed slap caught me across the temple, and I lunged toward Doytchevsky as he leaned over me. My teeth snapped together a fraction of an inch away from his leg.

"Bitch!"

His fingers dug into my shoulders as he flung me back. A moment later, he ground his knee into the centre of my chest, agony stopping my lungs.

He leaned closer, breathing heavily through his teeth. "You stupid *bitch!*"

I drew the shallowest of breaths under his weight, my heart pounding as though it would explode. "Fuck... you... dickhead..." The words ghosted out of my mouth.

He grabbed my throat, iron fingers crushing the bruises

from the previous night, his face snarling inches from mine. "I should kill you right now!"

I slipped into that state beyond fear.

Christ, that hurt. Grabbed me in the same damn place.

Don't. Pass. Out.

A shallow inhalation, pain blasting through my ribs. "You... need... me..."

Another wisp of breath. "Asshole..."

A sharp backhand snapped my head sideways, but at least he let go of my throat. The star-spangled blackness cleared from my vision in time to see his lips twist in a sneer.

"Stupid bitch. Do you *like* pain? I'll oblige."

He rocked forward, grinning when the last of the air crushed out of my lungs in a squeak of agony.

His hateful face receded into a slowly darkening tunnel.

I had been wrong. He was going to kill me after all. Should have called Stemp. Or Arnie.

Kane.

Anybody...

My mind floated hazily up to the ceiling, the pounding of my heart deafening me. Too late.

My lungs strained for air that wouldn't come.

Too late...

Then I was breathing again, sucking in sobbing gasps of air that burned like liquid fire.

Doytchevsky scowled down from beside the bed, my waist pouch dangling from his hand. "Now I want you to listen very closely. I've placed a bug in your..." He eyed the pouch with distaste. "...purse. I'm talking about a listening device and not an insect, in case you're too stupid to know that."

I wheezed in another breath. "Fuck you."

"Shut up!" He grabbed a fistful of my hair, yanking my head back and shoving his face close to mine. "Your little granny is in a secure place. There's a bomb under her chair. The bomb is connected to a detonator wired to a cellular phone. If I dial that phone number, the circuit will complete and the bomb will explode. And that will be the end of your little friend."

He threw me back and pulled a phone out of his pocket, poising a finger over one of the buttons. "I have it on speed dial. Would you care to provoke me some more?"

Terror froze me.

He smiled. "That's better. I was expecting you this morning, but I had hoped you'd be reasonable. This whole melodrama was really quite unnecessary. Now, as I was saying about the bug. You will carry it all day. If you say anything ill-advised..." He shrugged. "Boom. Also, if the bug goes off-line, or if for some reason I can't hear what you're saying, or if you don't follow my instructions down to the last detail, I'll push the button and blow her to bits. Are we clear?"

The pain in my chest wasn't just from bruises. "Clear," I whispered.

"Good. When you leave here, you will go to Sirius and act as if nothing happened. When you're finished there, you'll leave your cell phone in your desk drawer, get in your car, and drive to Calgary without communicating with anyone. You'll go directly to the address I gave you, and you will drive around to the loading bay. You will wait there until the door opens, and then you will drive in. You will stay in your car with both hands on the steering wheel until I give you further instructions. If anyone approaches you in the meantime, get rid of them. If I think you've set me up, or if I feel threatened in any way, I'll detonate the bomb."

His eyes gleamed with triumph. "And don't think you're going to pull any cute moves like slipping a note to somebody. I've hacked every surveillance system inside Sirius. I'll have eyes on you at all times."

He reached into his pocket and tossed a key onto the bed beside me. "Lock up when you leave and push the key under the door. And don't mess up my apartment. That would annoy me."

The report of the trank gun was the last thing I heard.

I woke crumpled awkwardly on the bed, my wrists and ankles free but my arms still crushed by my own weight. A moan leaked out between my teeth as I hauled the deadened limbs out from under me. Pins and needles seared my arms while my entire upper body throbbed with bone-deep pain.

Holding fast to self-control, I pushed my emotions away and breathed slowly for a few moments, fighting the jerky breaths that wanted to become sobs.

Crush the fear. Reach for anger.

"You fucking prick." I spoke aloud for the benefit of the bug, my voice scouring my aching throat. "At least when I tranked you I laid you out comfortably and put some blankets on you. Dickhead."

I clenched my teeth on the urge to shower him with more abuse. Now wasn't the time. I patted my numb hands against the bed, trying to encourage more circulation into them despite the pain.

Think.

Lola would be safe as long as I cooperated. I held tightly to that knowledge while my mind swooped in dizzying arcs, unable to find a solid perch.

My fault. I had called his bluff on the rape and torture, so he'd switched to something he knew I'd believe.

Why the hell hadn't I told Stemp yesterday about the address change for the meeting? Oh, yeah, because I'd had all that spare time.

What if I had gone to Stemp this morning instead? But the outcome would have been the same. Doytchevsky would still have Lola. Stemp would still refuse to intervene. He'd just tell me to carry on with my mission as planned.

Stop rambling. Concentrate.

I fought the residual confusion of the tranquilizer. I had to find a way to transmit the new address to Stemp today. If I couldn't...

Well, who the hell cared? It wasn't like I owed Sherman anything. Tammy's memories wrenched a shudder out of me. So Doytchevsky killed him, so what? No loss.

My only responsibility was to get the wireless network generator from Sherman. That shouldn't be a problem. Doytchevsky hadn't shown any interest in obtaining it for himself.

I hauled myself slowly upright, ignoring the vertigo that whirled the room momentarily. Breathe through the pain. Just relax into it. Don't tense up. My muscles quivered on the edge of spasm.

I twisted carefully. Right, then left. A loud pop from my back administered an electric shock of pain followed by blessed relief, and I drew a deeper breath.

Bearable now.

I leaned over and spat on Doytchevsky's pillowcase. Leaving rusty stains on the white cotton, I cleaned the blood off my wrists before turning the pillow over to hide the mess.

So I have a passive-aggressive streak. So sue me. Asshole.

I dragged myself up off the bed and staggered into his bathroom to clean the shallow wounds properly. A quick survey in the mirror assured me he'd considerately avoided leaving any marks on my face, and I adjusted the turtleneck I'd selected in the morning to hide the livid bruises on my throat. The long sleeves would hide the new damage on my wrists as long as I didn't reach for anything.

Fine.

I left, locking up behind me and sliding his key under the door as he'd instructed.

Wrapping the protection of numbness around myself once again, I strode into my office and wished Spider and Jack a convincingly cheerful 'good morning'. Doytchevsky offered me a sardonic smile, which I didn't acknowledge.

You can't break me, you piece of shit.

I was just sinking onto the small sofa trying to look as though my body wasn't a glowing knot of pain when Stemp stuck his head in the door.

"Kelly, our analysts have identified some important communications that need to be decrypted. Those will be your top priority this morning. Webb has obtained floor plans of the Knights' office, and he'll give you those along with the access codes and a dossier on Sherman. I've requisitioned a trank gun and nylon restraints so you can apprehend him. Report to my office at noon for briefing."

He paused only long enough to receive my nod before vanishing down the hall.

"Oh." Jack looked relieved. "I guess you won't need me

today. That's good. I've been neglecting my own research lately, and I was going to be away this afternoon anyway. I'm meeting with Brendan's teacher."

I feigned warm interest. "How does he like kindergarten?"

Her beautiful face lit up with maternal pride. "He just loves it, and he loves his teacher. He's so excited to go to school every day. Poor Ivy misses her brother and she's just dying to go to 'real school', so I've enrolled her in an advanced nursery school. They're both doing so well!"

Her enthusiasm made me smile despite the weight of my pain. "I'm not surprised. They take after their mom."

She blushed, her smile luminous. "Thanks! See you later. Have a good day."

"You, too."

She hurried out, still smiling, and I turned a bland face to Doytchevsky. "I guess we won't need you today, either. Spider and I can handle the decryptions."

He out-blanded me. "I'd better stay. Without Kane, there's nobody to pull you out of the network if you get in trouble."

I might have imagined the emphasis on his last three words. But probably not.

I shrugged. Slowly and painfully. "Spider, let's get to it."

My mind wasn't fully on the decryptions, but I managed to deal with them competently enough. Thank God I could make my avatar pain-free inside the virtual reality network.

Returning my consciousness to my body was like being hit by a truck. One moment, fine; the next, pain exploding every nerve. I swore violently, instinctively grabbing for my aching head only to recoil from the pain of lifting my arms. Slumped on the sofa, I groaned and whimpered until the pain in my head subsided and the rest of my body equalized into a throbbing ache.

Spider's skinny fingers rubbed tentatively at my temples, and I pried my eyes open at last.

He leaned down to examine me worriedly. "That seemed worse than usual. Are you okay?"

I patted his hand and heaved myself upright, wincing. "I'm okay. Thanks, Spider. I'm just tired and sometimes it hits me harder then."

"Okay..." He eyed me doubtfully. "I've got those floor plans and Sherman's dossier on my laptop. You can go over them and I'll give you the access codes before you meet with Stemp."

"Thanks." I pulled up a chair beside him, ignoring Doytchevsky completely.

Doytchevsky rose and strolled for the door. "I'm taking the afternoon off, too."

I turned to face Spider's eager briefing, pretending to concentrate on the utterly useless information about the Knights' office. At least the dossier on Sherman was enlightening. Now I could put a face to the remembered feel of his hands.

I shuddered and hauled myself out of the chair. "Thanks, Spider. Guess I'll head for my briefing now."

"Good luck." He eyed me anxiously.

Boy, was I going to need it.

"Thanks."

I wandered down the hall and shut myself into the ladies' room, my mind racing. If I went to Stemp's briefing, he would mention Doytchevsky and it would be all over for Lola.

And if Doytchevsky was telling the truth about the surveillance, I couldn't even signal Stemp that anything was wrong.

No options left.

I peeped out the door at the empty corridor, and then strolled casually back to my office, my heart pounding.

CHAPTER 34

I tucked my cell phone into my desk drawer with trembling hands before hurrying down the hall. God, please don't let Stemp see me. The only thing worse than going to his briefing would be trying to explain why I was avoiding the briefing.

What was Doytchevsky planning? He hadn't told me to leave my gun behind, but surely he wouldn't let me keep it for long. And he had overheard Stemp, so he knew I'd be carrying a trank gun and restraints, too.

I scrubbed moist palms against my jeans. If he had told me to leave my weapons behind, I wouldn't be so worried. What the hell made him so confident? He must have some plan.

Too bad I couldn't say the same. God, I was so far out of my league.

I hesitated at the door to Stores. The longer I spent in the building, the greater the chance that Stemp would catch me. But if Doytchevsky expected me to be carrying the requisitioned items, he might not believe me if I told him I didn't have them...

Shit.

I ducked inside and picked up the trank gun and

restraints, tucking them into my jacket pocket with a shiver. They weren't exactly giving me warm fuzzies, but it was better to see them in my own hands than in Doytchevsky's.

When I emerged from the building, Doytchevsky was nowhere to be seen. I jittered for a moment on the sidewalk, wondering if he was watching me out here, too. Probably. I held back a shudder when icy gooseflesh rose on the back of my neck, and headed for the parking lot.

The ice spread to my veins at the sight of Hellhound's SUV parked next to my car. He got out, eyeing me anxiously as I approached.

Shit!

My feet carried me closer while my mind raced frantically. How the hell could I keep him from saying anything? If he mentioned last night's conversation or noticed the fresh wounds on my wrists...

I covered the last few yards completely devoid of inspiration, my pulse hammering.

"Aydan, what the-" he began, and I widened my eyes at him before silencing him in the only way that came immediately to mind.

He returned the kiss with interest. And then some. If I hadn't been so scared, I might have even enjoyed it.

Goddammit, I had to think of some way to warn him not to speak. I couldn't keep kissing him forever.

Although...

That was an extremely attractive option. The man was an artist. Those lips... and ohmigod, that magic tongue...

I pulled away, trying for a light tone. "You're 'way too tempting. I'd better get going. See you later."

Apparently my act wasn't going to win any Oscars. His smile dissolved into a worried frown.

"Darlin', what the hell-"

I widened my eyes at him again and gave him a tiny, desperate headshake. He stiffened, his gaze darting around the parking lot.

"...are ya doin' this afternoon?" he finished with only a slight hitch in the sentence. "Can ya sneak away for a little R and R?" He pulled me closer to fondle my ass. "I got a few things I wanna whisper in your ear."

He leaned down but I pulled away, afraid Doytchevsky's bug would be sensitive enough to overhear even a whisper.

"I'd love to, but I can't." I almost added 'I'm going down to Calgary', but changed my mind at the last instant. That might alarm Doytchevsky, and if Hellhound thought I was working the afternoon at Sirius, he'd probably go and hang out with Kane. Safer for everybody.

"I have to work," I said instead. "See you later." I gave him a quick peck on the lips and fled to my car.

When I turned out of the parking lot, Doytchevsky's car pulled onto the street behind me. Okay, at least I didn't have to guess what he was doing.

Hellhound's SUV turned in the opposite direction. Thank God. He'd gotten the message.

I hissed out a long breath and pressed my aching shoulders into the seat back, settling in for a long, uncomfortable drive.

Heading west on the highway, I had just passed the turnoff for my farm when a flash of movement made my eyes flick up to the rearview mirror. My heart sank at the sight of Hellhound's SUV overtaking Doytchevsky's car to tuck in behind me.

Dammit!

I drove on in an agony of indecision. Should I pull over?

Keep driving?

He'd probably follow me all the way to Calgary if I didn't stop. And Doytchevsky had likely recognized the SUV if he'd seen us in the parking lot.

What if Doytchevsky decided to eliminate the risk? A few bullets fired from a passing car; an unsolved shooting on a deserted country highway...

My decision was made for me when Hellhound overtook me a few minutes later and braked. For a split second I considered pulling out to pass, but decided against it. Safer to get rid of him now.

I followed his lead as he slowed and pulled over on the shoulder. In my rearview mirror, I watched Doytchevsky do the same about half a mile back. Out of pistol range, thank God.

By the time I returned my attention forward, Hellhound was striding toward me. I reached for the door handle, but changed my mind.

Stay in the car. Then even if Doytchevsky had binoculars, he wouldn't be able to read my facial expression or gestures.

I powered the window down and Hellhound leaned in. "Aydan, what's-"

"You can't take a hint, can you?" I snapped. "Don't you ever think about anything but sex? I told you, I'm busy this afternoon." I jabbed a finger at my waist pouch and cupped a hand behind my ear before cocking a thumb over my shoulder in Doytchevsky's direction.

Come on, Arnie, get it, please get it...

His eyes widened in comprehension. "Ya didn't seem to mind when ya were screamin' my name in bed," he growled. "Well, fine then. Lotsa other chicks out there. Don't need a goddam pissy bitch like you."

His fingertips brushed my cheek in the lightest of caresses before he turned and stomped back to the SUV. Moments later, its tires grated angrily on the pavement as it roared into a U-turn and headed back toward town.

I put my car into gear with a shaking hand and pulled out onto the highway again. My mind circled uselessly, considering and discarding plan after increasingly desperate plan. Doytchevsky could push that phone button far faster than I could draw a gun. I understood now why he had told me to leave my phone behind. I couldn't even text Stemp.

Maybe I should have held onto the phone instead of following his orders. How would he know?

But it was too risky. If it was my own life on the line, I might take a chance, but Lola was too important. To me. To everybody. Her warm smile hovered in my memory.

And anyway, it was a waste of time to second-guess myself. Too late now.

What could I do with what I had right now?

What if I crashed my car? It would attract attention. Take me out of the equation.

I thumped the steering wheel with an indecisive fist. Not really an option. He'd probably leave me if I was hurt badly enough, but then I likely wouldn't be capable of doing anything to help Lola, either. If I was only slightly injured, he'd haul me out of the wreckage and force me to cooperate anyway. No help for Lola and considerably more pain for me.

I squirmed in the seat again, trying to ease the burning ache in my arms and chest.

Speeding or attracting police attention in any other way would sign Lola's death warrant when I had to explain what I was doing. Driving anywhere except the address he'd given me would have the same result.

At last, I surrendered to the inevitable. Don't be a hero. Just do what he wants. Still, my hand crept to the zipper of my waist pouch.

Would he have inventoried all its contents when he placed the bug? And if he had, would he remember my knives? And would he think to take the pouch away from me and search it to make sure they were both still there?

I eased my folding knife free and tucked it inside the front waistband of my jeans. It was probably useless. I couldn't get to it before Doytchevsky pressed the button. But any weapon was better than nothing. If he found it, I'd cooperate and give it up without a fight. But if he didn't...

Despite my attempts to find a comfortable position, pain wracked my body by the time I pulled up at the address in a small semi-industrial strip mall. Groaning, I eased my hands off the steering wheel and slumped hopelessly in the seat while I stared at the storefront.

A pottery shop? This couldn't be the right place.

A few large urns and some smaller bowls with vivid glazes occupied the slightly grubby front window. The illuminated sign glowed determinedly 'Closed' despite the printed placard on the door that insisted it was open until four-thirty.

But apparently I'd gotten the address right after all. Doytchevsky pulled up beside me and pointed, and I drove in the direction he indicated. A few moments later I clenched my teeth, watching the overhead door roll up at the back of the building.

Maybe I shouldn't try to keep my knife. My heart bounded into my throat. What if he found the knife and blew Lola up out of spite?

Decide.

The door rolled down behind us and Doytchevsky got out of his car.

My hands tightened on the wheel. Too late now.

A fast glance around the bay revealed little hope. No potential weapons. No places to hide. No exits other than a door at the front that must lead to the storefront.

Some open shelves near the front of the bay held terracotta-coloured clay ware and large discoloured steel containers that looked like garbage cans. A potter's wheel stood beside the shelves, the concrete around it liberally spattered with dried clay. A huge stainless-steel chest squatted on the opposite side of the bay under a blackened ventilation hood. Probably the kiln. The only other furnishings were a plain desk with a computer on it and a small forklift with a long extension bar attached to the front.

Doytchevsky came up beside the car and stood several feet away, his phone in one hand, a trank gun in the other. Out of range of the door, even if I had considered swinging it open to hit him.

Despair soured my stomach. He had been a spy for decades. The fact that he was still alive was a testament to his skill. He wouldn't make stupid mistakes.

"Take your left hand off the wheel and open the door slowly."

I obeyed, and a hot metallic smell assailed my nostrils. I must have guessed right about the kiln.

"Keep your right hand on the wheel. Lay your weapons and restraints on the floor beside the car. Slowly."

I carefully laid out my Glock, the tranquilizer gun, and the nylon restraints. No sudden moves. Just like he said.

His finger hovered over the phone button and I swallowed hard. Thank God his hands were steady. Unlike mine.

"Take off your pouch and lay it down, too."

Holding my breath, I unfastened it and lowered it to the floor.

"Now step out of the car. Keep your hands in sight."

I hoisted my trembling hands and hauled myself out of the car. God, I should have eaten something before I left. Even if I did manage to get a gun into my hand, I'd probably miss just because I was shaking so badly.

"Nice and slow. Pull the chair into the middle of the floor and sit on it."

I was just sinking into the chair when a doorbell sounded. Doytchevsky glanced at his wristwatch, his eyes flicking down only for a fraction of a second before locking onto me again.

"He's early. You will follow my instructions to the letter. You'll walk out into the store and let him in the front door. You'll tell him Sam is back here. You'll lock the front door behind him and send him back here ahead of you. If you make any sign or warn him in any way, I'll blow your little granny to hell. Clear?"

I nodded, heart racing, and began to rise.

"Hold it!"

I froze, my legs locked at an awkward half-seated angle.

Doytchevsky laughed. "Oh, very good. I'm glad you've decided to be so cooperative. You may stand up."

I straightened slowly.

"If it's anyone else, get rid of them." He jerked his chin a fraction of an inch in the direction of the door, the phone and trank gun still rock-steady in his hands. "Go."

CHAPTER 35

The doorbell sounded again as I walked stiffly into the store, trying to hide my quivering knees. Outside, a tall, skinny silhouette made my heart leap into my throat.

Oh, God, no, Spider!

A moment later relief nearly melted my knees. It wasn't Spider. The bearded young man thumped on the door a couple times before spotting me. His frown lightened and he waved and pointed to the placard on the door.

"Sorry, we're closed," I called.

He frowned, gesturing and mouthing something unintelligible outside the glass.

"I said, we're closed!"

Come on, buddy, just fuck off.

No such luck. He rattled the door handle vehemently.

Doytchevsky's nasal voice floated out from behind the door. "You have ten seconds. Ten..."

I lunged for the door and shoved my face up against the glass. "The store is closed! We've had a death in the family! Show some respect!"

He stepped back uncertainly, and I turned and strode for the rear of the shop.

Just leave, buddy, come on, please. Just go away.

Thank God, he did. When I glanced back over my shoulder, I could see his disconsolate figure wandering away, scratching his head.

I eased the door open, not wanting to surprise Doytchevsky. "He's gone."

"Good. Back in the chair."

I sat. Several minutes of silence made me wonder if I was supposed to be engaging him in conversation or something. What would a real agent do? Try to talk her way out of trouble?

Somehow I couldn't see that happening. He needed me to suck Sherman in, so he wasn't going to let me go. And I seriously doubted he'd gloat like a movie villain and spill all his dastardly plans.

But I had to try. "Do you own this shop?" I ventured.

Silence.

"The glazes are beautiful on those pieces in the front window," I tried again. "Do you just paint them on?"

"How stupid are you?" he snapped. "That's raku."

Okay, if he wanted to insult me, fine. As long as it got him talking.

"You mean it's... spaghetti sauce?"

"You're pathetic." He peered down his nose at me. "I said *raku*, not Ragu. R-A-K-U. It's a complex glazing and firing technique."

"It's spectacular. How do you get those metallic patches?"

He drew himself up, smirking. Unfortunately, neither his gun nor his phone wavered in the slightest. "It takes a great deal of practice and expertise, and even then I never quite know how they'll turn out. Each piece is a surprise."

Well, what do you know? Doytchevsky had a hobby.

"They're beautiful. Tell me about the firing technique."

Oops, maybe that was a little too obviously chummy.

He glared and jabbed the phone in my direction. "Shut up."

I shut.

Many silent minutes later, I wondered if his hands were getting tired. He was leaning comfortably against my car, gun and phone still at the ready. No sign of fatigue.

For the first time, I realized his usual roll of soft belly fat was gone. It must have been fake all along. His body looked hard and fit and his movements were smooth and confident, his former jerky awkwardness gone without a trace.

Bastard. Fooled us all.

And idiot me, underestimating him even after I knew his background.

The sound of the doorbell yanked me out of my useless recriminations.

Doytchevsky straightened. "Go. Same instructions as last time."

This time when I approached the door, surprise made my step falter. The man on the other side of the glass was definitely Terry Sherman. No mistaking the shock of thick white hair I'd seen in his dossier. But the rest of him was startlingly small and frail. Somehow in Tammy's mind he was bigger and stronger.

I shook my head and reached for the lock. Tammy's memories, not mine. She must be a much smaller woman than I.

When the door swung open, a chime sounded in the back. Sherman shot a nervous glance around the shop. "Where's Sam?"

I held my voice level. "He's in the back. Go on through.

I'll just lock up behind you." I waved in the direction of the back door and turned to reach for the lock.

"No, you first."

Something in his voice made me turn slowly, cold fear slithering down my spine. A gun trembled wildly in his hands, his finger quivering on the trigger.

My heart kicked my chest. Great, just fucking great. After all this, I was going get shot accidentally by some little old fart who couldn't handle a gun.

"Okay, Terry, you don't need to point that at me. I'm going."

I spoke a little louder than necessary. At least Doytchevsky's spy skills might do me some good.

No such luck. The shithead didn't make an appearance.

Gulping at the large hairy lump apparently lodged in my throat, I moved in the direction of the door.

Who would get me first? Shot in the back by Sherman or in the face by Doytchevsky?

I opened the door slowly. No sign of Doytchevsky by my car.

As I stepped forward, a whisper of movement alerted me to his presence right beside the door, inches away.

Maybe if I had been Kane, I could have done some spectacular martial arts move. Disarmed Doytchevsky and thrown him into the path of Sherman's bullet or something.

I wasn't Kane. Not even close.

Staring straight ahead, I walked farther into the bay, my back prickling with the expectation of a bullet.

A quick shuffle of motion behind me; a cry of pain and a thud.

"Restrain him." Doytchevsky didn't even sound out of breath. "Use the ties on the shelf beside him."

When I turned, Sherman lay on the floor, his wrist bent at an unnatural angle. His face was white with shock and pain, his breathing quick and shallow. Doytchevsky stood several feet away looking unperturbed, his trank gun and phone steady in his hands. A surreptitious glance revealed Sherman's gun lying on the floor beside the shelves, at least fifteen feet away.

Dammit, I should have done something. He would have had to put both the phone and the gun down in order to disarm Sherman.

Common sense asserted itself.

If I had tried, he probably could have dealt with me just as easily as Sherman. And he might have pressed the button in the process. Not an option.

I turned back to make my way to the shelf, eyeing Sherman's gun. Only fifteen feet away. I glanced at Doytchevsky, who shook his head slowly, smiling his vicious smile. I eased out a sigh. That gun might as well be fifteen miles away.

Nylon ties in hand, I pulled Sherman's arm around behind him. He let out a cry, sweat glistening on his face. His hand flopped horribly on his obviously broken wrist, already mottled and swelling. I shot a glance at Doytchevsky.

"I said tie him." He made a threatening gesture with the phone, and I hurried to obey despite the sickness that squirmed in my belly while I tightened the tie around the puffy flesh.

Don't listen to his whimpers. Don't look at his injuries.

Don't feel.

I clamped down on control.

"Good." Doytchevsky jerked his chin in the direction of

the desk. "Bring that case over and put the leads on his forehead."

The small case he indicated sent a shock of recognition through me. Jack's lie detector.

Doytchevsky smiled at my expression. "On temporary loan. Since Dr. Travers wasn't using it this afternoon." His smile vanished. "Hurry up."

I had seen Jack use it often enough. A few moments later, the crown of electrodes was fastened around Sherman's sweaty forehead, the ready light glowing.

As I leaned over him he met my gaze, tears puddling in his white-rimmed eyes. "Please," he quavered. "My wrist... Can you-"

"No, she can't. Now you're going to tell me where your wireless network generator is." Doytchevsky cut across Sherman's plea.

Sherman tensed. "No."

"Break his fingers." Doytchevsky's voice cracked like a whip. "One at a time, until he feels more cooperative."

"No!" I recoiled instinctively, guts clenching.

"What did you say?" Doytchevsky's finger moved slowly toward the phone button.

"Wait!" My gaze bounced between Doytchevsky's deadly face and Sherman's pallor. My stomach twisted into a sick knot.

He was just a skinny, helpless old man. The thought of breaking his fingers sent hot bile surging into my throat.

"Do it." The phone described an ominous arc.

My quivering knees dropped me beside Sherman. "Just tell him. He tortured Rex Rimmel until he told everything. You'll end up telling him anyway. Please, just tell him!"

Sherman must have seen the truth in my face. His

shoulders slumped. "It's in my pocket."

Doytchevsky barked out a laugh. "Stupid old man. That was too easy. I didn't even need the lie detector." His gaze snapped to me. "Take it."

I groped through Sherman's pockets and extracted a small USB device. Doytchevsky jerked his chin toward the shelves. "Put it there."

I had only taken a couple of steps when the sound of the trank gun made me whirl to see Sherman go limp.

"Hurry up. Put it on the shelf. Then lie face down on the floor."

Adrenaline stinging my veins, I froze. Take my chances and jump him now? He was too damn far away. He'd shoot me before I could take a step.

Doytchevsky snorted. "Don't be stupid. Do it."

I watched my hand rise to place the USB stick on the shelf. He was right. Getting tranked would be stupid. I lowered myself to the floor.

"Put your hands on your head. If you move, I'll detonate the bomb. Clear?"

"Clear," I mumbled into the dirty concrete. The chemical smell burned my nose and my eyes began to water.

A few moments later, I heard movement in the corner and the forklift started. What the hell was he doing?

The sound of the engine approached and I swallowed hard, my hands trembling on my head, overworked muscles screaming. How could Tammy bear blindness? It was torture not to be able to see what was coming.

The forklift stopped. Close. A roll of canvas hit the floor beside me, making me jerk involuntarily.

"Get up."

I hauled myself upright, trying to hide my shivering.

Cold concrete, low blood sugar, too much adrenaline. My mind drifted lightly in a sea of fear.

"Take off the electrodes. Unroll the sling and get him in it."

I stood staring stupidly at Doytchevsky in the driver's seat of the forklift, one hand on the controls, one hand on the phone. Shit, if he'd just put the phone down for an instant...

"Hurry up!" Doytchevsky's command was accompanied by another threatening wave of the phone, and I bent stiffly to remove the lie detector. The canvas unrolled into a smallish square with webbing loops at the corners. I laid it out beside Sherman and bent to heave at his limp form.

Clenching my teeth, I managed not to groan while I rolled and dragged him into the middle of the canvas. Thank God he was small and skinny. Knives of pain stabbed my chest and sweat soaked my shirt. I knelt for a moment, panting and trembling while Doytchevsky manoeuvred the forklift's extension over the sling with one hand on the controls, the other still holding the phone.

"Loop it over the extension and tuck his arms in."

I obeyed and the extension whined upward, raising the corners of the sling to roll Sherman into an uncomfortable-looking semi-fetal position inside the hammock of canvas.

Doytchevsky picked up a small control box from the floor of the forklift and a moment later, a blast of fierce heat rolled from the kiln as its lid opened.

Sudden horrible comprehension paralyzed me, my sweat freezing in the heat. "You... you can't..." My voice came out as an unrecognizable croak, my hands clenching on the canvas.

"Watch me." He brandished the phone. "Let go." He reached for the forklift controls. "Or keep holding on, and

I'll put you in the kiln along with him. That might actually be a better-"

The sound of the door chime made us both tense. Not the doorbell. The chime that sounded when the door opened. A moment later, the crash of breaking pottery shattered the air.

"Go!" Doytchevsky hissed, the phone slashing between us. "Deal with it."

As I turned away, I heard the forklift moving.

The whine of hydraulics.

I was almost at the door.

A sizzling roar and the stench of burning.

My knees went weak, my stomach heaving. I clung to the shelves for support. More pottery smashed in the store.

Another mechanical whine and the roaring was muffled. The reek pervaded the entire bay, burning my nose, searing my mind.

Another crash from the front of the shop brought me back to my senses. Too late to help Sherman now. Protect Lola.

I stumbled through the door.

Kane's gun swung up to point at me, his finger already tightening on the trigger.

CHAPTER 36

It happened too fast. Kane's eyes widened and he jerked his chin in a 'get-out-of-the-way' gesture, the muzzle of his gun searching for a target. Gaping in shock, I stood stupidly.

An instant later, Kane dove sideways as Doytchevsky's weight smashed into my back, his forearm crushing my throat, his gun hand swinging out beside me. The trank gun spat its small, venomous report.

Kane crumpled, his body sprawling into the broken pottery.

"Idiot." Doytchevsky shoved me away, his voice barely penetrating the cocoon of horror that held me motionless. "Bring him."

Staring at Kane lying limp on the floor, I stood frozen. How could I have failed him like this? I'd only had to get out of his line of fire. A single side-step...

This couldn't be happening.

Blood etched a shining red thread down his bicep, a scratch from one of the shards. My mind flew irrationally to my waist pouch. I had adhesive bandages in there. I should get one for him...

A slap to the back of my head jolted me into reality again. "I said, bring him. Hurry up."

My trembling knees dropped me beside Kane. "I can't. He's too big." I held out a shaking hand. "I have blood sugar problems. I can barely stand up. I can't carry him."

"Your problem, not mine." Doytchevsky pushed his toe at the shards. "Damn, that was one of my better pieces." He stooped to pick up Kane's gun and straightened, tucking it into his waistband. His phone threatened me again. "Drag him." His finger moved closer to the phone button. "Now."

I grasped Kane's wrists, my hands slick with sweat. Somehow I managed to heave his body across the floor and through the door into the bay before I collapsed beside him, gasping. My pulse battered my eardrums.

Another canvas roll dropped onto the floor beside me. "Get him onto it."

My heart contracted to a single point of incandescent pain before extinguishing completely.

If necessary, I would have chosen Lola over Sherman. I couldn't... wouldn't... choose between Kane and Lola.

Think of something. Anything to delay the inevitable.

"I thought you wanted him to suffer." My voice spoke from outside myself. "This is too easy. A few minutes of pain."

I looked up at the sound of Doytchevsky's snort. "There's no pain at all. Unfortunately. That kiln is over two thousand degrees right now. Hotter than a crematorium. Wood combusts spontaneously at only around six hundred degrees. He'll be dead after his first breath. In less than an hour, there's nothing left but fine gray ash."

I wrestled my terror into submission and stuffed it deep under the remains of my heart. Stall. It was my only hope.

"So like I said, it's too easy." My voice was horribly level. "Let him wake up. I've got a bone to pick with him."

"Have you, now?" Doytchevsky eyed me narrowly. "And what might that be?"

The cold voice spoke again from my mouth. "I hate the bastard. He raped me."

Doytchevsky's face lit with an unholy grin. "Well, well. The great and virtuous John Kane has feet of clay after all."

He gazed into middle distance for a few moments before returning his attention to me. "How convenient. I'll get to use that lie detector after all." He tossed a couple of nylon ties on top of Kane's body. "Tie him. Then lie on the floor and keep your hands on your head."

He moved toward the desk, the phone aimed at me like a weapon while I slid a tie onto Kane's ankles with shaking hands. I feigned yanking it tight, hoping I was convincing. It had to be tight enough to fool Doytchevsky, but maybe a little slack would be enough to give Kane something to work with.

Doytchevsky's watchful gaze never left me while I moved up to Kane's wrists. I strained at his limp body, dragging his wrists behind him and propping his back against my hip while I fumbled with the tie.

Maybe, just maybe.

I hunched lower, letting out a grunt of effort. Under the cover of Kane's broad back, I fished my knife out of my jeans and tucked it into the waistband of Kane's. He should feel its hard shape against his back when he woke. With his hands behind him, he might be able to free himself.

"Hurry up!"

I twitched at Doytchevsky's command and let out another pitiful grunt. "He's too damn heavy... there, got it."

I snugged the tie barely closed and let Kane flop onto his back again before lying down beside him, hands on my head. My heart battered the cold concrete under me. If

Doytchevsky checked my work...

But he didn't seem inclined to approach. After a short interval of silence, his footsteps stopped several feet away. "I've set up a webcam. It won't be the quality of my usual work, but it should suffice." I could hear the smile in his voice. "When he wakes up, you can force him to admit his transgressions. I'll signal you when to start and stop."

His footsteps receded again, and I lay shivering in silence while my mind skittered wildly. Stall. Draw out the 'questioning' to give Kane a chance to realize my knife was there and free himself.

But if Doytchevsky hooked Kane up to the lie detector, how could I make him admit to something he hadn't done? Unless...

Ignoring waves of shivering that ignited fiery pain in my shoulders, I gave myself over to frantic thought.

Kane stirred beside me only a few short minutes later, groaning. Doytchevsky's footsteps stopped at a safe distance again.

"Get up."

I wasn't sure which of us he was addressing, so I moved slowly and carefully. When he didn't object, I crept to my knees, biting back a whimper of pain as I lowered my arms.

Still shivering, I hauled myself to my feet. Kane's eyes opened, his muscles bulging as he tested his bonds.

"Don't bother," I snapped. "I tied them tight."

His unfocused gaze sharpened on me and I blessed his instant comprehension when he stopped struggling. In just a few moments, he'd find the knife.

I hoped.

"Put the electrodes on him."

Kane's head snapped around to face Doytchevsky.

"Doytchevsky," he said levelly. "What do you want?"

"I want you to answer some questions," Doytchevsky replied as I settled the band around Kane's forehead.

"And why would I do that?"

Doytchevsky grinned and hefted the phone. "Because I'm holding the detonator for a bomb that will blow up an innocent little old lady if you refuse. I believe you know the little purple-haired granny from the sex shop?"

Kane's face set like iron. "I'll answer."

"Good. After discovering your less-than-stellar personality traits, I was afraid that might not have been sufficient inducement. But you're a knight in shining armour after all." He sneered. "Or so you like to pretend."

Doytchevsky cut his eyes at me and stepped back to the computer. "Go ahead."

Kane's gaze met mine, and I forced my face into a stony expression. When I spoke, my voice was deadly cold. No hint of my quaking insides.

"Answer yes or no. You've been following me. Disobeying a direct order."

A flash of pain twisted his face, gone in an instant. The look of a man stabbed in the guts and left to bleed.

His face was impassive, his voice expressionless as he replied. "Yes."

The green light flashed with the same vile glee as Doytchevsky's smile.

"You've followed me before, haven't you? Lots of times."

"Yes."

"It wasn't enough, was it?" I went on before he could respond, holding onto my icy calm. "Even after you raped me the first time, you still wanted more."

He stiffened, but his wooden expression didn't alter.

I lunged toward him, shoving my face close to his. "Admit it! Tell everybody how you broke into my house in the middle of the night!"

For a single naked moment we locked eyes before he dropped his gaze.

"You did, didn't you?" I demanded. "You broke into my house in the middle of the night!"

"Yes." His voice was barely audible.

"What did you say? I didn't hear you."

"Yes." He spoke louder and the green light flashed its assent.

"You came into my bedroom. I was asleep. Naked."

"Yes."

"I begged, but it was no use. You didn't stop, did you?"

His shoulders bulged with tension, his gaze glued to the floor. "No."

"Afterward, when I was lying there crying, covered with bruises, you knew what you'd done. Didn't you?" When he didn't answer immediately, I jerked his head up by the hair. "*Didn't you?*"

"Yes." His voice was raw. The green light flashed its damnation.

I spared a glance at Doytchevsky. His eyes glittered, his lips stretched in a feral grin. I let my hatred leap onto my face before turning the expression toward Kane.

"But that wasn't enough for you, was it? You did it again. And then you abandoned me in the woods, even though you knew I could barely walk afterward. Didn't you?"

"Yes." His face was barren, his voice bleak.

"And you've been following me. Hounding me. Waiting for another chance. Haven't you?"

Kane's shoulders slumped. "Yes."

I stabbed a finger at the green light. "See? He admits it. He's a filthy scumbag rapist and stalker."

Doytchevsky drew a finger across his throat and reached for the keyboard.

Dammit, had Kane freed himself yet?

"I have more," I blurted. "Stemp was in on it, too..."

Doytchevsky tapped some keys, apparently ending the recording. "Fascinating. I'd love to hear you take down Stemp, since he's the one who gave the order to kill Robert in the first place. But we're out of time. Right about now, Stemp will be realizing that you're not coming to his party at the Knights' office. Take the headset off him."

As I removed the wires from Kane's forehead, Doytchevsky stabbed a finger at Kane. "Get on the sling."

Kane's shoulders flexed. He must be free by now. But until Doytchevsky came closer...

Doytchevsky brandished the phone, his finger moving toward the button. "Get on the sling. Now."

Kane heaved awkwardly onto his knees and squirmed slowly toward the square of canvas, his hands still behind his back. I eased a step away from him. Then another. Adrenaline seared my veins, my brain floating weightlessly. A little closer to Sherman's gun, still lying on the floor only a few feet away...

"Hurry up," Doytchevsky snapped.

An ear-splitting crash erupted from the front of the shop.

CHAPTER 37

The din seemed to go on forever. The high-pitched shattering of glass, the grating thunder of falling bricks, all underscored by a deep rumble that shook the building.

Earthquake? Bomb?

My overloaded mind grappled with the possibilities for an instant until I realized Doytchevsky had snatched Kane's gun from his waistband, the muzzle swinging toward us. A gunshot exploded. I hadn't even seen him pull the trigger.

Kane lunged toward me, arms wide, as another shot rang out. His body twisted in the air, a grunt ripping from his lips. His weight slammed me forward onto the concrete.

I thrashed free, straining toward Sherman's gun. Doytchevsky whirled to face the back of the bay as Hellhound's bulk crashed through the door.

Scrabbling desperately toward the gun, time slowed. My fingers touched its handgrip as Doytchevsky's weapon tracked around toward Hellhound. I flinched at the deafening report of another gunshot. Kane hauled himself up, a crimson stain blooming on his leg like some obscene flower.

Hellhound's gun jerked, the shot echoing off the hard walls of the bay. Doytchevsky pitched backward, his gun hand flinging open. The gun spun through the air.

Then Sherman's gun was hard in my hand and I sprang to stand over Doytchevsky. Blood welled from his useless shoulder and his lips stretched into a hellish grin. He thrust the phone in my direction with his good hand.

Its sound annihilated the last of my hope. The last of my humanity.

Ring.

Ring.

Ring.

I watched my gun swing around to point at Doytchevsky's face and fire again and again.

Arnie spoke close beside me, his voice curiously isolated in the soft, puffy silence. "Gimme the gun, darlin'. It's over."

I stared down at the mess of blood and splintered bone that had once been a man's face. Felt nothing.

The gun was heavy in my hand. Cold. Lethal.

Good.

"Aydan, it's done." Arnie's touch on my face felt distant. Somebody else's face. Not mine.

"Come on, darlin'-"

The silence shattered into bedlam, black-clad figures pounding into the bay, shouting.

So much shouting.

Rough hands seized my shoulders, twisting the gun out of my grasp, shoving me to the floor and yanking my hands behind me into the familiar pain of restraints.

Oh, hooray.

The good guys had arrived.

Feet rushed back and forth. More shouting. Hellhound

knelt under guard a few yards away, his hands bound. A knot of activity around Kane parted to reveal a dressing on his leg, his hands secured behind him as they hoisted him to his feet to limp out of the bay.

The ride back to Silverside was a blur. Our body-armoured escorts kept us separated. I could see only a sliver of Hellhound's shoulder. I glimpsed another man, but couldn't identify him. Probably just some poor bastard who happened to be walking by at the wrong moment. They must have had orders to grab everybody and let Stemp sort us out.

My body vibrated beyond pain, a deep thrumming torment enlivened by fiery slashes when my flayed wrists twisted in their bonds. I concentrated on numbness, refusing to hear Lola's laughter, see her sweet wrinkled face, feel her arms around me.

One word echoed in my brain, pounding slowly with the beat of my useless heart.

Failed.

Failed.

Failed.

At last the truck jolted to a halt. More loud voices. More insistent hands half-guiding, half-shoving me into Sirius Dynamics. I fell once, my rubbery legs refusing to hold my weight, pain tearing my muscles when the hands caught me and dragged me upright again.

Then suddenly I was standing in Stemp's office. Stemp sat behind his desk as usual, but General Briggs rose from the chair beside him as my body-armoured escort towed me into the room. I took a small measure of comfort from Briggs's ramrod-straight posture and steady eyes.

He inclined his head toward the chair, his seamed face set in grim lines. "Please sit down, Agent Kelly. I'll be observing this meeting."

I perched awkwardly, trying not to put pressure on my throbbing arms. The guard laid my waist pouch on the floor beside me, but my Glock was nowhere to be seen.

Whatever. Sooner or later I'd get it back. And when I did...

Across the desk, I studied Stemp's reptilian features as if seeing him for the first time, distantly noting the strained lines around his mouth.

What a fucking prick. No, not even a prick. I couldn't think of any word foul enough to describe him. A monster. Trading a vibrant, loving woman for nothing more than a scrap of technology.

Some day I'd meet him in hell. A hell we both richly deserved.

"Kelly." His abhorrent voice stirred the seething vat of my hatred. "If I release your hands, do I have your word that you'll behave?"

"No." My cold dead voice fell from my lips like rotting flesh from a corpse. "I'll kill you the first chance I get. Shoot your fucking face off just like I shot Doytchevsky."

The body-armoured man stiffened beside me and Briggs shifted in his chair. Even Stemp's expressionless face tightened perceptibly.

"I see." Stemp nodded to my escort. "Cut her loose and wait outside."

He stiffened to attention. "But, sir..."

Stemp lifted a wry eyebrow. "I presume you searched Agent Kelly for weapons before you brought her here. And General Briggs and I are both armed."

"Yes, sir."

The guard didn't sound convinced, but he cut the ties on my wrists and marched out without further comment, swinging the door shut behind him.

I tried to bite back my whimpers while I dragged my aching arms around into my lap, but a small moan leaked out despite my best efforts. I eased back in the chair and breathed.

General Briggs crossed the room. "Agent Kelly, may I look at your wrists?"

I forced my burning muscles to extend my arm, and he gently peeled back the bloodstained sleeve. His face hardened as we both regarded the mess beneath.

"Did our men do this to you?" he snapped.

"No." A few shiny beads of fresh blood oozed up in one of the cuts, belying my words. "They couldn't help it," I amended. "I was cut up before they put the restraints on."

His firm hand closed on mine. "I'm sorry."

I retrieved my hand. "It's okay. It's just a few little cuts."

"I believe that is the least of the apologies we owe you." He retraced his steps to his chair and sat, frowning.

I had only a few moments to puzzle over that cryptic remark before Stemp leaned forward. "Kane raped you repeatedly. And you believe I encouraged him. I did not. I didn't know it was happening, and I would have acted to protect you if I had known. Why didn't you tell me?"

Another wound opened in my heart. It might have even bled if there had been anything left inside.

Doytchevsky. That bastard. That's what he had been doing with the computer at the pottery shop. He hadn't just been recording...

"Doytchevsky sent you the video." I couldn't summon up

enough energy for anything but a dead-flat statement.

"Yes. He sent it to the entire chain of command, including General Briggs," Stemp confirmed.

"That fucking bastard." My voice floated in from a great distance. "It was all faked. Kane has never done anything wrong, and he certainly didn't rape me. It's all lies."

"Agent Kelly..."

It might have been compassion in Stemp's eyes. I didn't care. I didn't want his compassion. Only his blood and his suffering.

"You recorded the video yourself." His voice was soft. "His confession was confirmed by Dr. Travers's lie detector. We both know the lie detector is accurate. You can't deny this anymore, and you shouldn't try. He's in custody. You're safe from him now."

"We spoofed the lie detector." Anger thawed the edges of my icy detachment. "Don't you dare frame him with this bullshit."

"Aydan." General Briggs leaned forward, holding me with his gaze. "If we hooked Kane up to another lie detector, one we knew was working correctly, and if you asked him the same questions, would his answers be the same?"

I closed my eyes for a moment, excruciatingly weary. "Yes." When I opened my eyes again, I read the pain in his face. "But the questions themselves were misleading," I added. "Watch the video again. Listen to the questions. Kane was giving truthful answers about missions and briefings we've had over the past several months. The way I phrased the questions made it sound like forced sex, but I can give you a full explanation of the circumstances around each question. None of those circumstances involve rape or sexual harassment or any improper behaviour at all on

Kane's part."

I met General Briggs's eyes. "You know damn well he wouldn't do that."

He eased back in his chair. "I want to believe that."

"Believe it."

"And your allegations regarding Director Stemp's improper conduct?"

I shot Stemp a poisonous look, wishing I could force myself to lie solely for the vicious pleasure of watching him suffer.

"If necessary, I could have made it sound as though he colluded with Kane to arrange for my rape and subsequent sexual harassment." I held his gaze for a moment. "But that would have been lies, too."

Both men relaxed almost imperceptibly.

"Then may I ask why you expressed such... animosity toward Director Stemp?" General Briggs pinned me with his sharp gaze.

I turned to Stemp, hatred boiling over. "Have you retrieved the..." My voice broke and I gulped hard before continuing, my voice grinding like broken glass in my throat. "...remains from the explosion yet? You bastard."

"What?" He frowned at me for a moment before his impassive façade dissolved into a smile. "Oh. No. We got her out."

The air refused to enter my lungs. "You... what...?"

His smile widened, lightening his eyes to warm gold. "There was no explosion. Lola Ives is safe. We got her out."

CHAPTER 38

I should have been laughing and crying and jumping up and down.

I sat paralyzed in the chair, staring at Stemp's smile.

At last I drew a breath, sweet air soothing the pain in my chest. "You... she's safe? How...?"

"Apparently your neighbour was driving by your house around noon when he noticed your gate was open. He knew you always close it, so he drove into your yard. He knocked and rang the doorbell but got no reply, so he was suspicious already when he saw the torn paper taped to your garage door. He discovered the crumpled threat and called the police."

"Thank you, Tom," I murmured.

"I presume that threat was the reason you vanished without attending my briefing?"

"No. I would have come straight to you if it was just that threat. But Doytchevsky planted a bug on me and hacked the surveillance cameras here in Sirius so he could see and hear everything I did. I couldn't communicate with you in any way without risking Lola."

His brows snapped together as he snatched up the phone. "Webb. Kelly says our surveillance cameras have been hacked. Check it." He hung up. "Any other security breaches I should know about?"

"No." I still couldn't quite believe she was safe. "How did you find Lola?"

"The police contacted Mrs. Ives's business to see if she had arrived for work. Her business partner is her granddaughter, Linda Burton, who is currently dating Webb. She immediately called him, and he came to me..." Stemp cleared his throat. "...*insisting* that I intervene. Since you had already notified me of the situation, I dealt with the police and acquired the photograph for analysis. I pulled our best people onto it, but it was Webb who recognized the background once we had enhanced the photo."

"And..." I prompted.

"Apparently Webb's family is quite civic-minded. His parents frequently volunteer at community functions, and Webb often participates, too. He recognized the basement storage room at the community hall."

Stemp shrugged. "It was an ideal location. The treasurer of the community association confirmed that she received an anonymous phone call on Monday morning from a man wondering if the community hall had been booked for any functions this week. When he discovered nobody would be there, it would have been an easy task for him to pick the lock and set up his bomb inside. Abducting Mrs. Ives was an easy matter with his trank gun."

I swallowed nausea. So close to disaster.

"So the bomb...?"

"It was quite a simple improvised explosive device," Stemp said. "Our bomb techs went in through the side wall in case there was a trigger on the door, but there wasn't one, nor was there a booby trap on the device itself. Disarming it was a matter of snipping a wire."

"So she's safe." I couldn't seem to get it through my head.

"She's safe."

Lola, safe. My mind repeated the words over and over like a talisman.

"What... um..." I gave my head a shake and marshalled my wits. "What did you tell her? About why she'd been abducted?"

"Fortunately, Doytchevsky tranked her without letting her hear or see him. When she regained consciousness, she was already tied up in the storage room. We told her she had been abducted by a disturbed member of an extremist religious group who thought sex shops were the work of the devil."

I blew out a sigh. "Good. That'll work." My conscience prodded me. "Thank you."

"You're welcome. And thanks to you, we have the wireless network generator."

I blinked. "Um. It was on the shelf in the back bay of the pottery shop."

"Yes, the team retrieved it from exactly where you described it."

"From where..." I frowned. "I didn't describe it. I didn't think of it until just now."

Stemp raised a puzzled eyebrow. "You described it to the team who retrieved you. You were extremely insistent. You made them show it to you several times to confirm that they had it."

"Oh." I hoisted an aching arm to massage my forehead. "Right... I'd forgotten that. I remember now."

Dimly. But then, everything was distant. Even the news

of Lola's rescue barely warmed the ice in my soul.

Deal with it later.

I turned my attention back to Stemp, realizing he had spoken again. "Sorry, what?"

"I said, please brief us on all your activities to date."

"Right."

I plodded through the lengthy narrative, forcing my tired mind to concentrate. When I came to the part when Kane had appeared at the pottery shop, I hesitated, wondering if there was any way to protect him from his obvious defiance of a direct order.

No. They'd seen us together on the video and captured him a few feet away from me. No hope.

I laid it out exactly as it had happened.

At last I got to the arrival of the troops. "How did you find us?" I asked.

"The tracking device you planted on Doytchevsky. I saw the signal move to his apartment this morning, so I knew you had placed it. I had a team in position outside the Knights' office building, still believing you would be meeting Sherman there, and that Doytchevsky would attempt to intercept him. When the tracking device wasn't converging on the office in time for four-thirty, I pulled the team and scrambled them to the device's location."

The damn thing was still in my change purse. I'd completely forgotten about it. Again.

He didn't need to know that.

"I have it in my waist pouch now." I leaned over, clenching my teeth on a groan as I straightened and fished out the tiny device to hand it over. After a moment, I added, "What blew up in the front of the shop?"

Stemp smiled. "Perhaps we can get some answers." He

picked up the phone and dialled an extension. "Bring Helmand."

Several minutes later, a rap at the door made Stemp glance up. "Come."

The door swung open to reveal Hellhound with an armed escort, but I was glad to see Hellhound's wrists weren't bound anymore. He strode into the room and took up parade rest beside my chair, ignoring Stemp and nodding to General Briggs. Briggs returned the nod with a ghost of a smile.

Stemp seemed unfazed by the slight. He shot a glance at the guard. "Dismissed." The man withdrew, closing the door behind him, and Stemp added, "Helmand. Report."

Hellhound eyed him for a moment, his legs planted like stone pillars. "I knew Aydan was in trouble," he rasped. "I called Kane an' pushed him into helpin'. It's my fault he broke orders."

"Save it for the court-martial," Stemp said, and Hellhound shot him a murderous glare before continuing.

"I followed Aydan onto the highway an' stopped her. She signalled me that she was being followed an' bugged. I doubled back an' met Kane an' we used Kane's truck to tail 'em into Calgary to the pottery shop. Saw Aydan drive into the back of the bay, an' then some guy rang the bell an' she came out front by herself, so we just sat tight. Didn't wanna fuck it up if she had somethin' goin' down."

He shot me a glance and continued. "Then some old fart showed up an' pulled a gun on her an' they went in the back. That's when we figured she was in trouble, so Kane broke in the front door an' made noise to draw 'em out while I doubled around to cover the back. He told me to stay outside an' if I heard gunfire, to call it in. I heard fuck-all. So then I didn't know what to do."

"John got tranked," I said. "It was my fault. I stood there like an idiot blocking his shot and Doytchevsky got him."

Stemp ignored me. "Go on, Helmand."

"I went around to the front an' saw all the busted dishes, but everythin' was too quiet inside. So I called Dave and got him to bring his rig over an' drive it through the front a' the shop while I shot out the lock an' came in the back."

Light dawned. "That's why that first shot seemed to come out of nowhere. And I thought the crash was an earthquake or something."

Hellhound spared me a grin. "Nah. Just Dave."

Stemp's dry voice intruded. "And where did you get the gun? You don't have a restricted weapons license."

Hellhound's parade rest stiffened, his chin rising as he stared over Stemp's head. "Found it."

"You found it." Stemp's dryness rivalled the Sahara.

"Yeah. Didn't wanna leave it in case some kid picked it up an' got hurt."

"How selfless."

"Yeah." Hellhound stared at the wall, stone-faced. "An' then this guy pulled a gun on me. Hadta fire in self-defence."

"I see." Stemp's snakelike features swivelled to face me. "Did you see a gun lying outside the bay when you came in?"

I shrugged and met his eyes without a qualm. "I was driving, so I wouldn't have seen it. Arnie must have picked it up, because I was at his house when he packed to come here and I didn't see a gun then."

Which was true. I had been in the bathroom when he was packing.

"If he says he found it, I believe him," I added.

In fact, I knew it was the truth. He had 'found' it. Just not outside the door to the pottery shop.

Stemp studied us in silence for a few moments. Hellhound's impassive face could have stopped a truck. I was pretty sure my expression was equally unenlightening, since I couldn't summon up any emotion other than exhausted detachment.

"And what about Kane's gun?" Stemp asked. "He surrendered his firearm as part of his suspension. So he was carrying an illegal weapon."

Hellhound didn't flinch. "I never saw a gun in his hand. Far's I know, he didn't have one."

"Is that so?"

Hellhound didn't deign to answer, and Stemp turned to me instead. "Except that Kelly's report already stated that Kane had a gun."

I gave him a blank stare. "He had something in his hand that looked like a gun. It was probably fake. That would explain why he didn't fire. It all happened so fast and I only caught a glimpse of it before Doytchevsky picked it up. I couldn't state with any certainty whether it was or wasn't a real gun."

Behind Stemp, General Briggs's lips twitched. He smoothed a hand over his chin, wiping away the expression, but the twinkle in his steel-blue eyes gave him away.

"I see." I was pretty sure there was amusement in Stemp's eyes, too. "Very well." He lifted the phone to his ear. "Bring Shore."

When Dave's guard waved him into the room, he glanced at its occupants, paling slightly before copying Hellhound's stance on the other side of my chair.

"Mr. Shore." Stemp surveyed him emotionlessly. "We

meet again."

"Yeah." Dave shot a sidelong glance at me before pressing his lips shut and emulating Hellhound's distant stare.

"Tell us what happened."

Dave's jaw worked for a few moments as if he was chewing on his words. "Hellhound called. Said Aydan needed me. Bobtailed over. Waited for Hellhound's signal and then backed my tractor into the shop."

Stemp raised an eyebrow. "Bobtailed?"

Dave nodded. "Drove the highway tractor. Left the trailer at a truck stop."

"Do you have a gun?"

"Nope."

"Did you see Kane or Helmand carrying a gun?"

"Nope."

"Did you see anything else?"

"Nope."

Briggs's lips twitched again. Dave stared into the distance.

Stemp tried again. "What else can you tell us?"

Dave gave me another sidelong glance. "I showed up, backed into the building. That's it. Can I go now?"

Stemp leaned back in his chair. "What's the hurry?"

Dave's jaw muscles rippled again and he gave me an imploring look.

I reached out to touch his clenched fist. "It's okay, Dave, you can say whatever you need to say."

His hand closed around mine. "Aydan, I left Nichele holed up at the truck stop motel. These guys won't let me call her. Did I..." He swallowed, his grip tightening. "Is she still in danger? I gotta get back to her!"

The fear in his eyes made even my deadened heart squeeze in sympathy. "She's safe, Dave. It's over. You saved her."

He slumped, the lines of tension melting from his face. "Shit, I mean, crap, thank God! Jeez, Aydan, it's been killing me thinking I might've..." He broke off. "Can I call her now?"

This time General Briggs didn't bother to hide his smile. "Go and call her. You can use your cell phone in the main lobby."

"Thanks." Dave hurried out.

Stemp eyed me. "What was that all about?"

"I was afraid Doytchevsky would use Nichele as leverage the way he used Lola. I told Dave to keep her safe."

"I see." Stemp nodded at Hellhound. "Dismissed. Close the door."

When the latch clicked behind him, I turned to face Briggs and Stemp. "What about Kane?"

Stemp's dispassionate mask descended again. "He suffered a superficial gunshot wound to his leg. He was treated and remanded to the brig. He'll remain in custody until his court-martial."

Don't feel. Don't let the pain in.

"And the sexual harassment issue?"

"Because of Kane's recorded confession, he'll also have to stand trial for rape. Sexual harassment is the least of his worries."

"It's all bullshit, and you know it." My voice was completely flat.

"So you say." Stemp passed a hand over his face, suddenly looking as tired as I felt. "You'll have your chance to testify."

"When?"

"I don't know yet."

I could feel something after all. A slow, deep current of burning rage. Swelling up between my ribs, turning my spine to stone and searing my heart into ashes.

"Tomorrow." The word boiled from my lips like white-hot lava. I fixed Stemp with a deadly glare, my voice sizzling with menace. "You will arrange a hearing tomorrow. This ends *tomorrow*."

Briggs's hand drifted casually toward his sidearm. I held Stemp's gaze. "Do it. You know he deserves to have this over and done."

He eyed me, letting my anger roll impotently against his impervious façade. "You aren't threatening me, are you Kelly?"

"No. I'm *telling* you."

Stemp laughed suddenly, leaning back in his chair. He glanced over at General Briggs. "How many strings can you pull?"

A small smile. "Quite a few."

Stemp sobered, facing me again. "We'll do our best."

"Thank you."

Briggs rose, his piercing gaze assessing me. "Do you still plan to shoot the director's face off?"

I looked at Stemp's bland expression, my anger cooling to a leaden lump between my aching ribs. Fatigue washed over me, and I eased out a long and painful breath.

"Not today."

Stemp's lips quirked. "Good enough. Pick up your weapon at Stores on your way out. Dismissed."

CHAPTER 39

Hellhound detached himself from the wall beside Stemp's office when I staggered out into the hallway. "Darlin', when did ya eat last?" His arm encircled me and I leaned into his strength.

"About six this morning."

"Shit!" His arm tightened around me and I whimpered an involuntary protest at the pain.

"Shit, sorry, darlin'." He loosened his grip, hovering anxiously. "Just sit down right here. I'll go an' get ya somethin'."

"No, I'm fine, I'm not going to sit here. I can make it to the end of the hall."

"Okay..." He trod slowly beside me while I plodded down the hall and into the staff lounge. "Sit," he commanded. "Tell me what to get ya."

I slumped onto one of the sofas, too tired to argue. "There are some little cartons of orange juice in the fridge and some cereal bars in the cupboard."

He was back in a moment, pushing the straw into the orange juice and handing it over before sinking onto the sofa beside me.

I hunched over to rest my elbows on my knees and

ducked my head to sip. The acidic sweetness lashed my tastebuds and I gulped eagerly. When I raised my head, Hellhound was frowning again.

"You're hurtin' even worse than last night, aren't ya? Ya can't even lift your arms."

"I'm fine." The lie issued easily from my lips. Just like old times.

His frown deepened. "Aydan..." He paused. "Look, I know this ain't the time for a heart to heart, but ya promised ya wouldn't lie to me an' I know you're lyin' about that. What d'ya think I'm gonna do, laugh 'cause you're hurtin'?"

I hunched my shoulders against the sting of memory and took another gulp of juice, avoiding his eyes.

"Aw shit, Aydan." His arm settled around my shoulders and his lips brushed my hair. "That fuckin' asshole ex-husband a' yours liked it, didn't he? He liked to see ya hurtin'."

I swallowed the lump in my throat and tucked the fraying edges of my emotions back in. "I don't think so. I think he was just so unhappy himself that he couldn't see-"

"Bullshit." His voice was flat with anger. "He could see."

"I really don't want to talk about this. Would you open that cereal bar for me, please?"

He yanked the wrapper off and crushed it in his fist, handing me the bar without speaking. I shrank into myself.

They act sweet until you begin to trust them and that's when it starts. The cold, angry silences, the vicious words, the eternal walking on eggshells. Never again.

"Aw, darlin', I'm sorry." Arnie's voice was a soft rasp.

"Forget it." I took a savage bite of the cereal bar and spoke through the too-big mouthful. "It's no big deal."

"It is a big deal, Aydan. It's a really fuckin' big deal to

me."

I groaned, gulped my mouthful, and chased it with another swig of orange juice before turning to face him. "Why? Why is it such a big fucking deal?"

"'Cause it's like I just hit ya an' I'm standin' here watchin' ya bleed. Just like my fuckin' asshole ol' man."

"Oh, Arnie, no. I'm sorry." I reached to touch his cheek, trying not to grimace when I lifted my arm. "You're not. You're nothing like your da... old man."

He cupped his hand over mine and turned his head to kiss my palm, whiskers tickling the sensitive skin. "It's okay, darlin', I don't want ya to apologize. I just want ya to trust me a bit, okay? I ain't tryin' to hurt ya."

I leaned into his gentle embrace. "I know."

A moment later he spoke again. "So how're ya really feelin'?" I could hear the smile in his voice.

I groaned and slumped against his shoulder. "Everything I own hurts like a fucking bitch from hell."

"Yeah, I figured. Come on, darlin'. Let's get ya somethin' decent to eat an' get ya home."

I let him help me carefully to my feet. Reality crushed me a few moments later.

"Shit, my car's in Calgary."

"It's okay, darlin', I got the SUV here an' I'm stayin' with ya tonight even if ya try an' kick me out."

I leaned gratefully against him. "I won't kick you out."

Dave rose smiling from one of the chairs when we came through the security doors into the lobby. "Long time, no see."

"Yeah, a whole ten minutes." I plastered on a convincing

smile and surveyed him. "Have you lost weight?"

"Yeah, few pounds." He grinned. "Nichele's been making me eat healthy, and I started working out a bit."

"Well, you look great."

He did. Nichele was obviously a good influence. His wild hair had been tamed by a crisp cut that flattered its waves, and he wore a new collared T-shirt with well-fitting jeans.

"Speaking of Nichele, did you talk to her?" I asked.

"Yeah, she's fine. She's gonna get a cab home and I'll go there when I get back to Calgary." A flush climbed his neck and he gave me a bashful smile. "We're gonna give it another try."

"That's great, Dave."

Knowing Nichele's track record with relationships, I wasn't sure how great it would be in reality, but who knew? Stranger things had happened.

I changed the subject to his first love. "Is your truck okay?"

"Should be. I backed in so the fifth-wheel did all the damage." Anxiety tinged his voice. "Sure hope it doesn't make the news. Don't want people thinking I can't back up without running into a building. Pulled out right away, but somebody might've seen me."

I squeezed his hand. "I'll talk to Stemp. If anybody saw it, we'll figure out a way to make it go away."

"Thanks, Aydan." A ringtone sounded from his pocket, and he withdrew his phone to check the display. "Gotta go. Called one of my buddies in Drumheller and he's picking me up."

I hugged him, trying to hide how much it hurt to raise my arms. "Thanks, Dave. You saved my life again."

He patted my back and pulled away, flushing scarlet. "No big deal," he mumbled. "Any time you need me, you just call. So long."

He hurried out, and Hellhound smiled down at me. "Let's get somethin' to eat. Wanna go to Eddy's?"

No music. Music makes you feel. I couldn't afford to feel right now.

"Not tonight. Let's go to Fiorenza's and get Italian instead."

By the time we parked in front of my house, my dull exhaustion had been augmented by the stupor of a full belly and a warm vehicle. I dragged myself out of my slump against the door when Hellhound turned to me.

"Come on, darlin'. Just a few more stairs an' you're home."

I nodded silent acquiescence and got out to trudge into the house. Inside, my answering machine blinked insistently. I tried to sleepwalk past it, but Arnie stopped me.

"Prob'ly better check your messages."

I sighed. "Yeah."

When I pressed the button, Tom's voice made me groan. "Aydan, please call me as soon as you get this. It's urgent. Thanks."

"Shit." I sank onto a kitchen chair and stared at the phone. "I forgot I'd have to explain all this to him. I'll have to call Stemp and see if he has a cover story."

I had one of the secured phones in my hand before paranoia penetrated my fog of indifference. I might not have any useful secret agent skills, but there was no need to make stupid mistakes. Extracting my illicit bug detector from its hiding place, I scanned my whole house before dialling, just to be sure.

When Stemp answered on the first ring, I spared a moment to wonder if he ever took a vacation. On call, twenty-four/seven. What a life. And he had pulled in all the department resources to save Lola. Maybe I should cut him some slack.

A few minutes on the phone established a usable cover story, and I hung up with a sigh. Without giving myself time to think about it, I dialled Tom's number.

He picked up immediately, apparently watching the call display. "Aydan?"

"Hi, Tom. I got your message, and the police told me what you did. Thanks."

"I'm glad I could help. Are you all right? What happened? The police wouldn't tell me anything except that Lola was safe."

"It's a long story..."

God, how much more bullshit would he believe?

I crossed my fingers and channelled sincerity for all I was worth. "I was doing the books for a religious group. I can't say which one because the police are still investigating. But they were kind of creepy, and eventually I realized they had some really sick notions of morality, so I told them I didn't want to do their books anymore. They pressured me to come back, and eventually I did. But then I discovered some flyers in their office that made me really nervous, stuff about how their calling is to eradicate the work of the devil. It sounded like they might be planning attacks against businesses that they thought were doing the devil's work. So I called the police. That was a few days ago, but they must have realized I had figured out what they were doing. I had some threatening phone calls, and this morning that photo was taped to my garage door. I was so scared I just drove straight to the police station in Drumheller. I didn't even think to take the paper with me until I was on the road, and then I was too afraid to come back."

I stopped babbling, hoping I hadn't sounded too glib. Please let him swallow it.

"Aydan," he said gently. "If anything like this ever happens again, come to me, okay? You could have called the police from my house. You didn't have to drive all the way to Drumheller."

"I know, Tom, it was stupid, but I was so scared..."

Great, now I looked like a pathetic fluff-brain. I held back a sigh. Maybe he'd decide I was too dumb to live and give up on me...

No such luck.

"You must be really shaken up over this. Do you want me to come over?"

Damn sympathy. I swallowed hard. "Thanks, Tom, I really appreciate the offer. But Arnie's here, and I'll be fine."

"Okay. Call me if you need anything. No matter how big or small."

"Thanks. 'Bye."

I let my arm fall to my lap, blowing out a long breath. Hellhound's arms closed around me and I pressed my face into his shirt. "God, I hate lying to people," I mumbled.

"I know, darlin'. Come on, let's go sit somewhere more comfortable."

I let him help me to my feet and we wandered into the living room to sink onto the sofa. Leaning against him, I rolled my raw emotions into a ball and locked them down, letting my mind go blank.

Just let it all go away. My body throbbed with an ache that wasn't just bruises and sore muscles.

Gentle fingertips coaxed my chin up. "Ya still in there, darlin'?"

I closed my eyes and tucked my head down against him. "No. I'm taking a vacation. Back in a few years."

I had expected him to chuckle, but he didn't. "Ya beatin' yourself up over Kane?"

"I can't think about that right now."

"It ain't your fault, Aydan."

Just shut the hell up and let me sit here.

His voice was soft. "Ya really went to town on that guy today. Ya wanna talk about it?"

"No."

He sat in silence for a short time before speaking again. "Aydan, look at me."

Why couldn't he just sit there and be quiet the way he'd done before? I pried my eyes open and straightened to face him.

He studied me. "I'm worried about ya, darlin'."

Okay, fine. Convince him there was nothing to worry about and he'd shut up. I cranked on a smile.

"Thanks, Arnie. There's nothing to worry about. I'm just tired, that's all."

"That all it is?" His keen gaze looked into my soul, and I leaned in to kiss him before he could see too much.

"Yeah, that's all. In fact, I think I'll call it a night."

He caught my hand as I pulled away. "Hang on, Aydan. We gotta talk."

CHAPTER 40

God, not now.

I listened to my voice say 'What's wrong?' without inflection.

He laid gentle fingertips under my chin and looked into my eyes for a moment before letting out a sigh. "I dunno, darlin', but I can guess. How d'ya feel?"

"Fine." When he said nothing, I recanted. "Sorry, I'm not trying to lie to you, I just don't want you to worry." I summoned all my energy to paste on my best convincing smile. "My arms and chest hurt and those welts on my leg still sting a bit, but other than that I'm fine."

"But ya ain't scared or mad or anythin'?" His voice was very soft.

"No, I'm okay. Just tired." Another premium, Grade-A-convincing smile.

For shit's sake, just let it go and leave me alone.

"I need a beer." Hellhound rose abruptly and strode for the kitchen. I heard the fridge door and musical clinking, and a moment later he returned with two bottles, passing me one as he sank back onto the couch beside me.

I handed it back to him. "I'm not really in the mood for beer. Thanks anyway."

He laid an arm around my shoulders and pulled me close beside his warmth. "Drink it. Ya need it." He pressed the bottle back into my hand and took a deep swallow of his own.

"Um, no, actually I don't, Arnie. I'm okay."

He sighed and slouched down on the sofa, laying his head back to stare at the ceiling. "Can I tell ya somethin' personal?"

Miss Manners spoke before I could silence her. "Of course, you can tell me anything."

No. Not tonight. Please, just shut up.

He tipped the beer bottle up to his lips, its contents gurgling alarmingly. By the time the bottle came to rest on his knee again, it was half empty.

"When I was a kid an' the ol' man was on a shit-faced rampage..." he began.

I gulped a long swallow of beer and curled tighter behind my shield of indifference. Not tonight. I couldn't bear his pain tonight. I tried to block out his words, but his voice was inexorable.

"...Us kids used to hide, just stay outta the way, but he'd find us and whale on us just for the hell of it. Mean fucker."

He drank more beer. "I was about four. Don, he was six years older, an' one day he told me about his safe place. I didn't get it, 'cause the ol' man'd just beat the shit outta him. Knocked out a coupla teeth an' broke his arm. But he said he had a safe place in his mind, a place where he could go an' it didn't matter if anybody hit him or not."

I shivered and Hellhound pulled the throw blanket over me, cuddling me closer against him. But he didn't stop talking.

"After that it made sense," he went on. "I always knew when he was in his safe place. I could see it in his eyes. I made a safe place in my mind, too, an' I went there whenever the ol' man got hold a' me."

He turned to study me. "Your ex was a mean motherfucker, too, an' I bet ya got a safe place a' your own. An' I think you're there now."

I said nothing, clinging to my shield.

Hellhound sighed and chugged more beer before leaning back to speak to the ceiling again. "It's good to have that place. It gets ya through shit. But one day Don went to his safe place an' he just never came back. Kept on livin', but he was just goin' through the motions. One night years later he was shit-faced as usual. We were kicked back shootin' the shit, an' he said the only time he felt really alive was when he was hurtin' somebody."

I already knew the rest of that story. How Don had perpetuated the cycle of violence and addiction in his own family. How Arnie had tried over and over to get help for them until the night his brother turned on him. The twisted scar on his forearm told the story more eloquently than he ever could.

So much pain.

Hellhound drained his bottle and sat up to face me. "Aydan, ya gotta come outta that place now. It's okay to go there when ya need to, but it ain't a good place to live."

I shrugged. "I told you, I'm fine."

"Maybe." He took my hand, stroking it gently. "Darlin', ya said ya never lied to me."

"I haven't."

"Ya said ya trusted me."

"I do."

"So tell me the truth now." He searched my face. "Ya know what I'm talkin' about, don't ya?"

Leave me alone. Just go away and leave me alone.

Stubborn honesty forced a reply out of me.

"Yes."

"Ya know ya can't stay there, don't ya?"

I pulled my hand out of his grasp. "Why not? I lived there for years. It works."

"Darlin', it doesn't work. Ya think it's workin' 'cause ya can't feel the pain, but the truth is ya can't feel anythin'."

"Yeah, and you know what? I'm just fine with that." I tipped up my beer bottle for a defiant gulp.

"But I ain't." His quiet intensity froze me. "Aydan, that place's always gonna be there inside ya. Ya can go back if ya need to. But the longer ya stay there, the harder it is to leave. Ya gotta come back now."

Sudden tremors rocked me, long waves shaking me to my core. "Arnie, please don't ask me to do that right now. I just need a bit of time. Later I will, I promise. I'll deal with it. Just not now."

He straightened, holding me with his gaze. "Darlin', I never asked ya for anythin' before, but I'm askin' ya now. Come back to me. Please."

The touch of his fingertips on my cheek breached my defences.

"No!" I jerked away, my throat tightening, tears blurring my vision. "Goddamn it, you have *no right* to ask me that! It's... I won't..." Sobs caught in my aching chest. "Shit..."

I sprang up to run, but for the first time since I'd known him, Arnie didn't let me go. He was on his feet in an instant, his hands firm on my shoulders. I tried to twist free, but he held me fast.

"Aydan," he said urgently. "Ya said ya trusted me. Trust me now."

"To... do... *what*?" I thumped my fists against his chest. The tears were spilling over onto my cheeks. "*What?* You can't... protect me... you can't..." A sob tore from my throat. "Let me *go*..." I tried to push him away, my arms screaming with the effort.

His voice was so soft I barely heard him. "Trust me to hold ya when ya cry."

He released me and stepped back, his powerful arms dropping to his sides, his palms turned toward me in silent entreaty.

I had been wrong all these years. There was still something left inside me that could break.

My legs wobbled and I slumped to the floor, raw sobs tearing my throat. When Arnie's arms closed around me, I clung to him as if to a life raft in a hostile ocean, my tears soaking his shirt.

Cradled in his arms, I wept helplessly until at last I subsided into hiccups and sniffles while he muttered comfort, stroking my hair over and over. Humiliation heated my already-burning cheeks.

God, how could I be such a pathetic mess? I should have made him leave. *I* should have left. Idiot.

Damn weak stupid idiot.

"Aydan?"

At the sound of his soft rasp, I pressed my face tighter against his soggy shirt.

Why couldn't I just vanish?

"Darlin', I know what you're thinkin', an' you're dead wrong."

"No, you don't," I mumbled.

"Yeah, I do. You're kickin' yourself an' tellin' yourself I'm gonna laugh at ya an' never let ya forget this. An' you're wonderin' how to pretend it never happened, an' maybe you're thinkin' ya should dump me 'cause I'm gettin' too close."

I gulped. Okay, so maybe he did know what I was thinking.

"Aydan, your ex was fucked up. I ain't him. I ain't gonna use this to hurt ya. I already forgot it happened, an' if you're thinkin' this's gonna turn us into a couple, tell me now so I can run like hell."

In spite of myself, I snickered wetly against his chest. "I love your fear of commitment."

He chuckled. "I'm gonna take that as a compliment." He caressed my hair away from my cheek. "Come on, darlin', sit up."

I burrowed closer. "No. I've got snot all over my face."

"Wipe it on my shirt."

"Gross! No."

Hellhound laughed. "Well, ya better figure out somethin' before it dries or you'll be stuck to me for good."

I snickered again. "Joined by the sacred bonds of crusty snot."

"Jesus, darlin', ya should write weddin' poetry." He dropped a kiss on the top of my head. "I'll get the snot-rags. Be right back."

He rose while I fiddled with the blanket, hiding my face. Before I had a chance to get embarrassed all over again, the tissue box plopped down in front of me and he sat on the sofa.

After some mopping and blowing, I couldn't delay the inevitable any longer. Arnie leaned forward to raise my chin.

"Lemme see your face, darlin'."

I focused on the binding of my blanket, picking at a few

loose threads. "No. I'm sure it's not a pretty sight."

His fingers were gentle but insistent. "Look at me, Aydan. Look me in the eye."

When I met his gaze at last, he smiled, his shoulders easing. "You're right, it ain't pretty. It's beautiful. Come here, darlin'." He held out his arms and when I curled beside him on the couch, he pulled me close and pressed his lips against my hair.

"Thanks for comin' back," he murmured.

I hid my face against his clammy shirt. "It wasn't like you gave me a choice."

"It's always your choice, darlin'." His hand smoothed my hair. "Ya know there's another choice ya should think about makin'. Ya been through some bad shit lately. Ya might wanna think about talkin' to somebody. I know ya got trust issues, but a shrink ain't gonna use your feelin's against ya."

"I know." I blew out a breath of surrender. "I'll call Dr. Rawling tomorrow."

"Promise?"

"Promise." I pulled away to meet his eyes. "How about you?"

"Me?" He shrugged. "I'm fine."

"You called me on my bullshit, now I get to call you on yours. You shot a man today, too. Doesn't that bother you?"

He sighed, looking through me into the past. "Hate to say it, darlin', but no, not really. Kinda wish it did, but I ain't gonna lie to ya." His gaze faltered and he picked up my half-empty beer bottle, squinting at it. "Just like my fuckin' ol' man." He raised the bottle in a bitter toast and poured the contents down his throat.

"Arnie, that's not true."

He shrugged.

"Arnie." I cupped his face in my hands to look into his eyes. "You lived in a war zone before you were even old enough to go to school. You saw combat in the army. Defending yourself without remorse doesn't make you like your old man. I know you don't enjoy causing pain. He did. It's totally different."

"Just seems like it's pretty fucked up to put a bullet in a guy an' not give a shit."

I turned away, unable to meet his eyes. "Well, you're not as fucked up as me," I mumbled. "I shot his face off."

His voice was soft behind me. "I got a feelin' there was a reason. That the guy that beat ya?"

"Yeah." I didn't turn around. "It wasn't just that, though. He burned a man to death in the kiln." I shuddered, sickness rising at the memory. "The kiln was so hot he just..." Hellhound's arms closed around me and I turned to hide against his chest.

"I heard him *sizzling*, Arnie. Like... like a steak on a barbecue. It was... just... He was going to do the same to John. And I thought he'd blown Lola up with a bomb. And because of him, John's facing a court-martial and rape charges."

Hellhound stiffened. "Rape? What the fuck, Aydan, how'd that happen?"

I pulled away to face him. "It was my fault. John was unconscious and Doytchevsky was going to put him in the kiln. I had to find a way to stall. I knew how much Doytchevsky hated John, so I told him John raped me and I wanted to get revenge. It kept him from killing John, but..."

I wrapped my aching arms around my body. "I might as well have killed him myself. John faked a confession, and Doytchevsky recorded it and sent the video to his entire chain of command."

Hellhound slumped back on the sofa. "Aw, shit."

CHAPTER 41

The phone woke me in the grey half-light of early morning. I jerked violently, my heart leaping into a frenzied drumming as I wrestled free of the blankets and scrambled over Hellhound's barely-stirring bulk to grab the handset.

The call display did nothing to soothe my fear. I punched the Talk button. "What?"

Stemp's voice didn't sound as urgent as I'd feared. "The hearing is arranged for ten-hundred hours today. Briefing in my office at zero-nine."

"I'll be there."

He disconnected without another word and I collapsed back onto the bed, waiting for my heart rate to slow.

Hellhound heaved up on one elbow to peer anxiously down at me. "What, darlin'?"

"Stemp has arranged a hearing for Kane at ten o'clock. He wants a briefing with me at nine."

He flopped back on the pillow, scrubbing his hands over his face. "Is that good or bad?"

"I don't know." I stared at the ceiling, crushing a handful of blanket in my fist. "Oh, God, Arnie, I pressured Briggs and Stemp into having a hearing today, but what if I can't convince them John's confession was faked? And even if I do convince them, he'll get court-martialled anyway for disobeying an order. Maybe I should have just shut up and let it drag on a little longer..."

"No, darlin'." He slid an arm around my shoulders. "Kane'd wanna get it over with. Ya did the right thing."

I sighed and propped my chin on his chest, following the lines of his tattoos with my fingertip. "I don't know anything about military law. Do you think there's any chance he can avoid the court-martial? Or be acquitted?"

His silence confirmed my fears.

"Prob'ly not," he rasped at last. "It's pretty straightforward. Direct order, an' he broke it." He caressed my hair. "Dunno how important ya are in the big picture an' I know ya can't tell me, but if you're as important as I think, he might be able to argue he was protectin' national security tryin' to keep ya safe."

His chest rose and fell under me in a deep sigh. "Doubt if they'll go for it, though. If somebody'd had ya at gunpoint, maybe, but not when ya were just drivin' down the highway. They'll say he shoulda called it in to Stemp an' stayed away." He pounded a fist against the mattress. "Fuck, I told him to stay put an' let me deal with it, but he wouldn't fuckin' listen."

"I thought you said you'd dragged him into it."

"Nah. After he saw that fuckin' sick video, there was no way he was gonna sit back an' let that fucker get another shot at ya. I thought I'd talked him outta it the night before, but he was watchin' ya by the time I met ya in the parkin' lot at Sirius. I didn't even know he was there 'til he phoned me after ya pulled out. I tried to get him to break off, but then when ya turned me back I hadta either get in the truck with Kane or give it up completely. He was tailin' ya a few miles back."

I pulled the blankets up over my shoulders, shivering. "I can't believe they'd court-martial him. He's the best agent they've got."

"Yeah, darlin', it sucks shit. But the army doesn't make exceptions."

Arnie's gloomy words hung in my memory while I signed for my security fob at Sirius Dynamics. Absorbed in rehearsing all the arguments I might offer in Kane's defence, I realized I was bracing myself for the sight of Doytchevsky's face as I hurried upstairs.

When I remembered he was dead, the surge of relief made my stomach twist with a peculiar mixture of guilt and satisfaction. Arnie was right. How fucked up was it to feel nothing but fierce elation at the memory of the gun kicking in my hand; the sudden horrible relaxation of taut muscles into death?

I gave my head a vigorous shake. Deal with it later. Kane needed me now.

On the dot of nine o'clock, I tapped on Stemp's door.

He glanced up from his computer, an intent frown clearing from his forehead. "Come in. Close the door."

He nodded in the direction of the chair and I sank into it as he withdrew the bug detector from his drawer and scanned the room. Including my waist pouch. I shot him a twisted smile and received a wry quirk of his mouth in response.

Assured that the room was clear, he resumed his seat behind the desk.

"How about the security cameras?" I asked.

"Webb went over the system with a fine-toothed comb. Doytchevsky was bluffing."

"That fucking bastard." I caught myself. "Sorry. I'll try to watch my mouth in the hearing."

Stemp raised a shoulder in one of his tiny shrugs. "It's unlikely to matter. It's not a trial or court-martial or any sort of official tribunal, merely a meeting of the chain of command to determine appropriate action. Fortunately, Kane's chain of command is relatively short. There will only be two other men there besides General Briggs and myself. We hope to be able to establish and document a valid reason why charges are not appropriate. But it will have to be a unanimous decision."

He eyed me levelly. "As you are likely aware, discipline is vital in a military organization. It would be virtually unprecedented to cancel a court-martial. Arbitrarily allowing that sort of special treatment would deal a severe blow to the credibility of the leaders and consequently, morale."

I bit my tongue to keep from blurting out a detailed and explicit description of exactly what the army could do with its discipline and morale.

I held my voice level. "Do you think there's any hope?"

"I have a strategy in mind. Doytchevksy followed you to Vegas and made contact in a way that made you realize he was a threat to our agents and to our internal security. I issued orders to Kane to meet you in Vegas. It won't be necessary to mention I issued those orders before I was aware it was Doytchevsky who was following you."

He eyed me expressionlessly. "It could be argued that you used Kane to draw Doytchevsky out of hiding. That both you and Kane were acting under orders to pretend the sexual harassment complaint and Kane's subsequent suspension were true in order to bait Doytchevsky. In that case, the suspension order preventing Kane from contacting you would be rendered invalid by his standing mission orders to work with you to expose Doytchevsky."

Hope rose, temporarily short-circuiting my breathing. After a moment I managed to inhale, trying not to wince at my tightening bruises. "That could work."

"It could. It will all depend on how the meeting proceeds and whether anyone asks awkward questions. Kane is in the brig and we will have no contact with him until the hearing, so he won't know we've discussed this. He may inadvertently say something that makes this strategy unworkable."

Stemp met my eyes. "I will do everything in my power to sway the discussion, but I won't mislead anyone or perjure myself. I suggest you do the same unless you want to risk the consequences."

He paused. "That only solves half the issue, of course. The other half hinges on your ability to convince the chain of command that Kane didn't engage in any improper conduct. Though you have been sufficiently convincing to General Briggs and myself, the other two members of the tribunal are unknown quantities."

I eased out a long breath. "I have an idea that I think will work. Can we use Jack's lie detector?"

Stemp sat in silence for a moment. "Are you certain you want to go down that path?" He leaned forward, holding me with his unsettling amber gaze. "If there is any little thing at all in your dealings with Kane that could be misconstrued, the lie detector might prove more harmful than helpful."

Oh.

Little things like screwing each other's brains out?

I swallowed the dryness in my throat and held my voice level. "We might as well go for broke. If I can't convince this group, there's no hope of convincing a judge or jury if he ends up going to trial."

Stemp leaned back in his chair. "I'll make sure the lie detector is available, but I'll leave the final decision to you."

He glanced at his watch. "We've gathered some more information that may or may not be relevant. Doytchevsky apparently took up pottery as a hobby several years ago, taking particular interest in a form of glazing known as raku, which involves firing the pottery to extremely high temperatures and then plunging it into flammable materials which then combust, creating desirable but unpredictable finishes."

"Yes, he mentioned that," I agreed. "He seemed quite proud of his work."

Stemp's lips twitched into a wry grimace. "His work; but perhaps not necessarily his pottery. Apparently that type of top-loading kiln is rarely used for raku because of the difficulty in unloading the hot pieces. Doytchevsky acquired the shop and hired an assistant to run it part-time. The assistant says on several occasions Doytchevsky asked him to fire the kiln to a high temperature and then leave the shop. He also said the other tenants in the strip mall had complained about excessive smoke and odour on those days. Doytchevsky explained it away as part of the raku process."

My stomach rolled queasily, the sound and smell of Sherman's cremation still lingering like greasy fog in my memory. I gulped down nausea. "So Sherman probably wasn't the first."

"Probably not, though we have no way of proving that. If not for the fact that Sherman's stainless steel medical alert bracelet didn't melt, we would have only your word that those were his ashes in the kiln. There was nothing left but fine grey powder."

I swallowed again, willing my breakfast back into place. "Doytchevsky said it took less than an hour. As if he had already tested it."

Stemp shrugged. "We'll never know."

His expressionless façade descended again and I braced myself. That was never a good sign.

"When we searched Doytchevsky's apartment, we discovered some..." He hesitated. "...disturbing products and video footage. We also discovered blood on his pillow and bloodstained nylon restraints beside the bed. The blood type matches yours. In your briefing yesterday..." He hesitated again. "Did you provide a complete and accurate account of your interactions with Doytchevsky? More to the point, did you get medical attention?"

"No, I'm fine. The video was faked and the blood was from my wrists." I held them up for corroboration. "He just beat me and choked me. No big deal."

Stemp eyed me in silence for several long moments before speaking. "I've made an appointment for you with Dr. Rawling tomorrow at zero-nine-hundred. I expect you to attend and to cooperate with him fully, including any and all follow-up appointments he deems necessary. That's an order."

I eased back in my chair. "Okay. I was going to call him this morning anyway."

He relaxed visibly. "I'm glad. I was hoping I wouldn't have another fight on my hands."

"I'm saving it for the hearing." I shot him a grim smile.

He returned an equally mirthless grimace. "Good."

CHAPTER 42

Released from Stemp's presence, I prowled back and forth behind the closed door of my office, preparing arguments in my mind only to discard them and start over.

Far too soon, my remaining minutes evaporated. Kane's remaining minutes.

Dammit.

I squared my shoulders despite the pain and hiked up my sleeves to expose the bruised flesh of my wrists crisscrossed with scabbed cuts. Might as well go for the sympathy vote, if there was such a thing.

I tossed my hair back and strode for the conference room, head held high.

I realized my mistake as soon as I stepped through the door. It hadn't even occurred to me that I'd be under-dressed. Stemp was in one of his usual quiet suits, but General Briggs and the other two men wore dress uniforms loaded with braid and insignia. I knew nothing about military ranks, but it sure as hell looked daunting.

And wouldn't you know I'd be the last to arrive, making a grand entrance in my faded jeans, scuffed hiking boots, and waist pouch.

Before I had a chance to shrivel into the nearest

knothole, all four men rose and General Briggs extended a gracious hand. "Agent Kelly, thank you for attending. This is Colonel Talbot..." He indicated a tall, sallow-skinned man. "...and Colonel Brinder."

I shook their proffered hands, sizing them up. Talbot's thin face was drawn in long lines of boredom, or maybe pain. If it was pain, I hoped it wouldn't make him cranky. Brinder looked as though he'd been inflated with a bicycle pump, his jacket straining over his belly, his bulging chins obscuring his crisp white collar. A prim cupids-bow mouth huddled under the inadequate shelter of his tiny black moustache.

"Please have a seat," General Briggs invited.

"Thanks," I mumbled, slinking into the nearest chair.

The room seemed to have been arranged for maximum intimidation. The five of us sat in a semicircle around the head of the table, while a single forlorn chair floated on the barren expanse of carpet well beyond the foot.

Sweat prickled my armpits and moistened my hands, my heart rate ratcheting up to drum in my ears. Shit, this was worse than facing Doytchevsky. And I wasn't even the one on trial.

Approaching footsteps in the hall made me lick my dry lips, trying to summon up enough spit to swallow. A moment later, an armed guard marched in, taking up a position against the wall.

Kane filled the doorway next, and I momentarily forgot my discomfort in the effort to keep my jaw from dropping.

My God.

I'd never seen him in full dress uniform before.

My. God...!

He stiffened to attention and threw a salute that threatened to melt my cerebral cortex. Or some part of my body, anyway.

I tore my gaze away from him long enough to belatedly identify a second guard behind him, stepping into position in the hallway and swinging the door closed.

By the time I'd recovered enough to resume breathing, some exchange had apparently taken place between Kane and the other officers. Kane stepped forward with only a slight limp and lowered himself into the lone chair, back straight, shoulders square, eyes front.

If I hadn't known him so well, I might not have noticed the hard lines around his mouth that betrayed the pain he was hiding. It was impressive acting, but I was pretty damn sure gunshot wounds didn't feel better the next day.

General Briggs addressed us. "This is not a trial or court-martial or a formal proceeding of any nature. We're here because Agent Kelly insists that the accusations against Captain Kane are completely fabricated. This chain-of-command meeting is only to hear her explanation and decide whether a formal inquiry is warranted."

He eyed Kane gravely for a moment. "That said, if it is decided that formal proceedings are warranted and if you are found to have made statements in this meeting that are subsequently proven to be untrue, additional charges will be laid. Is that clear?"

"Yes, sir." Kane's voice was steady, his eyes never wavering from some invisible point on the back wall.

"Good." Briggs paused, the force of his authority holding us all motionless for a moment. "Captain Kane, do you have anything to say before we begin?"

"No, sir, not at this time."

I drew a short breath of relief. I hadn't truly expected him to break down and spill a confession about our consensual sex. After all, this was Kane. Mr. Super-cool James Bond. But some little part of me felt reassured nevertheless. So far, so good.

"Agent Kelly?" Briggs gestured. "You have the floor."

I rose, then wondered whether I was supposed to stand or sit.

Well, too bad. They could tell me to sit down if they wanted me to sit. Flustered, I drew a deep, calming breath, forgetting my bruised chest. I couldn't quite suppress my wince.

"Sorry," I said reflexively.

Oh, for shit's sake, get it together. I drew myself up to face the gauntlet of eyes.

"It's quite all right," Briggs said gently. "We know you've been injured, and this is not an official proceeding. Just relax and take your time."

A little of my nervousness subsided. At least two people were rooting for me in this room. Well, probably three, counting Kane.

"Thanks." I drew another, more careful, breath.

Might as well jump in at the deep end.

"I'd like to address the videotaped rape confession first," I began.

Just stay calm. I could do this.

"First I'd like to point out that I've never formally accused Kane of rape. If he, or anyone for that matter, had raped me, I would have filed charges immediately."

I eyed the impassive faces around the table. "The only reason you're considering charges against Kane is because this video was recorded and the lie detector indicated his statements were true. If this video hadn't existed, you would have simply accepted a statement in my mission report that we fooled Doytchevsky by faking a confession."

General Briggs gave me a nod that looked like approval. Talbot and Brinder looked thoughtful.

Good.

I drew a slow breath. "I'm going to provide an explanation for why Kane answered the way he did. Can we run the video now?"

Stemp nodded, pressing some keys on a laptop computer and turning it so we could all see. I concentrated hard while the video ran, double-checking my strategy. God, I could barely remember saying those things. And Kane was an amazing actor. He looked guilty as sin in the recording.

Shit.

I turned to face the group. "First, you need to understand the context of the video. We were both under extreme duress..."

I hesitated. "Um... I'm sorry, I don't mean to offend anybody, but I don't know how much I can tell about, um... the technology involved...?"

"Everyone here has a top-level security clearance," Stemp reassured me. "And this room is completely secure. There is no audio or video surveillance active."

"Okay." I plunged in, explaining Doytchevsky's background as a Russian spy and his connection to my dead husband and the Knights. I could feel Kane's eyes boring into me as I spoke, and I avoided his gaze.

If we were still friends when this was all over, I was going to owe him some major apologies for withholding that information from him. Oh, and for getting him captured and shot and accused of rape and...

Shut up.

I forced my concentration back to my narrative, laying

out Doytchevsky's threats and not skimping on the details of what I had suffered. The more despicable he looked, the better for Kane.

"So anyway," I concluded, "Doytchevsky hated Kane because he executed Robert... my husband, Doytchevsky's best friend. And after Doytchevsky burned Sherman in the kiln, I knew he wouldn't hesitate to do the same to Kane. I was desperate to find a way to stall him until Kane regained consciousness. I had been pretending to dislike Kane anyway in order to build rapport with Doytchevsky, so I appealed to Doytchevsky's hatred by offering a way to make Kane suffer. This video was the result."

I eased out a long breath, willing my pulse to slow. Stay calm. Stay focused.

"You'll notice that Kane didn't admit to sexual contact at any time in the video. I accused him of rape and then followed the accusation with statements that sounded like they were related but weren't. Let's look at what he actually admits to."

I ticked the points off on my fingers. "He followed me. He broke into my house when I was sleeping. He didn't listen when I begged. Notice I didn't specify what I was begging for; it only sounds as though I was begging him not to rape me because I'd just finished mentioning I was naked. And I always sleep naked-"

None of their damn business. I willed the heat out of my cheeks and carried on.

"Next, I say I was bruised and crying, but the only accusation he actually answers is 'you knew what you had done'. Then I say he 'did it again'..." I made air quotes around the words. "...but the only thing he actually admits to is leaving me in the woods barely able to walk. Then he admits to following me again."

I met their eyes, each in turn. "So what have we got? Obviously he could truthfully say he followed me many times; our mission reports confirm all the times he showed up just in time to save my a..." I stopped myself just in time. "...skin."

Deep breath.

"If you read our mission reports from last summer, you'll find that Kane did break into my house when he was hiding after he'd been supposedly killed. We discussed strategy..."

... which had involved some begging on my part that sounded suspiciously like 'Oh God, John, harder'...

Focusing my full attention on my audience, I summoned up all my bravado and continued. "...and at the time I begged him to let me tell his father that he was still alive."

Which was also true, fortunately.

"I was bruised and, um..."

Dammit, it was none of their business. I didn't admit to *anybody* that I cried. Ever.

Arnie's gentle words came back to me. He didn't think less of me. I drew myself up. Normal people wouldn't use my emotions to attack me.

And fuck them if they did.

I met their eyes defiantly. "The mission reports will confirm that I'd been severely beaten twice in a short period of time. Watching Kane apparently killed and then attending his funeral was very difficult. I was bruised, and crying in bed."

No visible reaction from my audience. I concluded with relief, "We agreed that Kane would hide in the woods on my farm. We had a briefing there and went our separate ways. As I've already noted, I had been badly beaten. I could barely walk."

Both of which were true, though not related. My wobbly knees at the time had more to do with the activities included in our so-called briefing. More like a 'de-briefing'...

I yanked my attention back to the room. No questions yet, thank God.

"So now you understand the depth of Doytchevsky's hatred for the Knights and for Kane. He wanted to damage Kane's reputation and make him suffer. Since we conveniently provided him with a kiss to photograph, he seized the opportunity to file the bogus sexual harassment charge in my name. Which played right into our hands."

This time Stemp gave me an almost-imperceptible nod.

Almost there. I clasped my shaking hands in front of me and drew another deep, painful breath. "So the two pieces of so-called evidence against Kane were both fabricated by Doytchevsky. I've never filed a rape charge against Kane, I've never accused him of any improper behaviour, and I have no reason to."

I couldn't read Brinder or Talbot. Were they sufficiently convinced? I met Stemp's eyes. Should I or shouldn't I?

Go for broke.

I faced the officers. "I realize this isn't a trial, but since the lie detector is what made you suspect Kane, I'd like to use it to clear him instead."

My pulse thumped in my throat as Stemp rose to hand over Jack's small case. I laid it out on the floor beside Kane and secured the band around his head, firmly resisting the urge to let my fingertips drift over his hair in reassurance. He stared straight ahead, his cop face unreadable.

I drew a deep breath. "Please answer yes or no. Have you ever raped me?"

"No." Green light. True.

"Have you ever sexually harassed me?"

"No."

I swallowed a surge of relief when the green light flashed. That had been a dangerous question. I had been afraid he might actually believe he had.

I turned back to him with renewed confidence. "In fact, have you repeatedly initiated conversations with me to make sure that neither you nor any members of your team have acted in ways that might make me feel harassed or intimidated?"

"Yes." Green light.

"So Doytchevsky's fabrications are completely groundless and false."

"Yes."

The beautiful green light shone once more, and I quickly removed the band of electrodes from Kane's forehead.

I turned to the officers. "Now I'm going to ask Kane to face his so-called accuser." I fumbled with the headband, trying to secure it around my own forehead.

"If I may?" At Briggs's nod of assent, Kane rose to fasten the band.

"Why don't you sit down?" Kane indicated the chair. "You look as though you need to."

I realized my hand tremors had spread to my legs and clammy sweat was collecting on my forehead.

"Not as much as you. Nobody shot me."

"It's fine. Please." He gestured, and I sank gratefully onto the chair. If there was any sympathy to be had, I was going for it.

Kane surveyed me dispassionately for a moment. "I'll keep this short," he said. "Have I ever raped you?"

"No."

"Have I ever done anything to make you feel harassed or intimidated?"

"No."

"Did you file a sexual harassment complaint against me?"

"No."

There might have been a softening at the corners of his mouth. "So all accusations of rape and sexual harassment are completely groundless and false?"

"Yes."

Green light all the way.

"Thank you, those are my only questions."

He removed the electrodes from my head with as much alacrity as I'd removed them from his. I had a feeling we were both thinking the same thing.

Please don't ask us any direct questions about sexual contact...

General Briggs rose. "Thank you, Agent Kelly. Captain Kane, you are dismissed." He nodded at the guard. "Take him away."

Kane stiffened into another magnificent salute before striding out ahead of the guard, straight-backed.

When the door closed behind the guard, Briggs spoke again. "I'm satisfied that no charges are warranted in this case. Are we agreed?"

Both Stemp and the roly-poly Brinder nodded.

Talbot spoke in a nasal twang far too similar to Doytchevsky's voice.

"No."

CHAPTER 43

The oxygen vanished from the room. I tried fruitlessly to draw a breath, my heart thundering in my ears. The thin colonel's drawl continued.

"I'm satisfied there has been no sexual misconduct. But Kane blatantly disobeyed a direct order. He has to answer to that charge in a court-martial."

Brinder spoke in a deep basso voice completely at odds with his prissy little mouth. "Come on, Talbot, there were extenuating circumstances. The accusation was false, and all parties knew it. There was no reason for him to stay away from her. And it wasn't public insubordination. If we drop it here, nobody outside this room will ever know about it."

I managed to suck in some air at last. A distant humming floated between my ears.

"That's not the point." Talbot's voice drilled an ugly hole in the silence of the room. "The point is that regulations exist for a reason. Arbitrarily ignoring them is a step down the road toward chaos and anarchy."

Chaos and anarchy? You pompous, self-important prick...

I jerked forward, my fists clenching. I was just opening my mouth when Stemp rose, quelling me with a glance.

His bland tones neutralized the poisonous atmosphere. "Perhaps I can clarify the situation. Kane was under orders to follow Kelly. Those orders were standing at the time the harassment complaint was filed. Kelly immediately informed me that the complaint was fake and that Doytchevsky was a potential threat to our security and to Kane."

He swept the others with his emotionless gaze and continued, "I decided to trap Doytchevsky instead of immediately reporting the falsified complaint. I filed a full time-stamped report at that time, but redacted it until such time as I could determine the extent of the security breach surrounding Doytchevsky. Therefore, though the rest of the chain of command was unaware of it, Kane's standing orders to follow Kelly rendered the orders of the suspension invalid."

I traced the convoluted logic trail, holding my breath. I wasn't sure it all followed, but he had delivered the final sentence with such calm conviction I hoped Talbot would just cave.

"There are no grounds for court-martial," Stemp said quietly. "I recommend that all references to this matter be expunged from Kane's record and transferred instead to a mission report, which is where they belong." He resumed his seat.

The sour lines deepened on Talbot's face. "Of course you recommend that. You're just a civilian. You don't understand the importance of military discipline."

"Christ, Talbot, get the stick out of your ass." Brinder spoke with tolerant humour, but Talbot's sallow cheeks flushed to an unhealthy hue nevertheless. Before he could respond, Brinder added, "Stop tripping over your army hard-on and think for a minute." He shot me a cursory glance. "Sorry for the language."

I managed a jerky gesture of pardon, and he turned back to Talbot. "What good does it do to make an example of Kane over a technicality like this? We lose our best agent, and that won't do any damn good for your precious morale."

Talbot stiffened. "If everyone blatantly disregarded orders that inconvenienced them, our fighting forces would be reduced to the equivalent of a troop of monkeys with sharpened sticks. We'd be the laughingstock of-"

"Yeah, the world, I know." Brinder leaned back in his chair. "And if everybody blindly obeyed without challenging inappropriate orders, we'd have Nazi Germany all over again. Just let it go."

Silence made the air too thick to breathe.

"Fine," Talbot snapped at last. "It's against my better judgement but-"

"So we have a unanimous agreement," General Briggs interrupted.

Two firm nods and one reluctant one made me suck in a tentative breath.

Briggs lifted the phone. "Please bring Captain Kane back to the meeting room."

Several minutes of delay did nothing for my nerves. What if Talbot changed his mind? Could he even do that now that he'd agreed?

A rap on the door made me jump.

"Come in."

The guard reappeared, followed by Kane. He saluted before stiffening to attention, his grey gaze locked on an unseen horizon.

General Briggs rose. "Captain Kane, we have concluded

our discussion and come to a decision. We agree unanimously that no charges of any kind are warranted. You are restored to active service effective immediately. All entries pertaining to these events will be expunged from your record and transferred instead to your mission reports."

He smiled. "Congratulations, Captain Kane. Consider yourself on medical leave for the rest of the week. Report for light duty Monday morning as usual. You are dismissed."

"Thank you, sir." Kane's face betrayed no emotion whatsoever as he saluted and marched out.

I slumped in my chair, my bones melting into jelly.

Over.

It was over.

"Agent Kelly?" General Briggs extended his hand. "Thank you for your testimony. And for your good work on this mission."

I dragged myself out of my stupor to shake his hand. "You're welcome," my mouth said automatically.

The men filed out. Stemp paused in the doorway to survey me. "Kelly?"

"Uh. I'm just..." I drew a deep, quavering breath. "I'm just going to sit for a minute."

He appraised me for a moment. "Take your time. When you're ready, go home. I'm placing you on medical leave until Monday as well." I managed a faint nod and he mercifully left without further comment.

I sagged in the chair, staring at the wall and schooling myself into slow, deep yoga breaths. Everyone safe. Doytchevsky dead. Kane reinstated.

Thank God.

A sound from the doorway made me snap around, my nerves still raw. The resulting jab of pain jerked a grunt out of me.

Kane stepped into the room, eyeing me with concern. "Are you all right?"

"Fine." I clamped down on the urge to leap up and fling my arms around him. "You?"

"Fine." He half-reached a hand toward me before letting it drop to his side again. "Thank you."

"You're welcome."

So much to say.

We regarded each other in silence for a moment before I pulled myself together. "Come on, let's get out of here. Stemp gave me the rest of the day off, too, and Arnie's waiting down in the lobby."

His limp was considerably more pronounced when we walked down the hallway toward the stairs.

I glanced up at his set face. "Let's take the elevator."

"It's all right. It's sutured. It's better if I keep moving. I don't want to lose strength in the surrounding muscles."

I clenched my fists to keep from reaching for his hand. "I'm so sorry. For everything."

"It's all right."

He descended the stairs slowly, his knuckles whitening on the handrail. I hovered anxiously beside him. No way to help. No way to make it better. He kept his gaze focused to the front, whether in pain or anger I couldn't tell.

When we emerged into the lobby, Arnie sprang up from one of the chairs, his worried gaze ricocheting between Kane and me.

I didn't keep him in suspense. "It's over. He's free. And he's on leave until Monday."

A grin split Hellhound's face and he let out a whoop. "Right on!" He pulled Kane into a rough embrace and pounded him on the back. "Right-fuckin'-*on!*"

Kane pulled away, grinning. "Don't make me disgrace the uniform by hugging a hairy ugly bastard like you."

Hellhound bellowed a laugh. "Ya fuckin' snotty officers are all the same. C'mon, I'll take ya home to change an' then I'm buyin' at Eddy's."

"Deal." Kane turned his smile on me. "Coming?"

Relief melted my tension. He wasn't mad.

I shot him a theatrically incredulous look. "Are you kidding? Arnie's driving, *and* he's buying? Hell, yeah, I'm coming!"

Happily ensconced at our usual table with my back to the wall, I took a deep swallow of ice-cold beer. Beside me, Kane eased out a long breath and carefully extended his leg before drawing from his pint glass with appreciation.

Across the table, Hellhound sat at a slight diagonal to the room, casting uneasy glances over his shoulder.

I took pity on him. "Come and sit beside me." I shuffled my chair closer to Kane. "There's room here."

"Thanks, darlin'." Hellhound rose with obvious relief and pulled his chair around beside me before sinking into it with a satisfied sigh. "That's better." He shot a glance at Kane and me. "We look like fuckin' idiots lined up against the wall like this."

"Yeah, but we're happy idiots." I raised my bottle. "Here's to being dumb and happy."

"I'll drink to that." Hellhound clinked his bottle against mine, and Kane reached over from the other side, smiling, to complete the toast with his glass.

We sipped companionably for a while, letting the

excellent blues music wrap around us. Then Hellhound placed his half-empty bottle on the table, leaning forward to survey Kane and me with his shrewd gaze.

"I gotta take a dump," he announced, and rose. "Gonna be a while."

We watched his bulky figure stride toward the men's room, and Kane raised an amused eyebrow. "Subtle as a brick."

I grinned. "Yep, that's why we love him."

We met each other's eyes and looked away hurriedly. An awkward silence hung between us for a few moments before we spoke at the same time.

"I'm really sorry, John-"

"Aydan, I'm sorry-"

Pause.

We tried again.

"You don't need to-"

"It wasn't your-"

Kane shook his head ruefully. "You first."

I reached for his hand, but stopped myself. Even the smallest public display of affection was too dangerous. I wouldn't risk that again.

"John, I'm sorry I put you through this. It was all my fault."

He shook his head, raising a hand in protest, but I overrode him. "The harassment complaint, the way I froze at the pottery shop and got you captured and..." My throat closed with the memory of how close a call it had been. My voice came out in a quaver. "...and got you shot and damn near court-martialled; I nearly cost you everything and I'm so, so sorry-"

"Aydan, no! None of this was your fault. It was my fault

for..." His gaze flicked over the room and he lowered his voice. "...for what I did in Vegas. I was careless and you paid the price." His hand moved toward mine before retreating to clench around his glass. "When I saw that video Doytchevsky made, I..." He fell silent, his powerful hands flexing on the glass until I feared it would shatter in his grasp.

"But it was all fake," I said in my most reassuring tones. "No big deal."

"But it could just as easily have been real."

I swallowed some beer, groping for a reply. "John..." I returned my bottle to the table a little more firmly than necessary. "It wasn't your fault. It's just my stupid job and my stupid life and there's nothing you or anybody else can do about it."

"Aydan..."

I turned to face him. "Look, just let it go. Walk away while you still can. I told you I'll only end up hurting you, and this was the proof. You nearly lost everything. Your career, your pension, your good name..." I gulped. "Your life..."

"Aydan, you know I'm not the kind of guy who plays it safe. I'd do it again in a heartbeat if I knew I was the only one who'd suffer for it."

"No!" The word wrenched out of me before I could stop it. He flinched as if I'd slapped him, and my heart twisted. "John, it would kill me to know you were suffering because of me. Don't do that to me. Please."

"Stop panicking." His hand closed briefly around mine, warm and reassuring. "I didn't say that because I expect anything from you. I'm not asking you to change."

He released my hand, but his grey gaze held me like an

embrace. "I said it because I want you to know that if the worst had happened, or if it does happen in the future, it's worth it to me. And I don't ever want you to think otherwise."

"Oh. Um." I hid my sudden self-consciousness in a gulp of beer. "Thanks."

The laugh lines crinkled around his eyes as he leaned back in his chair. "You're welcome."

"There you are!" Spider's buoyant smile lit up the room as he bounded over. He flung his lanky arms around me, nearly knocking over Hellhound's beer bottle in the process. "I'm so glad you're okay!" He turned his grin on Kane. "And I'm so glad *you're* okay! And your mission is over! It's so good to see you together again..."

His enthusiasm faltered. "Um, I'm not, um... interrupting anything, am I?"

"No, of course not," I reassured him. "We're just having a beer with Arnie, and you're welcome to join us."

"Great!" He plopped into the opposite chair.

I rose. "Actually, I'm just going to return some of this rental beer. Back in a flash." I wandered in the direction of the washrooms.

When I ducked into the corridor, Hellhound straightened from where he had been leaning against the wall. His gaze searched my face. "Everythin' okay, darlin'?"

I slid my arms around him as I turned to look back at Kane, his injured leg propped on a chair, smiling at Spider's chatter. The tension drained from my body in a long, slow breath. "Yeah. I think everything's going to be..."

Movement caught my eye and a chill shook me when Paul sat down a few tables away. He inclined his head in my direction and flashed a sardonic smile before turning to speak to the waitress.

"...just fine," I finished with determination.

Book 7 is available!

Visit my Books page at dianehenders.com/books for progress updates and announcements.

A Request

Thanks for reading!

If you enjoyed this book, I'd really appreciate it if you'd take a moment to review it online.

Here are some suggestions for the "star" ratings:
Five stars: Loved the book and can hardly wait for the next one.
Four stars: Liked the book and plan to read the next one.
Three stars: The book was okay. Might read the next one.
Two stars: Didn't like the book. Probably won't read the next one.
One star: Hated the book. Would never read another in the series.

You can help prospective readers by writing a few sentences about what you liked or disliked about the book.

Thanks for taking the time to do a review!

About Me

Before I started writing fiction, I had a checkered career: technical writer, computer geek, and interior designer. I'm good at two out of three of those. Fortunately, I had the sense to quit the one I sucked at (interior design).

When my mid-life crisis hit, I took up muay thai and started writing thrillers featuring a middle-aged female protagonist. ('Walter Mitty', you say? Nope, never heard of him.)

Writing and kicking the hell out of stuff seemed more productive than more typical mid-life-crisis activities like getting a divorce, buying a Harley Crossbones, and cruising across the country picking up men in sleazy bars; especially since it's winter most months of the year here in Canada.

It's much more comfortable to sit at my computer. And Harleys are expensive. Come to think of it, so are beer and gasoline.

Oh, and I still love my husband. There's that. So I stuck with the writing.

Diane Henders

And here's my "professional" bio, in case you need something more suitable for mixed company:

Diane Henders is the Kindle best-selling author of the NEVER SAY SPY series: Sexy thrillers packed with tension, laughs, profanity, and sometimes warm fuzzies.

The first book in the series, NEVER SAY SPY, has had over 450,000 downloads to date, and stayed on Kindle's 'Women Sleuths' Top 100 list for 60 consecutive months.

Diane enjoys target shooting, gardening, auto mechanics, painting (art, not walls), music, and martial arts; and loves food and drink almost as much as she loves her husband. They live in the wilds of British Columbia, Canada, where they get all the adrenaline rush they could ever want by growing fruit trees in bear country.

Want to know what else is roiling around in the cesspit of my mind? Drop by my blog and website at dianehenders.com, check out the extras, and don't forget to leave a comment in the guest book to say hi – I love hearing from you! Or you can connect with me on Facebook at:
https://www.facebook.com/authordianehenders.
See you there!